REI HIROE

It's hard to believe, but here's the book! Four years since my last on Seems like I get these published once every four year Olympics. Will it be another four mo joking.) Hope you'll e

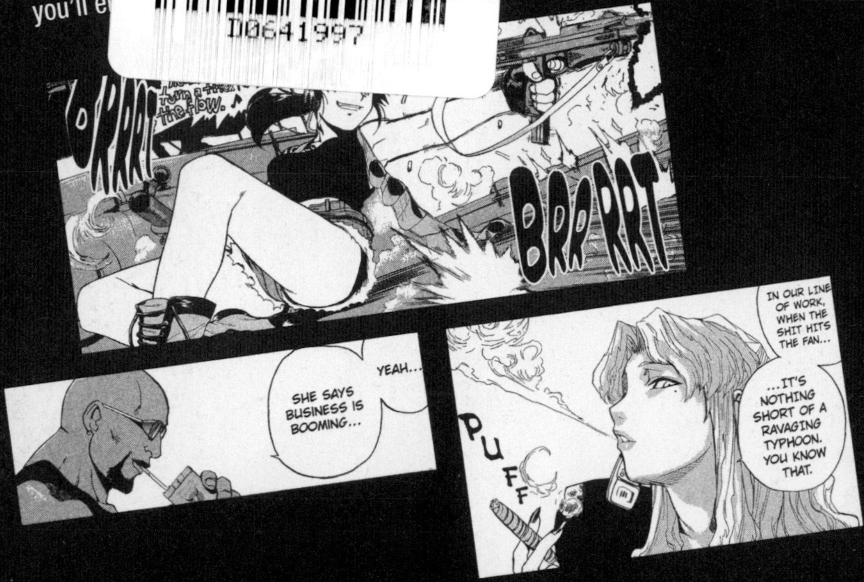

BRRRRT
IN OUR LINE OF WORK, WHEN THE SHIT HITS THE FAN...
...IT'S NOTHING SHORT OF A RAVAGING TYPHOON. YOU KNOW THAT.
PUFF
YEAH...
SHE SAYS BUSINESS IS BOOMING...

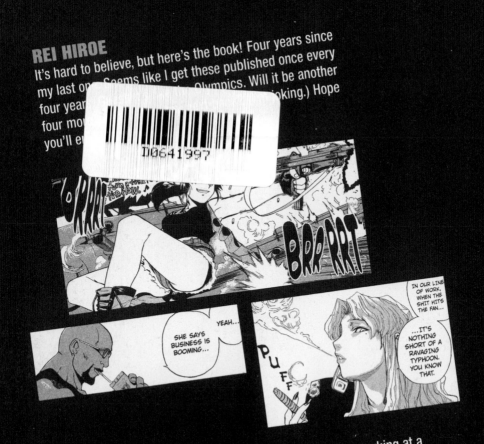

Rei Hiroe was born on December 5, 1972. After working at a game company, he debuted as a mangaka in 1993. He has been an active illustrator and dojinshi, and has created many titles released through the dojin community. He is best known for his works, *Hisuikyoukitan* and ***SHOOK UP!*** (both currently available in new formats published by Shogakukan) and his first artwork collection, *Barrage*.

BLACK LAGOON 001

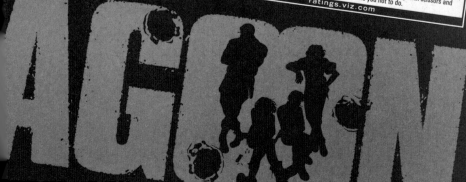

BLACK LAGOON
VOL. 1
VIZ Signature Edition

Story and Art by
REI HIROE

Original Japanese edition "BLACK LAGOON"
published by SHOGAKUKAN Inc.

Logo design by Mikiyo KOBAYASHI + Bay Bridge Studio

Translation/Dan Kanemitsu
Touch-up Art & Lettering/John Hunt, Primary Graphix
Design/Sam Elzway
Editor/Mike Montesa

Printed in the U.S.A.

Published by VIZ Media, LLC
P.O. Box 77010
San Francisco, CA 94107

10 9 8 7 6 5 4
First printing, August 2008
Fourth printing, June 2011

VIZ SIGNATURE
www.vizsignature.com

VIZ media
www.viz.com

RATED M FOR MATURE

PARENTAL ADVISORY
BLACK LAGOON is rated M for Mature and is recommended for mature readers. This volume contains graphic violence, strong language, nudity, adult situations, drinkin', smokin', ass-kickin', law breakin', gun-love, running with scissors and just about everything your mother ever told you not to do.

ratings.viz.com

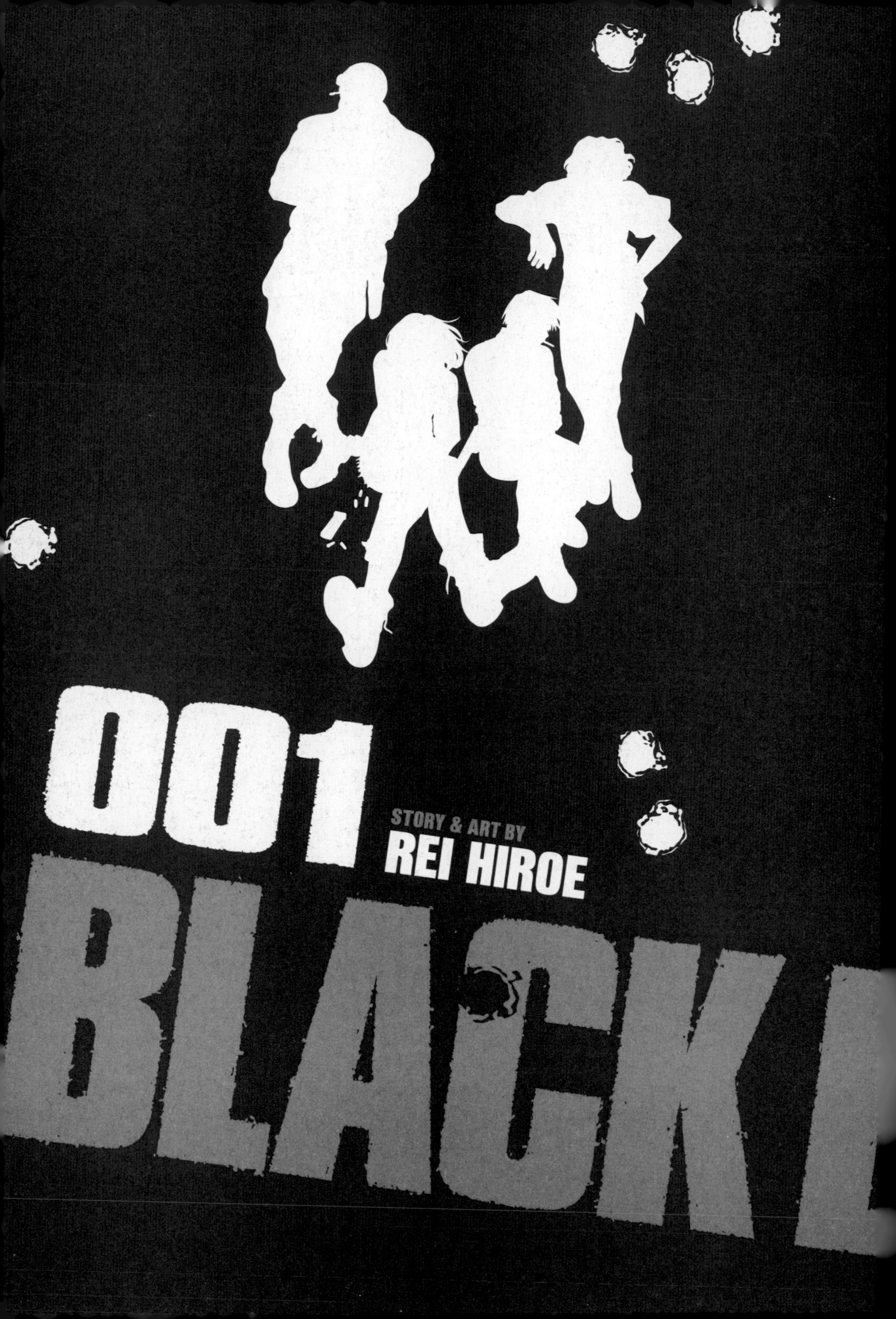
001
STORY & ART BY
REI HIROE
BLACKL

BLACK LAGOON

STORY & ART BY

REI HIROE

001

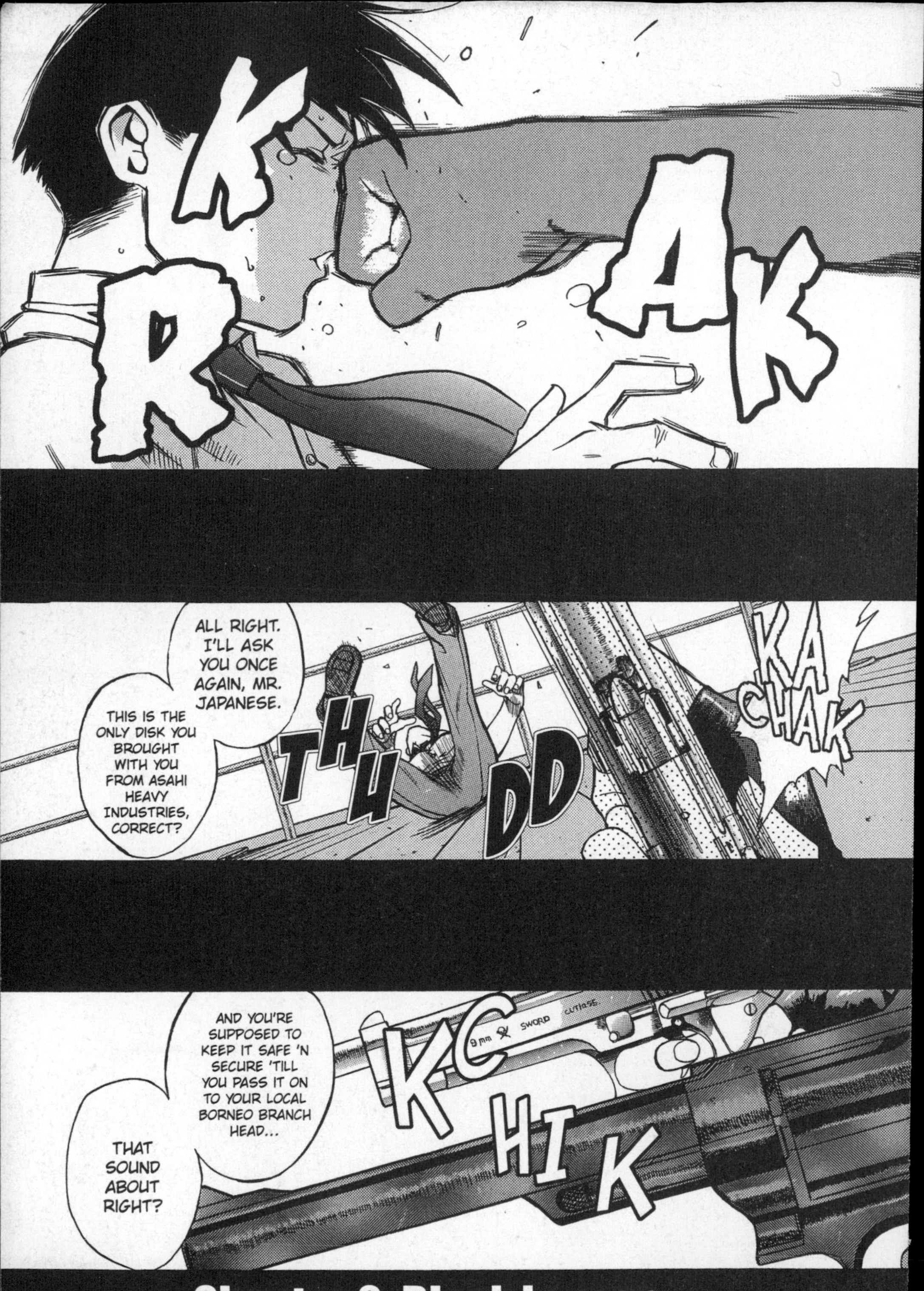
KRAK
KA CHAK
THUDD
ALL RIGHT. I'LL ASK YOU ONCE AGAIN, MR. JAPANESE.
THIS IS THE ONLY DISK YOU BROUGHT WITH YOU FROM ASAHI HEAVY INDUSTRIES, CORRECT?
KCHIK
AND YOU'RE SUPPOSED TO KEEP IT SAFE 'N SECURE 'TILL YOU PASS IT ON TO YOUR LOCAL BORNEO BRANCH HEAD...
THAT SOUND ABOUT RIGHT?

Chapter 0: Black Lagoon

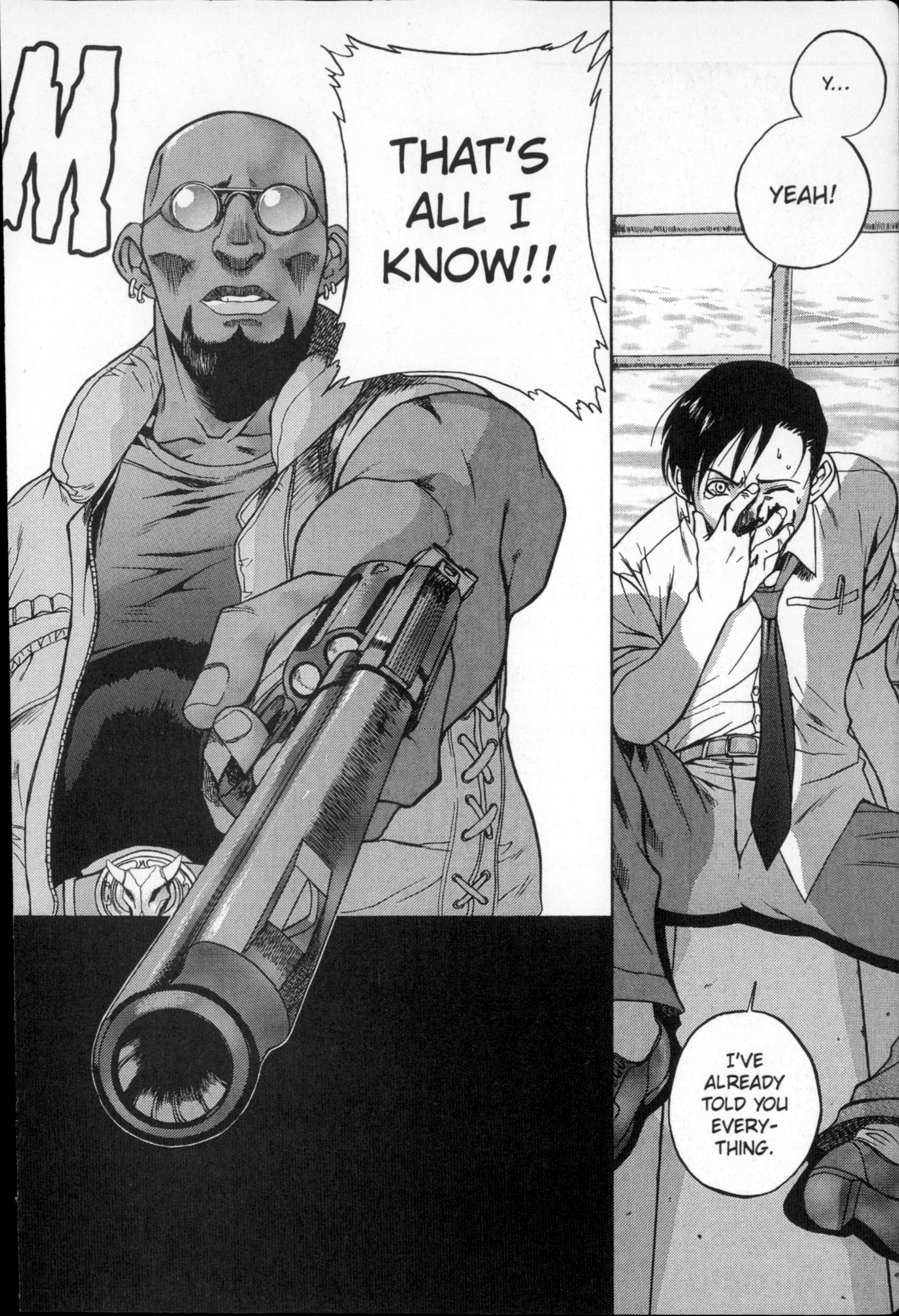
Y...
YEAH!
I'VE ALREADY TOLD YOU EVERY-THING.
M
THAT'S ALL I KNOW!!

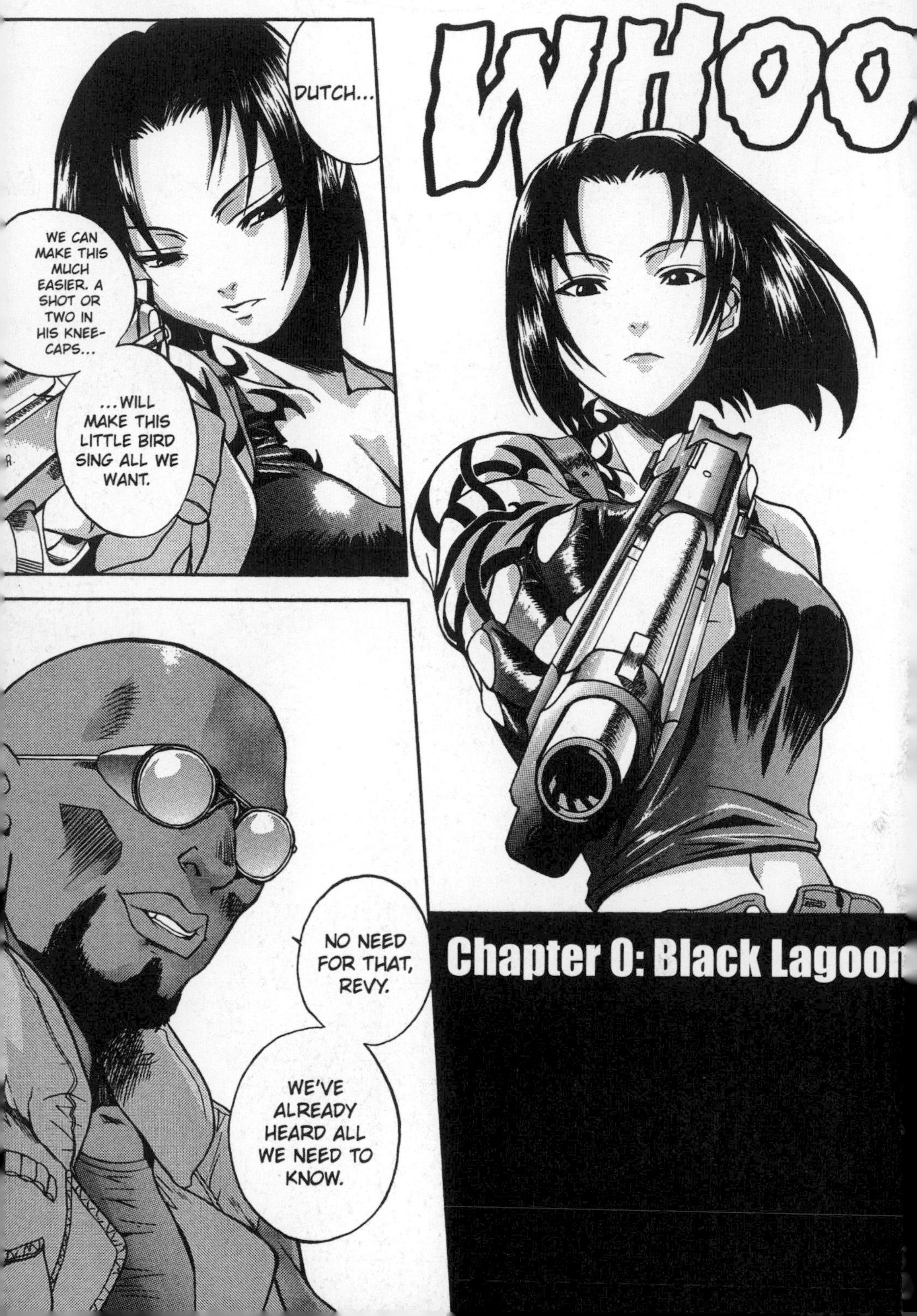
WHOO
Chapter 0: Black Lagoon
DUTCH...
WE CAN MAKE THIS MUCH EASIER. A SHOT OR TWO IN HIS KNEE-CAPS...
...WILL MAKE THIS LITTLE BIRD SING ALL WE WANT.
NO NEED FOR THAT, REVY.
WE'VE ALREADY HEARD ALL WE NEED TO KNOW.

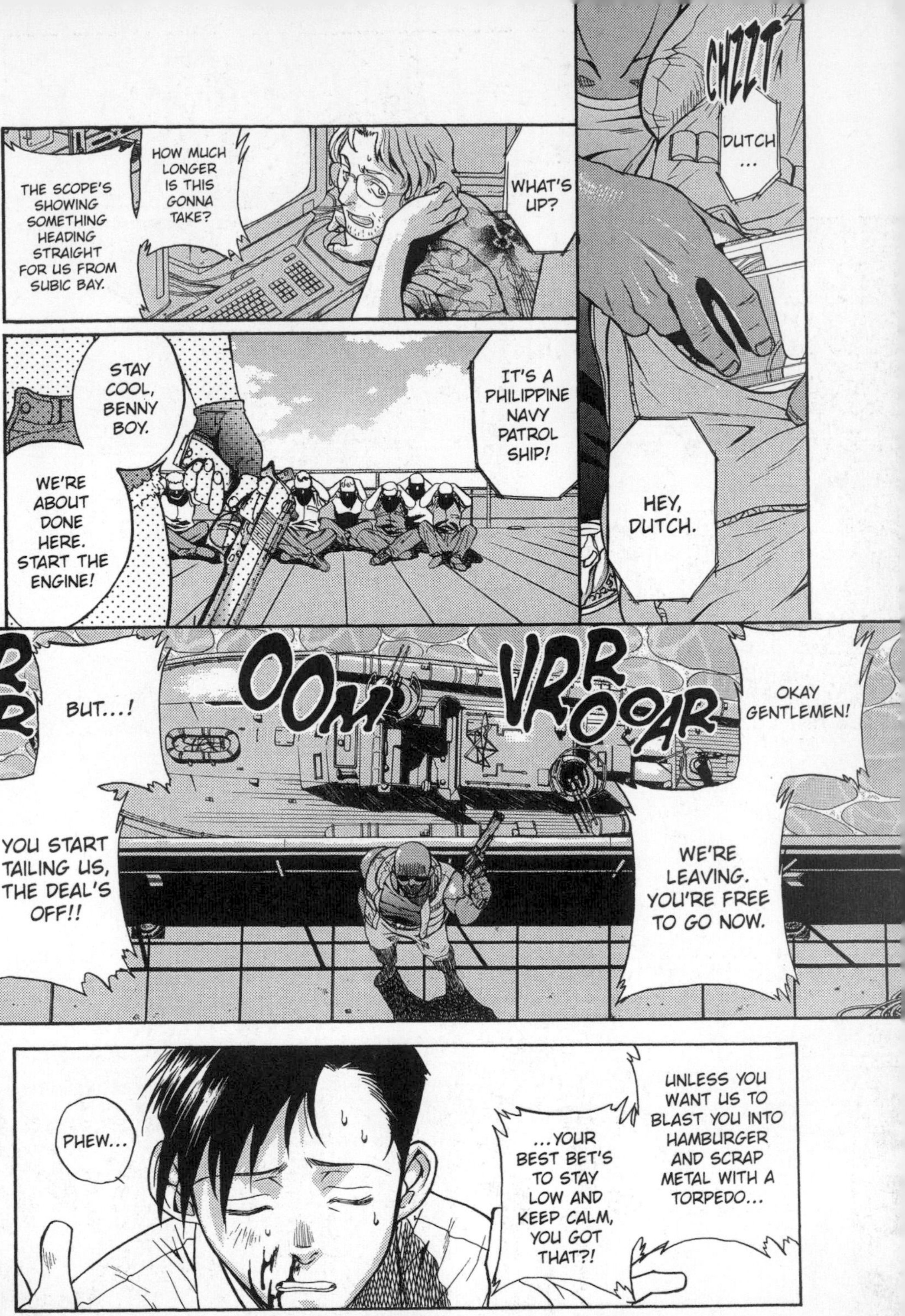
CHZZT
DUTCH ...
HEY, DUTCH.
WHAT'S UP?
HOW MUCH LONGER IS THIS GONNA TAKE?
THE SCOPE'S SHOWING SOMETHING HEADING STRAIGHT FOR US FROM SUBIC BAY.
IT'S A PHILIPPINE NAVY PATROL SHIP!
STAY COOL, BENNY BOY.
WE'RE ABOUT DONE HERE. START THE ENGINE!
OKAY GENTLEMEN!
WE'RE LEAVING. YOU'RE FREE TO GO NOW.
VRROOAR
RROOM
BUT...!
YOU START TAILING US, THE DEAL'S OFF!!
UNLESS YOU WANT US TO BLAST YOU INTO HAMBURGER AND SCRAP METAL WITH A TORPEDO...
...YOUR BEST BET'S TO STAY LOW AND KEEP CALM, YOU GOT THAT?!
PHEW...

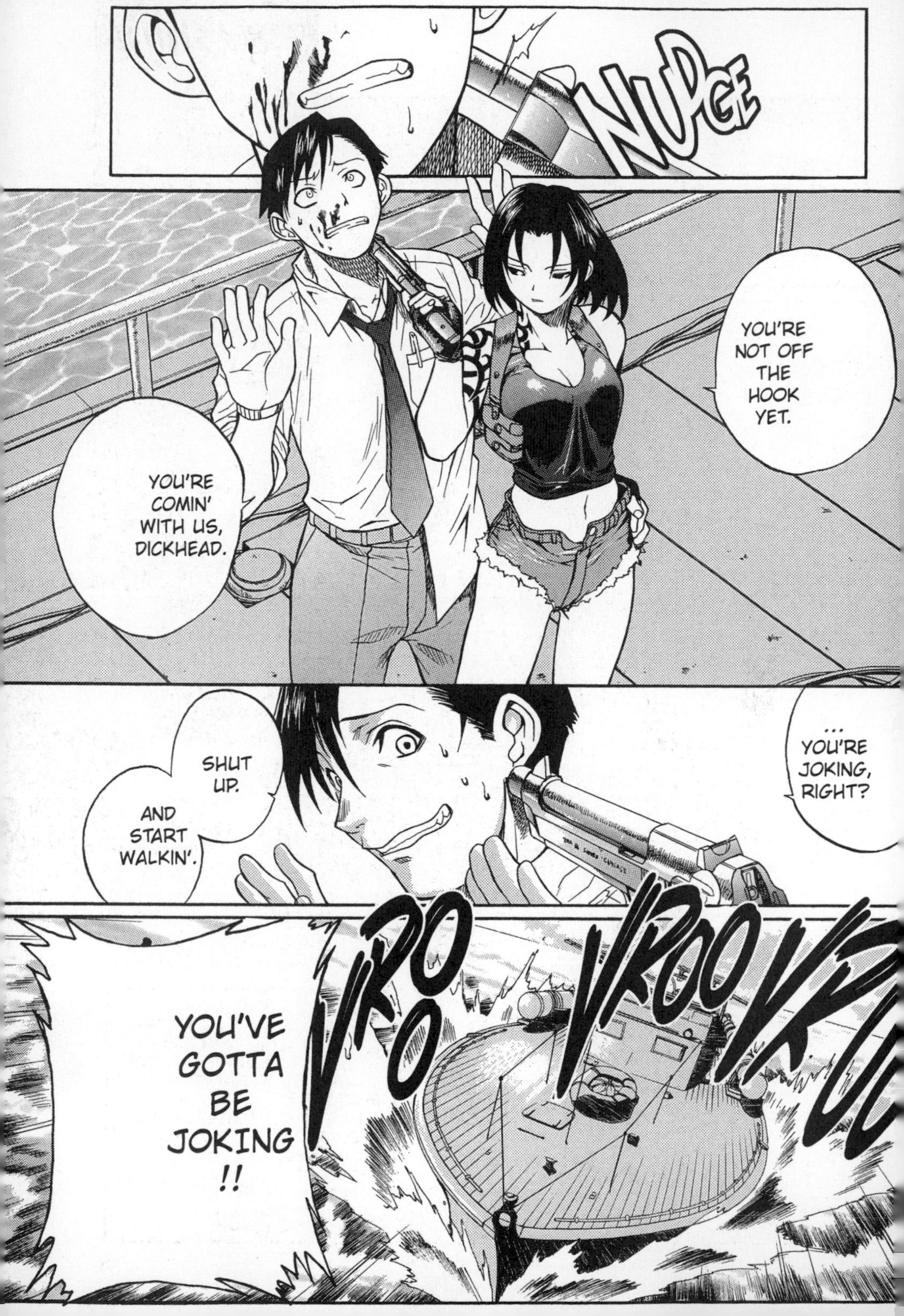
NUDGE
YOU'RE NOT OFF THE HOOK YET.
YOU'RE COMIN' WITH US, DICKHEAD.
... YOU'RE JOKING, RIGHT?
SHUT UP.
AND START WALKIN'.
VROOO
VROO
YOU'VE GOTTA BE JOKING !!

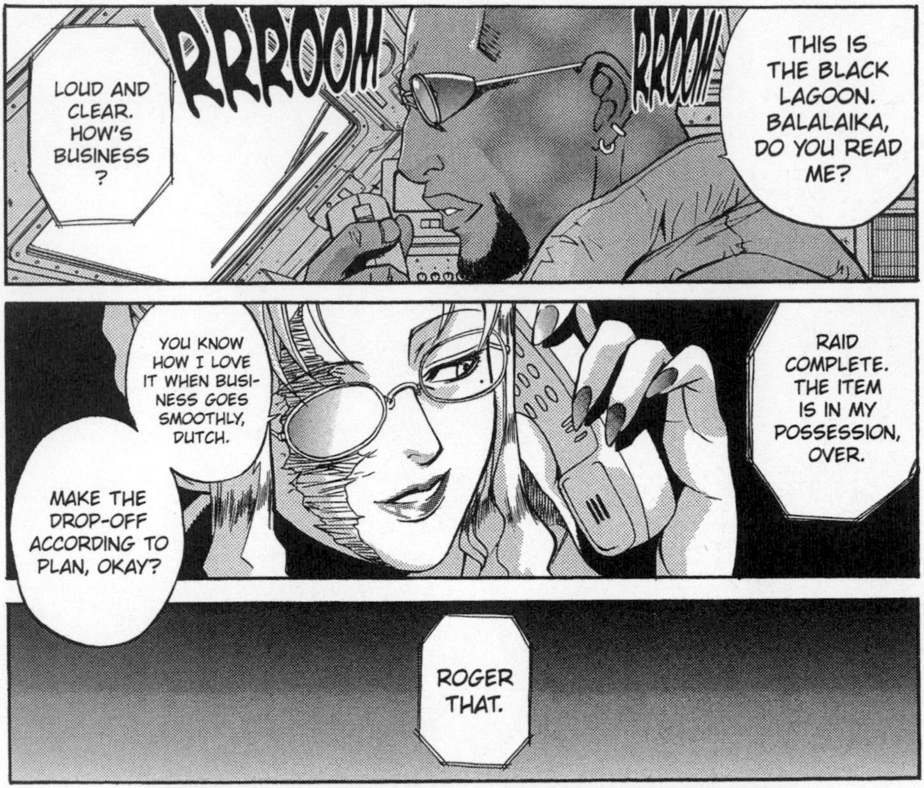
THIS IS THE BLACK LAGOON. BALALAIKA, DO YOU READ ME?
RROOM
RRROOM
LOUD AND CLEAR. HOW'S BUSINESS?
RAID COMPLETE. THE ITEM IS IN MY POSSESSION, OVER.
YOU KNOW HOW I LOVE IT WHEN BUSINESS GOES SMOOTHLY, DUTCH.
MAKE THE DROP-OFF ACCORDING TO PLAN, OKAY?
ROGER THAT.

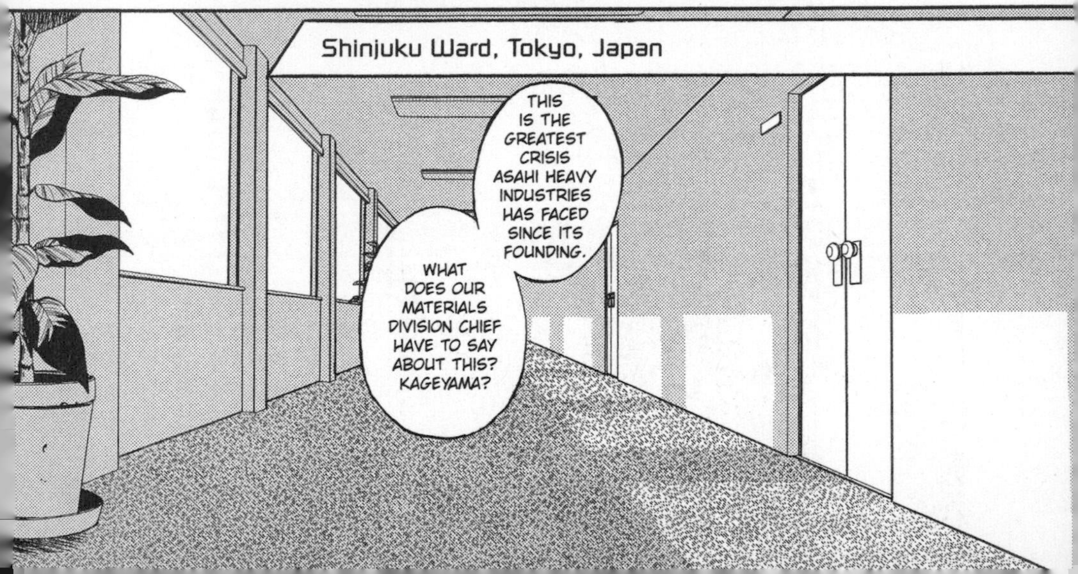
Shinjuku Ward, Tokyo, Japan
THIS IS THE GREATEST CRISIS ASAHI HEAVY INDUSTRIES HAS FACED SINCE ITS FOUNDING.
WHAT DOES OUR MATERIALS DIVISION CHIEF HAVE TO SAY ABOUT THIS? KAGEYAMA?

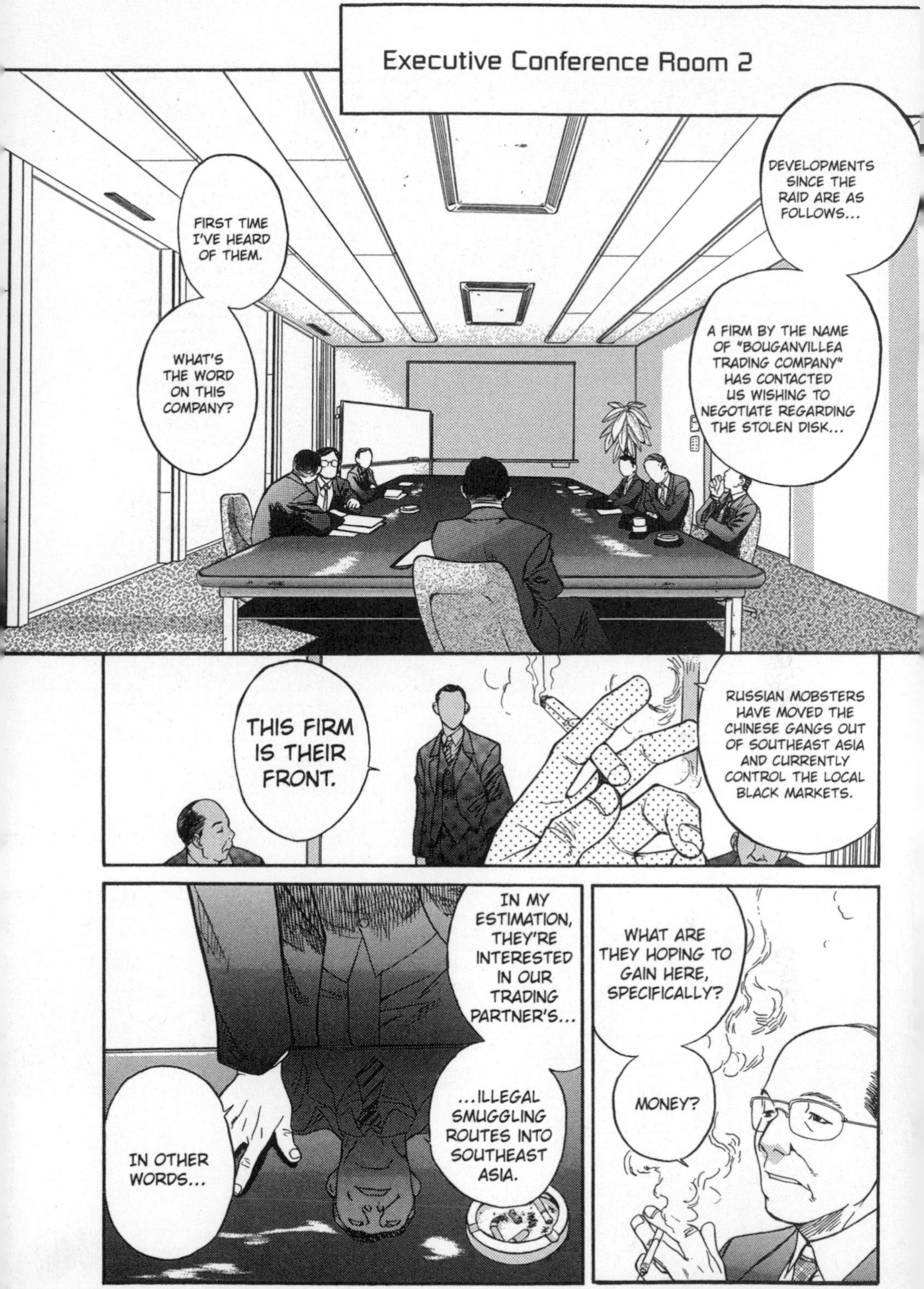
Executive Conference Room 2
DEVELOPMENTS SINCE THE RAID ARE AS FOLLOWS...
A FIRM BY THE NAME OF "BOUGANVILLEA TRADING COMPANY" HAS CONTACTED US WISHING TO NEGOTIATE REGARDING THE STOLEN DISK...
FIRST TIME I'VE HEARD OF THEM.
WHAT'S THE WORD ON THIS COMPANY?
RUSSIAN MOBSTERS HAVE MOVED THE CHINESE GANGS OUT OF SOUTHEAST ASIA AND CURRENTLY CONTROL THE LOCAL BLACK MARKETS.
THIS FIRM IS THEIR FRONT.
WHAT ARE THEY HOPING TO GAIN HERE, SPECIFICALLY?
MONEY?
IN MY ESTIMATION, THEY'RE INTERESTED IN OUR TRADING PARTNER'S...
...ILLEGAL SMUGGLING ROUTES INTO SOUTHEAST ASIA.
IN OTHER WORDS...

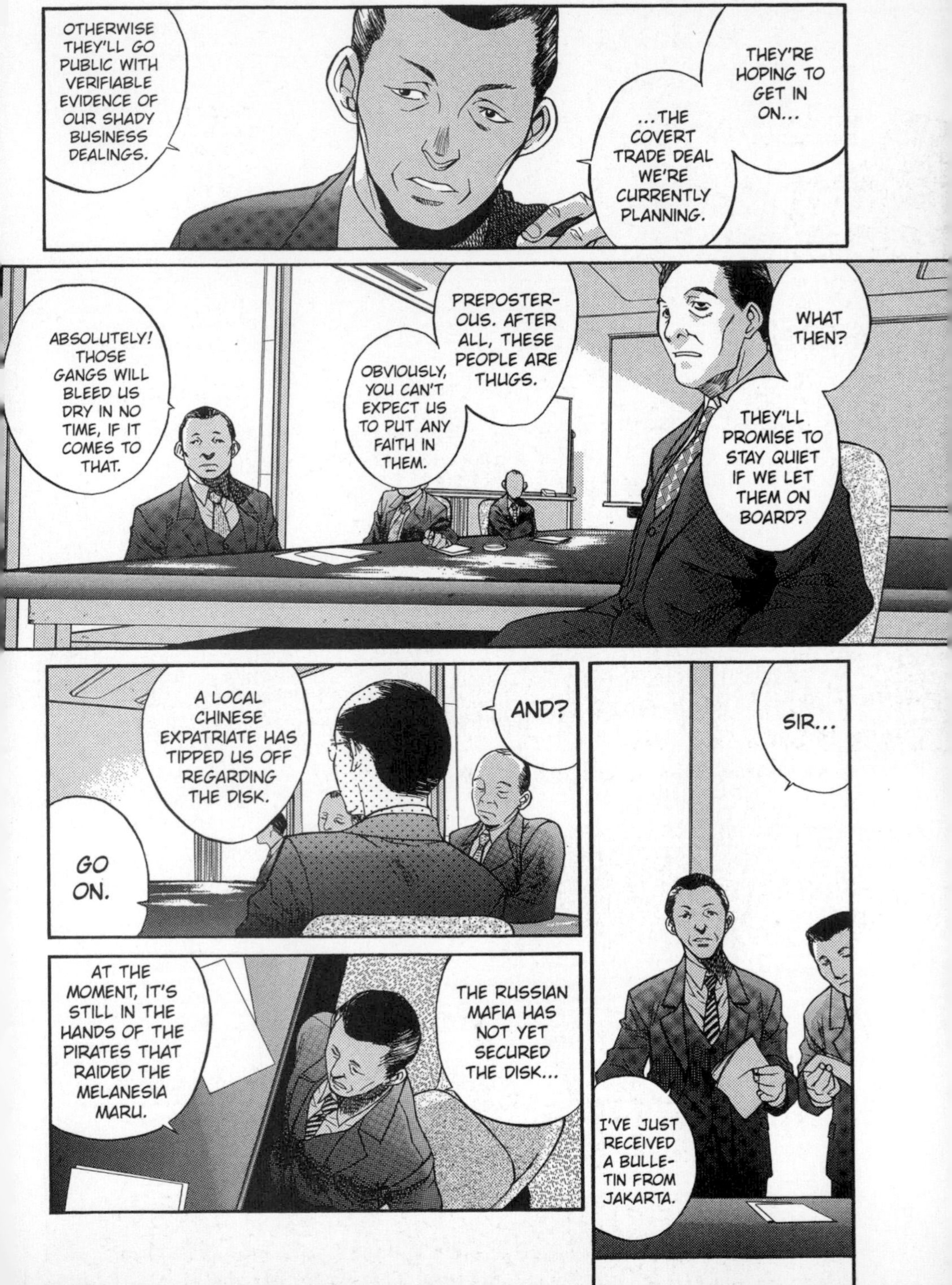
THEY'RE HOPING TO GET IN ON...
...THE COVERT TRADE DEAL WE'RE CURRENTLY PLANNING.
OTHERWISE THEY'LL GO PUBLIC WITH VERIFIABLE EVIDENCE OF OUR SHADY BUSINESS DEALINGS.
WHAT THEN?
THEY'LL PROMISE TO STAY QUIET IF WE LET THEM ON BOARD?
PREPOSTER-OUS. AFTER ALL, THESE PEOPLE ARE THUGS.
OBVIOUSLY, YOU CAN'T EXPECT US TO PUT ANY FAITH IN THEM.
ABSOLUTELY! THOSE GANGS WILL BLEED US DRY IN NO TIME, IF IT COMES TO THAT.
SIR...
I'VE JUST RECEIVED A BULLE-TIN FROM JAKARTA.
AND?
A LOCAL CHINESE EXPATRIATE HAS TIPPED US OFF REGARDING THE DISK.
GO ON.
THE RUSSIAN MAFIA HAS NOT YET SECURED THE DISK...
AT THE MOMENT, IT'S STILL IN THE HANDS OF THE PIRATES THAT RAIDED THE MELANESIA MARU.

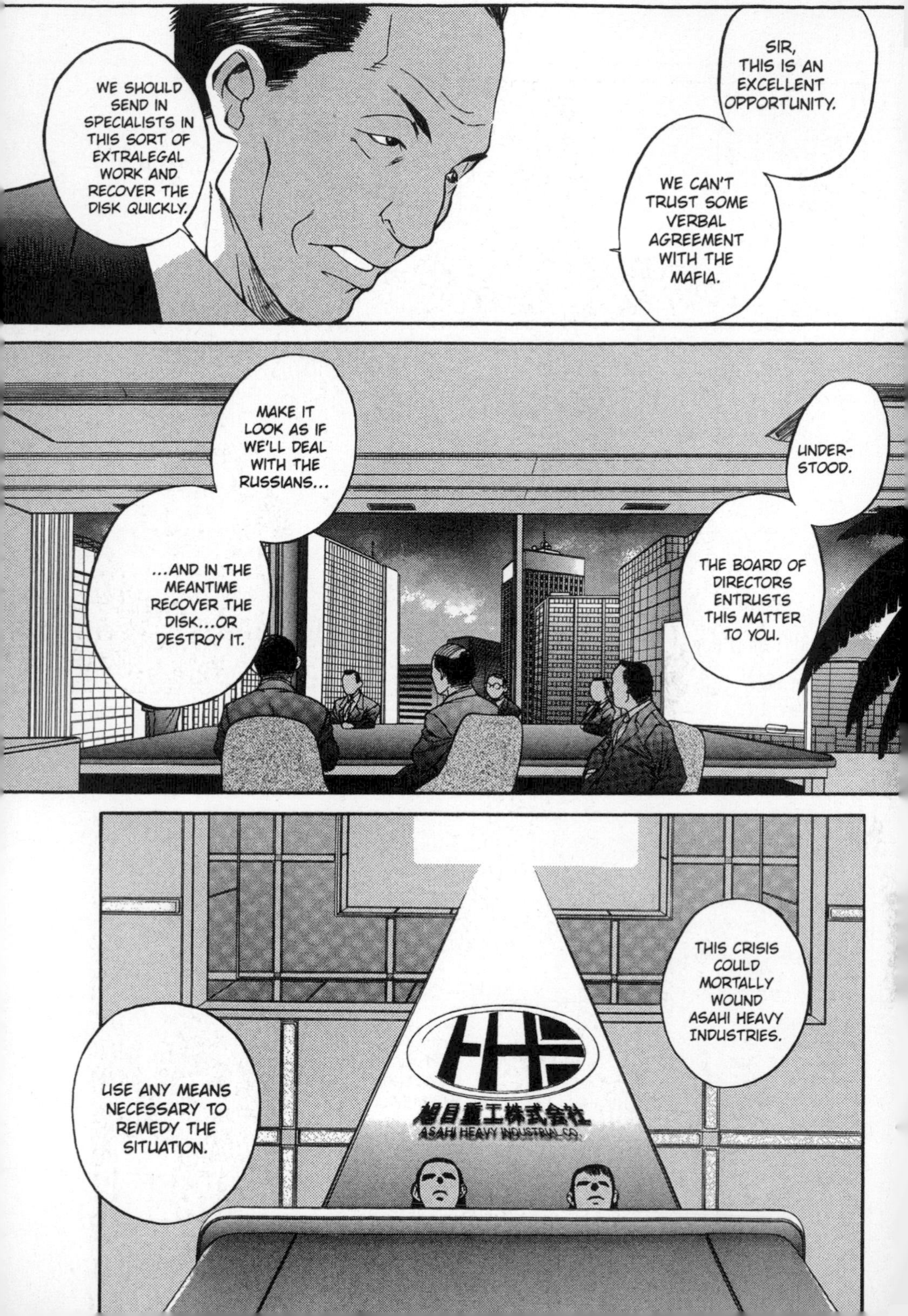
SIR, THIS IS AN EXCELLENT OPPORTUNITY.
WE CAN'T TRUST SOME VERBAL AGREEMENT WITH THE MAFIA.
WE SHOULD SEND IN SPECIALISTS IN THIS SORT OF EXTRALEGAL WORK AND RECOVER THE DISK QUICKLY.
UNDER-STOOD.
THE BOARD OF DIRECTORS ENTRUSTS THIS MATTER TO YOU.
MAKE IT LOOK AS IF WE'LL DEAL WITH THE RUSSIANS...
...AND IN THE MEANTIME RECOVER THE DISK...OR DESTROY IT.
THIS CRISIS COULD MORTALLY WOUND ASAHI HEAVY INDUSTRIES.
ASAHI HEAVY INDUSTRIAL CO.
USE ANY MEANS NECESSARY TO REMEDY THE SITUATION.

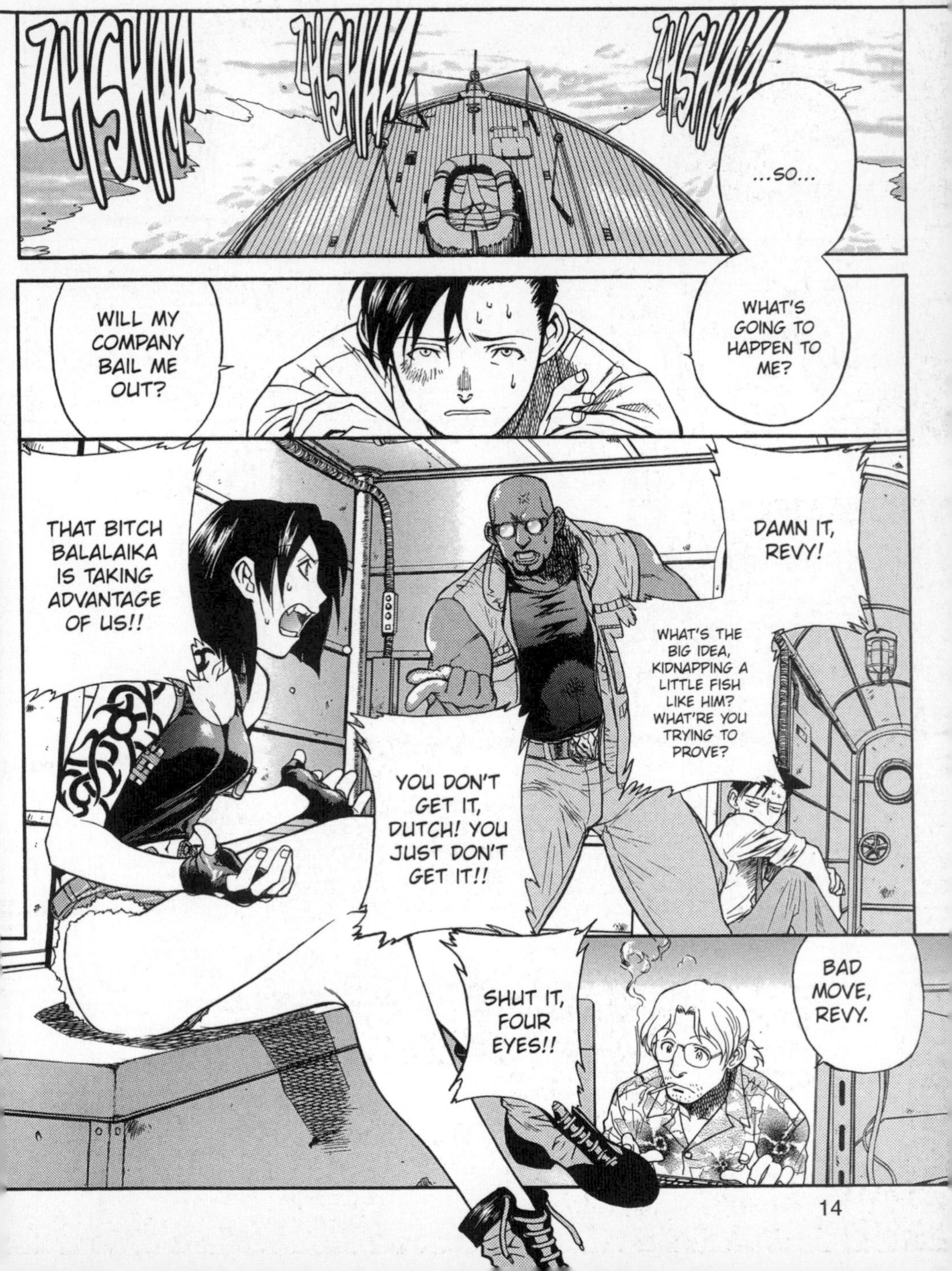
ZHSHAA
ZHSHAA
ZHSHAA
...SO...
WHAT'S GOING TO HAPPEN TO ME?
WILL MY COMPANY BAIL ME OUT?
DAMN IT, REVY!
WHAT'S THE BIG IDEA, KIDNAPPING A LITTLE FISH LIKE HIM? WHAT'RE YOU TRYING TO PROVE?
THAT BITCH BALALAIKA IS TAKING ADVANTAGE OF US!!
YOU DON'T GET IT, DUTCH! YOU JUST DON'T GET IT!!
BAD MOVE, REVY.
SHUT IT, FOUR EYES!!

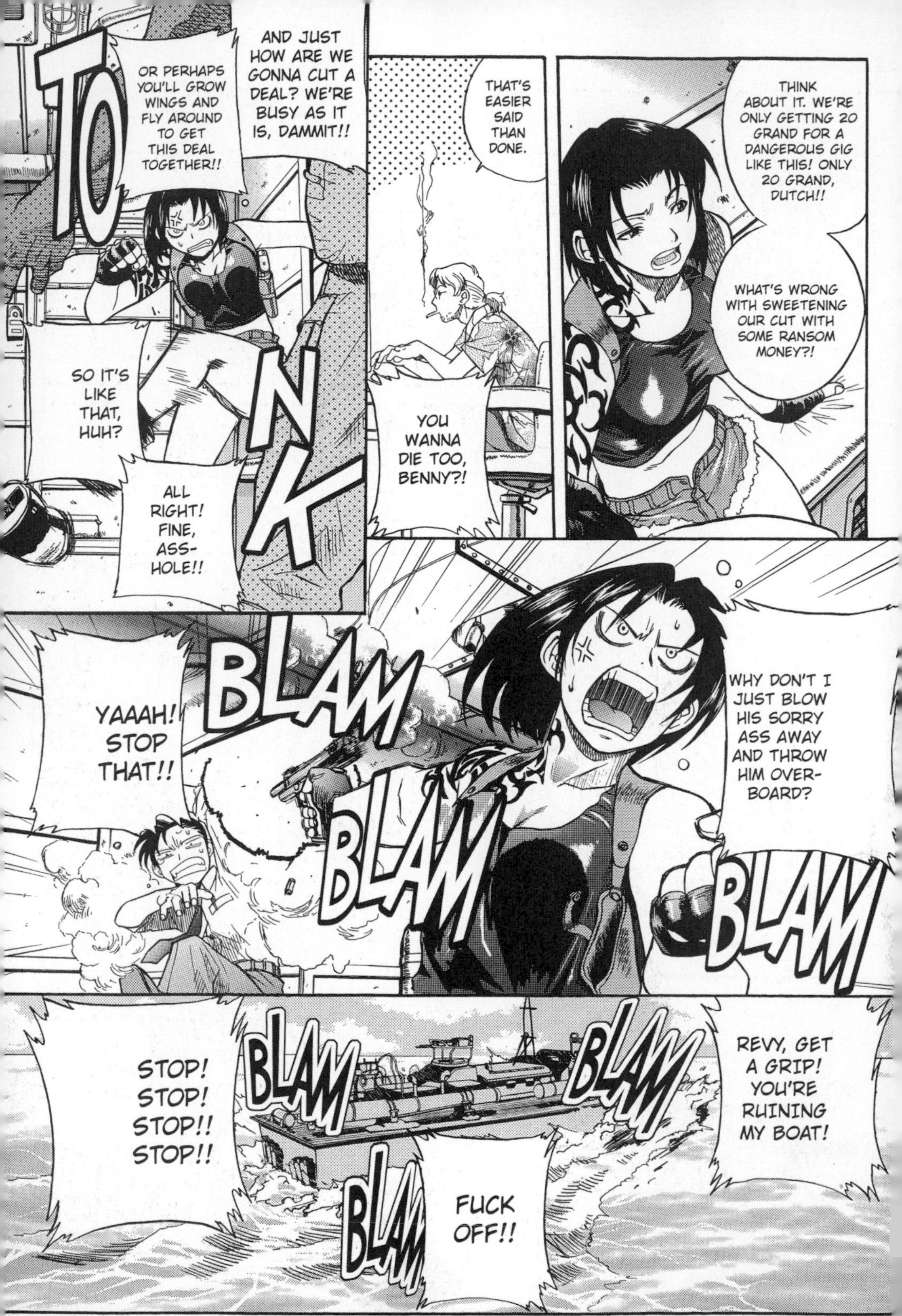
THINK ABOUT IT. WE'RE ONLY GETTING 20 GRAND FOR A DANGEROUS GIG LIKE THIS! ONLY 20 GRAND, DUTCH!!
WHAT'S WRONG WITH SWEETENING OUR CUT WITH SOME RANSOM MONEY?!
THAT'S EASIER SAID THAN DONE.
YOU WANNA DIE TOO, BENNY?!
AND JUST HOW ARE WE GONNA CUT A DEAL? WE'RE BUSY AS IT IS, DAMMIT!!
OR PERHAPS YOU'LL GROW WINGS AND FLY AROUND TO GET THIS DEAL TOGETHER!!
TONK
SO IT'S LIKE THAT, HUH?
ALL RIGHT! FINE, ASS-HOLE!!
WHY DON'T I JUST BLOW HIS SORRY ASS AWAY AND THROW HIM OVER-BOARD?
BLAM
BLAM
BLAM
YAAAH! STOP THAT!!
REVY, GET A GRIP! YOU'RE RUINING MY BOAT!
BLAM
FUCK OFF!!
BLAM
BLAM
STOP! STOP! STOP!! STOP!!

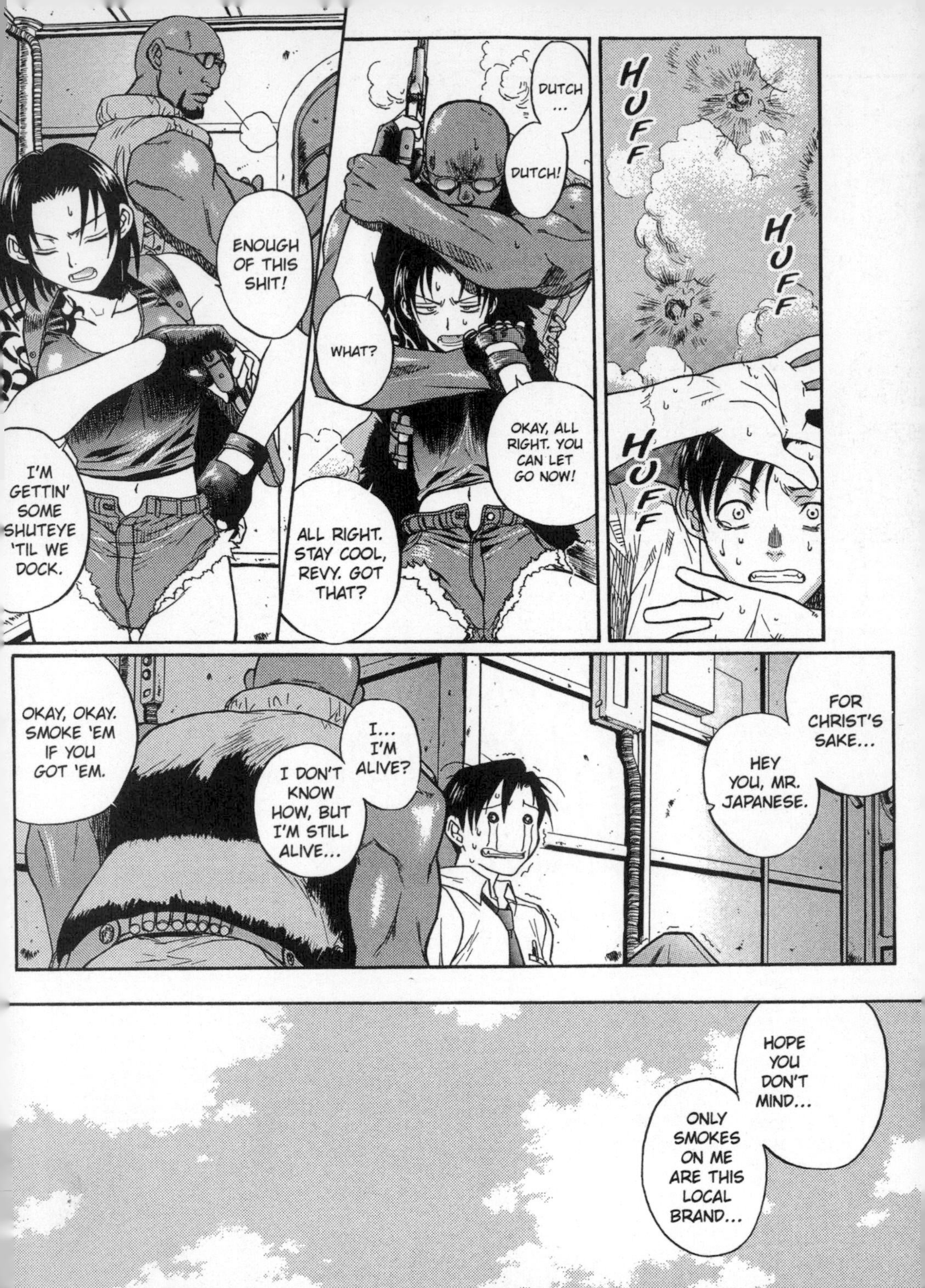
HUFF
HUFF
HUFF
DUTCH...
DUTCH!
WHAT?
OKAY, ALL RIGHT. YOU CAN LET GO NOW!
ALL RIGHT. STAY COOL, REVY. GOT THAT?
ENOUGH OF THIS SHIT!
I'M GETTIN' SOME SHUTEYE 'TIL WE DOCK.
FOR CHRIST'S SAKE...
HEY YOU, MR. JAPANESE.
I... I'M ALIVE?
I DON'T KNOW HOW, BUT I'M STILL ALIVE...
OKAY, OKAY. SMOKE 'EM IF YOU GOT 'EM.
HOPE YOU DON'T MIND...
ONLY SMOKES ON ME ARE THIS LOCAL BRAND...

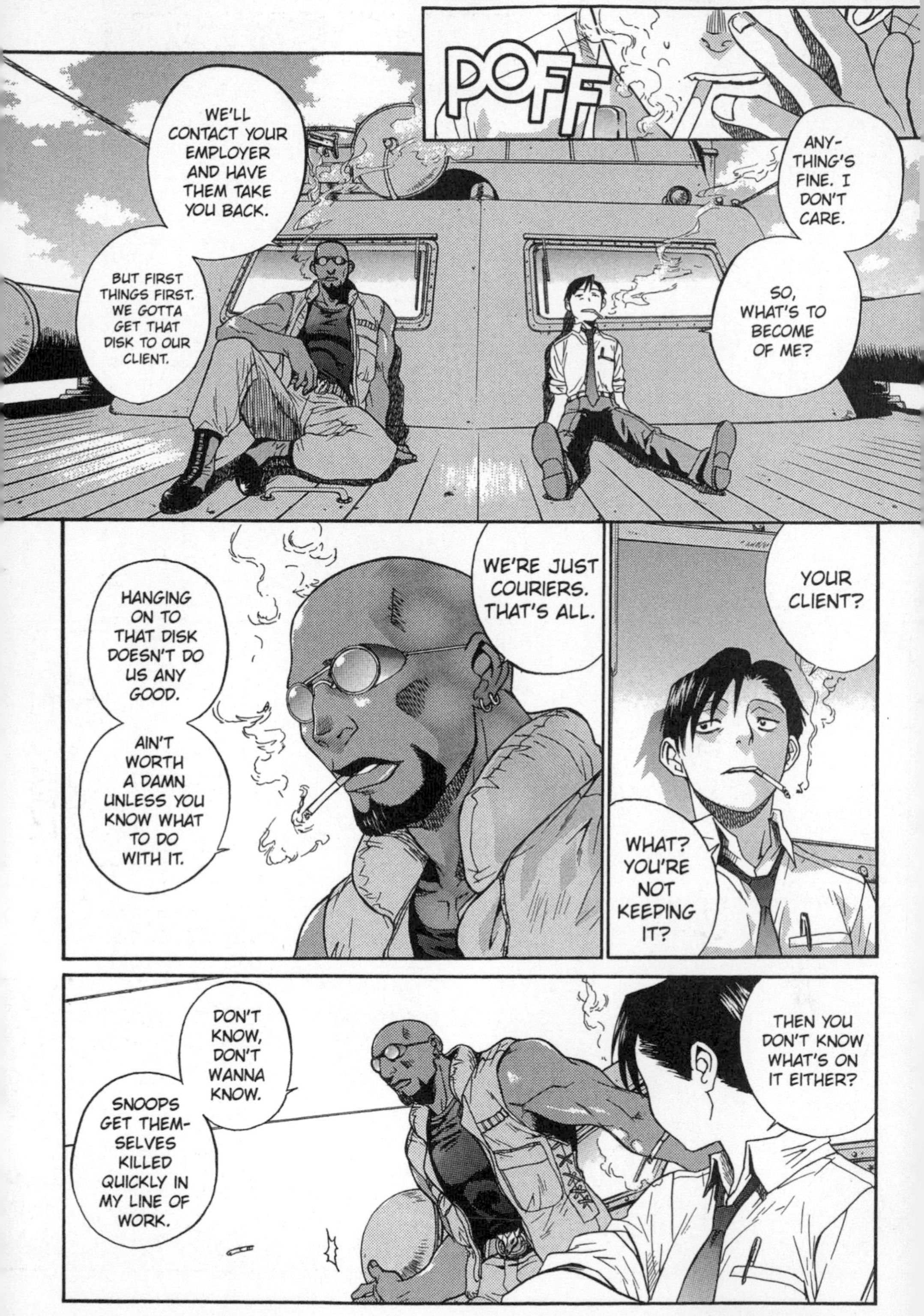
POFF
ANY-THING'S FINE. I DON'T CARE.
SO, WHAT'S TO BECOME OF ME?
WE'LL CONTACT YOUR EMPLOYER AND HAVE THEM TAKE YOU BACK.
BUT FIRST THINGS FIRST. WE GOTTA GET THAT DISK TO OUR CLIENT.
YOUR CLIENT?
WHAT? YOU'RE NOT KEEPING IT?
WE'RE JUST COURIERS. THAT'S ALL.
HANGING ON TO THAT DISK DOESN'T DO US ANY GOOD.
AIN'T WORTH A DAMN UNLESS YOU KNOW WHAT TO DO WITH IT.
THEN YOU DON'T KNOW WHAT'S ON IT EITHER?
DON'T KNOW, DON'T WANNA KNOW.
SNOOPS GET THEM-SELVES KILLED QUICKLY IN MY LINE OF WORK.

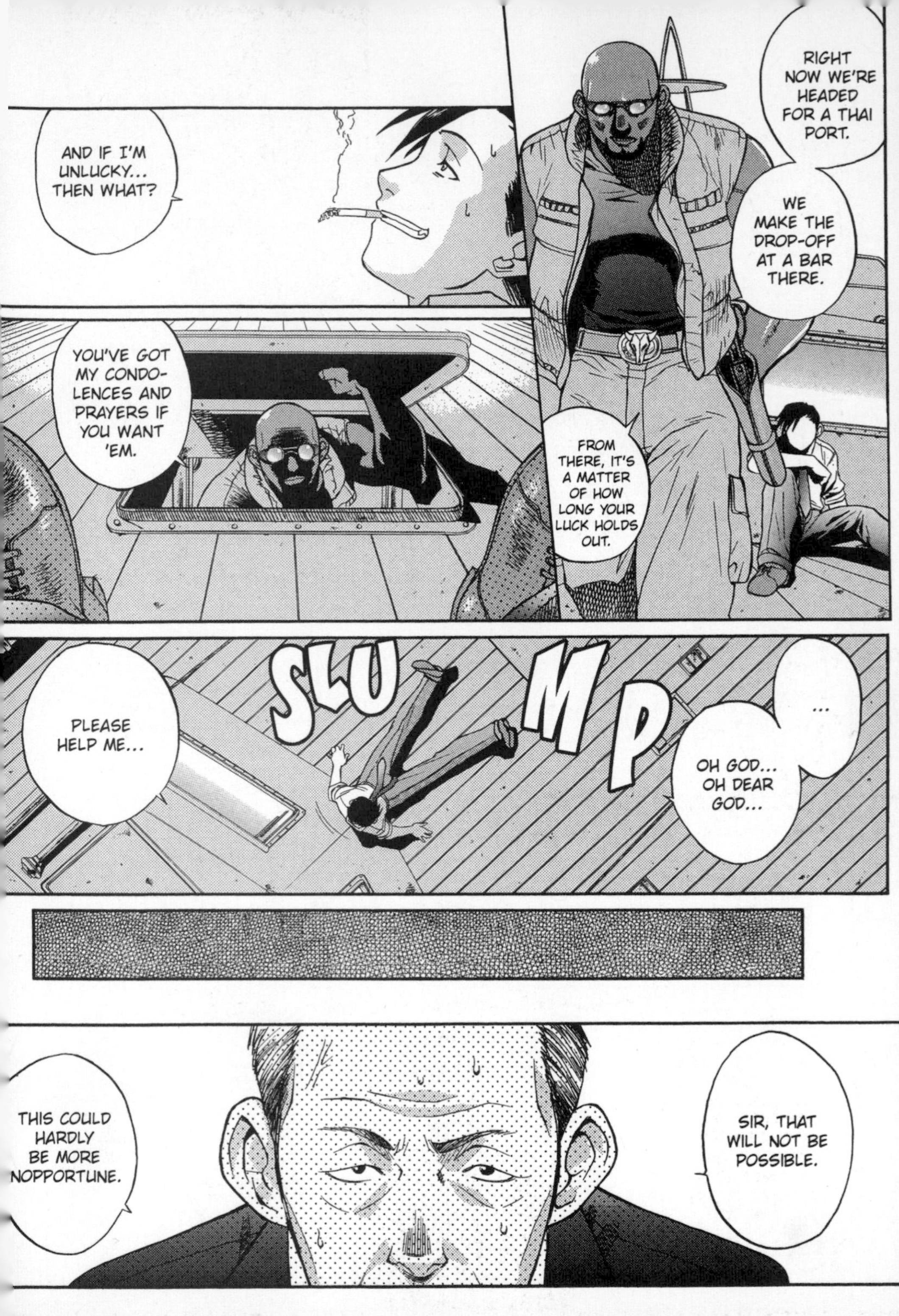
RIGHT NOW WE'RE HEADED FOR A THAI PORT.
WE MAKE THE DROP-OFF AT A BAR THERE.
FROM THERE, IT'S A MATTER OF HOW LONG YOUR LUCK HOLDS OUT.
AND IF I'M UNLUCKY... THEN WHAT?
YOU'VE GOT MY CONDO-LENCES AND PRAYERS IF YOU WANT 'EM.
...
OH GOD... OH DEAR GOD...
SLUMP
PLEASE HELP ME...
SIR, THAT WILL NOT BE POSSIBLE.
THIS COULD HARDLY BE MORE NOPPORTUNE.

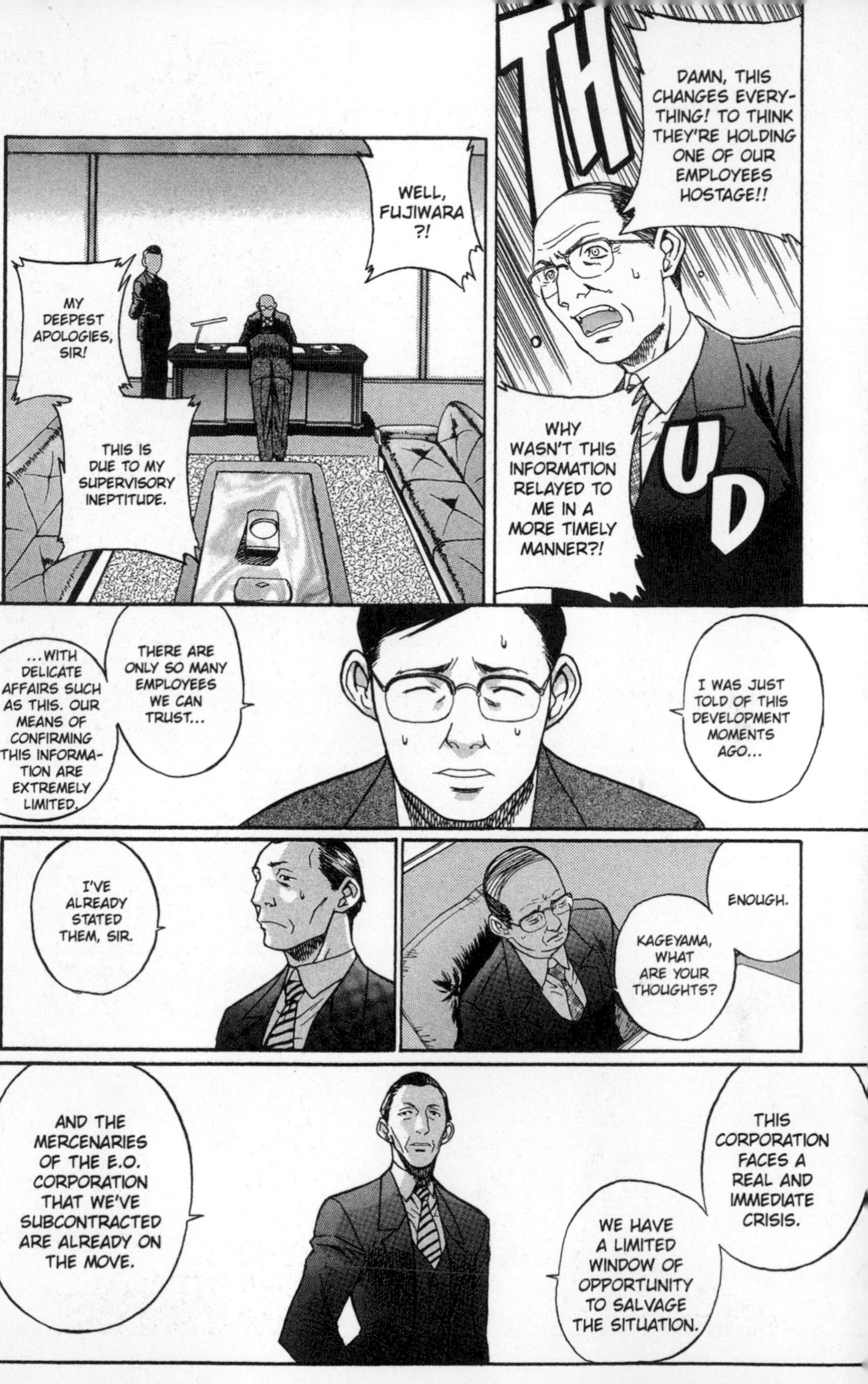
THUD
DAMN, THIS CHANGES EVERYTHING! TO THINK THEY'RE HOLDING ONE OF OUR EMPLOYEES HOSTAGE!!
WHY WASN'T THIS INFORMATION RELAYED TO ME IN A MORE TIMELY MANNER?!
WELL, FUJIWARA?!
MY DEEPEST APOLOGIES, SIR!
THIS IS DUE TO MY SUPERVISORY INEPTITUDE.
I WAS JUST TOLD OF THIS DEVELOPMENT MOMENTS AGO...
THERE ARE ONLY SO MANY EMPLOYEES WE CAN TRUST...
...WITH DELICATE AFFAIRS SUCH AS THIS. OUR MEANS OF CONFIRMING THIS INFORMATION ARE EXTREMELY LIMITED.
ENOUGH.
KAGEYAMA, WHAT ARE YOUR THOUGHTS?
I'VE ALREADY STATED THEM, SIR.
THIS CORPORATION FACES A REAL AND IMMEDIATE CRISIS.
WE HAVE A LIMITED WINDOW OF OPPORTUNITY TO SALVAGE THE SITUATION.
AND THE MERCENARIES OF THE E.O. CORPORATION THAT WE'VE SUBCONTRACTED ARE ALREADY ON THE MOVE.

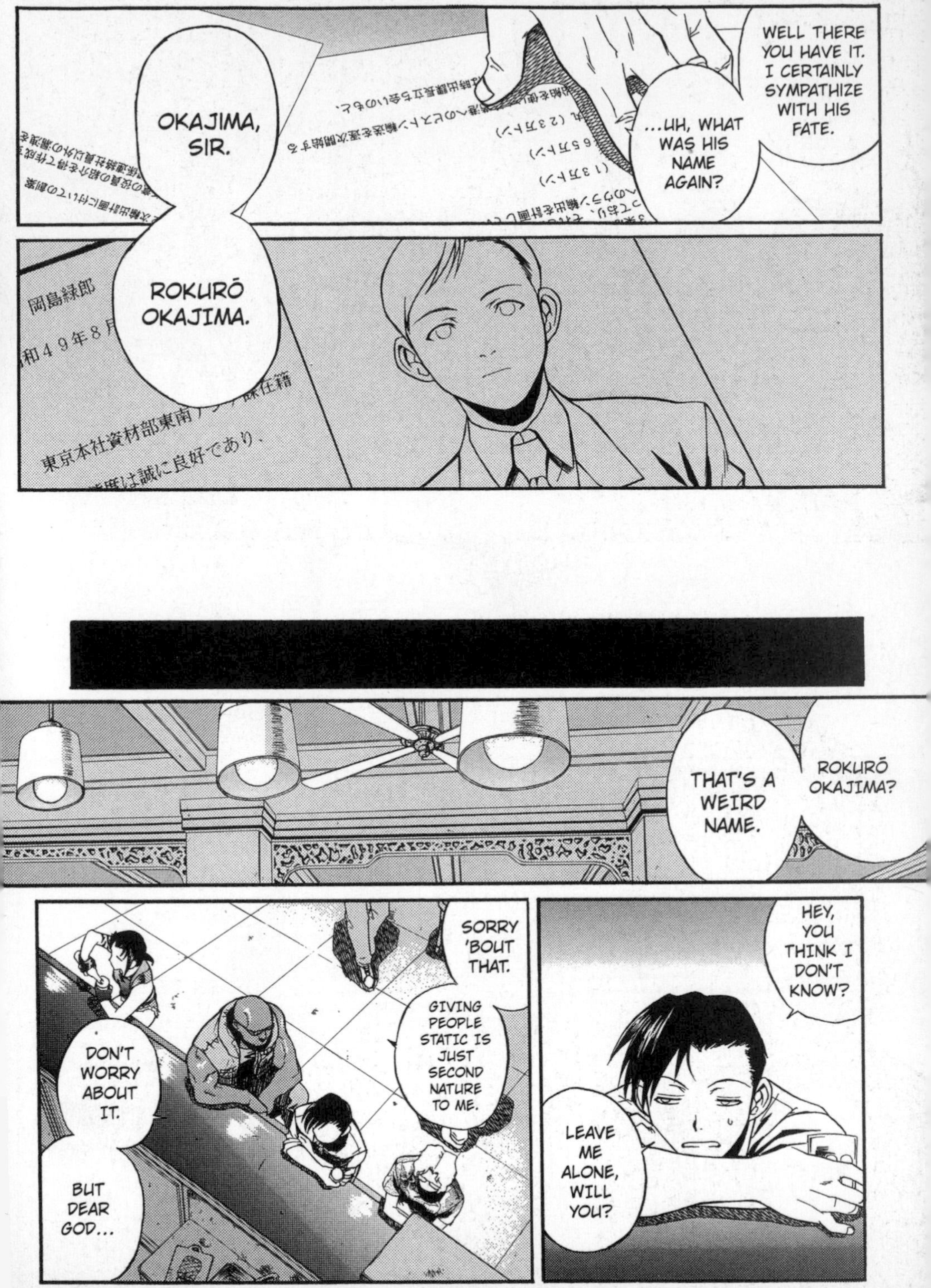
WELL THERE YOU HAVE IT. I CERTAINLY SYMPATHIZE WITH HIS FATE.
...UH, WHAT WAS HIS NAME AGAIN?
OKAJIMA, SIR.
ROKURŌ OKAJIMA.
岡島緑郎
ROKURŌ OKAJIMA?
THAT'S A WEIRD NAME.
HEY, YOU THINK I DON'T KNOW?
LEAVE ME ALONE, WILL YOU?
SORRY 'BOUT THAT.
GIVING PEOPLE STATIC IS JUST SECOND NATURE TO ME.
DON'T WORRY ABOUT IT.
BUT DEAR GOD...

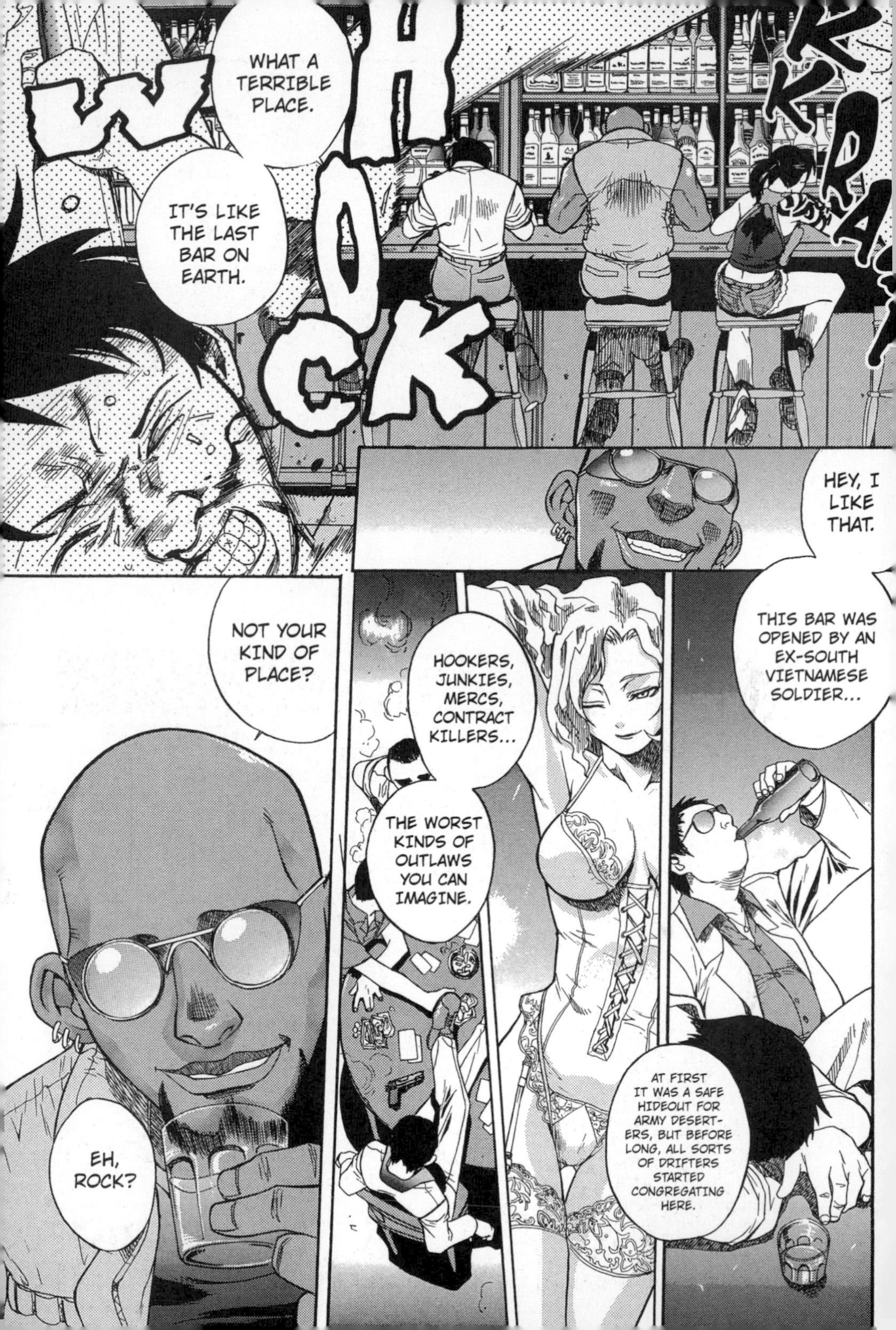
WHAT A TERRIBLE PLACE.
IT'S LIKE THE LAST BAR ON EARTH.
WHOCK
HEY, I LIKE THAT.
THIS BAR WAS OPENED BY AN EX-SOUTH VIETNAMESE SOLDIER...
AT FIRST IT WAS A SAFE HIDEOUT FOR ARMY DESERTERS, BUT BEFORE LONG, ALL SORTS OF DRIFTERS STARTED CONGREGATING HERE.
HOOKERS, JUNKIES, MERCS, CONTRACT KILLERS...
THE WORST KINDS OF OUTLAWS YOU CAN IMAGINE.
NOT YOUR KIND OF PLACE?
EH, ROCK?

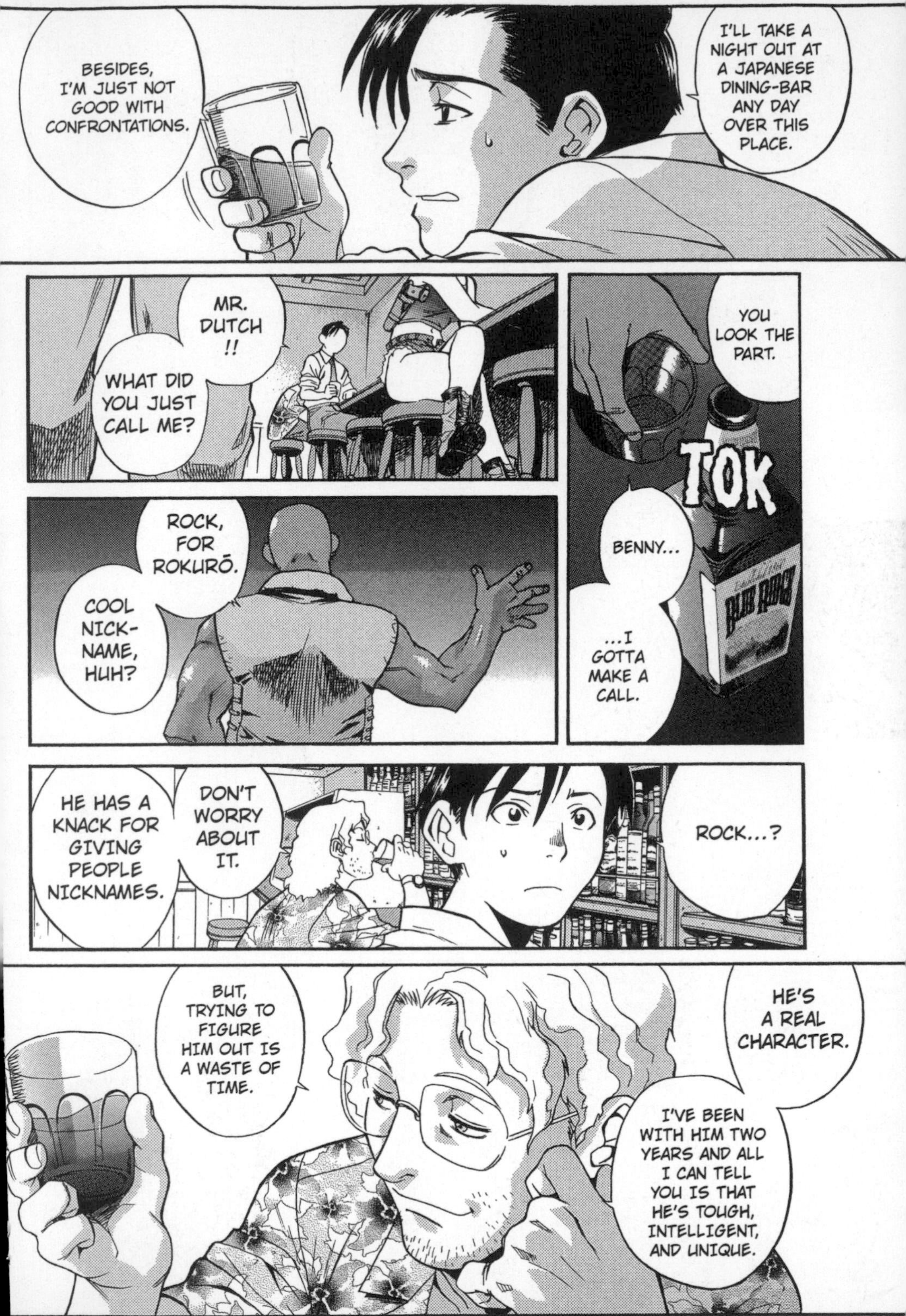
I'LL TAKE A NIGHT OUT AT A JAPANESE DINING-BAR ANY DAY OVER THIS PLACE.
BESIDES, I'M JUST NOT GOOD WITH CONFRONTATIONS.
YOU LOOK THE PART.
TOK
BENNY...
...I GOTTA MAKE A CALL.
MR. DUTCH !!
WHAT DID YOU JUST CALL ME?
ROCK, FOR ROKURŌ.
COOL NICK-NAME, HUH?
ROCK...?
DON'T WORRY ABOUT IT.
HE HAS A KNACK FOR GIVING PEOPLE NICKNAMES.
HE'S A REAL CHARACTER.
BUT, TRYING TO FIGURE HIM OUT IS A WASTE OF TIME.
I'VE BEEN WITH HIM TWO YEARS AND ALL I CAN TELL YOU IS THAT HE'S TOUGH, INTELLIGENT, AND UNIQUE.

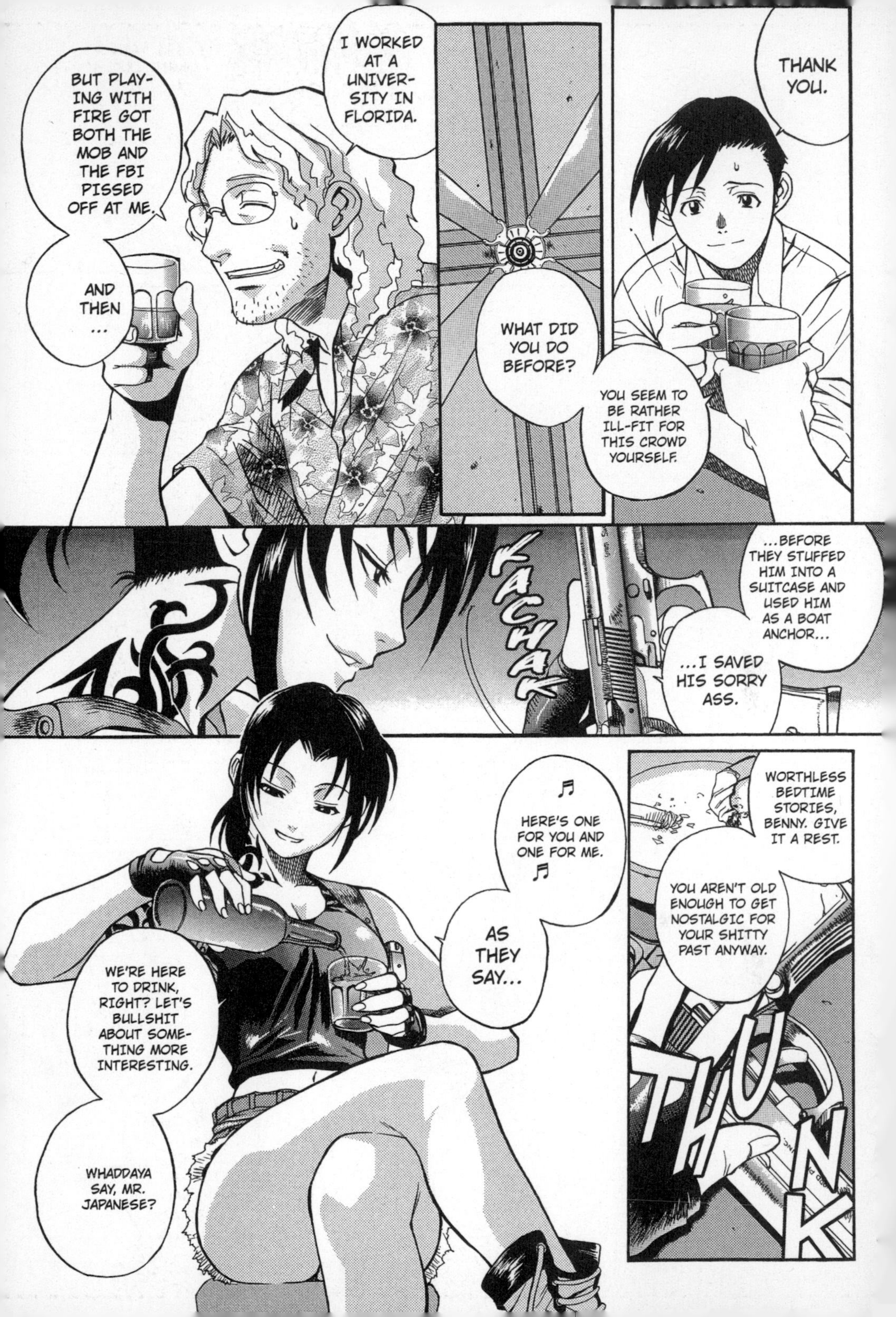
THANK YOU.
YOU SEEM TO BE RATHER ILL-FIT FOR THIS CROWD YOURSELF.
WHAT DID YOU DO BEFORE?
I WORKED AT A UNIVERSITY IN FLORIDA.
BUT PLAYING WITH FIRE GOT BOTH THE MOB AND THE FBI PISSED OFF AT ME.
AND THEN ...
...BEFORE THEY STUFFED HIM INTO A SUITCASE AND USED HIM AS A BOAT ANCHOR...
...I SAVED HIS SORRY ASS.
KACHAK
WORTHLESS BEDTIME STORIES, BENNY. GIVE IT A REST.
YOU AREN'T OLD ENOUGH TO GET NOSTALGIC FOR YOUR SHITTY PAST ANYWAY.
THUNK
♬ HERE'S ONE FOR YOU AND ONE FOR ME. ♬
AS THEY SAY...
WE'RE HERE TO DRINK, RIGHT? LET'S BULLSHIT ABOUT SOMETHING MORE INTERESTING.
WHADDAYA SAY, MR. JAPANESE?

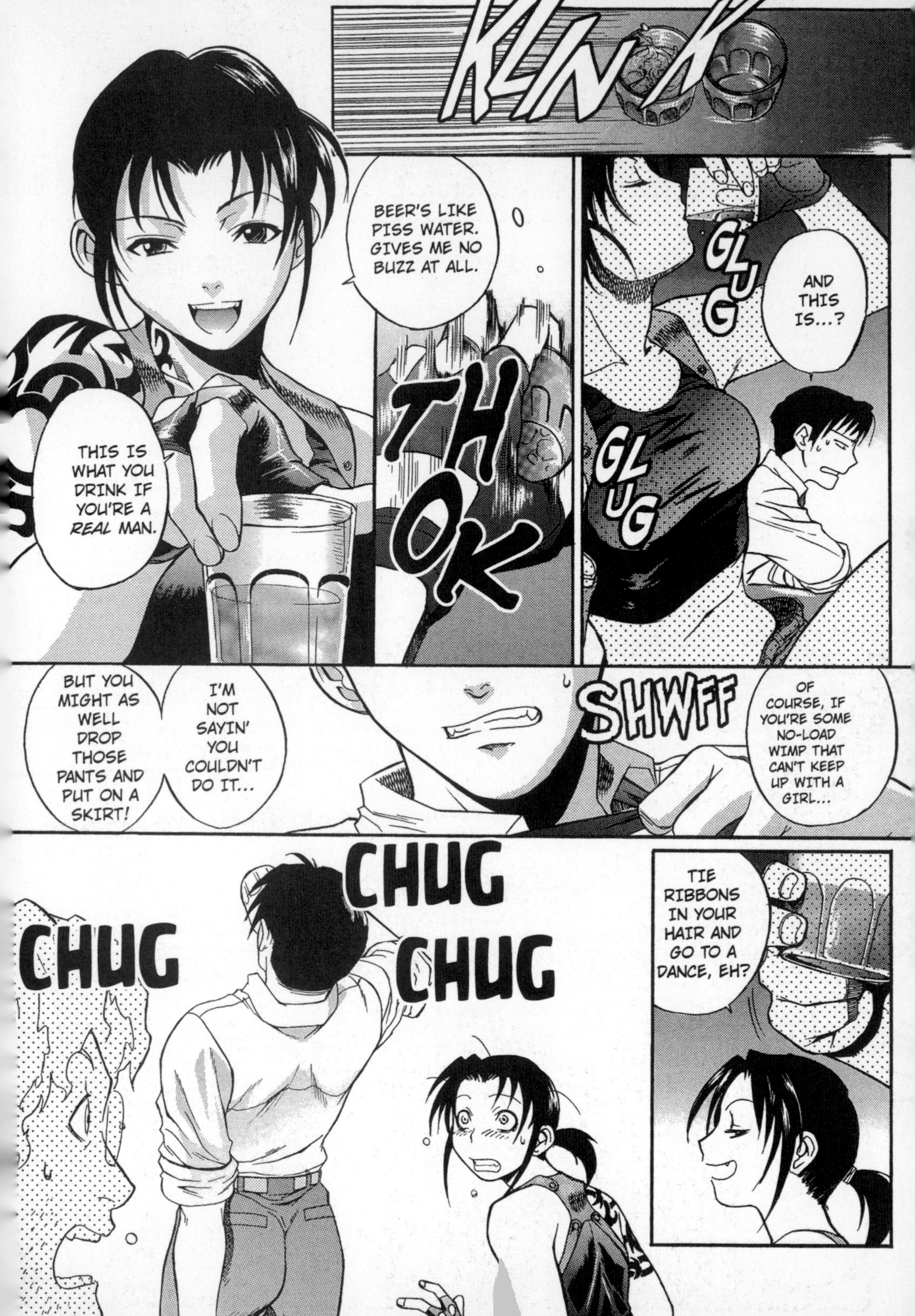
KLINK
GLUG GLUG GLUG GLUG
AND THIS IS...?
BEER'S LIKE PISS WATER. GIVES ME NO BUZZ AT ALL.
THOK
THIS IS WHAT YOU DRINK IF YOU'RE A *REAL* MAN.
OF COURSE, IF YOU'RE SOME NO-LOAD WIMP THAT CAN'T KEEP UP WITH A GIRL...
SHWFF
I'M NOT SAYIN' YOU COULDN'T DO IT...
BUT YOU MIGHT AS WELL DROP THOSE PANTS AND PUT ON A SKIRT!
TIE RIBBONS IN YOUR HAIR AND GO TO A DANCE, EH?
CHUG
CHUG
CHUG

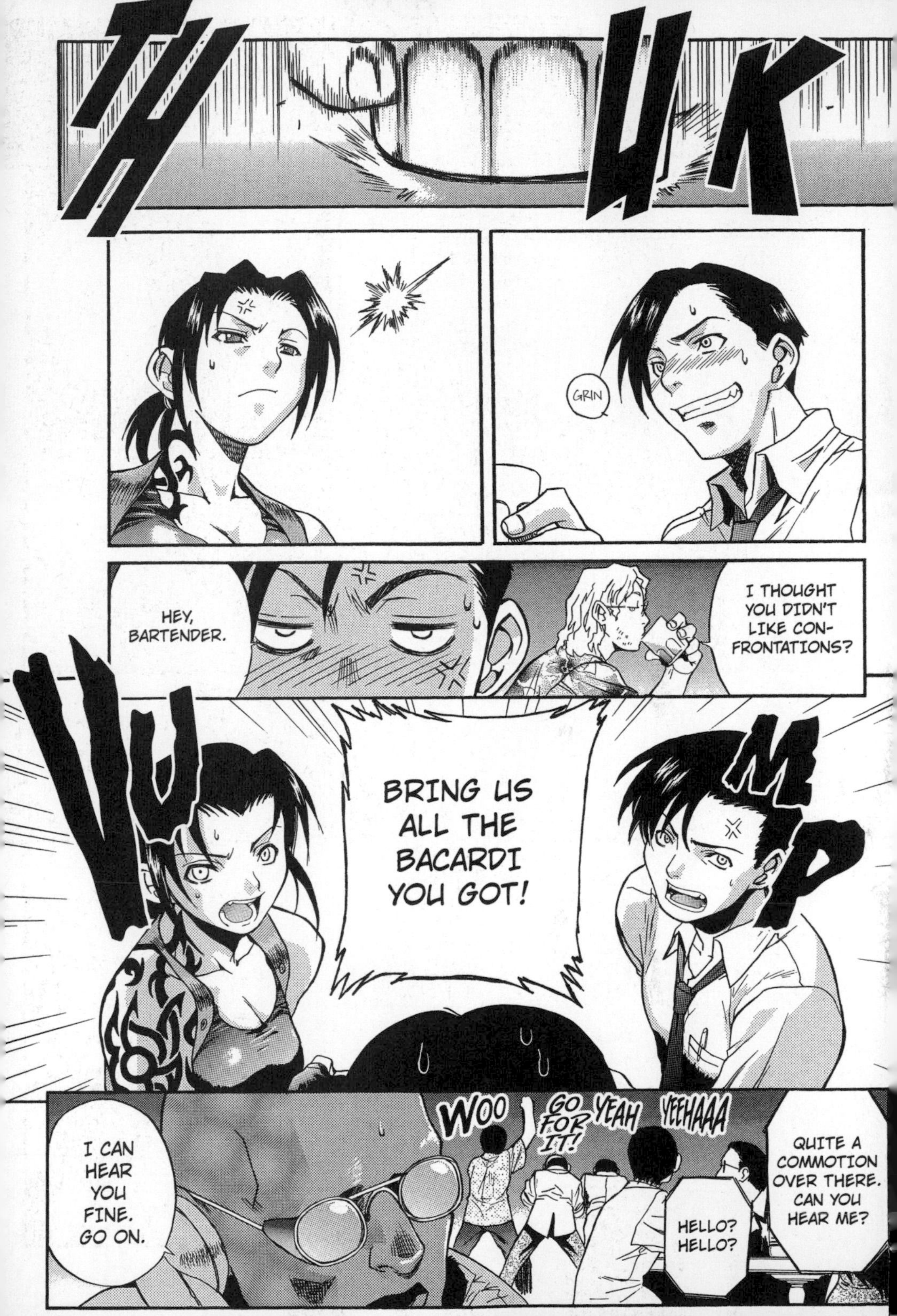
THUK
GRIN
I THOUGHT YOU DIDN'T LIKE CON-FRONTATIONS?
HEY, BARTENDER.
BRING US ALL THE BACARDI YOU GOT!
QUITE A COMMOTION OVER THERE. CAN YOU HEAR ME?
HELLO? HELLO?
YEEHAAA
YEAH
GO FOR IT!
WOO
I CAN HEAR YOU FINE. GO ON.

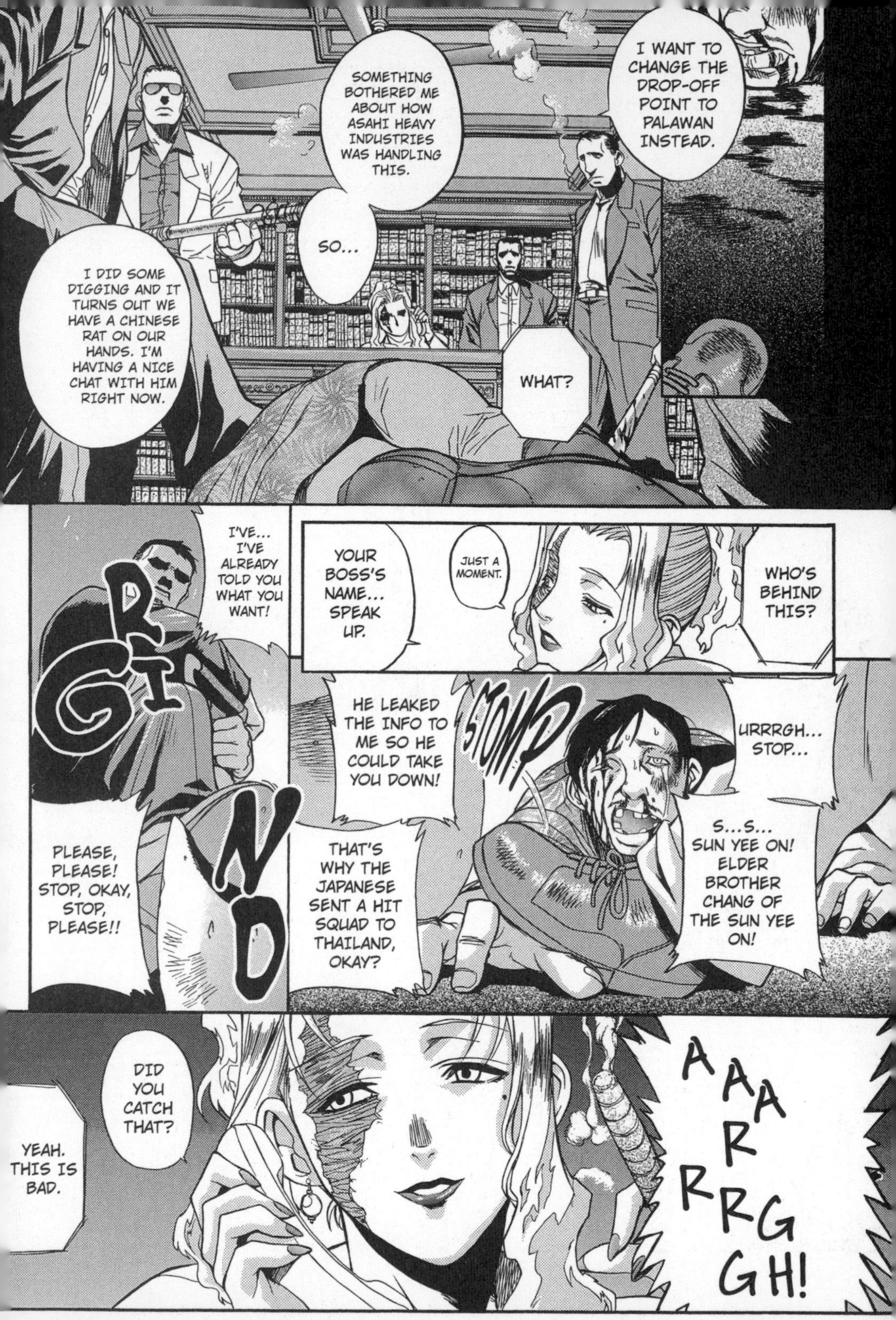
I WANT TO CHANGE THE DROP-OFF POINT TO PALAWAN INSTEAD.
SOMETHING BOTHERED ME ABOUT HOW ASAHI HEAVY INDUSTRIES WAS HANDLING THIS.
SO...
WHAT?
I DID SOME DIGGING AND IT TURNS OUT WE HAVE A CHINESE RAT ON OUR HANDS. I'M HAVING A NICE CHAT WITH HIM RIGHT NOW.
WHO'S BEHIND THIS?
JUST A MOMENT.
YOUR BOSS'S NAME... SPEAK UP.
URRRGH... STOP...
S...S... SUN YEE ON! ELDER BROTHER CHANG OF THE SUN YEE ON!
STOMP
HE LEAKED THE INFO TO ME SO HE COULD TAKE YOU DOWN!
THAT'S WHY THE JAPANESE SENT A HIT SQUAD TO THAILAND, OKAY?
I'VE... I'VE ALREADY TOLD YOU WHAT YOU WANT!
GRIND
PLEASE, PLEASE! STOP, OKAY, STOP, PLEASE!!
AAAARRRRGH!
DID YOU CATCH THAT?
YEAH. THIS IS BAD.

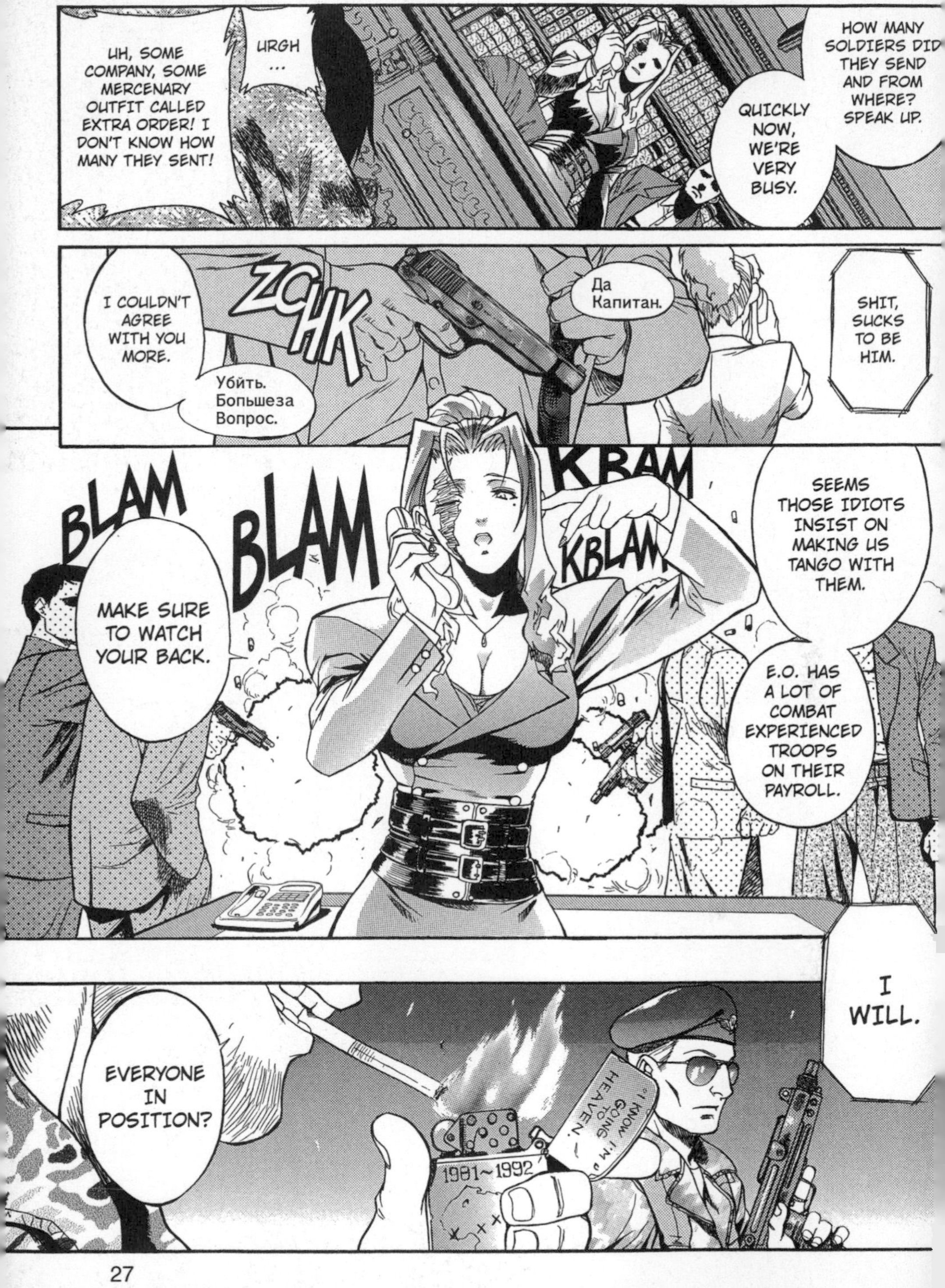
HOW MANY SOLDIERS DID THEY SEND AND FROM WHERE? SPEAK UP.
QUICKLY NOW, WE'RE VERY BUSY.
URGH ...
UH, SOME COMPANY, SOME MERCENARY OUTFIT CALLED EXTRA ORDER! I DON'T KNOW HOW MANY THEY SENT!
SHIT, SUCKS TO BE HIM.
Да Капитан.
ZCHK
I COULDN'T AGREE WITH YOU MORE.
Убить. Бопьшеза Вопрос.
KBAM
SEEMS THOSE IDIOTS INSIST ON MAKING US TANGO WITH THEM.
KBLAM
E.O. HAS A LOT OF COMBAT EXPERIENCED TROOPS ON THEIR PAYROLL.
BLAM
BLAM
MAKE SURE TO WATCH YOUR BACK.
I WILL.
"I KNOW I'M GOING TO HEAVEN."
1981~1992
EVERYONE IN POSITION?

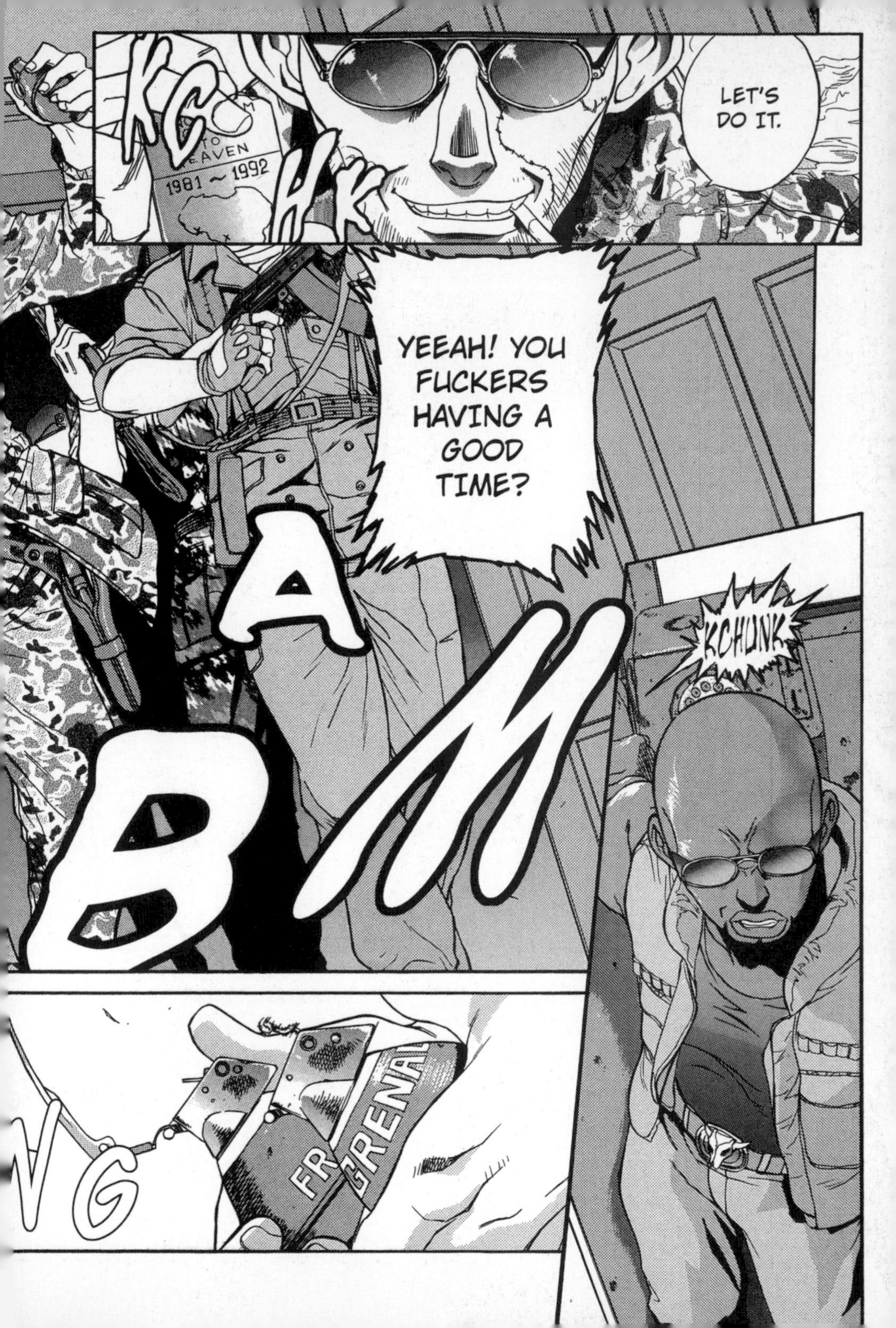

LET'S DO IT.
KCHK
1981 ~ 1992
KCHUNK
YEEAH! YOU FUCKERS HAVING A GOOD TIME?
BAM
NG

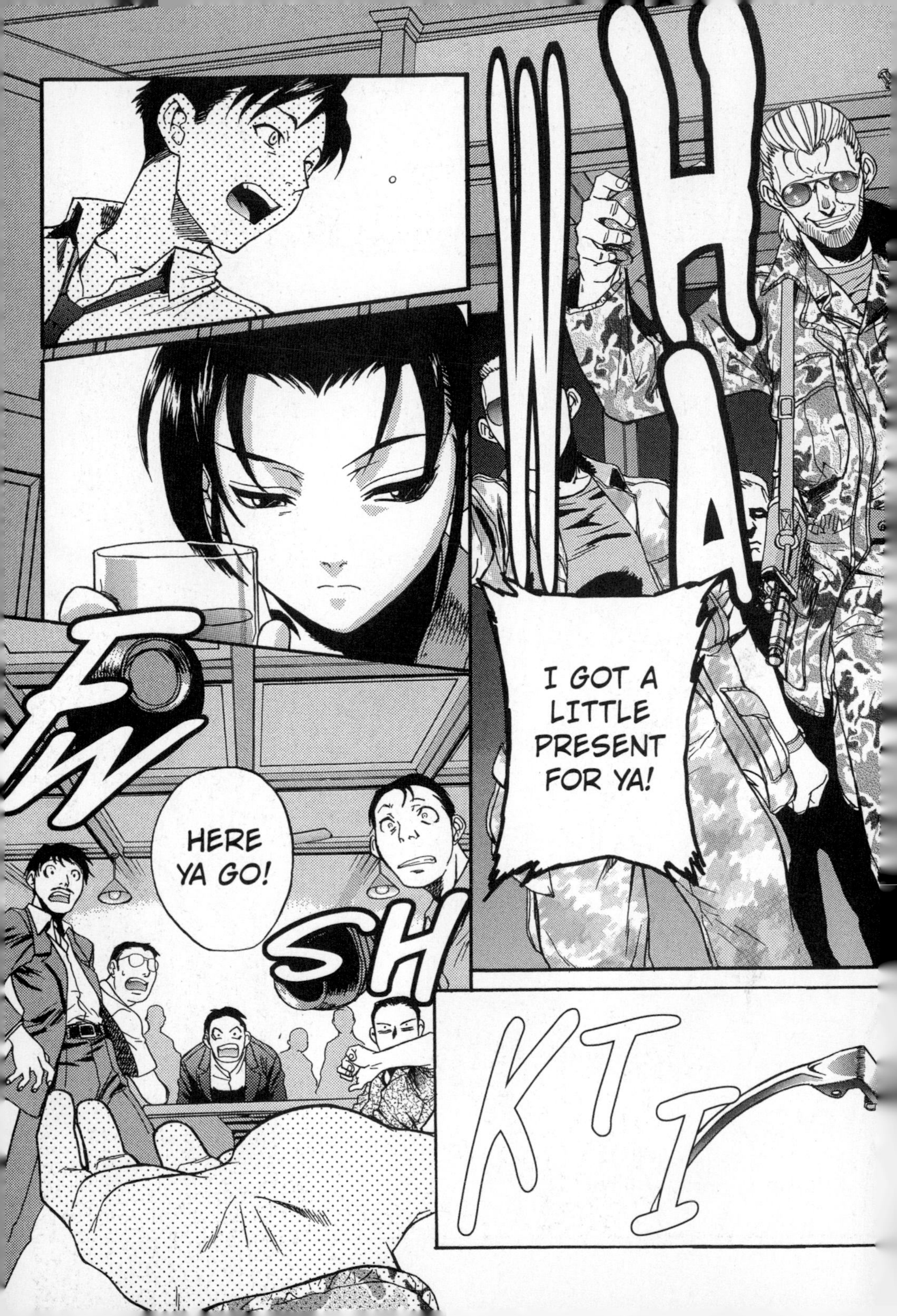
WHA
I GOT A LITTLE PRESENT FOR YA!
FWSH
HERE YA GO!
KTI

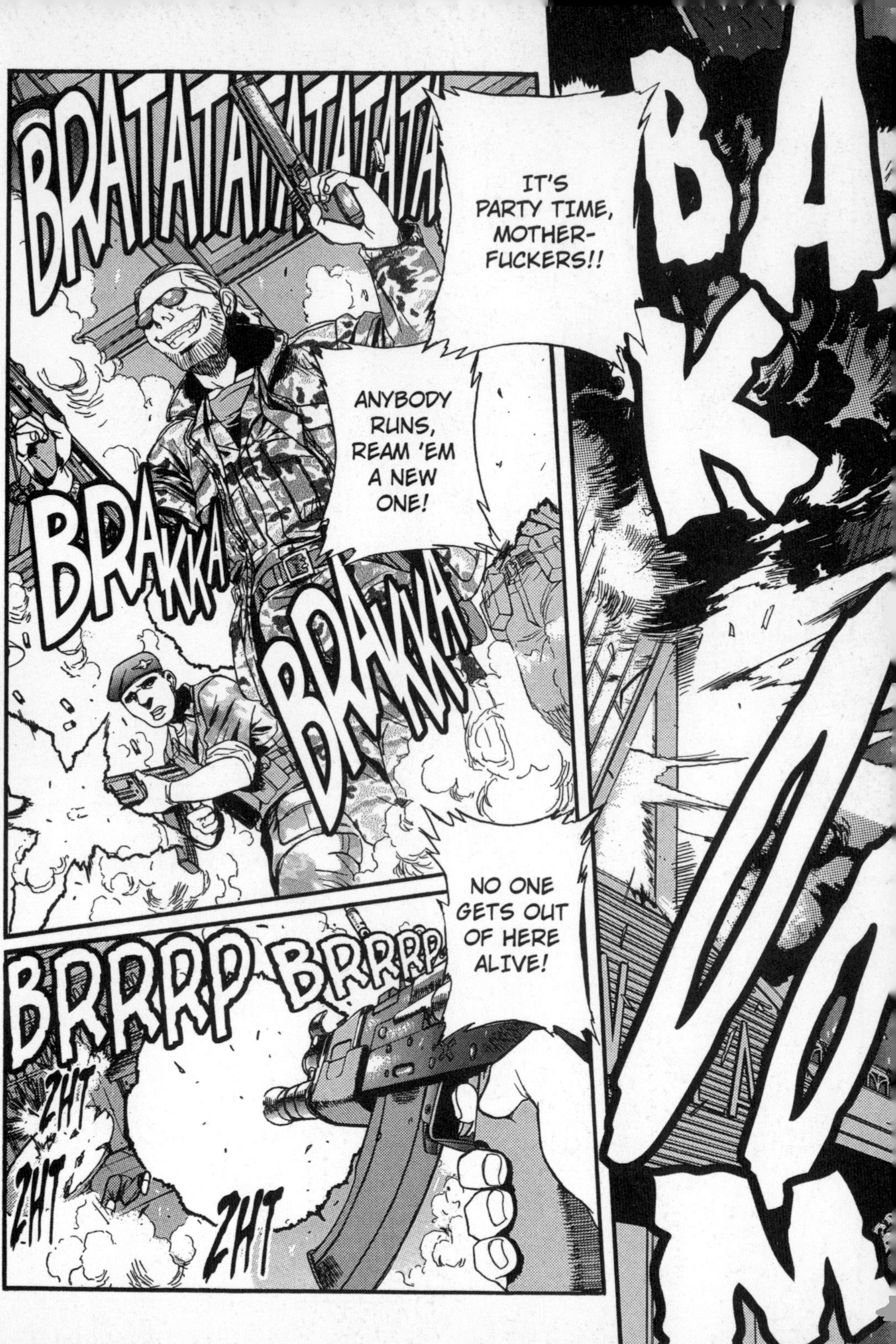
IT'S PARTY TIME, MOTHER-FUCKERS!!
BRATATATATATATA
ANYBODY RUNS, REAM 'EM A NEW ONE!
BRAKKA
BRAKKA
NO ONE GETS OUT OF HERE ALIVE!
BRRRRP
BRRRRP
ZHT
ZHT
ZHT
ZHT

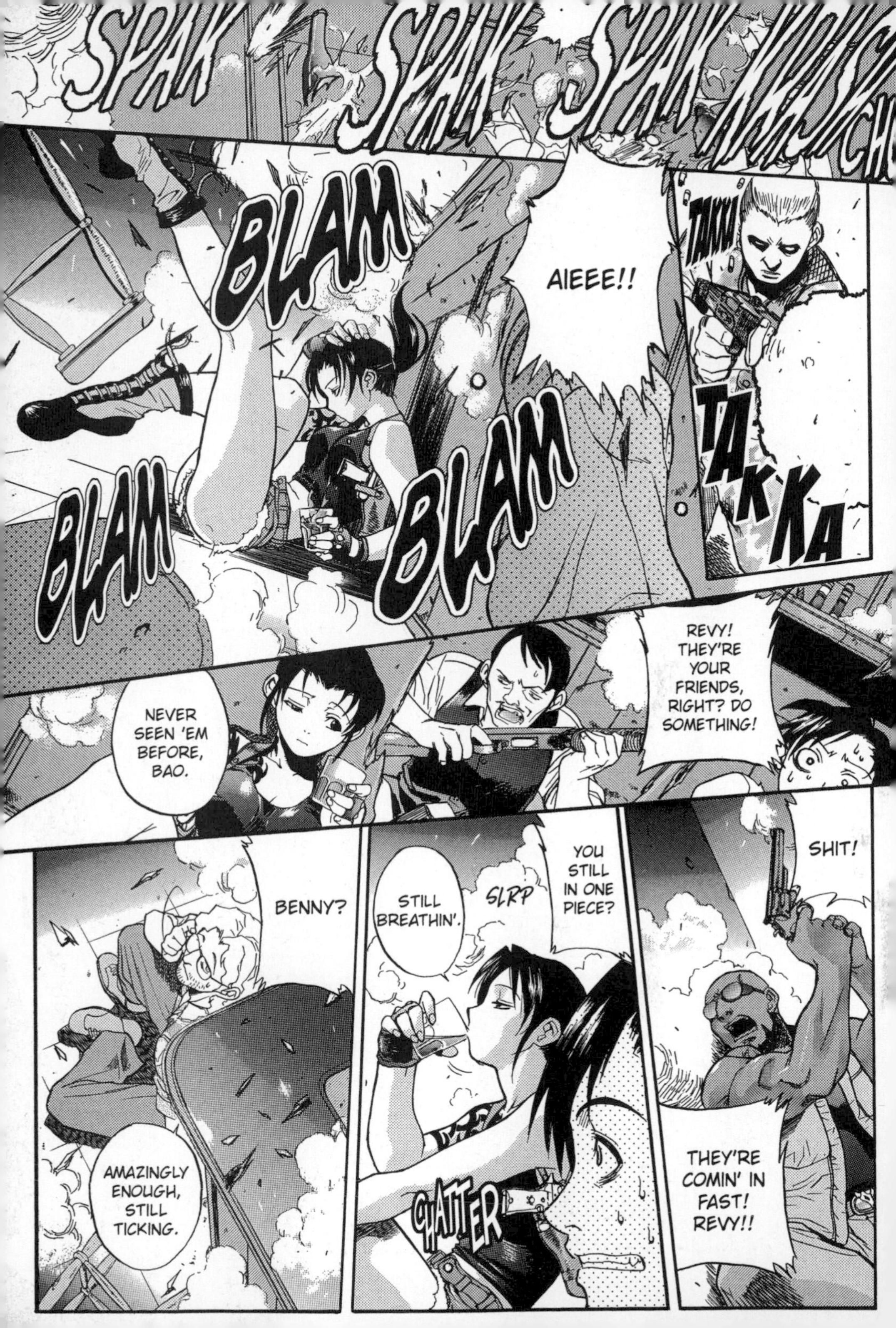
SPAK
SPAK
SPAK
TAKA
TAKKA
AIEEE!!
BLAM
BLAM
BLAM
REVY! THEY'RE YOUR FRIENDS, RIGHT? DO SOMETHING!
NEVER SEEN 'EM BEFORE, BAO.
SHIT!
THEY'RE COMIN' IN FAST! REVY!!
YOU STILL IN ONE PIECE?
SLRP
STILL BREATHIN'.
CHATTER
BENNY?
AMAZINGLY ENOUGH, STILL TICKING.

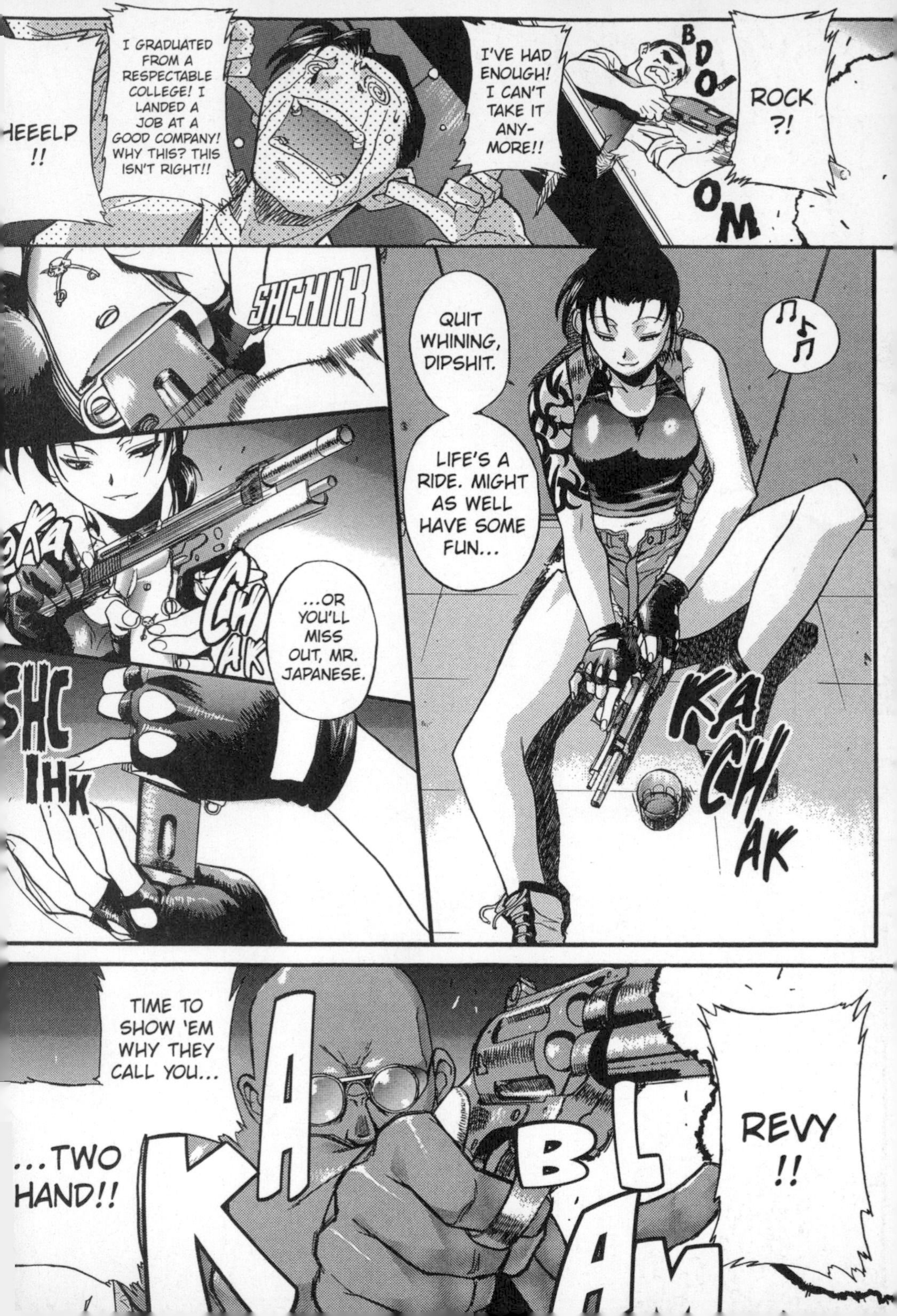
ROCK ?!
BDOOOM
I'VE HAD ENOUGH! I CAN'T TAKE IT ANYMORE!!
I GRADUATED FROM A RESPECTABLE COLLEGE! I LANDED A JOB AT A GOOD COMPANY! WHY THIS? THIS ISN'T RIGHT!!
HEEELP !!
QUIT WHINING, DIPSHIT.
LIFE'S A RIDE. MIGHT AS WELL HAVE SOME FUN...
KACHAK
SHCHIK
KA
CHAK
...OR YOU'LL MISS OUT, MR. JAPANESE.
SHCHIHK
REVY !!
TIME TO SHOW 'EM WHY THEY CALL YOU...
...TWO HAND!!
KABLAM

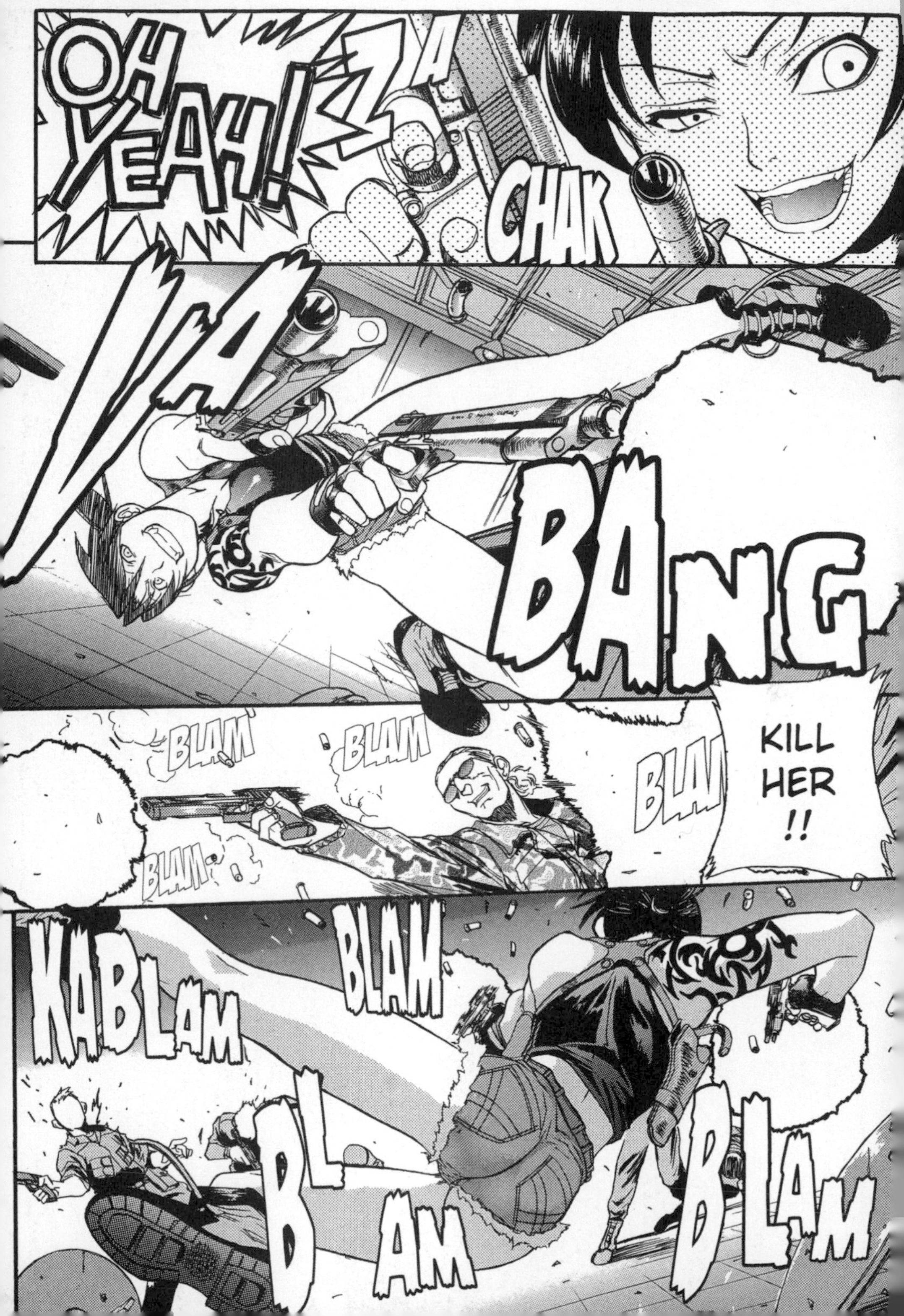
ZA
CHAK
OH YEAH!
YA
BANG
KILL HER!!
BLAM
BLAM
BLAM
BLAM
BLAM
KABLAM
BLAM
BLAM
BLAM

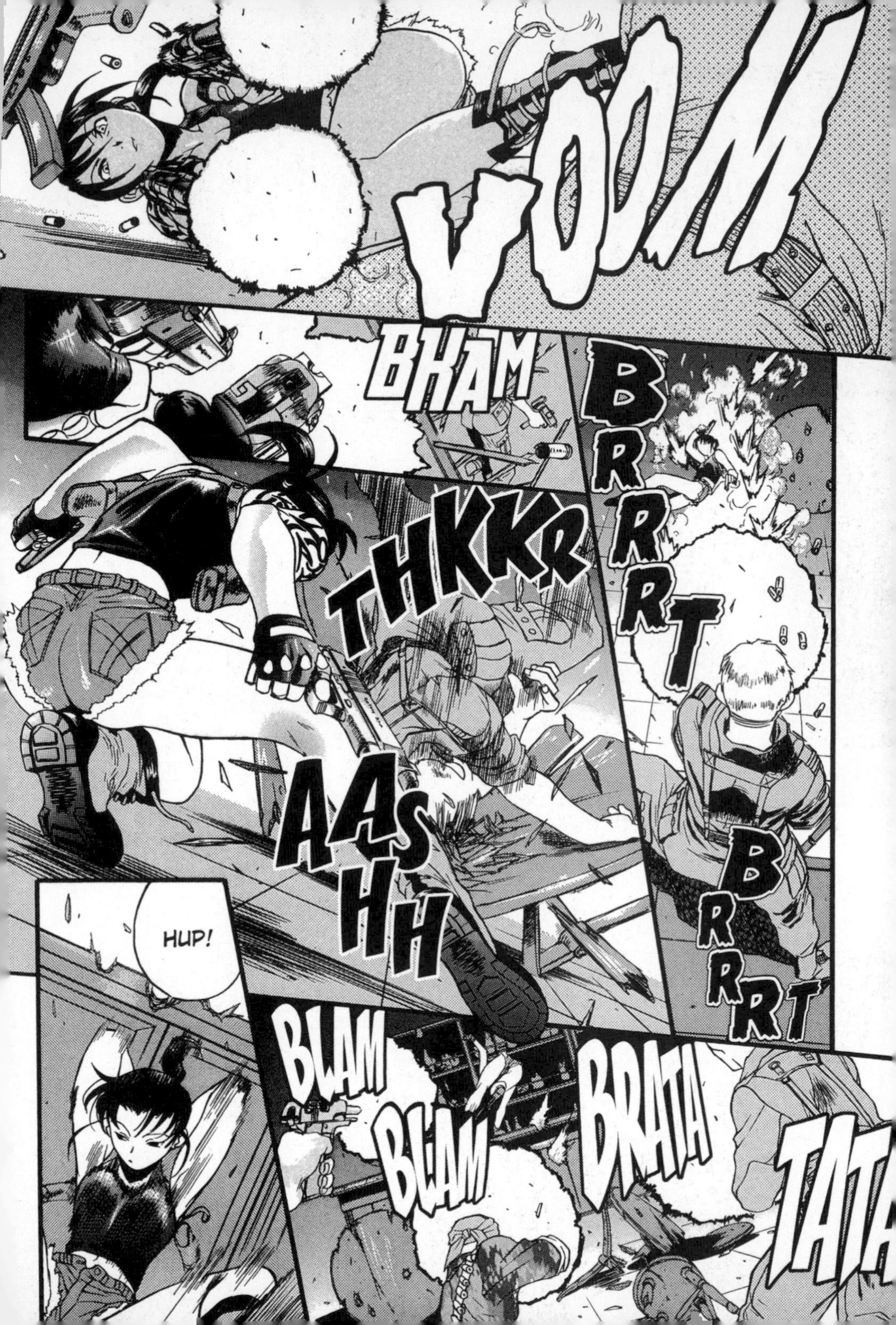
VOOM
BRRRT
BRRRRT
THKKR
AASHH
BHAM
TATA
BRATA
BLAM
BLAM
HUP!

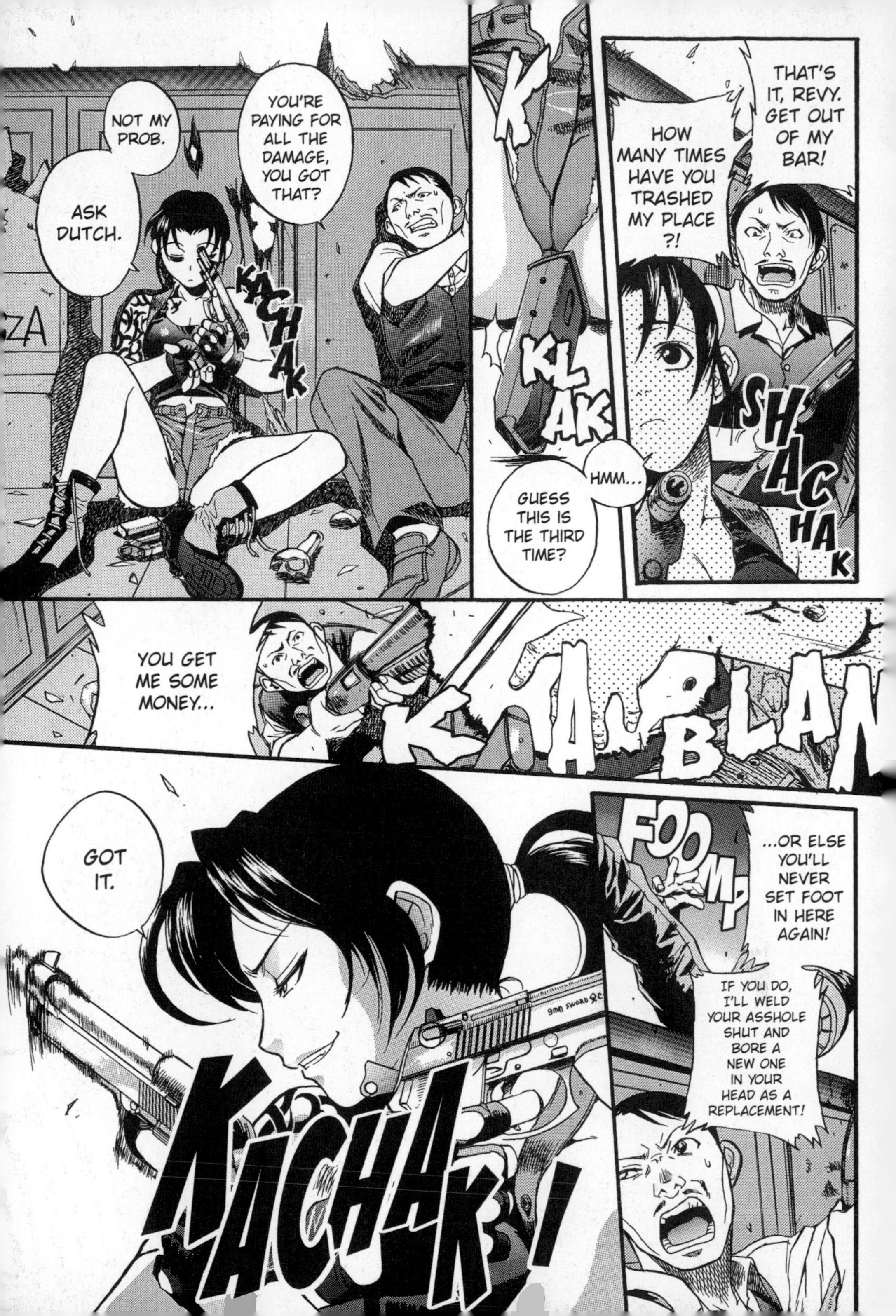

THAT'S IT, REVY. GET OUT OF MY BAR!
HOW MANY TIMES HAVE YOU TRASHED MY PLACE ?!
SHACHACHAK
HMM...
GUESS THIS IS THE THIRD TIME?
K
KLAK
YOU'RE PAYING FOR ALL THE DAMAGE, YOU GOT THAT?
NOT MY PROB.
ASK DUTCH.
KACHAK
KABLAM
YOU GET ME SOME MONEY...
FOOMP
...OR ELSE YOU'LL NEVER SET FOOT IN HERE AGAIN!
IF YOU DO, I'LL WELD YOUR ASSHOLE SHUT AND BORE A NEW ONE IN YOUR HEAD AS A REPLACEMENT!
GOT IT.
KACHAK!

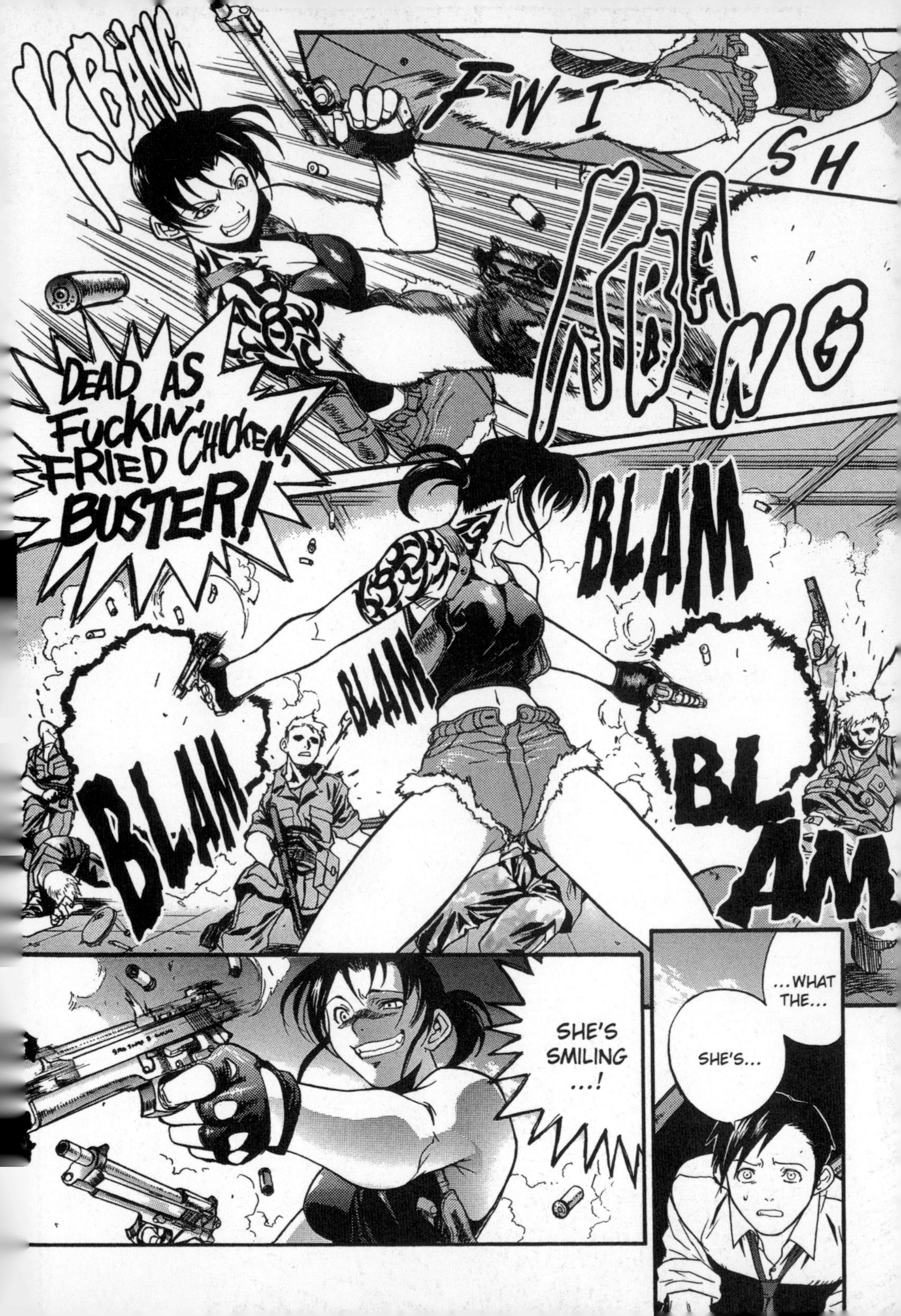
FWISH
BANG
BANG
DEAD AS FUCKIN' FRIED CHICKEN, BUSTER!
BLAM
BLAM
BLAM
BLAM
...WHAT THE...
SHE'S...
SHE'S SMILING ...!

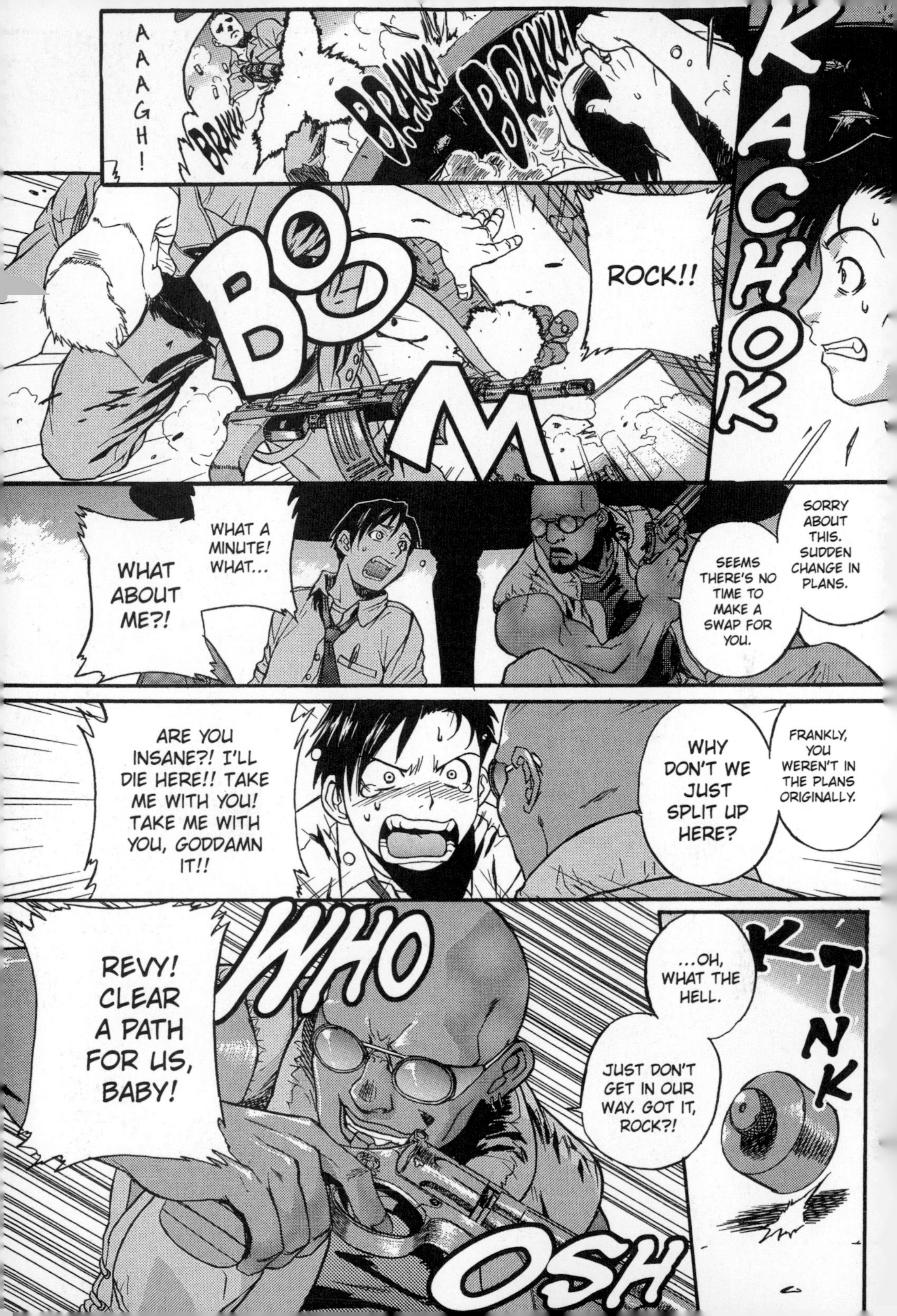
KACHOK
AAAAGH!
BRAKKA
BRAKKA
BRAKKA
BRAKKA
ROCK!!
BOOM
SORRY ABOUT THIS. SUDDEN CHANGE IN PLANS.
SEEMS THERE'S NO TIME TO MAKE A SWAP FOR YOU.
WHAT A MINUTE! WHAT...
WHAT ABOUT ME?!
FRANKLY, YOU WEREN'T IN THE PLANS ORIGINALLY.
WHY DON'T WE JUST SPLIT UP HERE?
ARE YOU INSANE?! I'LL DIE HERE!! TAKE ME WITH YOU! TAKE ME WITH YOU, GODDAMN IT!!
KTNK
...OH, WHAT THE HELL.
JUST DON'T GET IN OUR WAY. GOT IT, ROCK?!
REVY! CLEAR A PATH FOR US, BABY!
WHOOSH

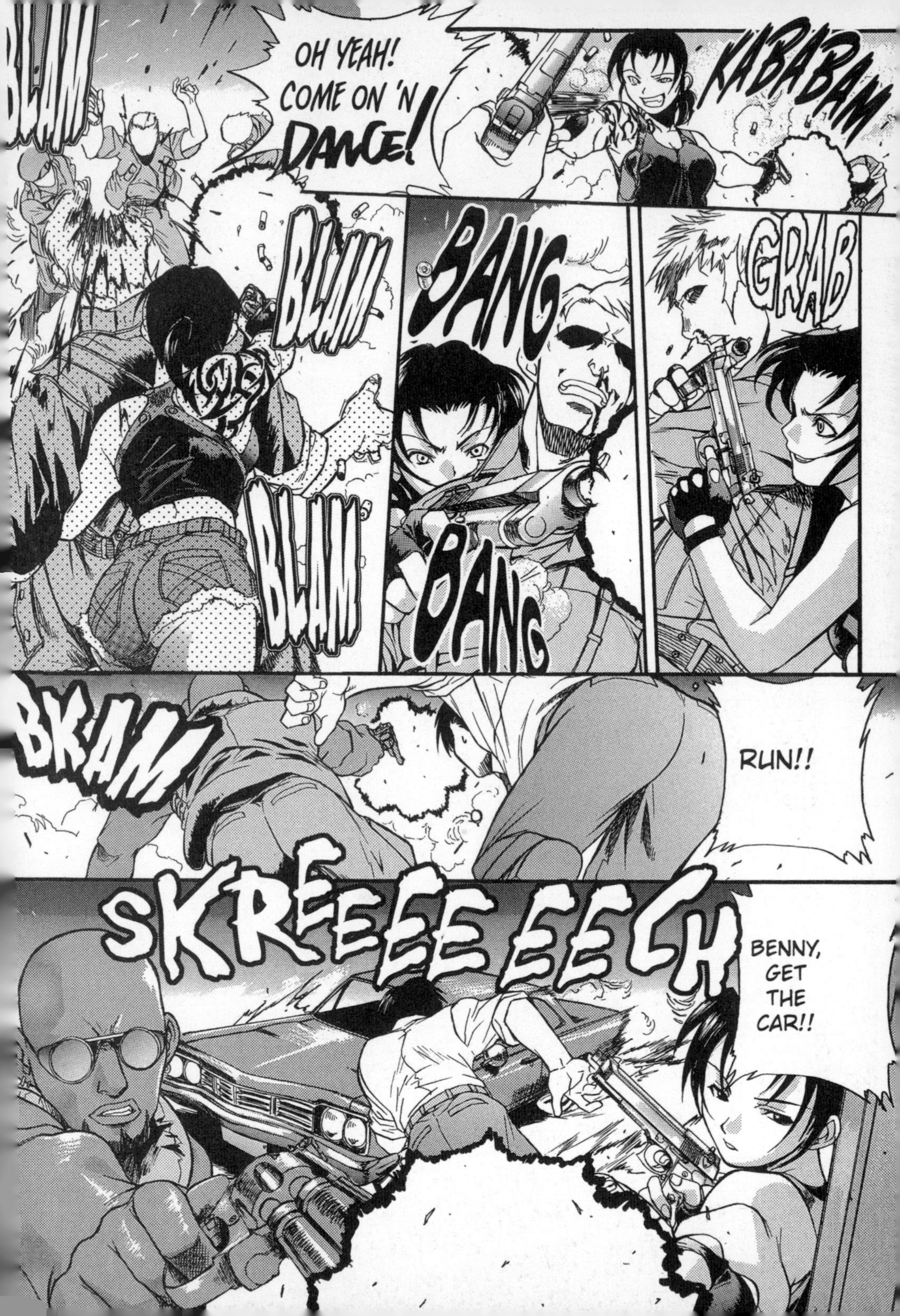
KABABAM
OH YEAH! COME ON 'N DANCE!
BLAM
GRAB
BANG
BANG
BLAM
BLAM
RUN!!
BKAM
BENNY, GET THE CAR!!
SKREEEE EEECH

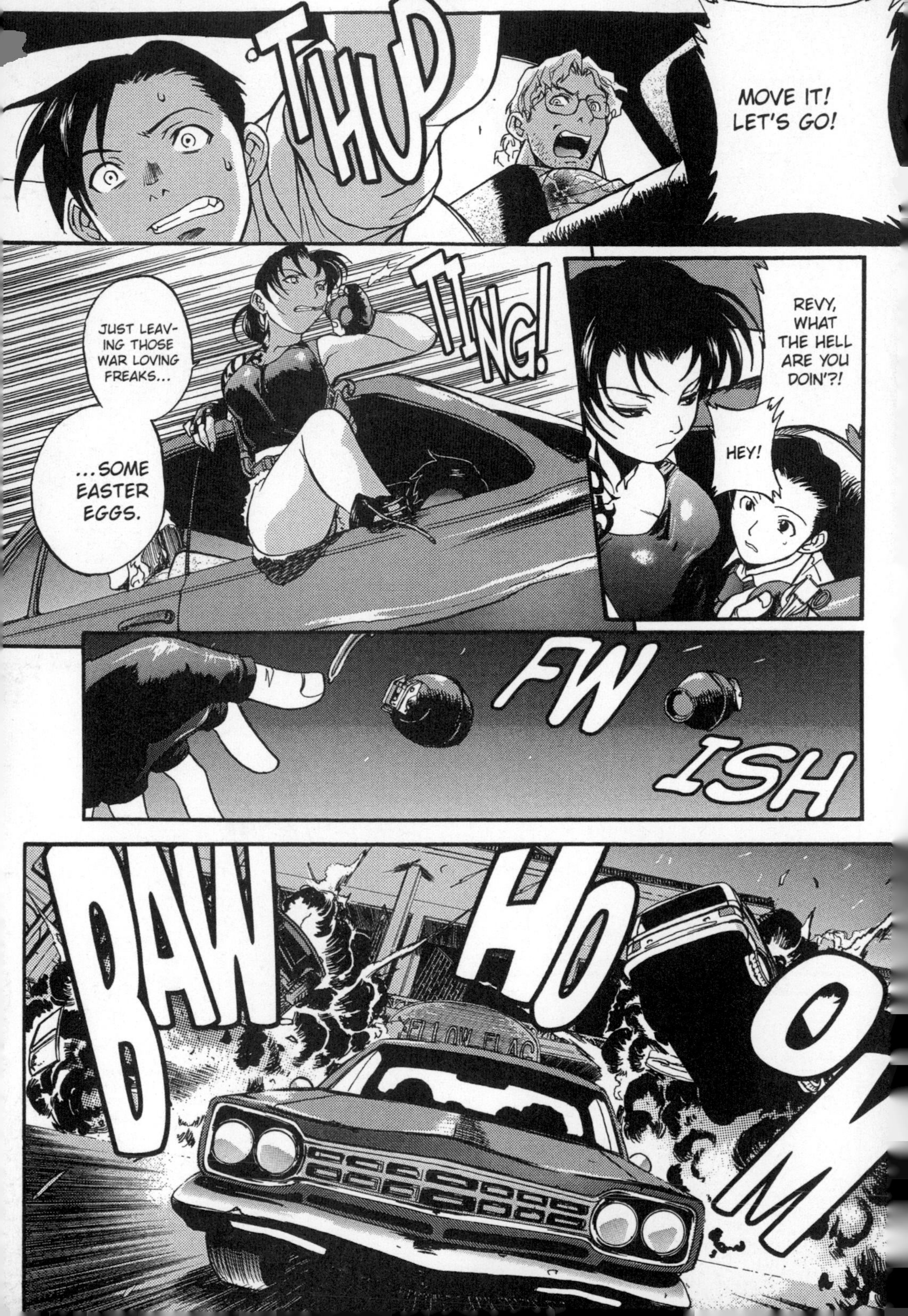
MOVE IT! LET'S GO!
THUD
REVY, WHAT THE HELL ARE YOU DOIN'?!
HEY!
TING!
JUST LEAV-ING THOSE WAR LOVING FREAKS...
...SOME EASTER EGGS.
FWISH
BAWHOOM

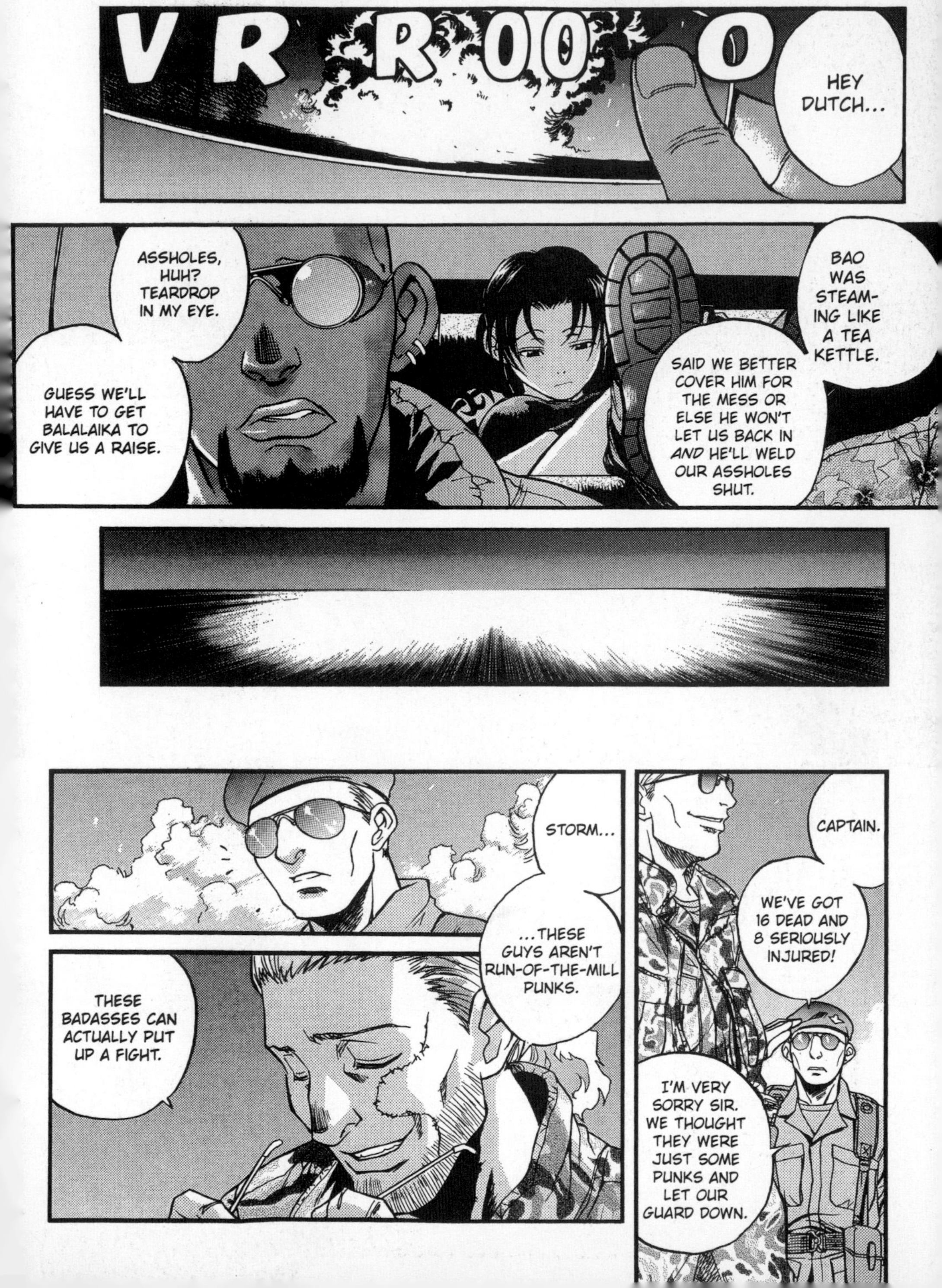
VRROOO
HEY DUTCH...
BAO WAS STEAMING LIKE A TEA KETTLE.
SAID WE BETTER COVER HIM FOR THE MESS OR ELSE HE WON'T LET US BACK IN *AND* HE'LL WELD OUR ASSHOLES SHUT.
ASSHOLES, HUH? TEARDROP IN MY EYE.
GUESS WE'LL HAVE TO GET BALALAIKA TO GIVE US A RAISE.
CAPTAIN.
WE'VE GOT 16 DEAD AND 8 SERIOUSLY INJURED!
I'M VERY SORRY SIR. WE THOUGHT THEY WERE JUST SOME PUNKS AND LET OUR GUARD DOWN.
STORM...
...THESE GUYS AREN'T RUN-OF-THE-MILL PUNKS.
THESE BADASSES CAN ACTUALLY PUT UP A FIGHT.

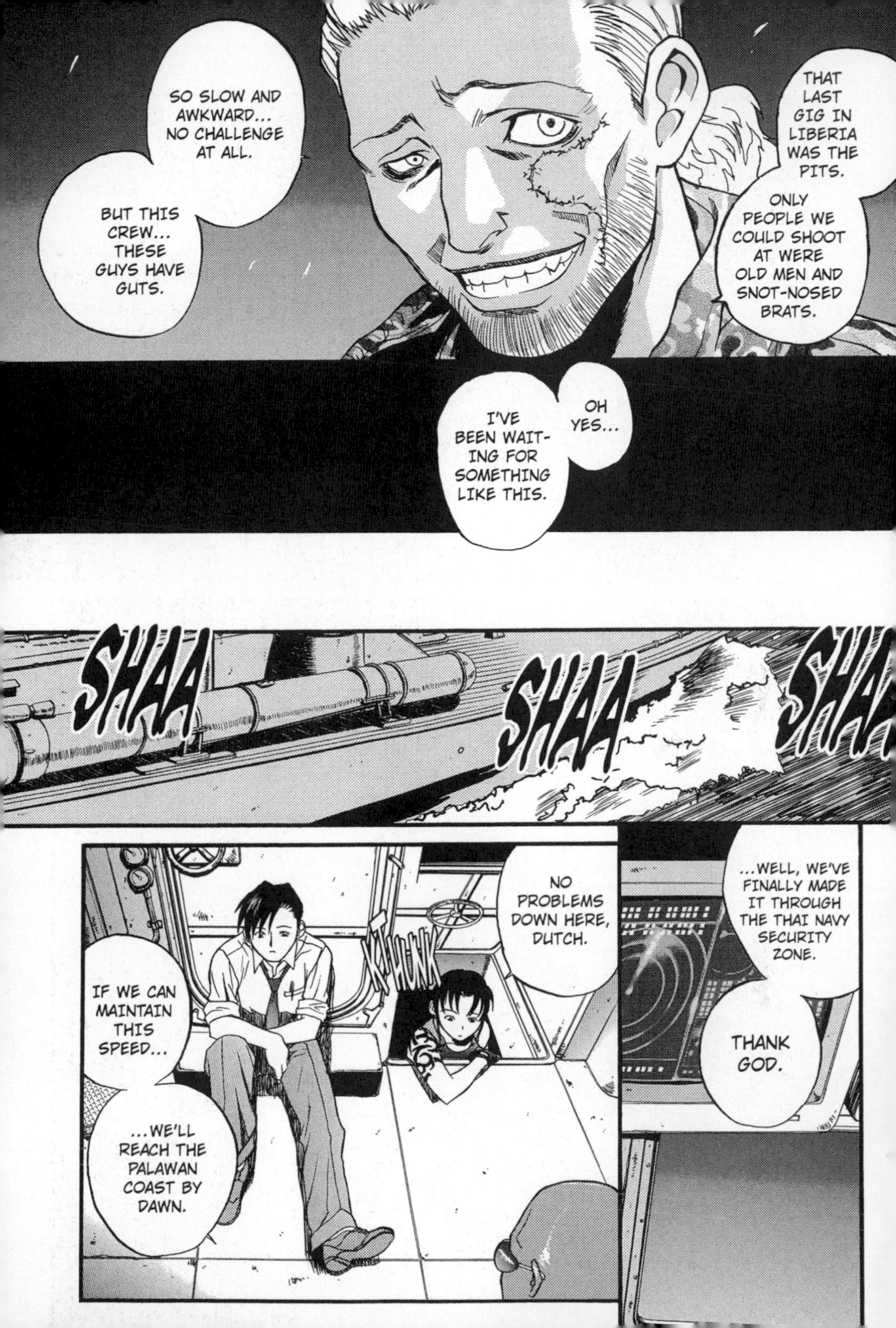
THAT LAST GIG IN LIBERIA WAS THE PITS.
ONLY PEOPLE WE COULD SHOOT AT WERE OLD MEN AND SNOT-NOSED BRATS.
SO SLOW AND AWKWARD... NO CHALLENGE AT ALL.
BUT THIS CREW... THESE GUYS HAVE GUTS.
OH YES...
I'VE BEEN WAITING FOR SOMETHING LIKE THIS.
SHAA
SHAA
SHAA
...WELL, WE'VE FINALLY MADE IT THROUGH THE THAI NAVY SECURITY ZONE.
THANK GOD.
NO PROBLEMS DOWN HERE, DUTCH.
KA-THUNK
IF WE CAN MAINTAIN THIS SPEED...
...WE'LL REACH THE PALAWAN COAST BY DAWN.

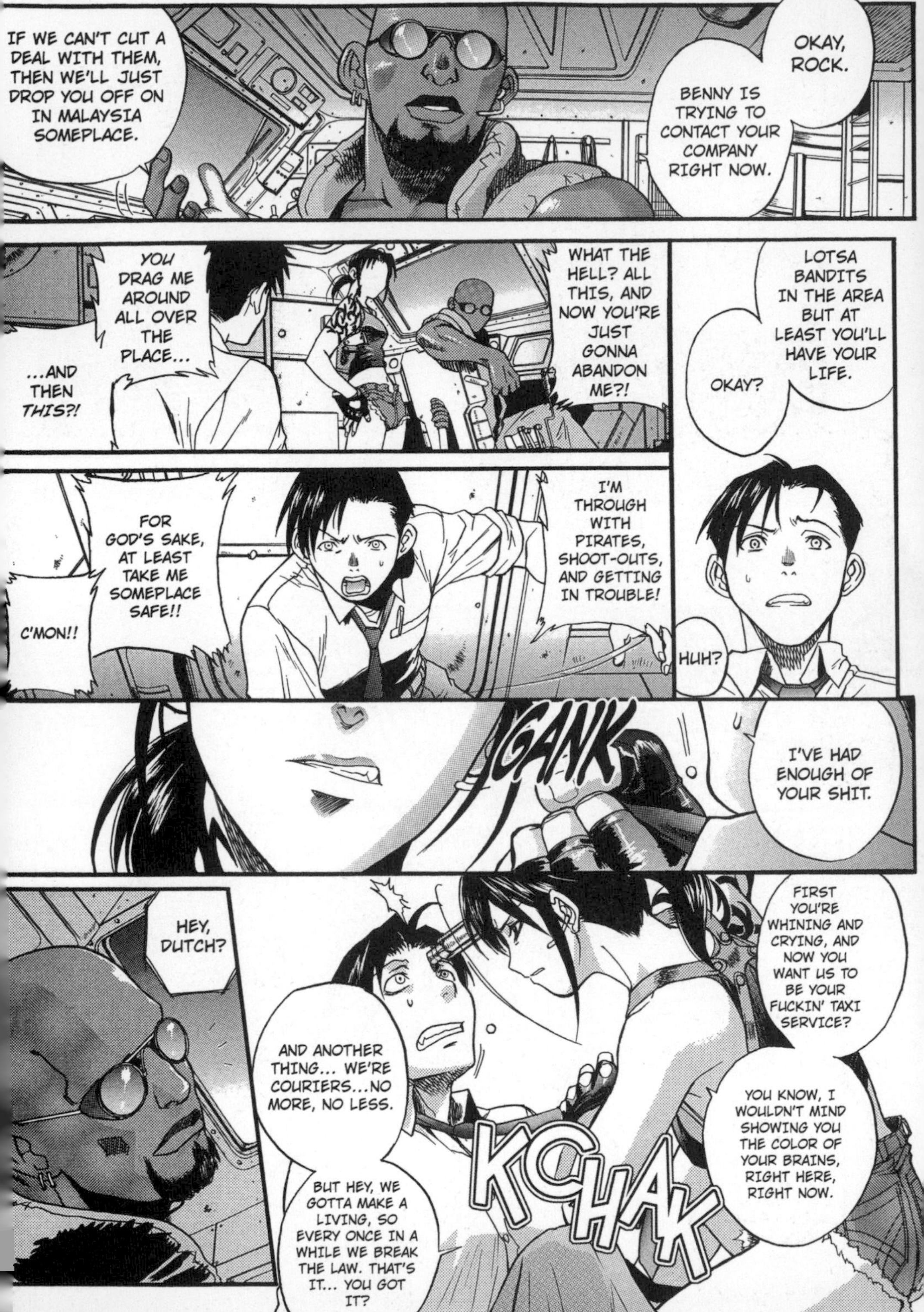
OKAY, ROCK.
BENNY IS TRYING TO CONTACT YOUR COMPANY RIGHT NOW.
IF WE CAN'T CUT A DEAL WITH THEM, THEN WE'LL JUST DROP YOU OFF ON IN MALAYSIA SOMEPLACE.
LOTSA BANDITS IN THE AREA BUT AT LEAST YOU'LL HAVE YOUR LIFE.
OKAY?
HUH?
WHAT THE HELL? ALL THIS, AND NOW YOU'RE JUST GONNA ABANDON ME?!
YOU DRAG ME AROUND ALL OVER THE PLACE...
...AND THEN *THIS?!*
I'M THROUGH WITH PIRATES, SHOOT-OUTS, AND GETTING IN TROUBLE!
FOR GOD'S SAKE, AT LEAST TAKE ME SOMEPLACE SAFE!!
C'MON!!
I'VE HAD ENOUGH OF YOUR SHIT.
GANK
FIRST YOU'RE WHINING AND CRYING, AND NOW YOU WANT US TO BE YOUR FUCKIN' TAXI SERVICE?
YOU KNOW, I WOULDN'T MIND SHOWING YOU THE COLOR OF YOUR BRAINS, RIGHT HERE, RIGHT NOW.
KCHAK
HEY, DUTCH?
AND ANOTHER THING... WE'RE COURIERS...NO MORE, NO LESS.
BUT HEY, WE GOTTA MAKE A LIVING, SO EVERY ONCE IN A WHILE WE BREAK THE LAW. THAT'S IT... YOU GOT IT?

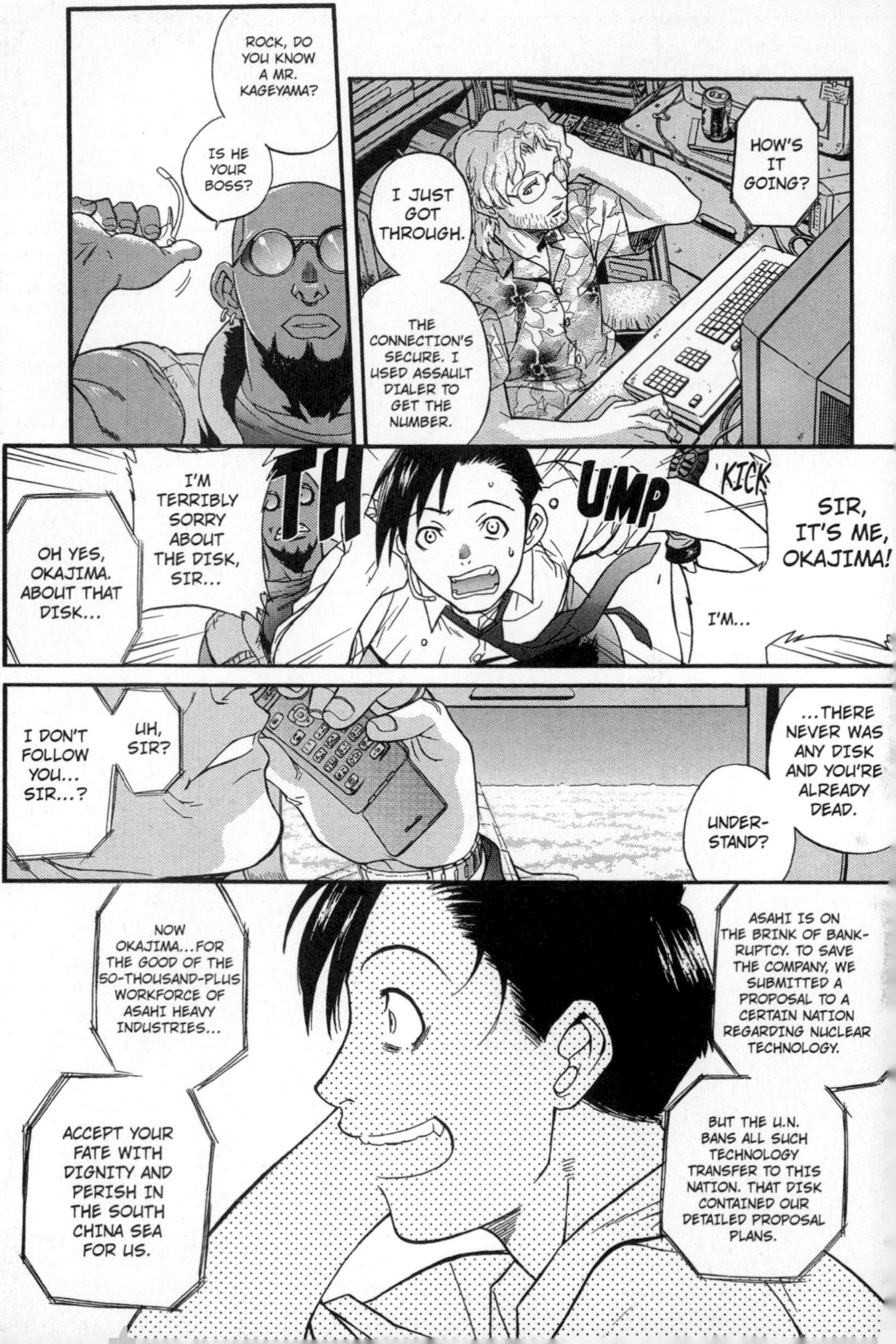
HOW'S IT GOING?
I JUST GOT THROUGH.
THE CONNECTION'S SECURE. I USED ASSAULT DIALER TO GET THE NUMBER.
ROCK, DO YOU KNOW A MR. KAGEYAMA?
IS HE YOUR BOSS?
SIR, IT'S ME, OKAJIMA!
I'M...
KICK
THUMP
I'M TERRIBLY SORRY ABOUT THE DISK, SIR...
OH YES, OKAJIMA. ABOUT THAT DISK...
...THERE NEVER WAS ANY DISK AND YOU'RE ALREADY DEAD.
UNDER-STAND?
UH, SIR?
I DON'T FOLLOW YOU... SIR...?
ASAHI IS ON THE BRINK OF BANK-RUPTCY. TO SAVE THE COMPANY, WE SUBMITTED A PROPOSAL TO A CERTAIN NATION REGARDING NUCLEAR TECHNOLOGY.
BUT THE U.N. BANS ALL SUCH TECHNOLOGY TRANSFER TO THIS NATION. THAT DISK CONTAINED OUR DETAILED PROPOSAL PLANS.
NOW OKAJIMA...FOR THE GOOD OF THE 50-THOUSAND-PLUS WORKFORCE OF ASAHI HEAVY INDUSTRIES...
ACCEPT YOUR FATE WITH DIGNITY AND PERISH IN THE SOUTH CHINA SEA FOR US.

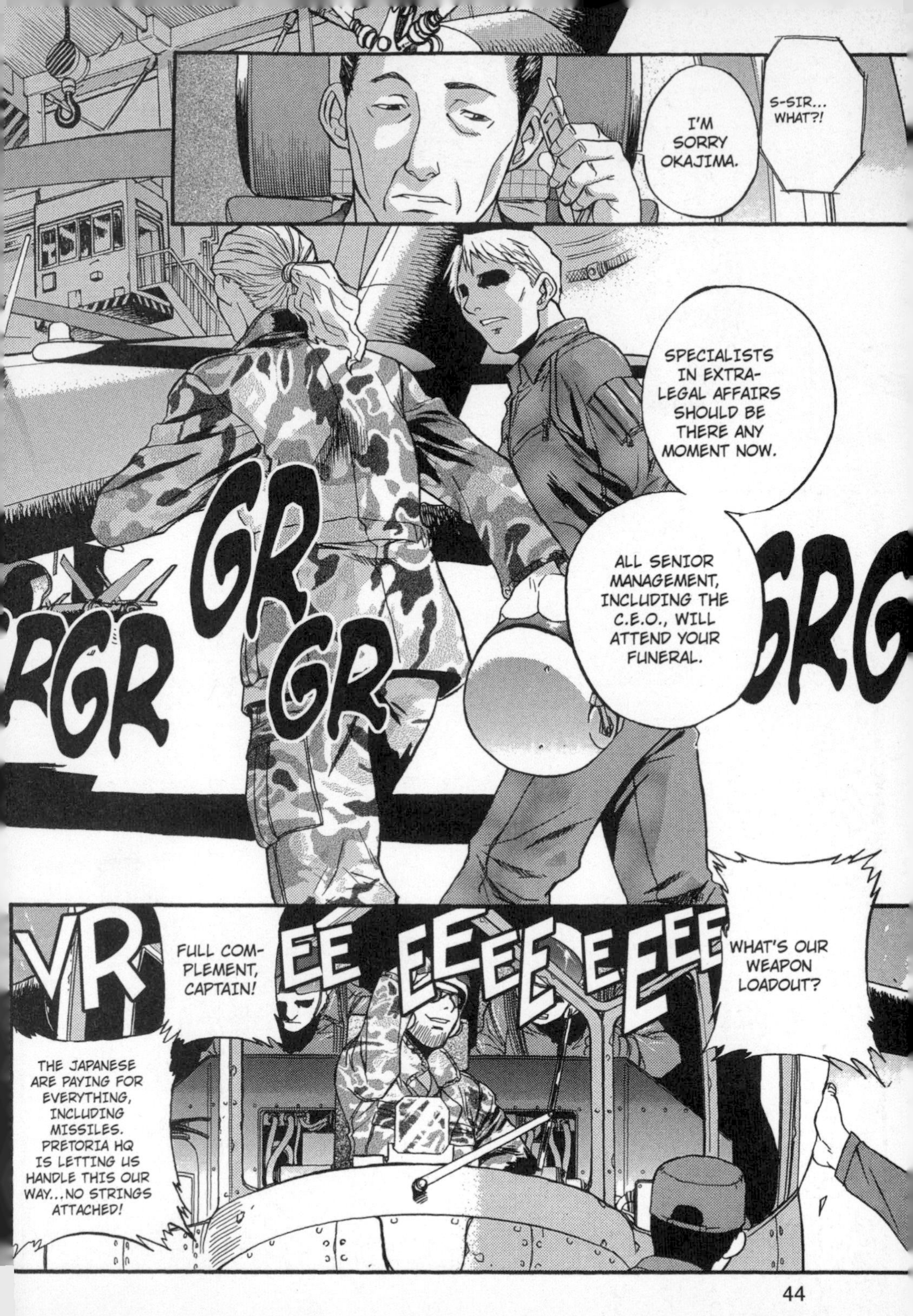
S-SIR... WHAT?!
I'M SORRY OKAJIMA.
GRG
SPECIALISTS IN EXTRA-LEGAL AFFAIRS SHOULD BE THERE ANY MOMENT NOW.
ALL SENIOR MANAGEMENT, INCLUDING THE C.E.O., WILL ATTEND YOUR FUNERAL.
GR GR
RGR
WHAT'S OUR WEAPON LOADOUT?
EEEEEEEEEE
FULL COM-PLEMENT, CAPTAIN!
VR
THE JAPANESE ARE PAYING FOR EVERYTHING, INCLUDING MISSILES. PRETORIA HQ IS LETTING US HANDLE THIS OUR WAY...NO STRINGS ATTACHED!

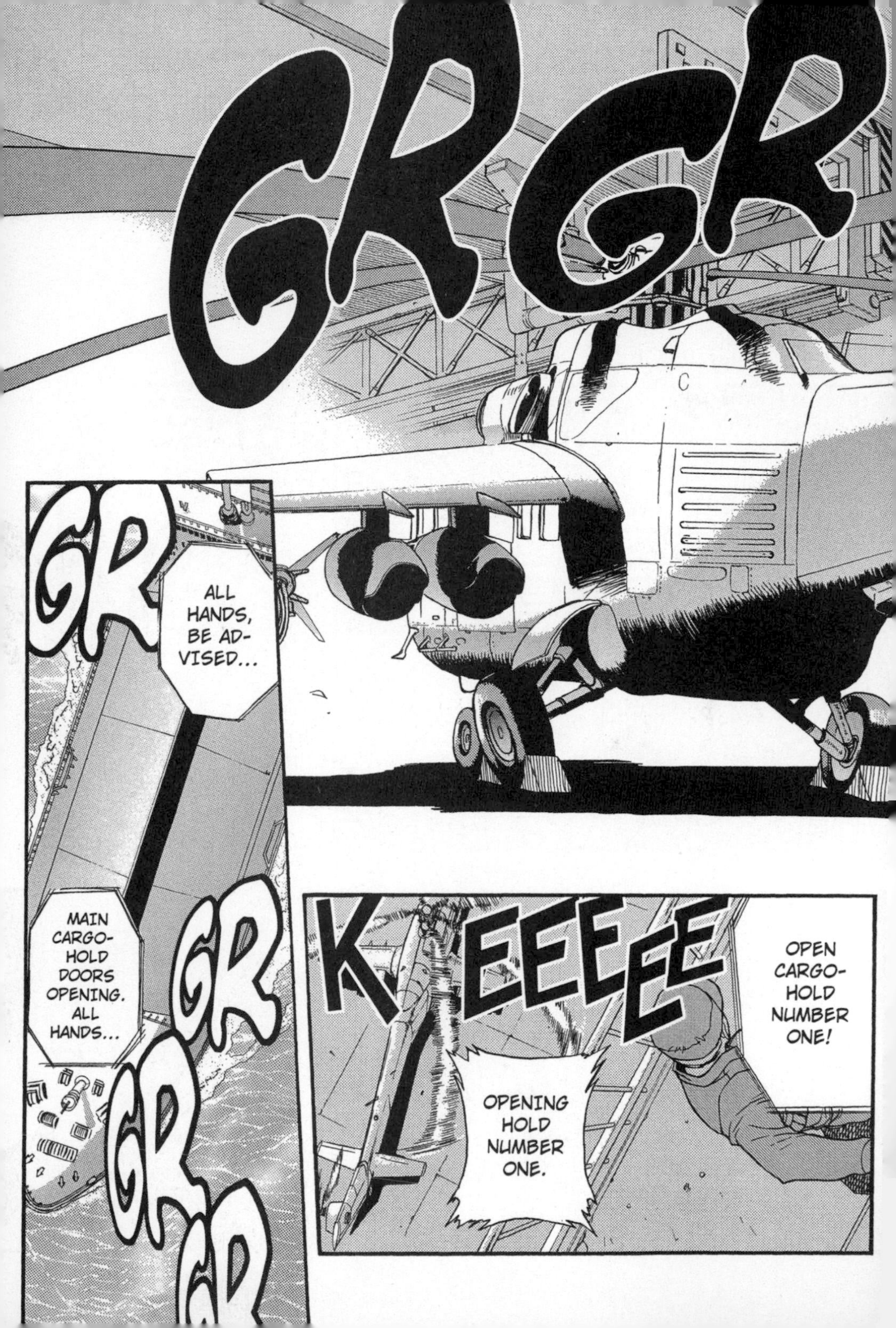
GRGR
KEEEEE
OPEN CARGO-HOLD NUMBER ONE!
OPENING HOLD NUMBER ONE.
GR
ALL HANDS, BE AD-VISED…
MAIN CARGO-HOLD DOORS OPENING. ALL HANDS…
GR
GR
GR

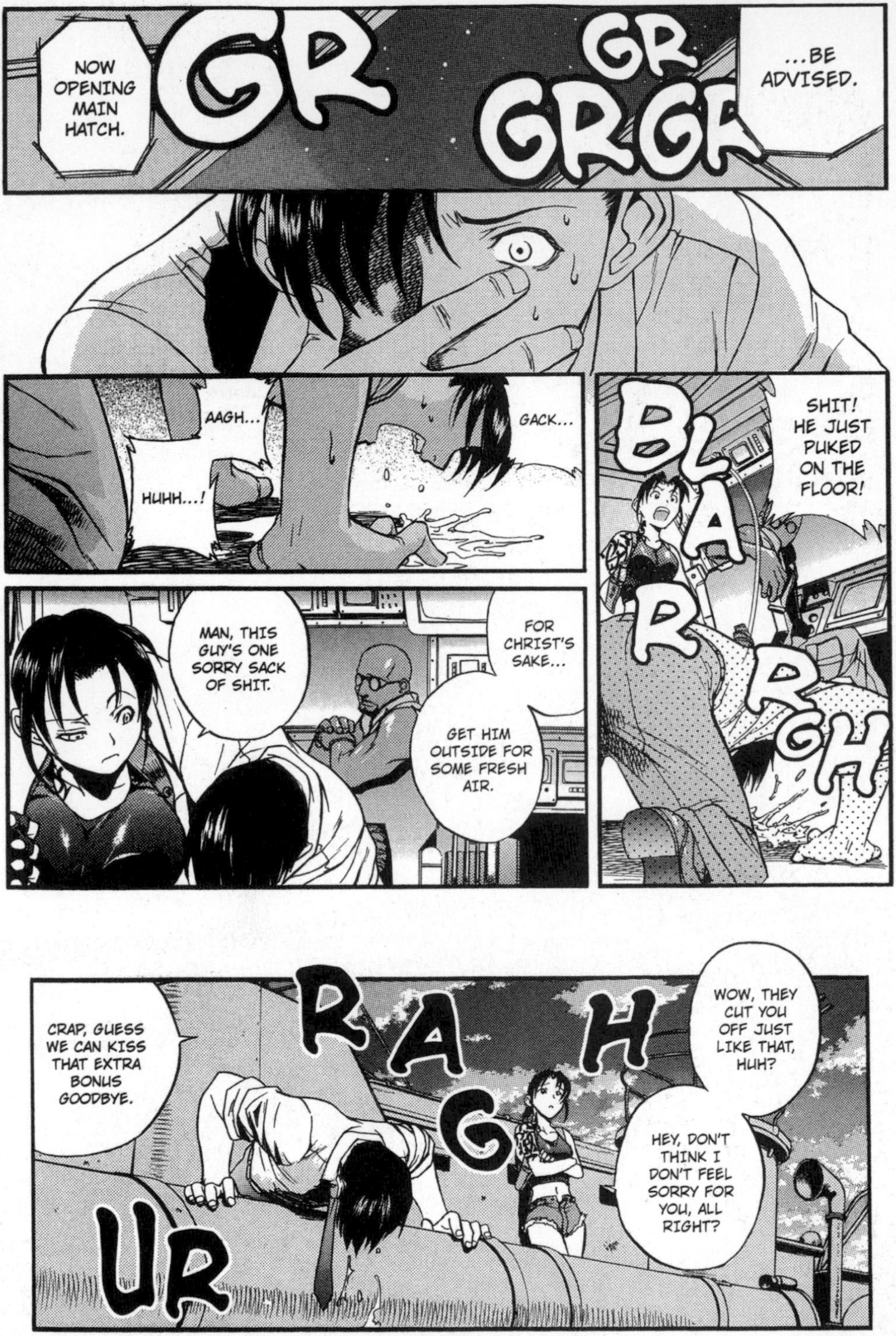
...BE ADVISED.
GR
GRGR
GR
NOW OPENING MAIN HATCH.
SHIT! HE JUST PUKED ON THE FLOOR!
BLARRRGH
GACK...
AAGH...
HUHH...!
FOR CHRIST'S SAKE...
GET HIM OUTSIDE FOR SOME FRESH AIR.
MAN, THIS GUY'S ONE SORRY SACK OF SHIT.
WOW, THEY CUT YOU OFF JUST LIKE THAT, HUH?
HEY, DON'T THINK I DON'T FEEL SORRY FOR YOU, ALL RIGHT?
RAH
G
CRAP, GUESS WE CAN KISS THAT EXTRA BONUS GOODBYE.
UR

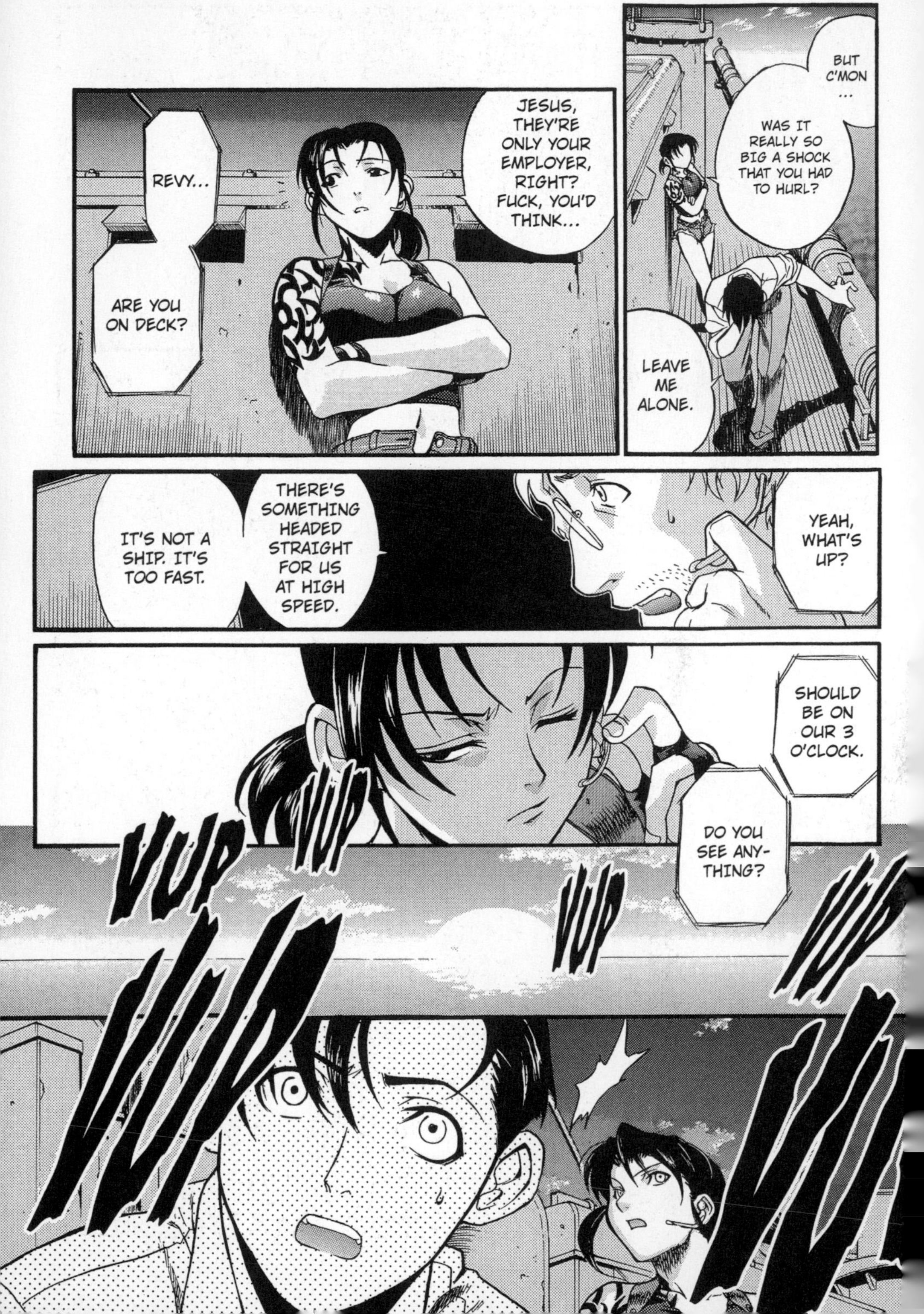
BUT C'MON ...
WAS IT REALLY SO BIG A SHOCK THAT YOU HAD TO HURL?
LEAVE ME ALONE.
JESUS, THEY'RE ONLY YOUR EMPLOYER, RIGHT? FUCK, YOU'D THINK...
REVY...
ARE YOU ON DECK?
YEAH, WHAT'S UP?
THERE'S SOMETHING HEADED STRAIGHT FOR US AT HIGH SPEED.
IT'S NOT A SHIP. IT'S TOO FAST.
SHOULD BE ON OUR 3 O'CLOCK.
DO YOU SEE ANY-THING?
VUP
VUP
VUP
VUP

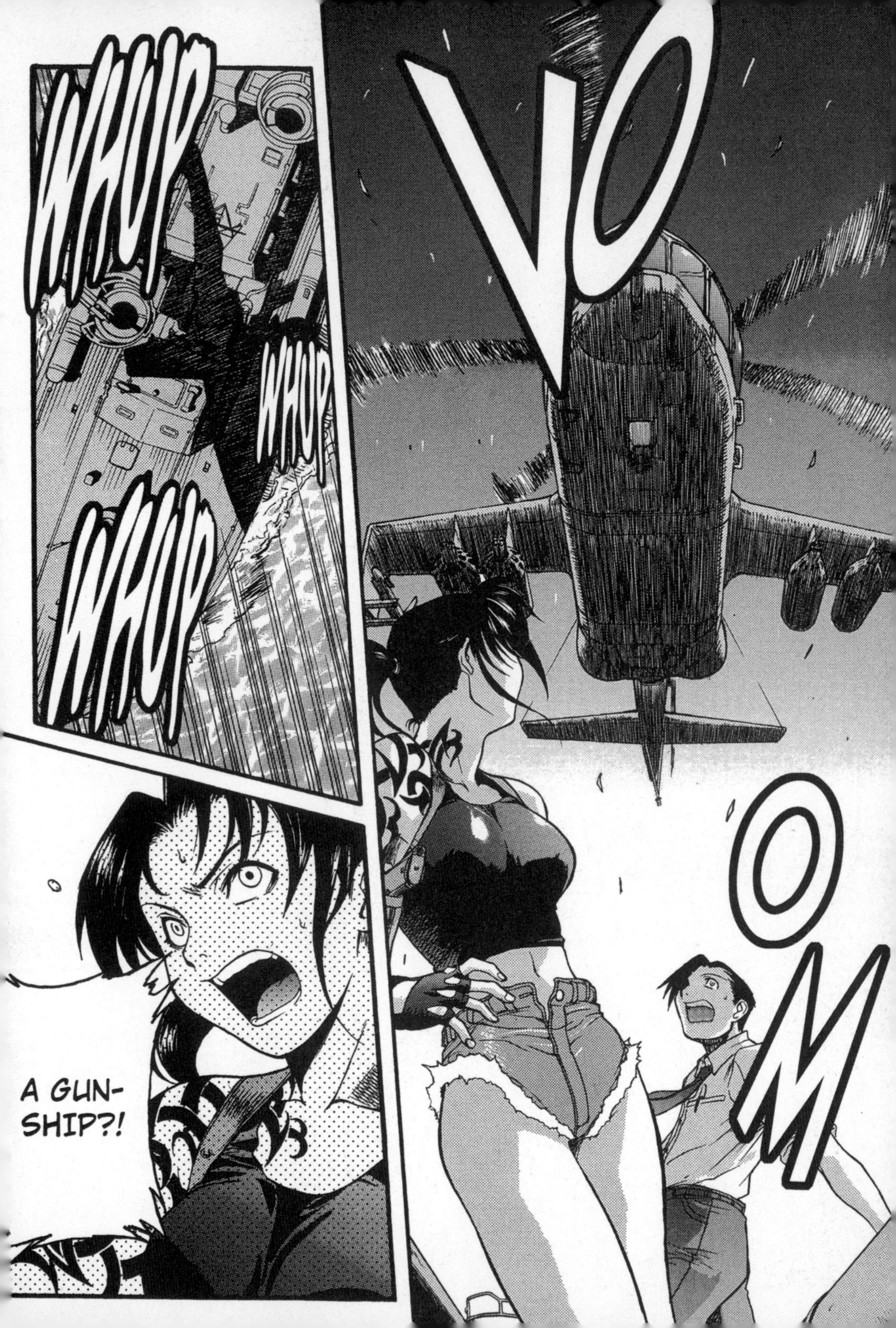
VO
OOM
WHOP
WHOP
WHOP
A GUN-SHIP?!

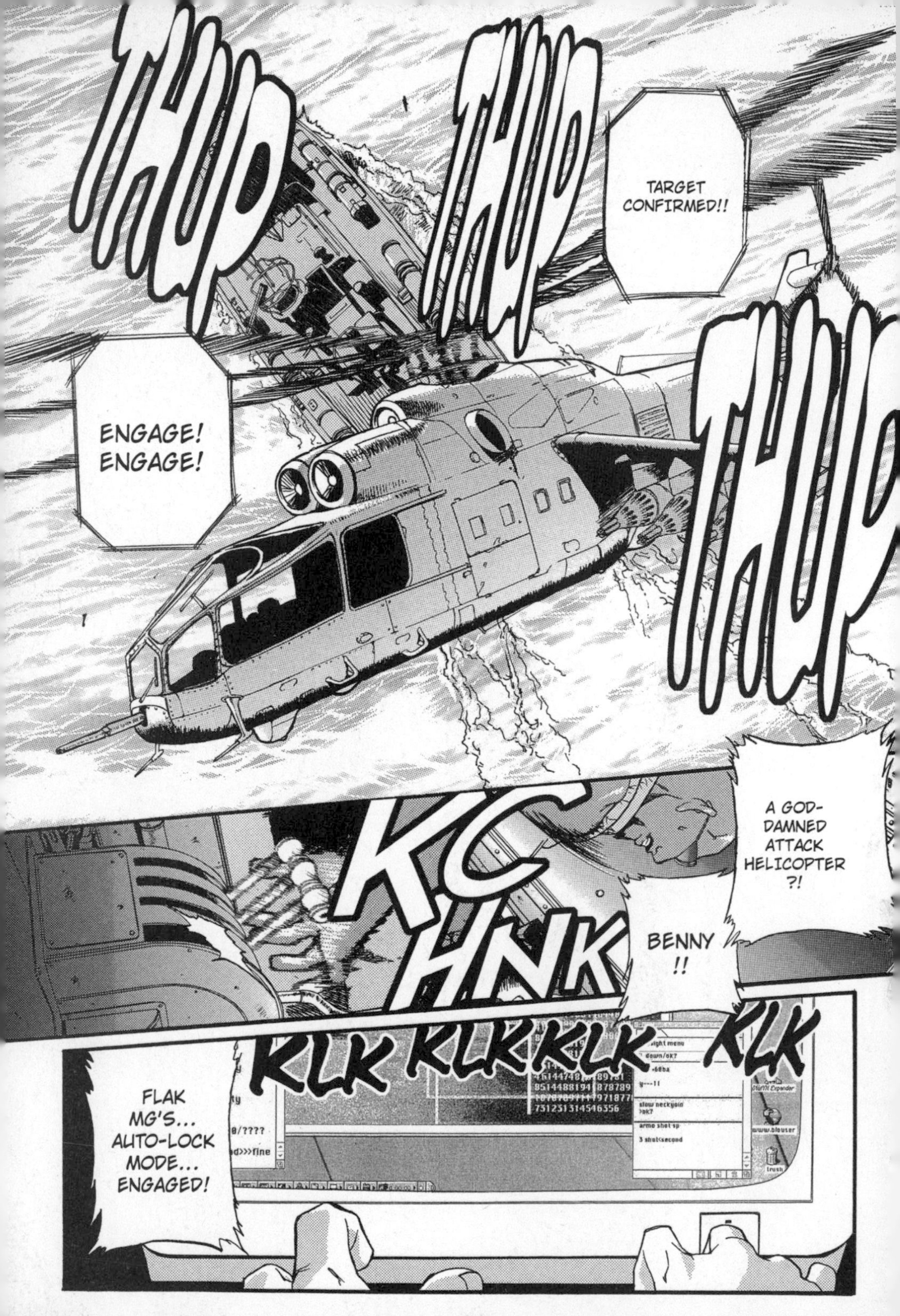
THUP
THUP
THUP
TARGET CONFIRMED!!
ENGAGE! ENGAGE!
A GOD-DAMNED ATTACK HELICOPTER?!
KCHNK
BENNY!!
KLK KLK KLK KLK KLK
FLAK MG'S... AUTO-LOCK MODE... ENGAGED!

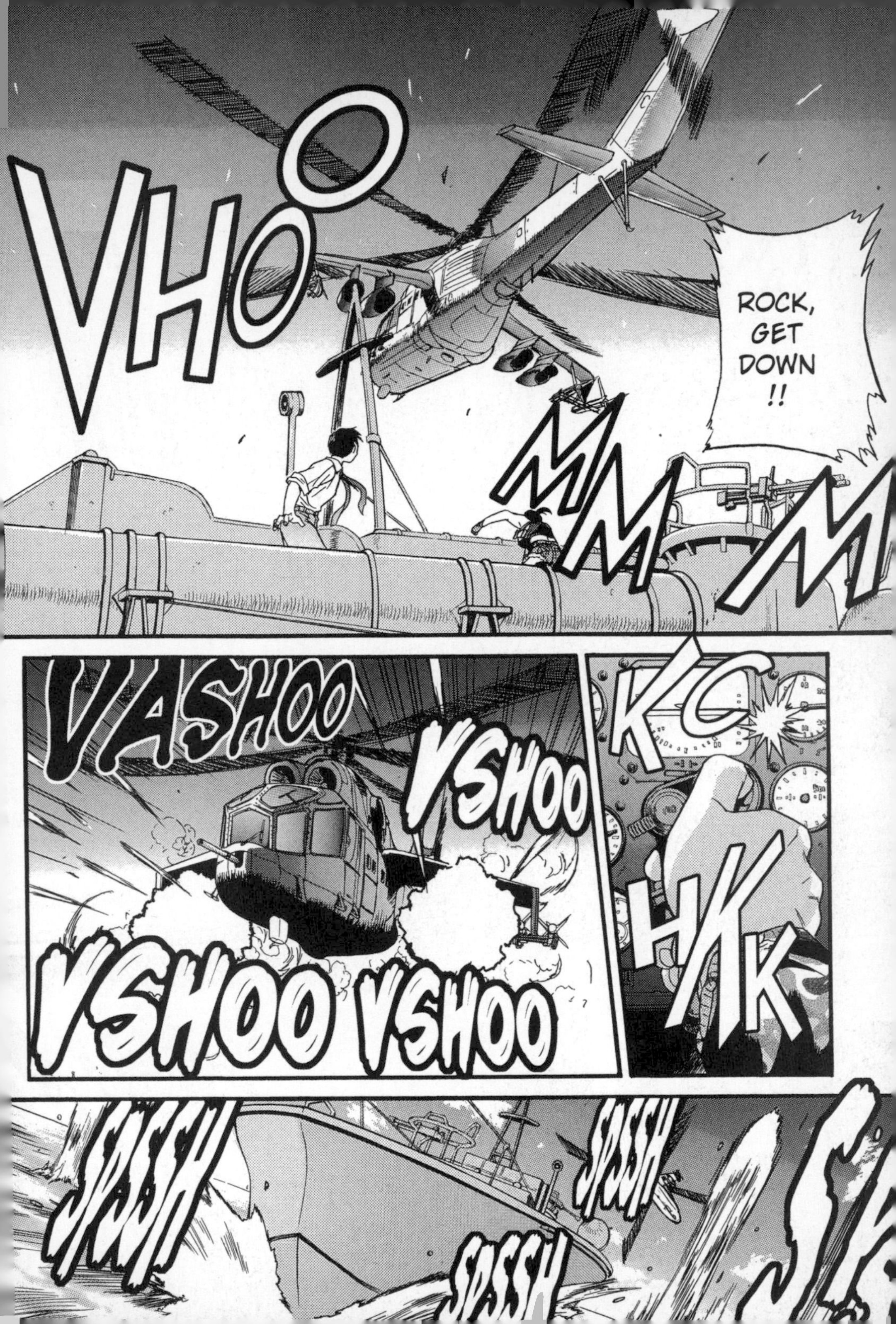
ROCK,
GET
DOWN
!!
VHOOO
MMMM
KC
HKK
VASHOO
VSHOO
VSHOO VSHOO
SPSSH
SPSSH
SPSSH

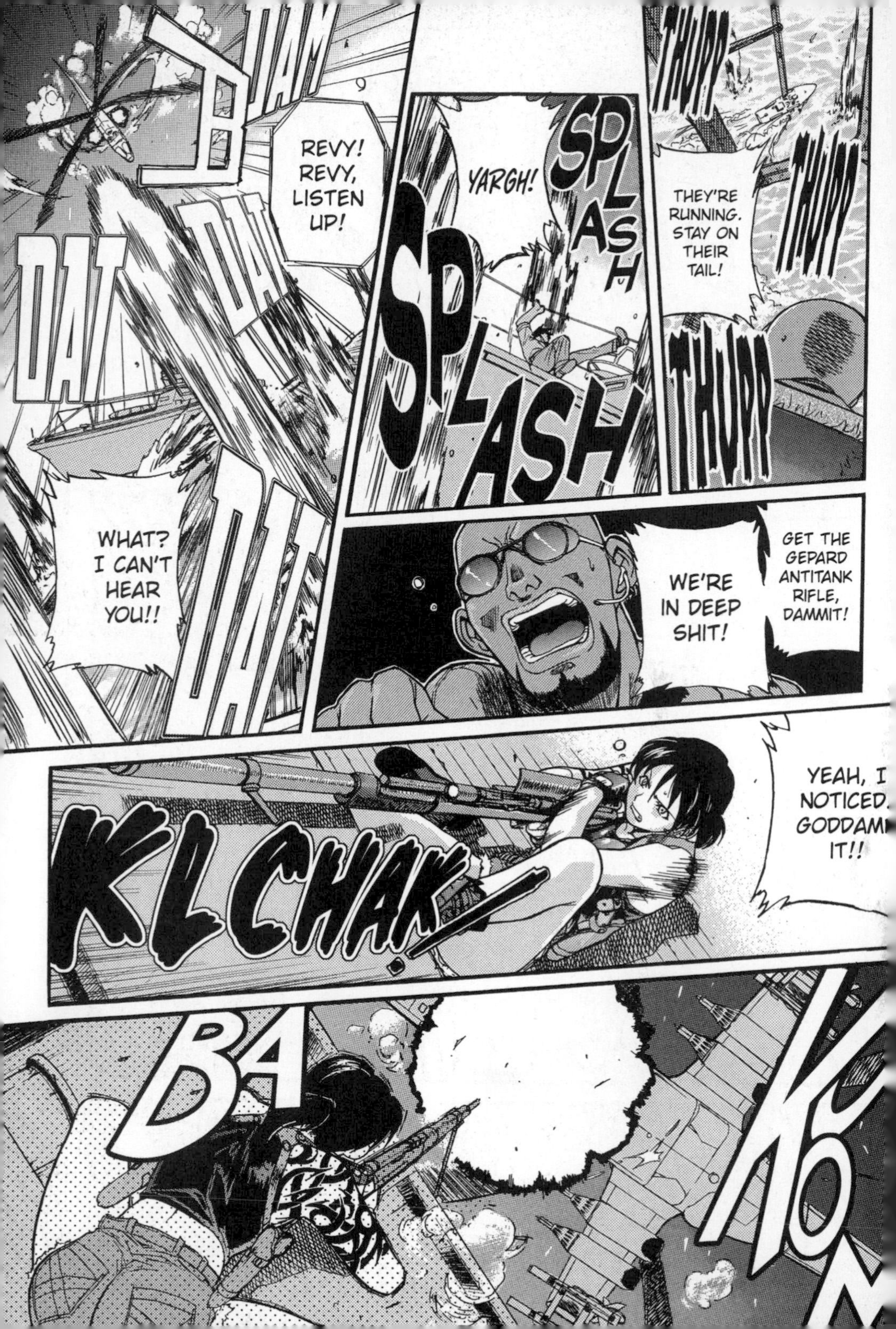
THURR
THURR
THEY'RE RUNNING. STAY ON THEIR TAIL!
THURR
SPLASH
YARGH!
SPLASH
GET THE GEPARD ANTITANK RIFLE, DAMMIT!
WE'RE IN DEEP SHIT!
REVY! REVY, LISTEN UP!
WHAT? I CAN'T HEAR YOU!!
YEAH, I NOTICED. GODDAMN IT!!
KLCHAK
BA

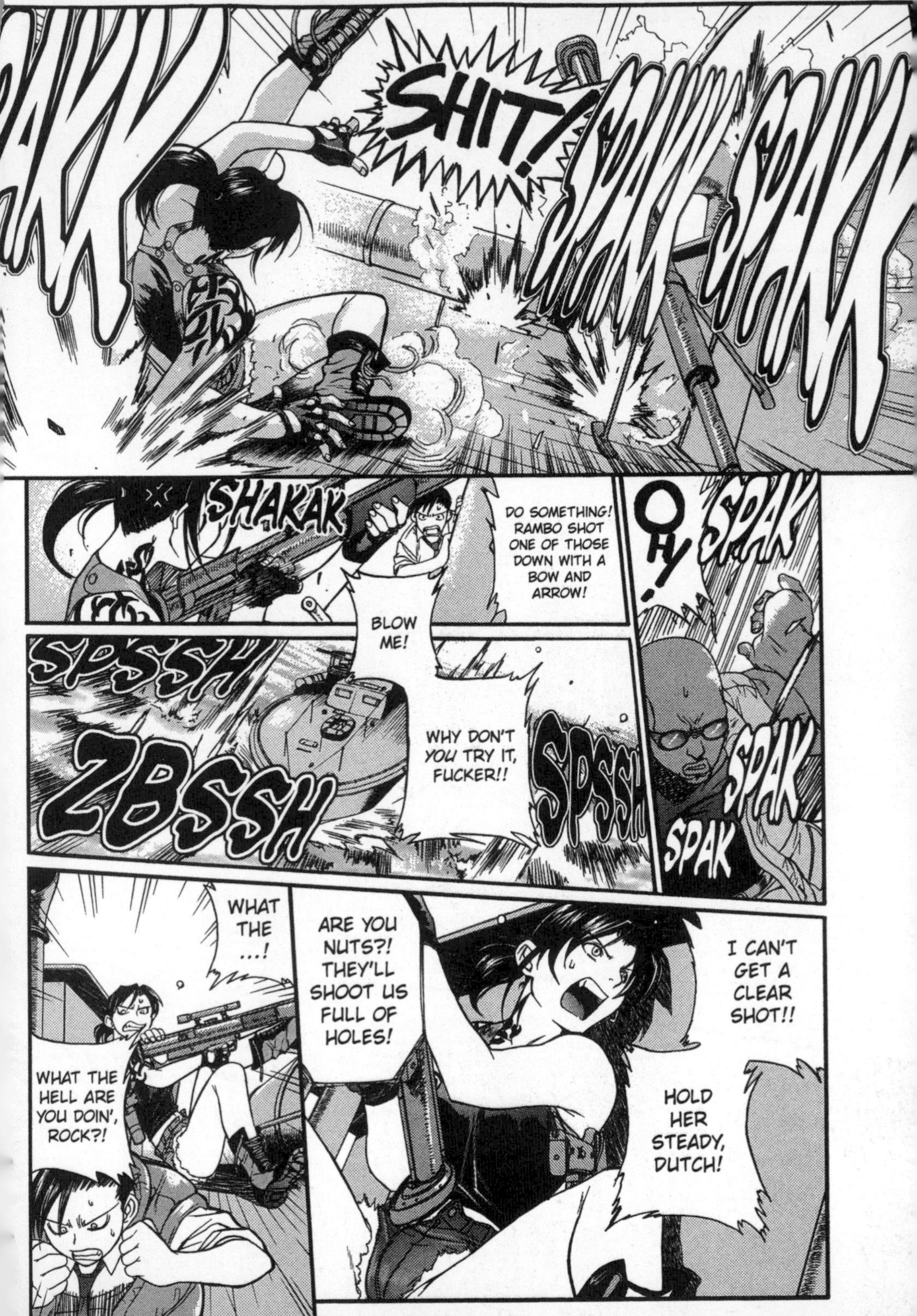
SHIT!
OH!
SPAK
DO SOMETHING! RAMBO SHOT ONE OF THOSE DOWN WITH A BOW AND ARROW!
SHAKAK
BLOW ME!
SPAK
SPAK
SPAK
WHY DON'T YOU TRY IT, FUCKER!!
SPSSH
ZBSSH
SPSSH
I CAN'T GET A CLEAR SHOT!!
HOLD HER STEADY, DUTCH!
ARE YOU NUTS?! THEY'LL SHOOT US FULL OF HOLES!
WHAT THE ...!
WHAT THE HELL ARE YOU DOIN', ROCK?!

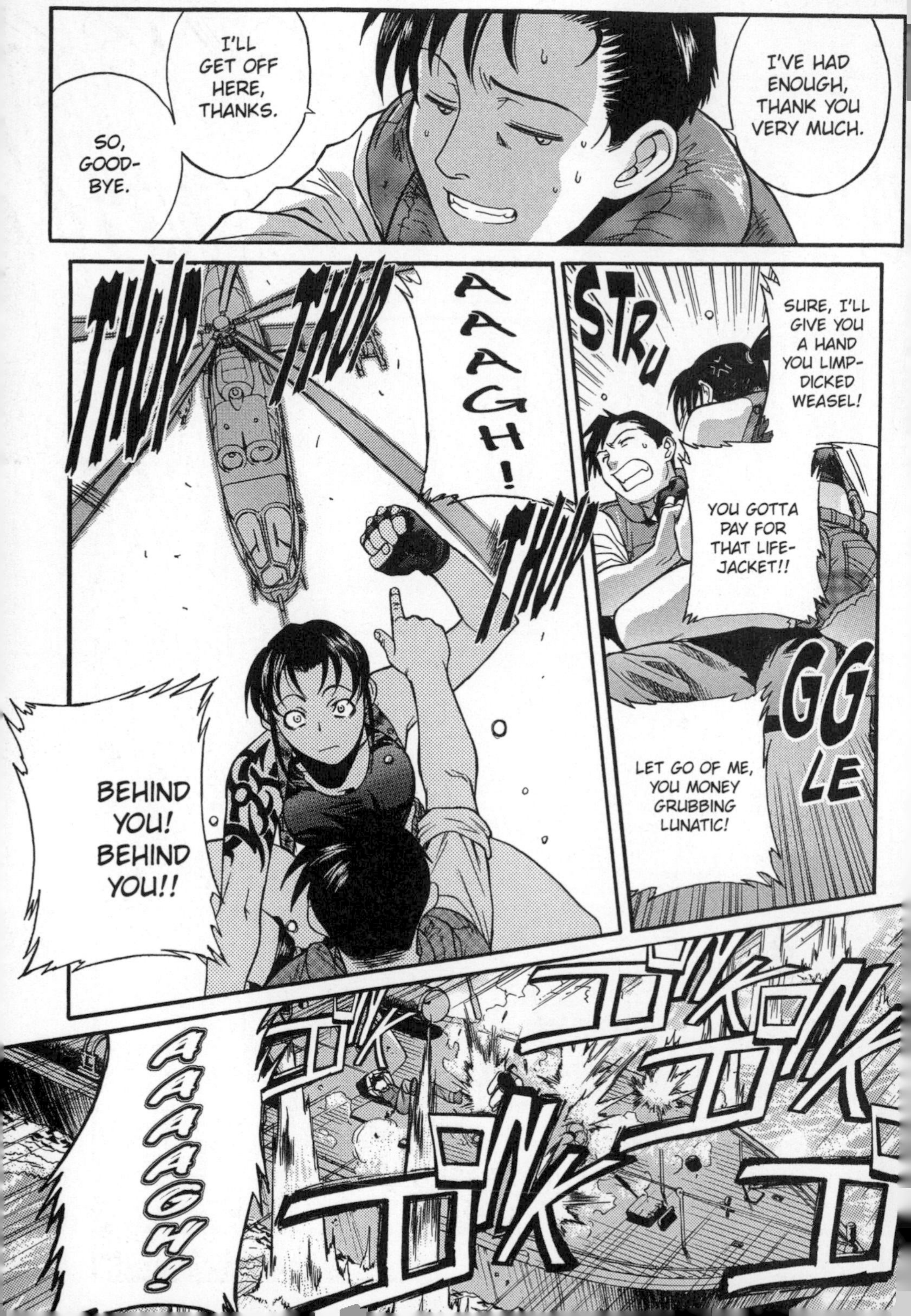
I'VE HAD ENOUGH, THANK YOU VERY MUCH.
I'LL GET OFF HERE, THANKS.
SO, GOOD-BYE.
STRU
SURE, I'LL GIVE YOU A HAND YOU LIMP-DICKED WEASEL!
YOU GOTTA PAY FOR THAT LIFE-JACKET!!
GG
LE
LET GO OF ME, YOU MONEY GRUBBING LUNATIC!
THUP
THUP
AAAGH!
THU
BEHIND YOU! BEHIND YOU!!
KONK
KONK
KONK
AAAAAGH!

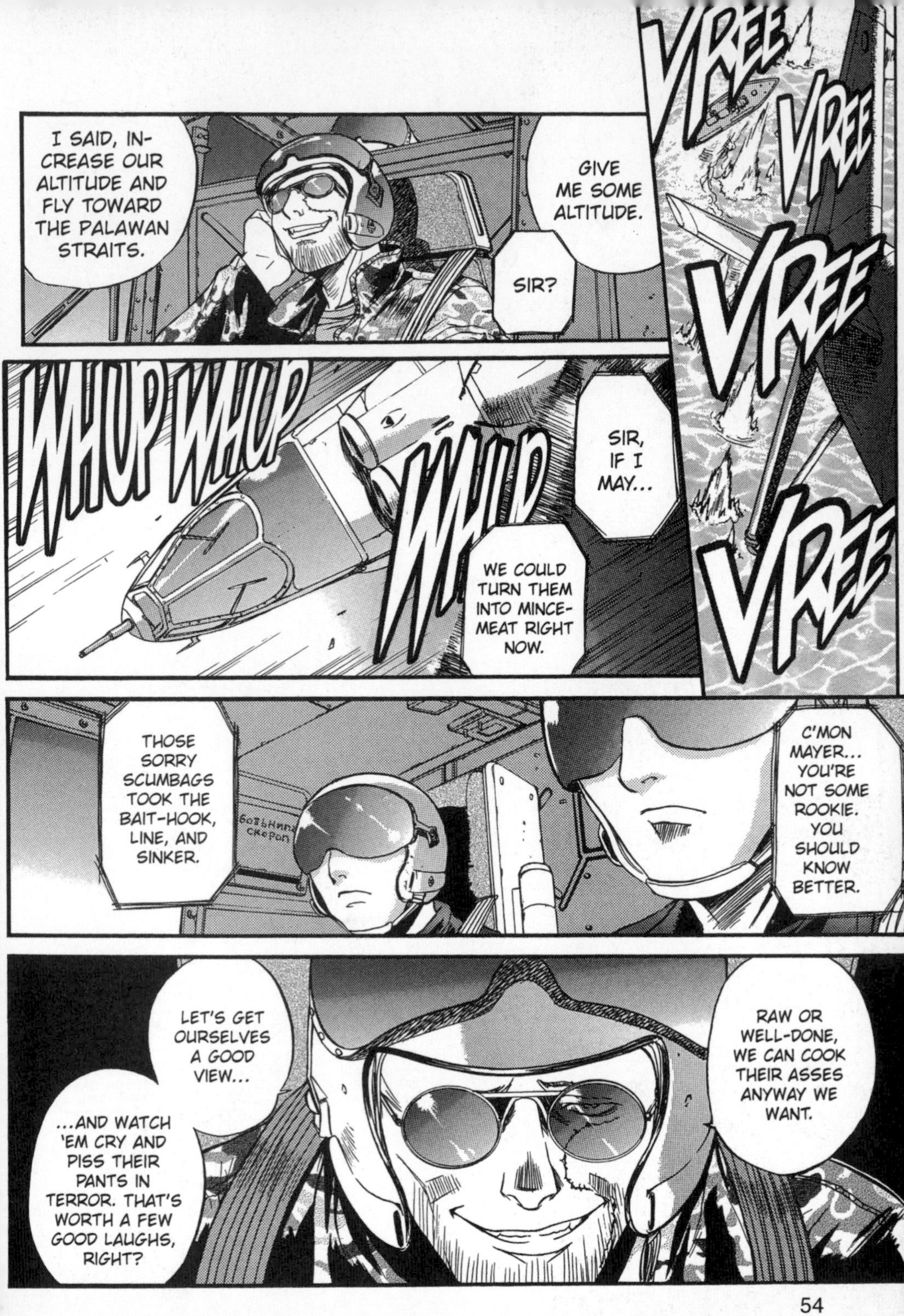

VREE
VREE
VREE
VREE
GIVE ME SOME ALTITUDE.
SIR?
I SAID, IN-CREASE OUR ALTITUDE AND FLY TOWARD THE PALAWAN STRAITS.
SIR, IF I MAY...
WE COULD TURN THEM INTO MINCE-MEAT RIGHT NOW.
WHUP WHUP
WHUP
C'MON MAYER... YOU'RE NOT SOME ROOKIE. YOU SHOULD KNOW BETTER.
THOSE SORRY SCUMBAGS TOOK THE BAIT-HOOK, LINE, AND SINKER.
RAW OR WELL-DONE, WE CAN COOK THEIR ASSES ANYWAY WE WANT.
LET'S GET OURSELVES A GOOD VIEW...
...AND WATCH 'EM CRY AND PISS THEIR PANTS IN TERROR. THAT'S WORTH A FEW GOOD LAUGHS, RIGHT?

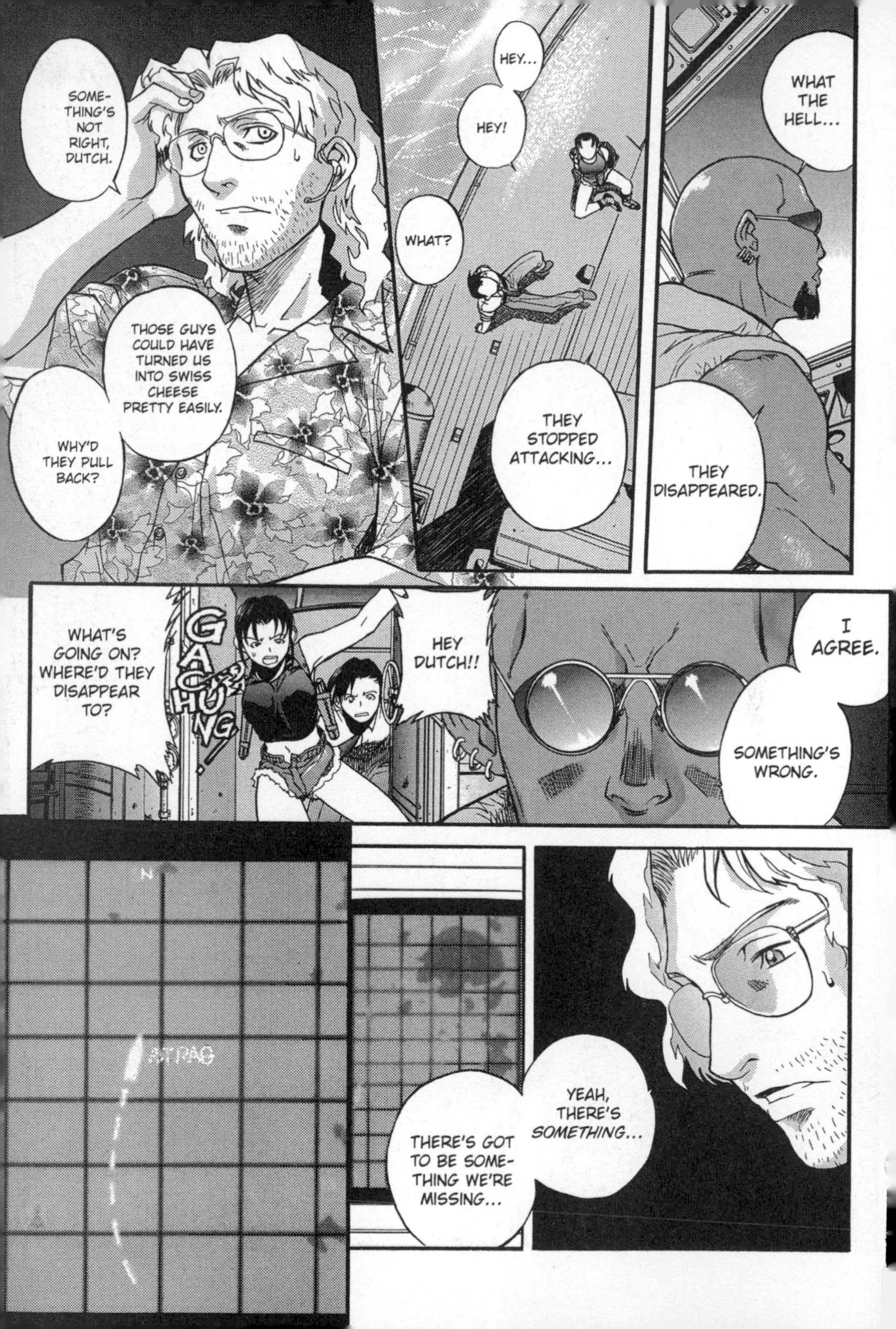
WHAT THE HELL...
THEY DISAPPEARED.
HEY...
HEY!
WHAT?
THEY STOPPED ATTACKING...
SOME-THING'S NOT RIGHT, DUTCH.
THOSE GUYS COULD HAVE TURNED US INTO SWISS CHEESE PRETTY EASILY.
WHY'D THEY PULL BACK?
I AGREE.
SOMETHING'S WRONG.
HEY DUTCH!!
GACHUNG!
WHAT'S GOING ON? WHERE'D THEY DISAPPEAR TO?
YEAH, THERE'S *SOMETHING*...
THERE'S GOT TO BE SOME-THING WE'RE MISSING...

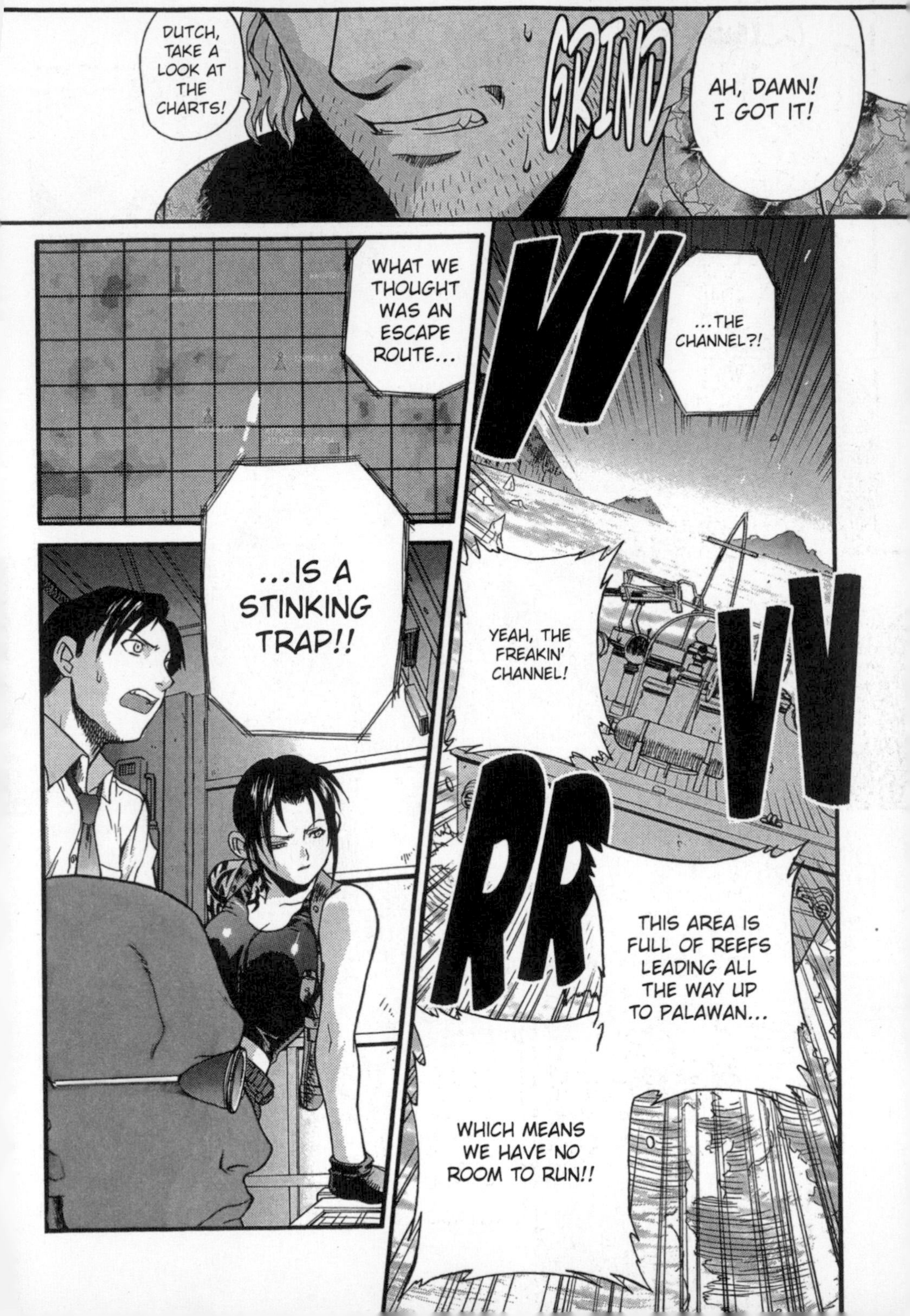
AH, DAMN! I GOT IT!
GRIND
DUTCH, TAKE A LOOK AT THE CHARTS!
VV
...THE CHANNEL?!
YEAH, THE FREAKIN' CHANNEL!
VV
RR
THIS AREA IS FULL OF REEFS LEADING ALL THE WAY UP TO PALAWAN...
WHICH MEANS WE HAVE NO ROOM TO RUN!!
WHAT WE THOUGHT WAS AN ESCAPE ROUTE...
...IS A STINKING TRAP!!

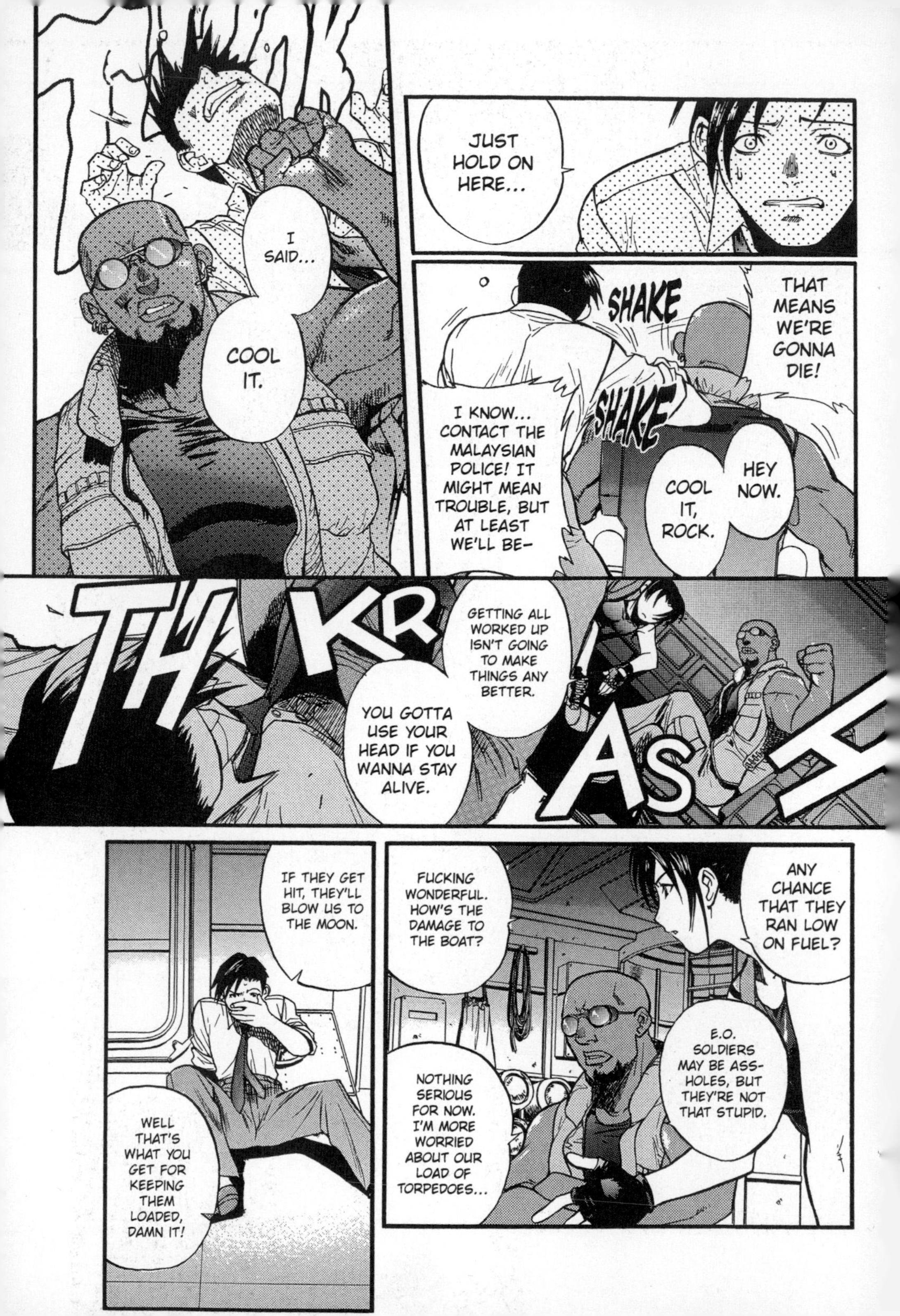
JUST HOLD ON HERE...
THAT MEANS WE'RE GONNA DIE!
SHAKE
SHAKE
I KNOW... CONTACT THE MALAYSIAN POLICE! IT MIGHT MEAN TROUBLE, BUT AT LEAST WE'LL BE-
HEY NOW.
COOL IT, ROCK.
I SAID...
COOL IT.
TH
KR
AS
H
GETTING ALL WORKED UP ISN'T GOING TO MAKE THINGS ANY BETTER.
YOU GOTTA USE YOUR HEAD IF YOU WANNA STAY ALIVE.
ANY CHANCE THAT THEY RAN LOW ON FUEL?
E.O. SOLDIERS MAY BE ASS-HOLES, BUT THEY'RE NOT THAT STUPID.
FUCKING WONDERFUL. HOW'S THE DAMAGE TO THE BOAT?
NOTHING SERIOUS FOR NOW. I'M MORE WORRIED ABOUT OUR LOAD OF TORPEDOES...
IF THEY GET HIT, THEY'LL BLOW US TO THE MOON.
WELL THAT'S WHAT YOU GET FOR KEEPING THEM LOADED, DAMN IT!

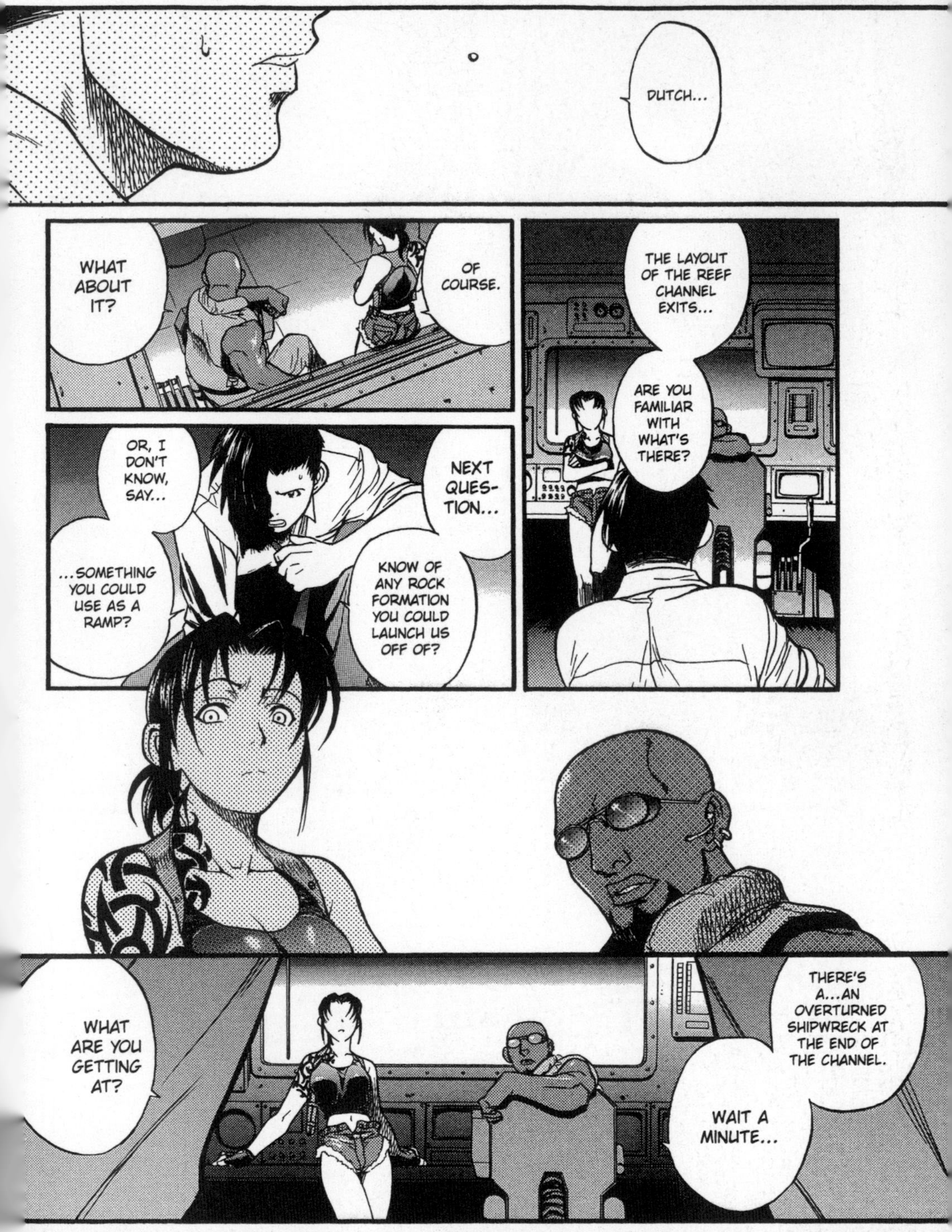
DUTCH...
THE LAYOUT OF THE REEF CHANNEL EXITS...
ARE YOU FAMILIAR WITH WHAT'S THERE?
OF COURSE.
WHAT ABOUT IT?
NEXT QUESTION...
KNOW OF ANY ROCK FORMATION YOU COULD LAUNCH US OFF OF?
OR, I DON'T KNOW, SAY...
...SOMETHING YOU COULD USE AS A RAMP?
THERE'S A...AN OVERTURNED SHIPWRECK AT THE END OF THE CHANNEL.
WAIT A MINUTE...
WHAT ARE YOU GETTING AT?

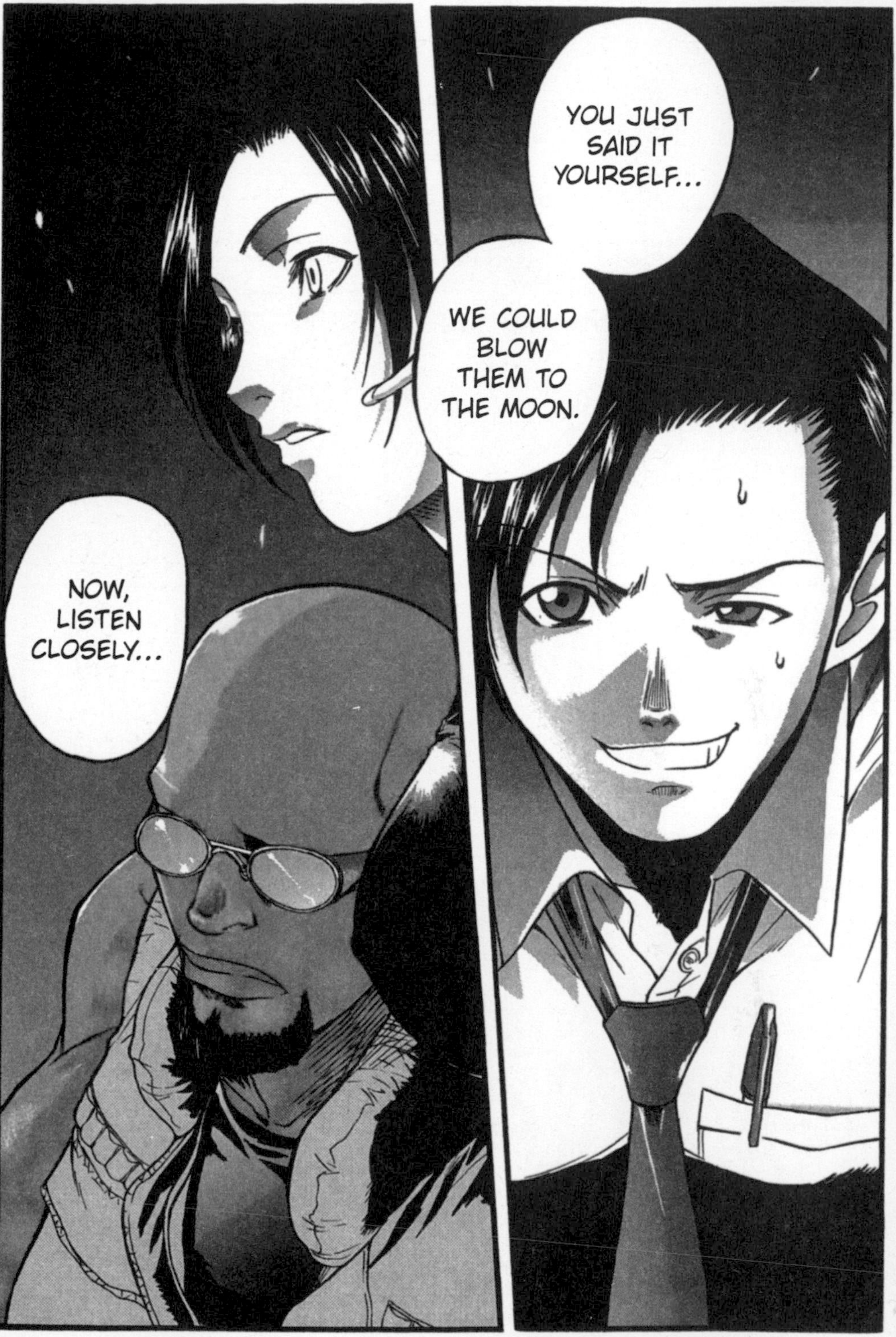
YOU JUST SAID IT YOURSELF...
WE COULD BLOW THEM TO THE MOON.
NOW, LISTEN CLOSELY...

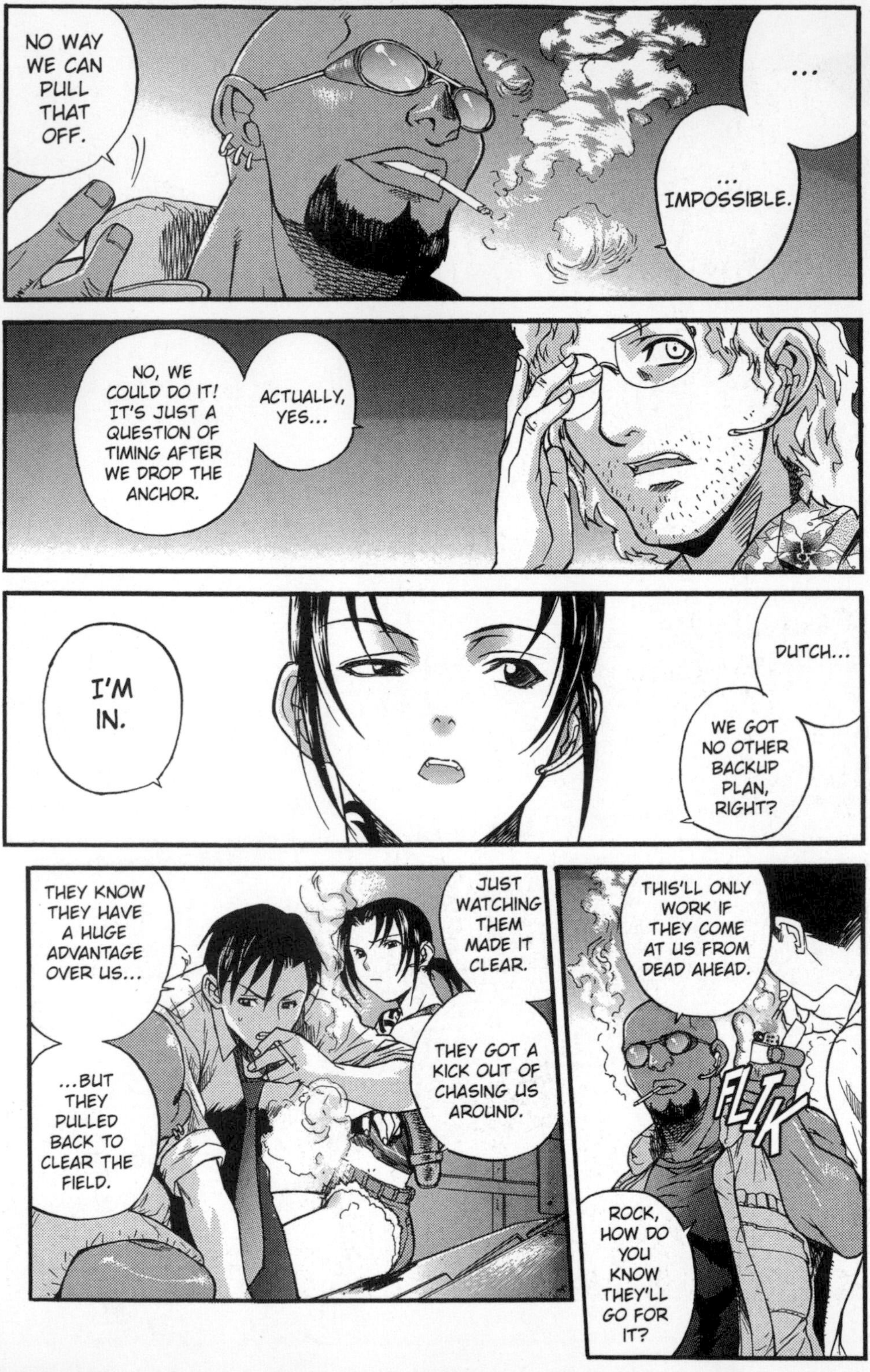
...
...IMPOSSIBLE.
NO WAY WE CAN PULL THAT OFF.
ACTUALLY, YES...
NO, WE COULD DO IT! IT'S JUST A QUESTION OF TIMING AFTER WE DROP THE ANCHOR.
DUTCH...
WE GOT NO OTHER BACKUP PLAN, RIGHT?
I'M IN.
THIS'LL ONLY WORK IF THEY COME AT US FROM DEAD AHEAD.
FLIK
ROCK, HOW DO YOU KNOW THEY'LL GO FOR IT?
JUST WATCHING THEM MADE IT CLEAR.
THEY GOT A KICK OUT OF CHASING US AROUND.
THEY KNOW THEY HAVE A HUGE ADVANTAGE OVER US...
...BUT THEY PULLED BACK TO CLEAR THE FIELD.

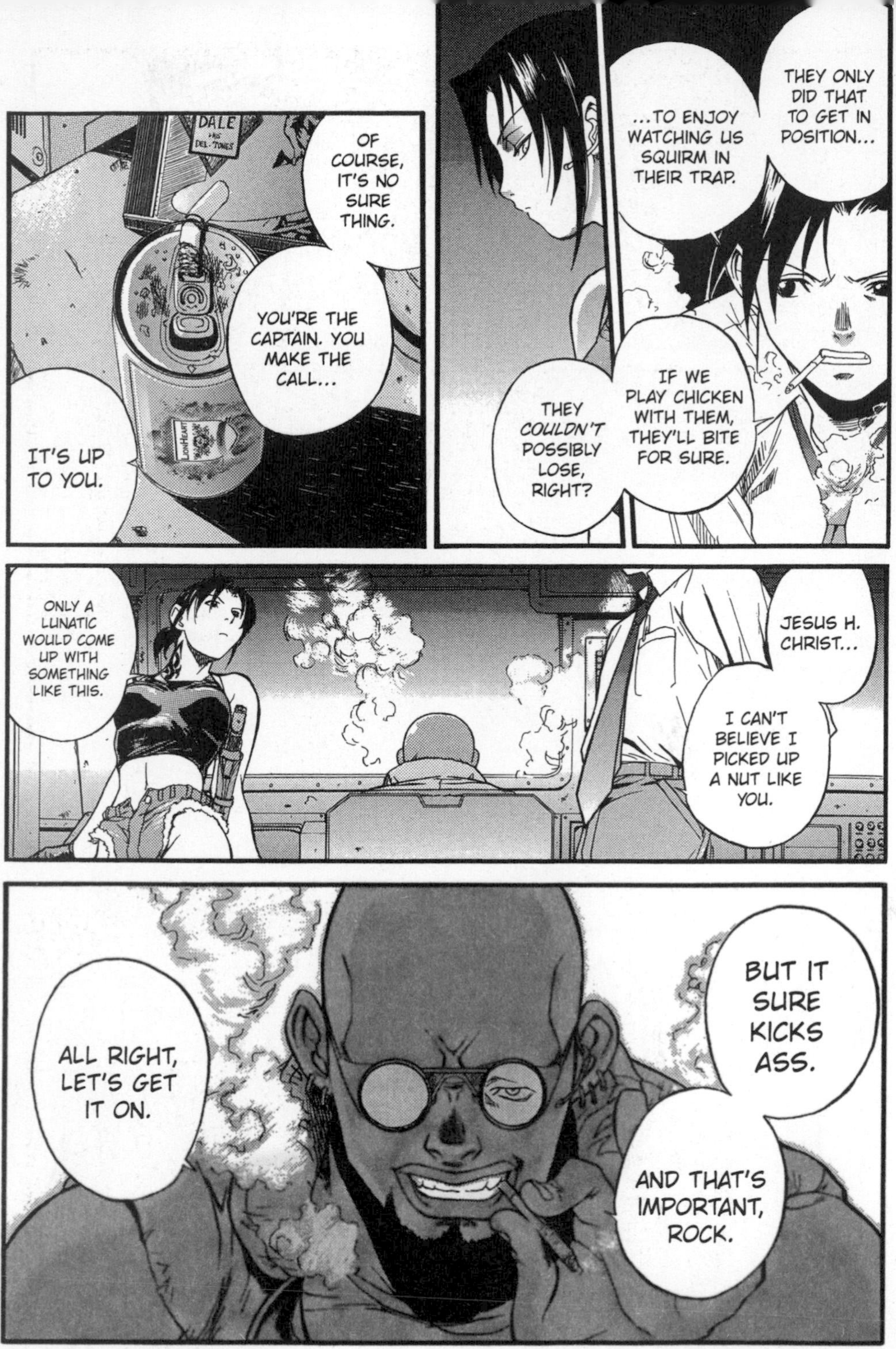
THEY ONLY DID THAT TO GET IN POSITION...
...TO ENJOY WATCHING US SQUIRM IN THEIR TRAP.
IF WE PLAY CHICKEN WITH THEM, THEY'LL BITE FOR SURE.
THEY *COULDN'T* POSSIBLY LOSE, RIGHT?
DALE
OF COURSE, IT'S NO SURE THING.
YOU'RE THE CAPTAIN. YOU MAKE THE CALL...
IT'S UP TO YOU.
JESUS H. CHRIST...
I CAN'T BELIEVE I PICKED UP A NUT LIKE YOU.
ONLY A LUNATIC WOULD COME UP WITH SOMETHING LIKE THIS.
BUT IT SURE KICKS ASS.
AND THAT'S IMPORTANT, ROCK.
ALL RIGHT, LET'S GET IT ON.

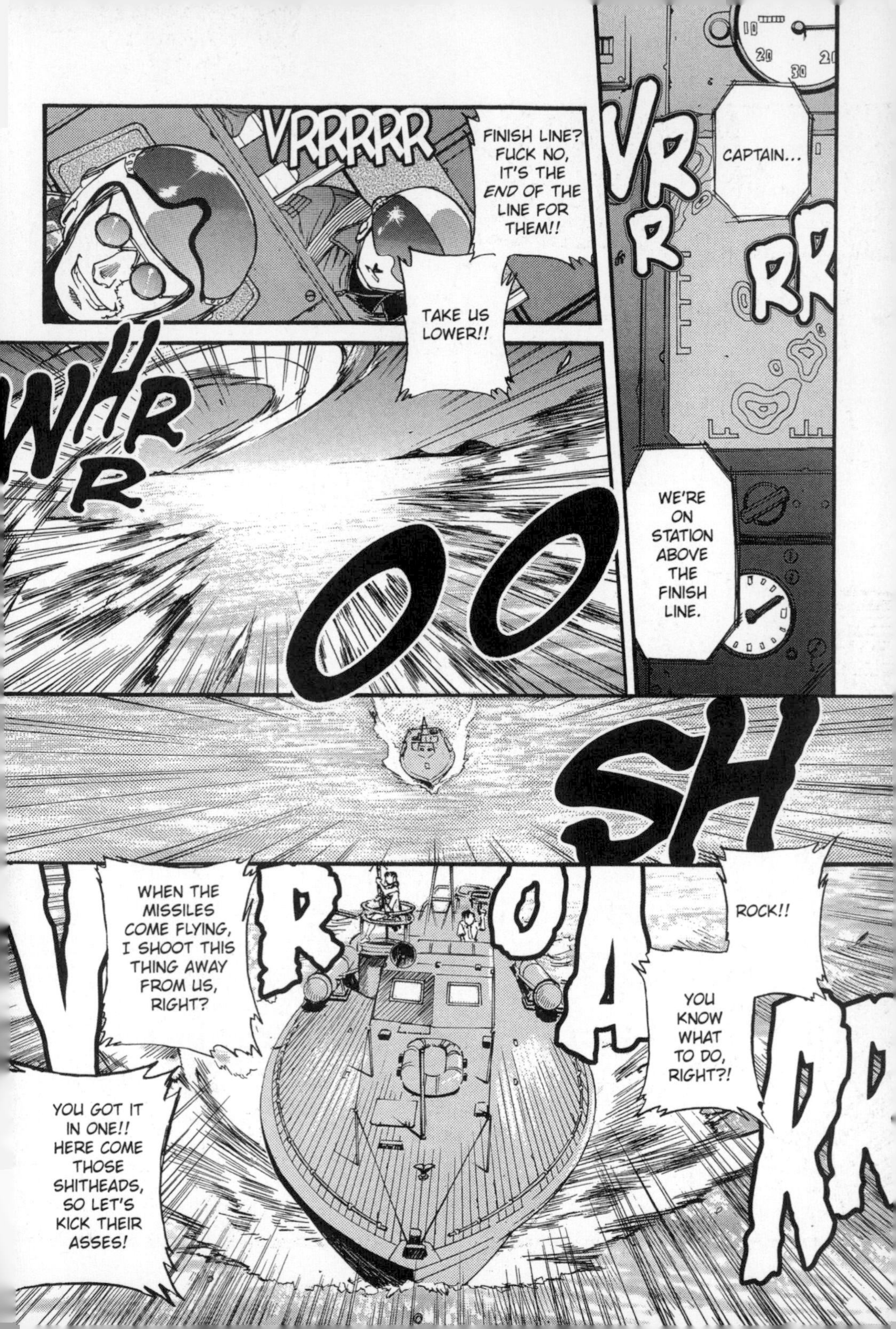

VR R RR
CAPTAIN...
WE'RE ON STATION ABOVE THE FINISH LINE.
VRRRRR
FINISH LINE? FUCK NO, IT'S THE *END* OF THE LINE FOR THEM!!
TAKE US LOWER!!
WHRR
OO
SH
ROCK!!
YOU KNOW WHAT TO DO, RIGHT?!
WHEN THE MISSILES COME FLYING, I SHOOT THIS THING AWAY FROM US, RIGHT?
YOU GOT IT IN ONE!! HERE COME THOSE SHITHEADS, SO LET'S KICK THEIR ASSES!
VROARRR

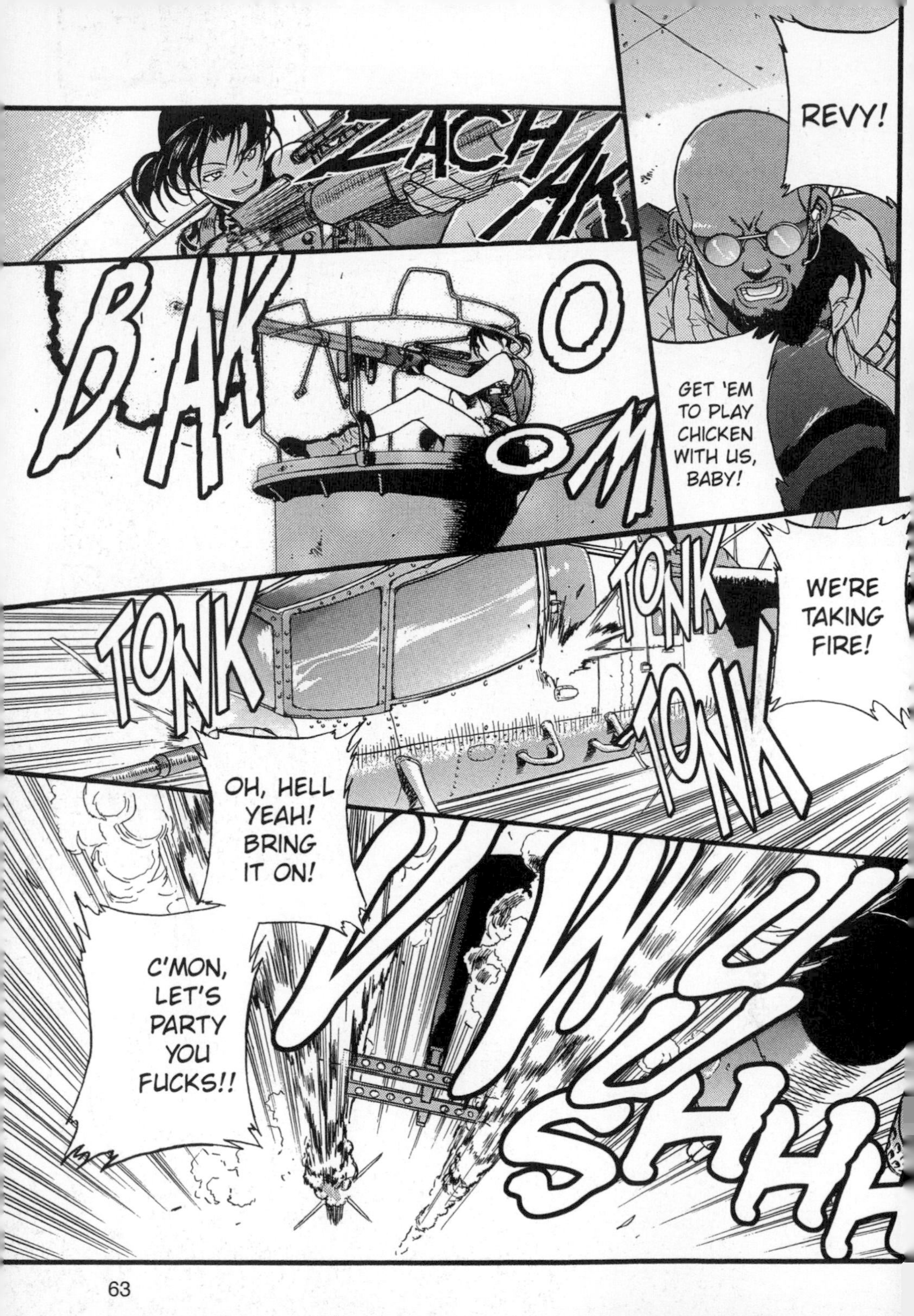
REVY!
GET 'EM TO PLAY CHICKEN WITH US, BABY!
ZACHAK
BAKOM
TONK
TONK
WE'RE TAKING FIRE!
TONK
TONK
OH, HELL YEAH! BRING IT ON!
C'MON, LET'S PARTY YOU FUCKS!!

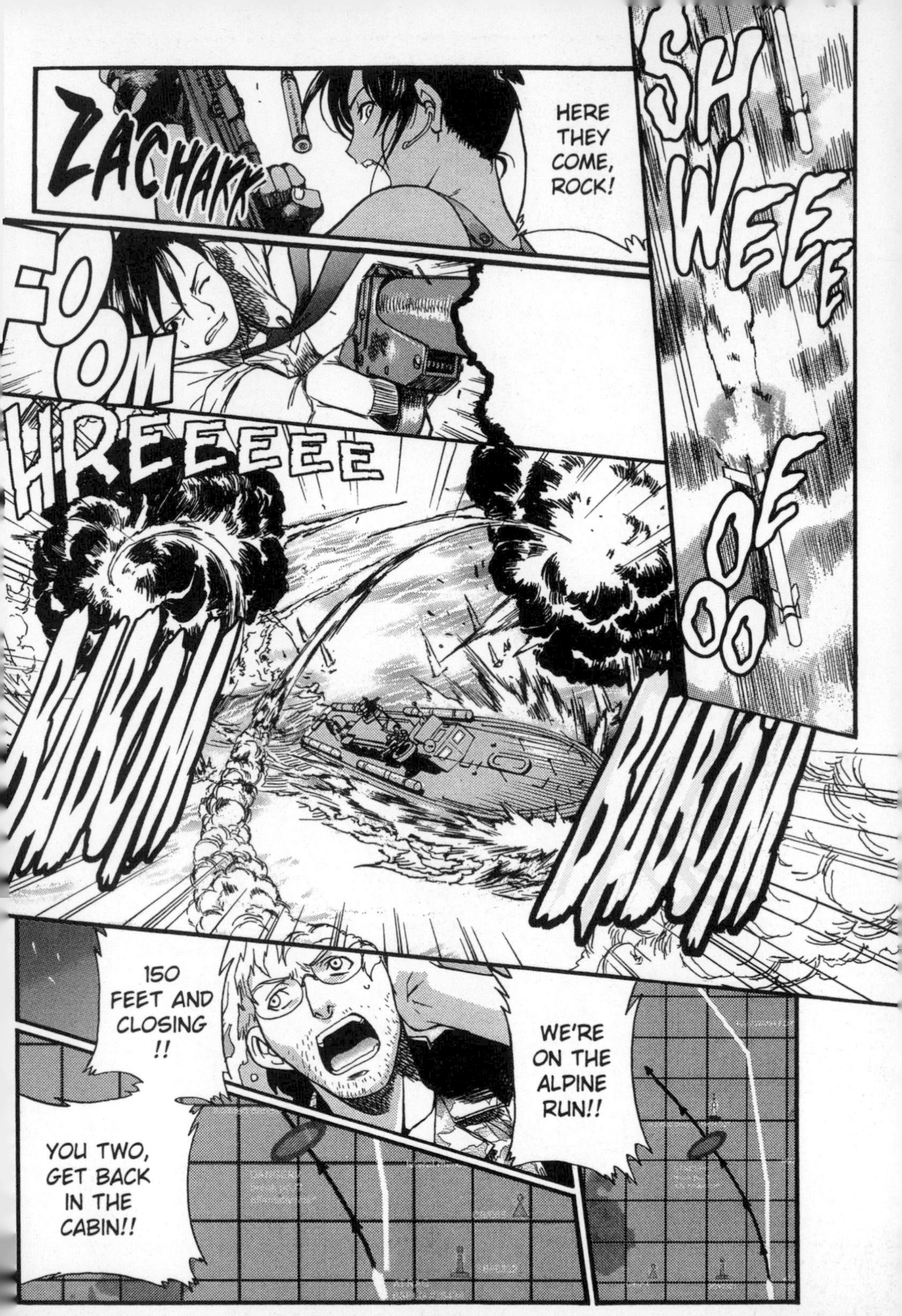
SHWEEE
HERE THEY COME, ROCK!
ZACHAKK
FOOM
HREEEEE
OOOF
150 FEET AND CLOSING !!
WE'RE ON THE ALPINE RUN!!
YOU TWO, GET BACK IN THE CABIN!!

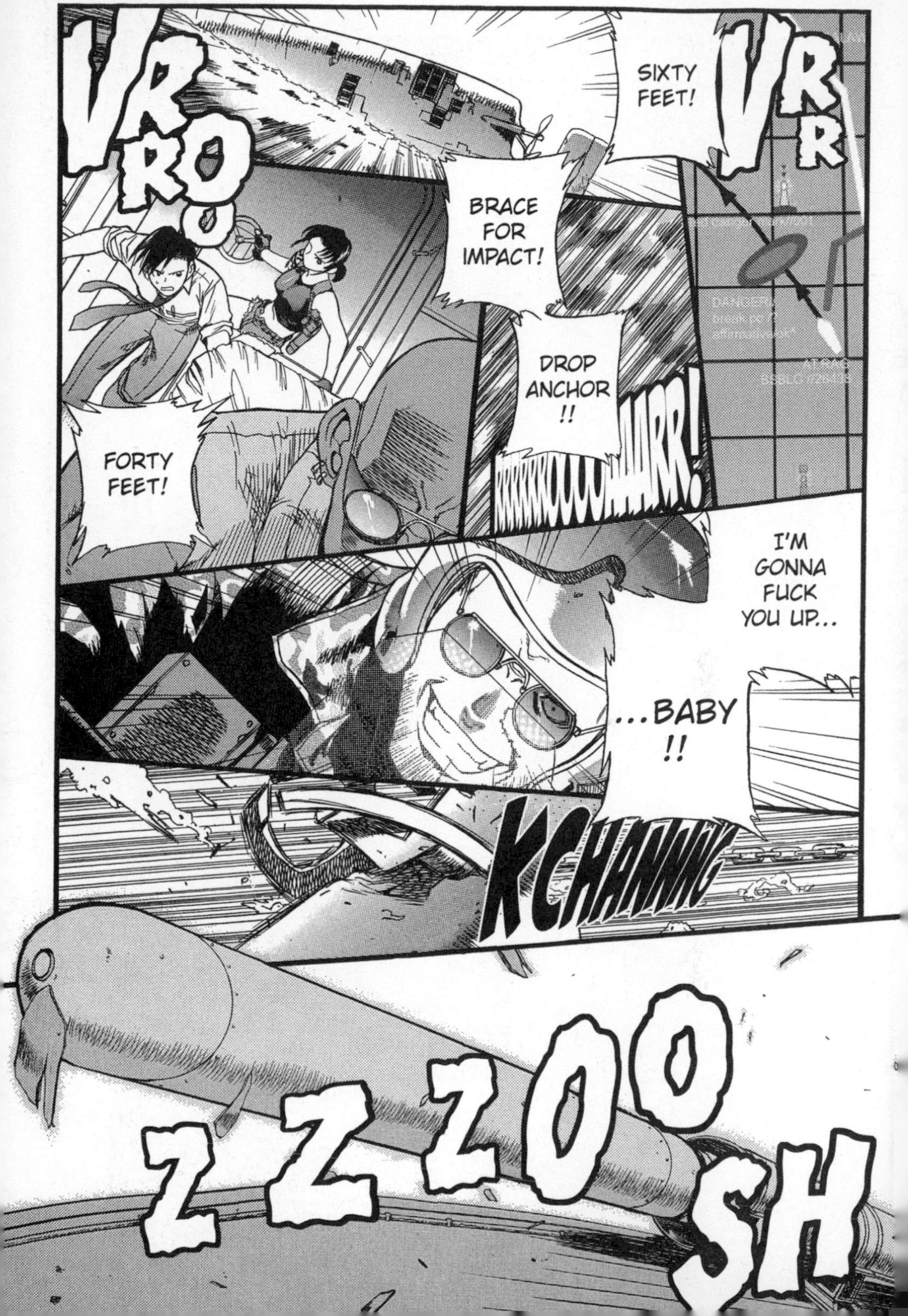
VRR
SIXTY FEET!
BRACE FOR IMPACT!
VROOO
DROP ANCHOR !!
RRRRROOOOHHARR!
FORTY FEET!
I'M GONNA FUCK YOU UP...
...BABY !!
K'CHANNNG
ZZZOOOSH

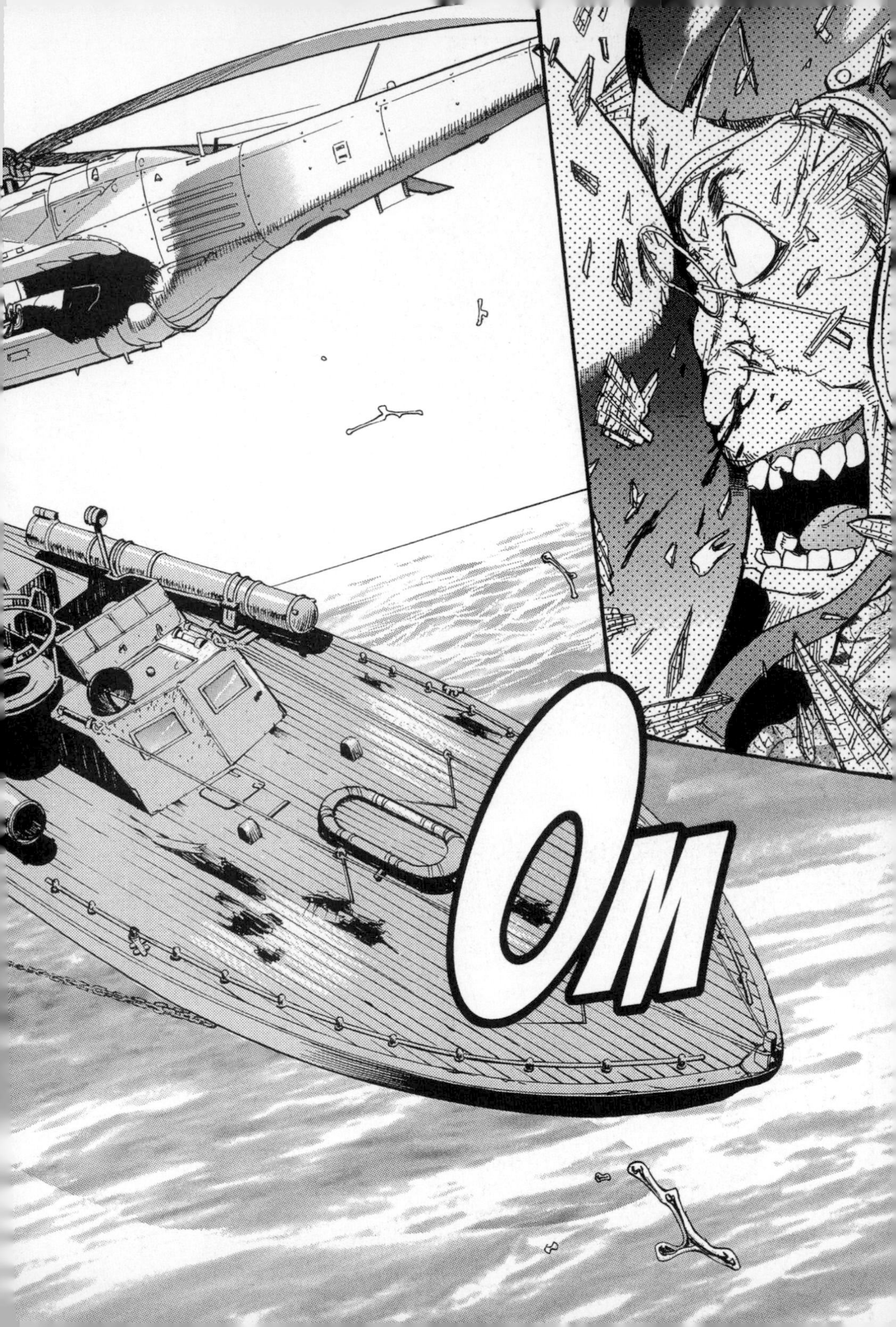
OM

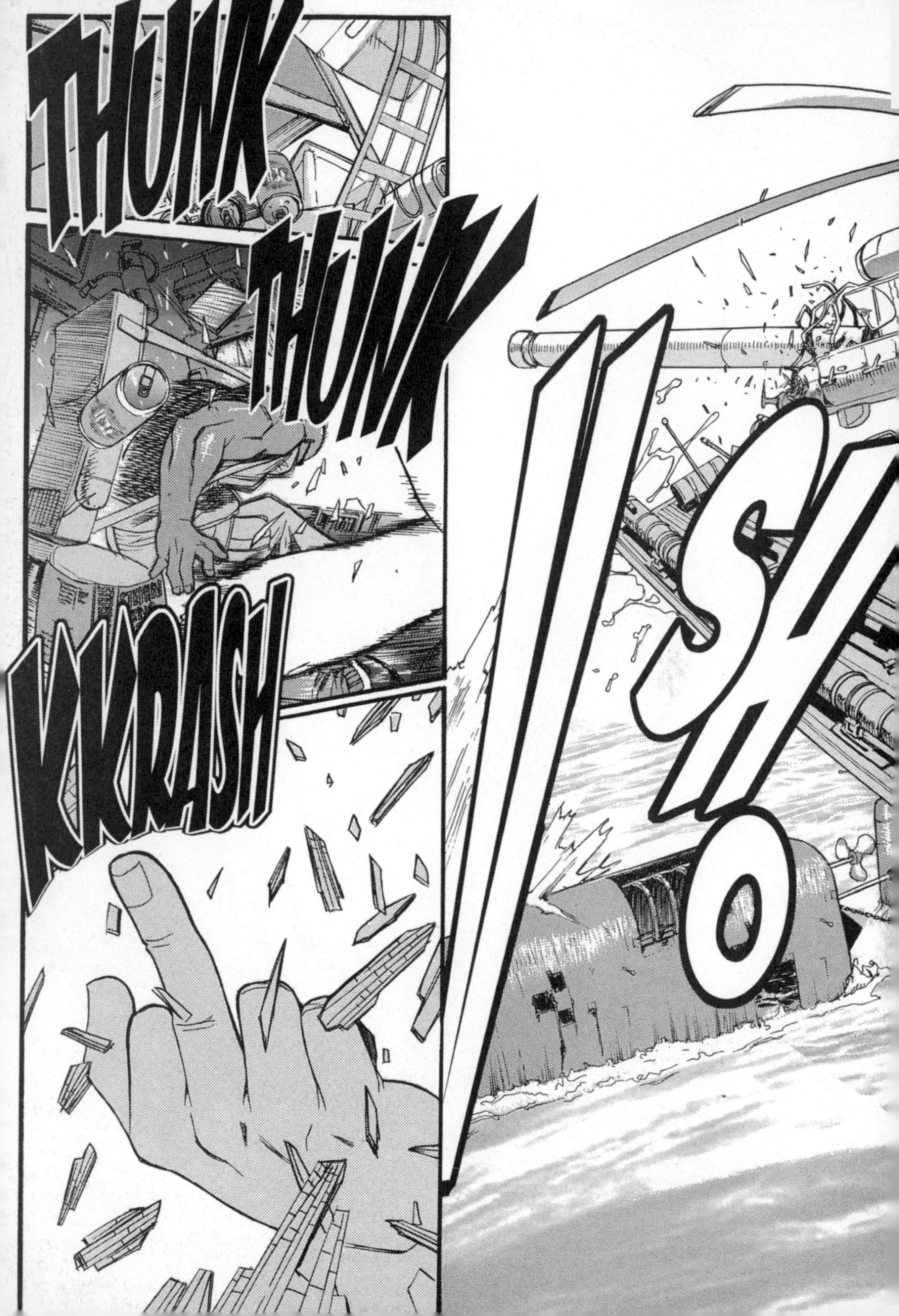
THUNK
THUNK
KKRASH

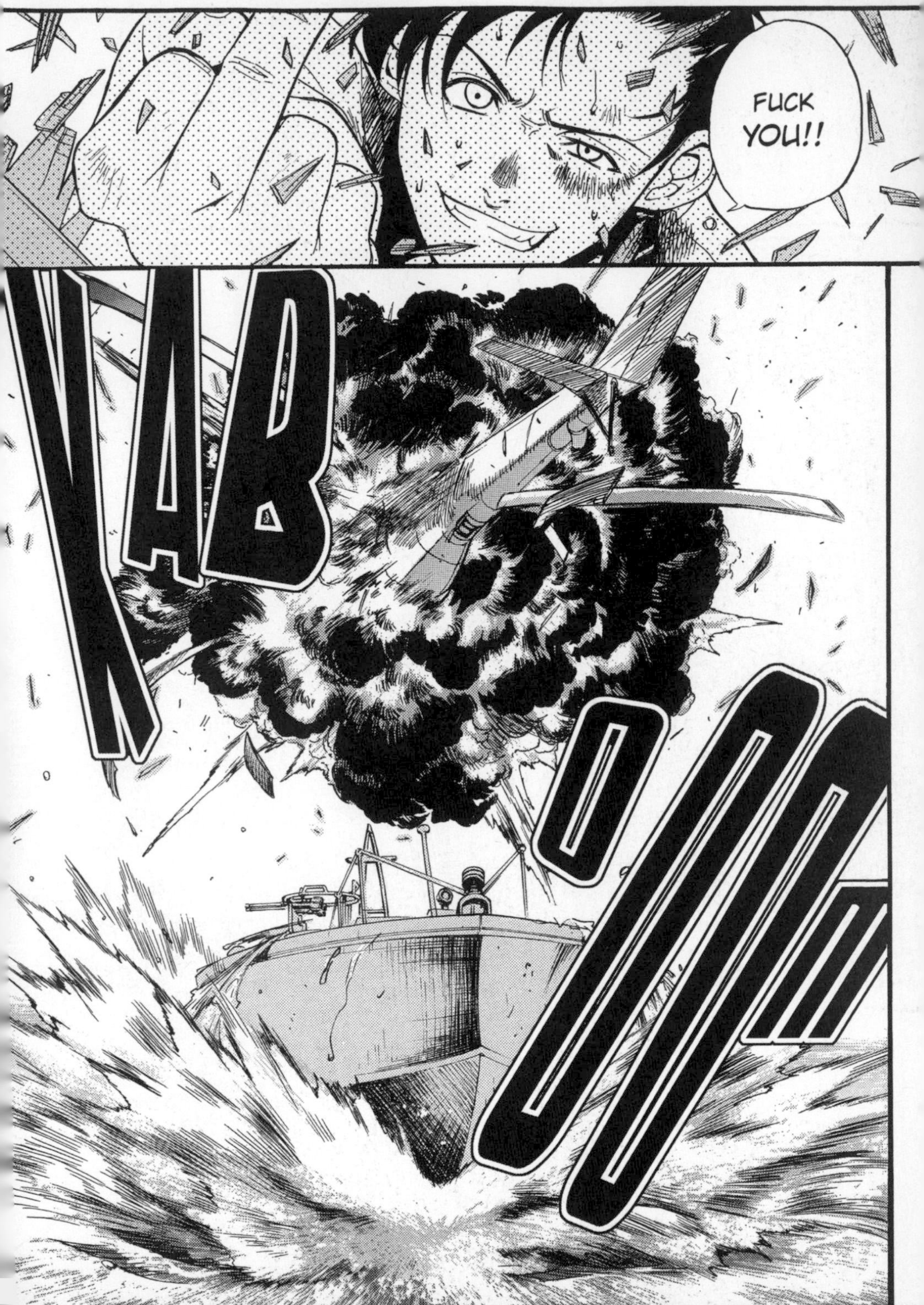
FUCK YOU!!
KABOOOM

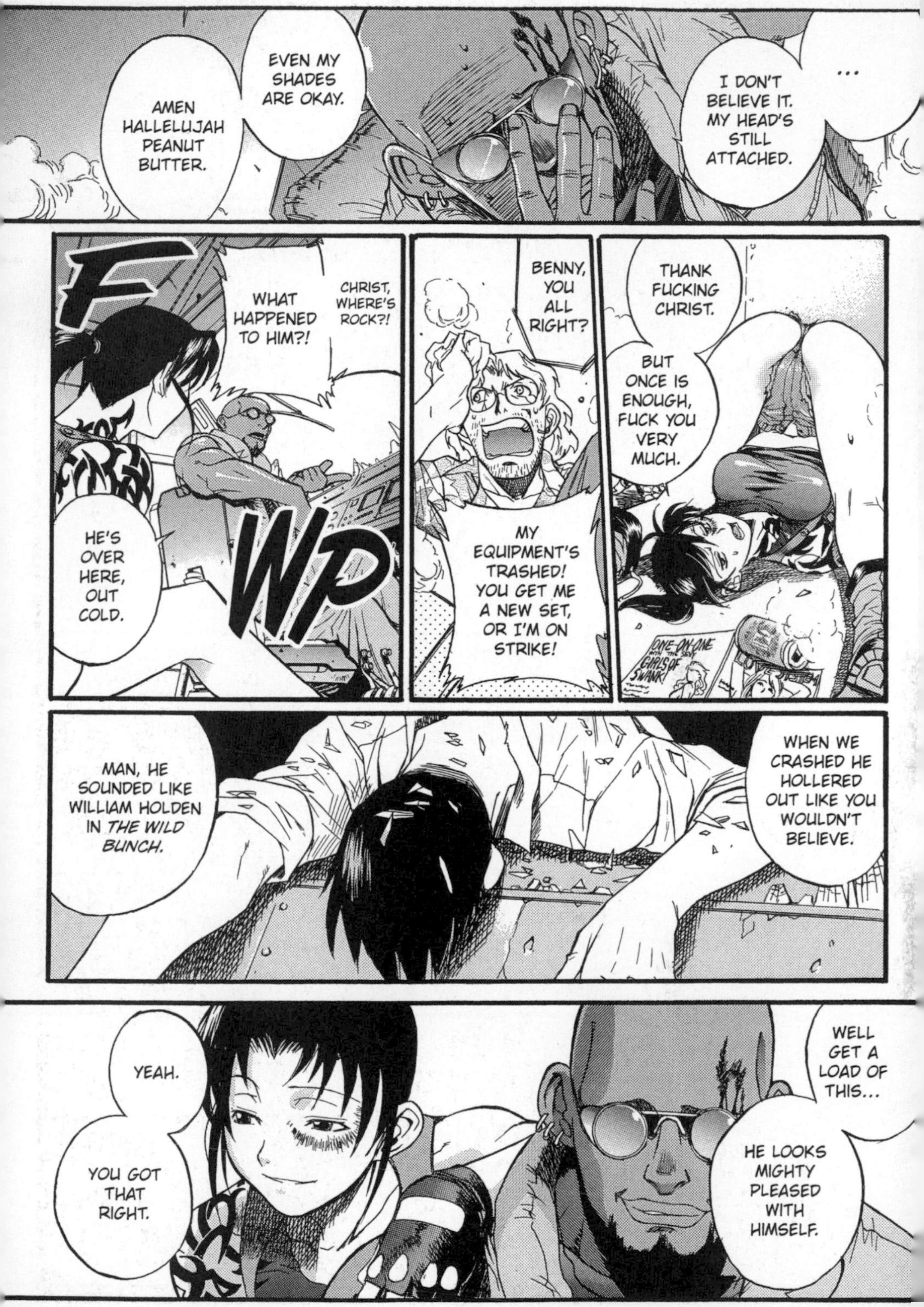
...
I DON'T BELIEVE IT. MY HEAD'S STILL ATTACHED.
EVEN MY SHADES ARE OKAY.
AMEN HALLELUJAH PEANUT BUTTER.
THANK FUCKING CHRIST.
BUT ONCE IS ENOUGH, FUCK YOU VERY MUCH.
ONE-ON-ONE
GIRLS OF SWANK!
BENNY, YOU ALL RIGHT?
MY EQUIPMENT'S TRASHED! YOU GET ME A NEW SET, OR I'M ON STRIKE!
CHRIST, WHERE'S ROCK?!
WHAT HAPPENED TO HIM?!
F
WP
HE'S OVER HERE, OUT COLD.
WHEN WE CRASHED HE HOLLERED OUT LIKE YOU WOULDN'T BELIEVE.
MAN, HE SOUNDED LIKE WILLIAM HOLDEN IN *THE WILD BUNCH.*
WELL GET A LOAD OF THIS...
HE LOOKS MIGHTY PLEASED WITH HIMSELF.
YEAH.
YOU GOT THAT RIGHT.

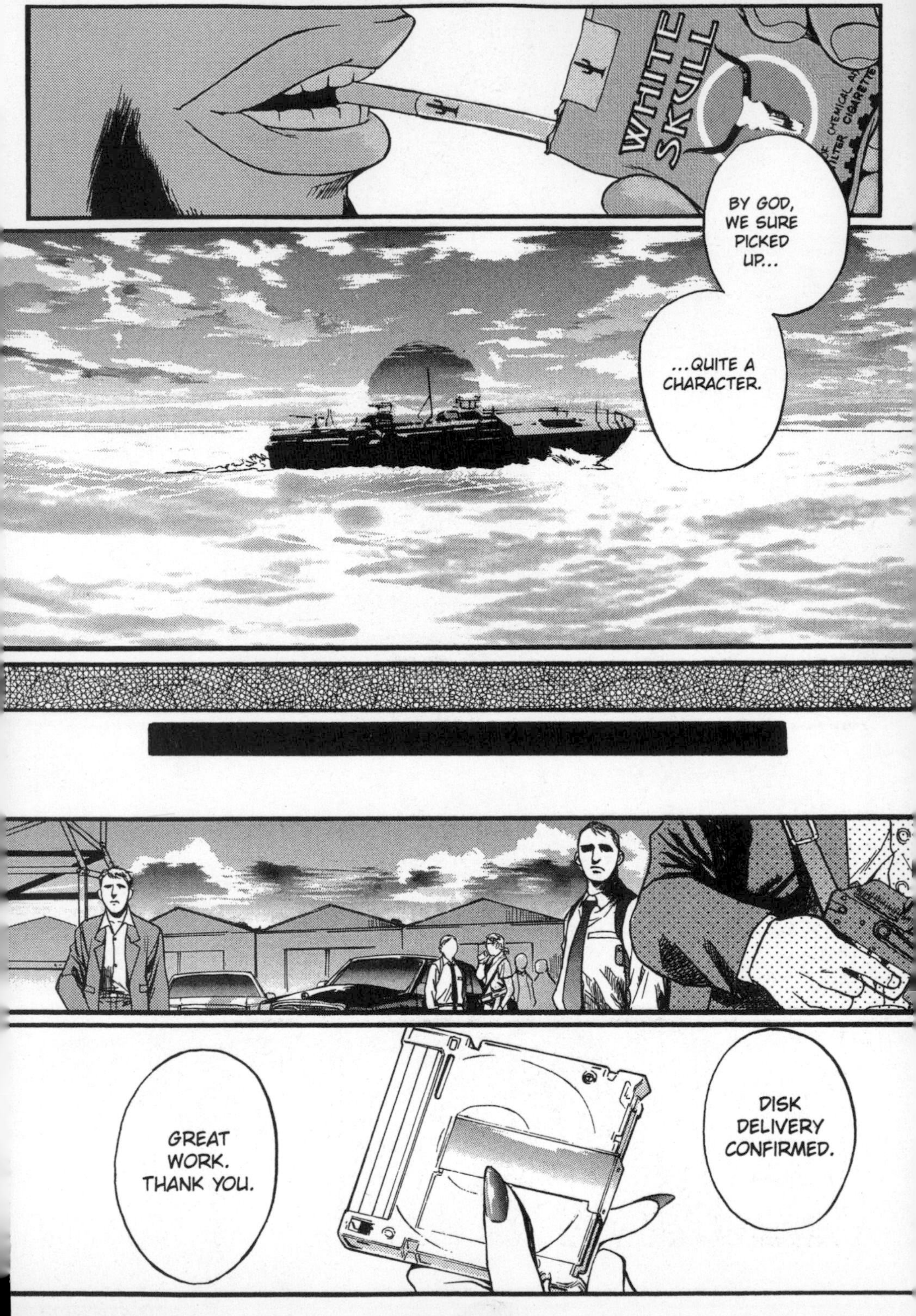
WHITE SKULL
BY GOD, WE SURE PICKED UP...
...QUITE A CHARACTER.
DISK DELIVERY CONFIRMED.
GREAT WORK. THANK YOU.

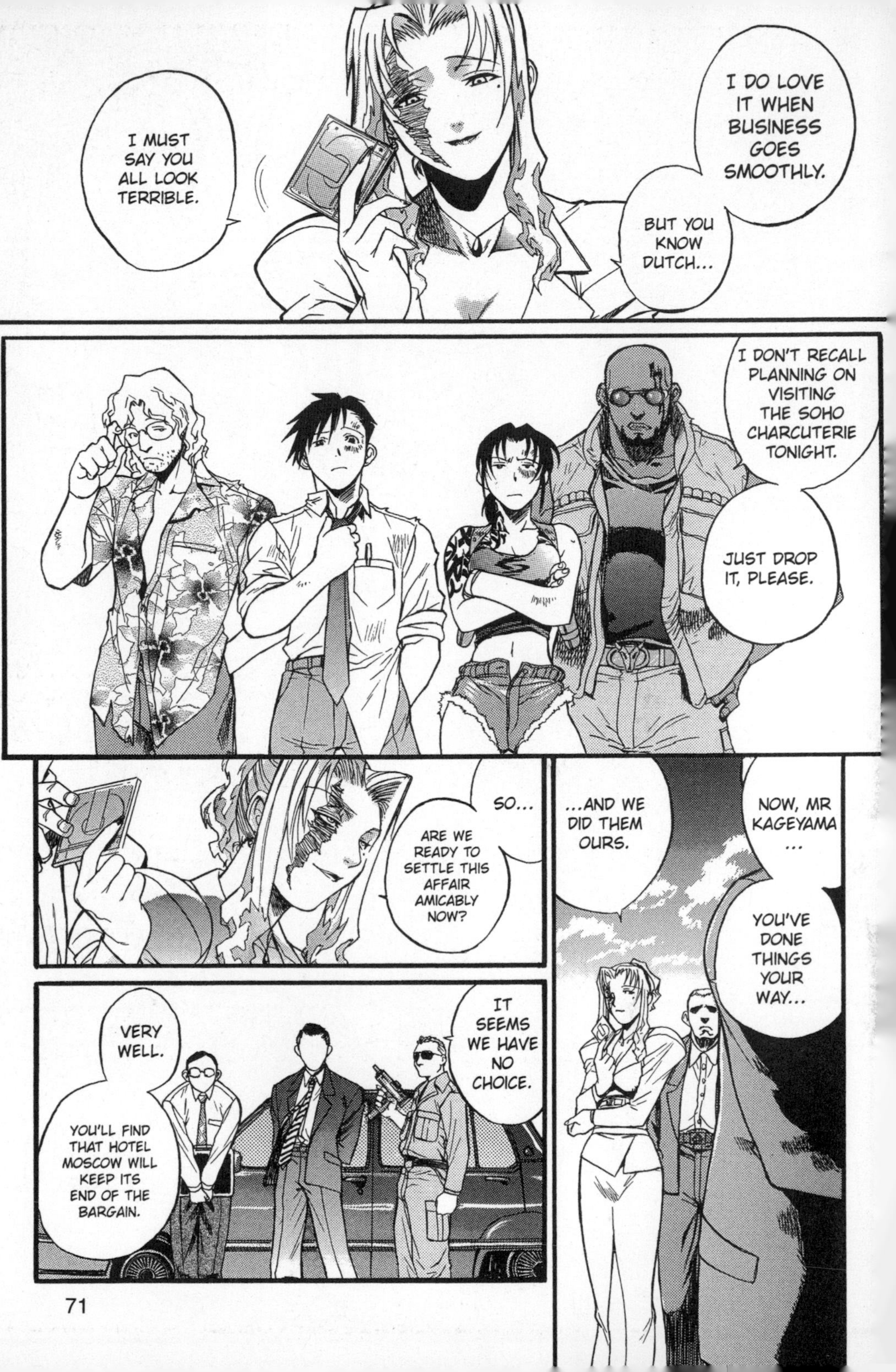
I DO LOVE IT WHEN BUSINESS GOES SMOOTHLY.
BUT YOU KNOW DUTCH...
I MUST SAY YOU ALL LOOK TERRIBLE.
I DON'T RECALL PLANNING ON VISITING THE SOHO CHARCUTERIE TONIGHT.
JUST DROP IT, PLEASE.
NOW, MR KAGEYAMA...
YOU'VE DONE THINGS YOUR WAY...
...AND WE DID THEM OURS.
SO...
ARE WE READY TO SETTLE THIS AFFAIR AMICABLY NOW?
IT SEEMS WE HAVE NO CHOICE.
VERY WELL.
YOU'LL FIND THAT HOTEL MOSCOW WILL KEEP ITS END OF THE BARGAIN.

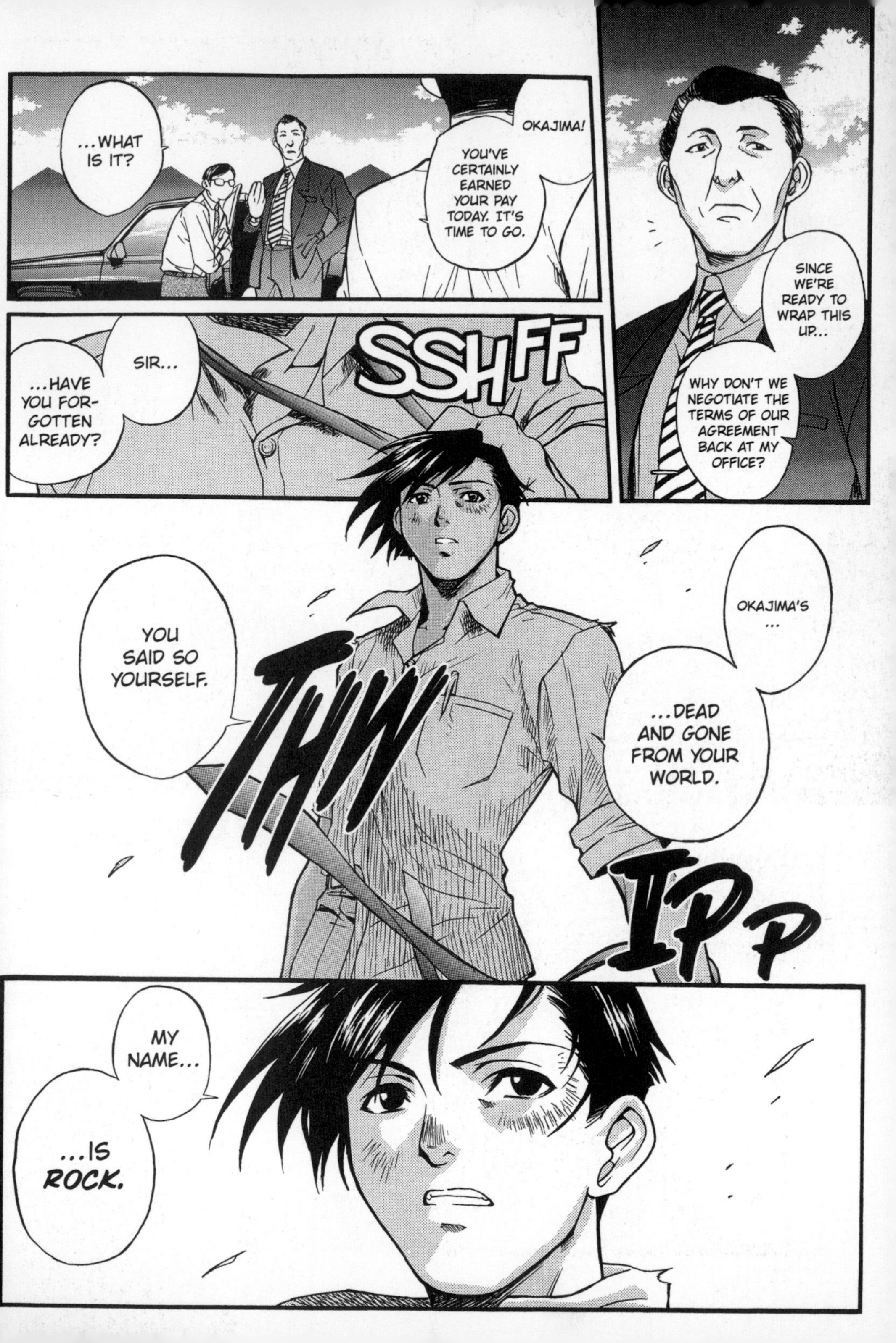
SINCE WE'RE READY TO WRAP THIS UP...
WHY DON'T WE NEGOTIATE THE TERMS OF OUR AGREEMENT BACK AT MY OFFICE?
OKAJIMA!
YOU'VE CERTAINLY EARNED YOUR PAY TODAY. IT'S TIME TO GO.
...WHAT IS IT?
SSHFF
SIR...
...HAVE YOU FOR-GOTTEN ALREADY?
OKAJIMA'S ...
...DEAD AND GONE FROM YOUR WORLD.
YOU SAID SO YOURSELF.
THWIPP
MY NAME...
...IS *ROCK.*

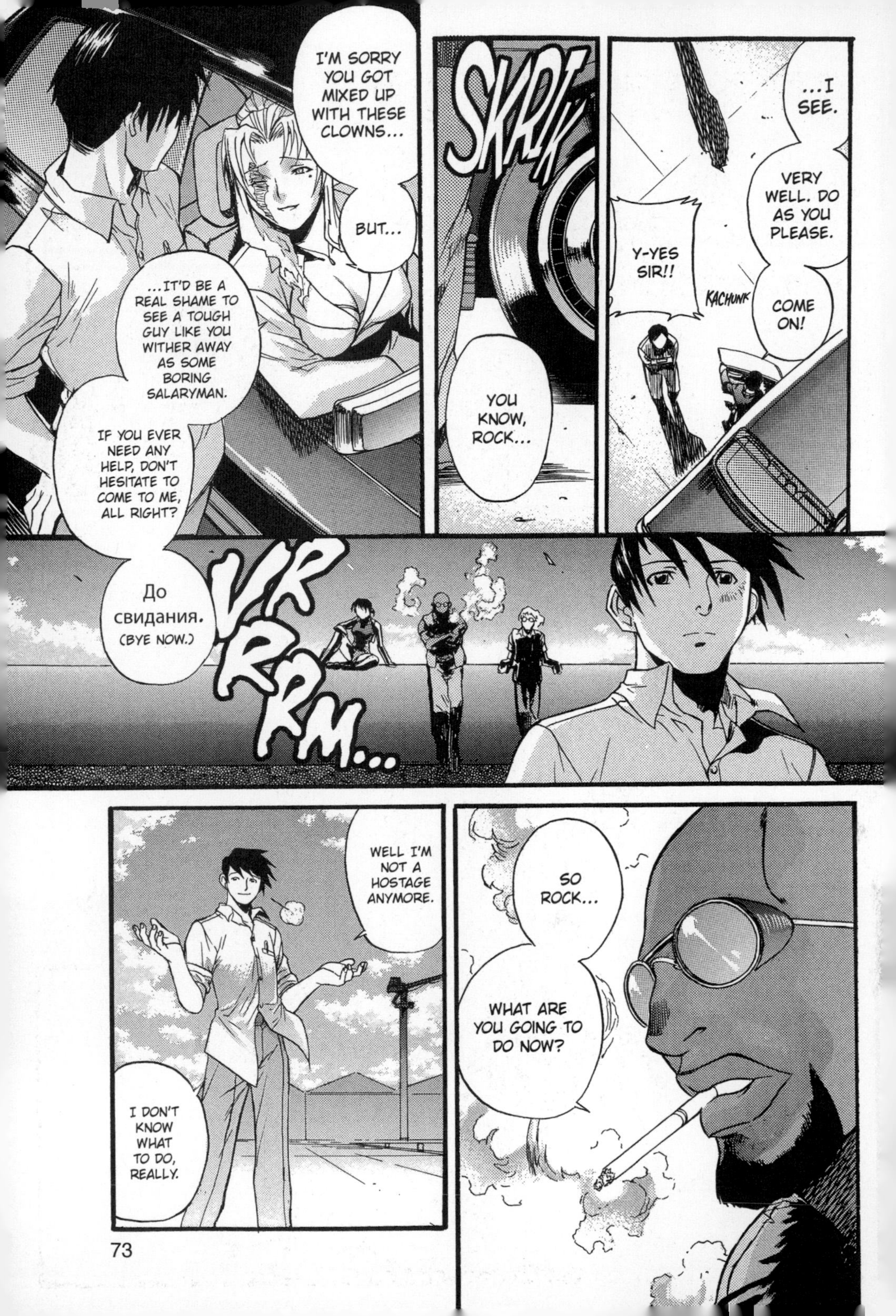
...I SEE.
VERY WELL. DO AS YOU PLEASE.
COME ON!
Y-YES SIR!!
KACHUNK
SKRIK
YOU KNOW, ROCK...
I'M SORRY YOU GOT MIXED UP WITH THESE CLOWNS...
BUT...
...IT'D BE A REAL SHAME TO SEE A TOUGH GUY LIKE YOU WITHER AWAY AS SOME BORING SALARYMAN.
IF YOU EVER NEED ANY HELP, DON'T HESITATE TO COME TO ME, ALL RIGHT?
До свидания. (BYE NOW.)
VRRRM...
SO ROCK...
WHAT ARE YOU GOING TO DO NOW?
WELL I'M NOT A HOSTAGE ANYMORE.
I DON'T KNOW WHAT TO DO, REALLY.

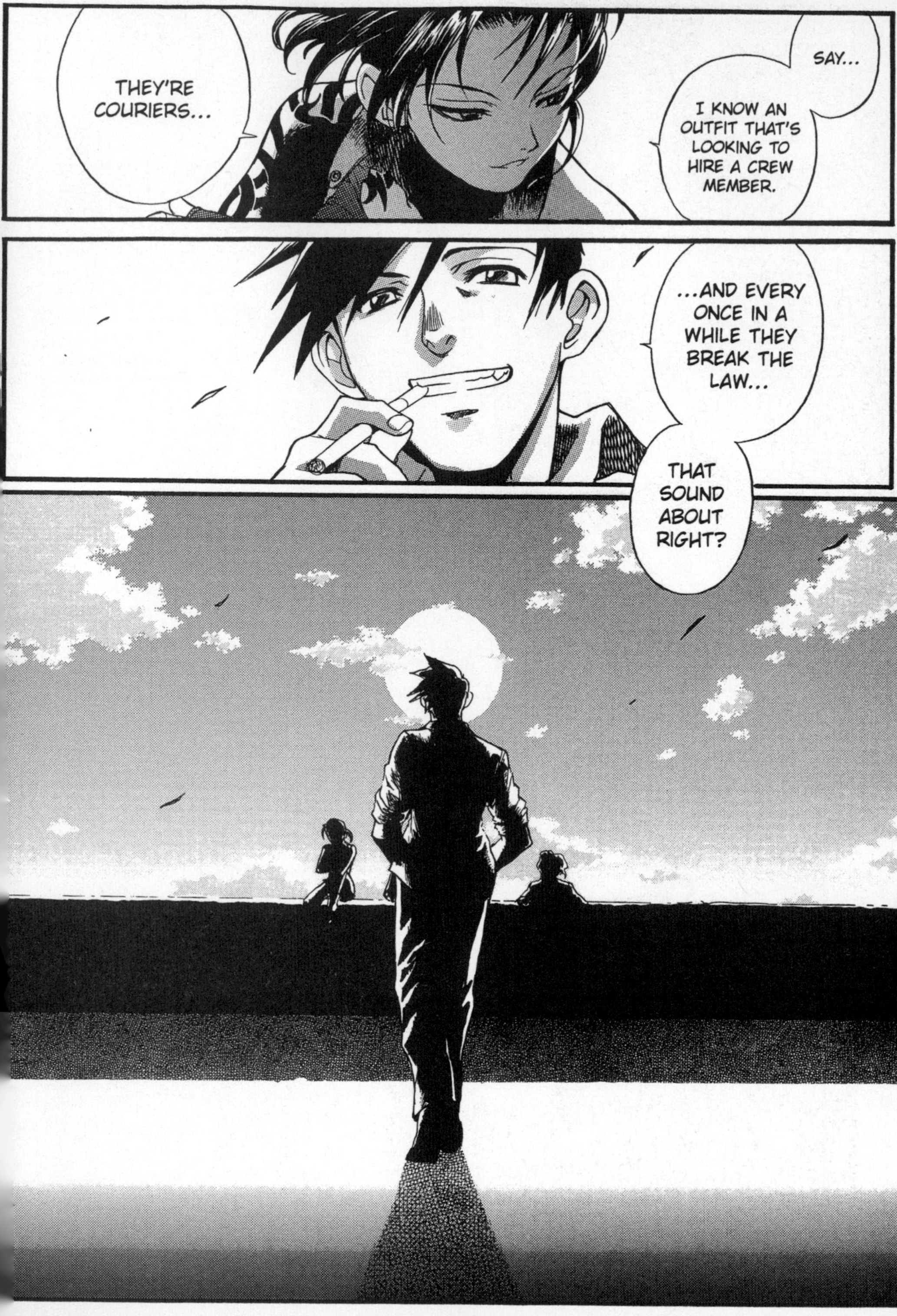
SAY...
I KNOW AN OUTFIT THAT'S LOOKING TO HIRE A CREW MEMBER.
THEY'RE COURIERS...
...AND EVERY ONCE IN A WHILE THEY BREAK THE LAW...
THAT SOUND ABOUT RIGHT?

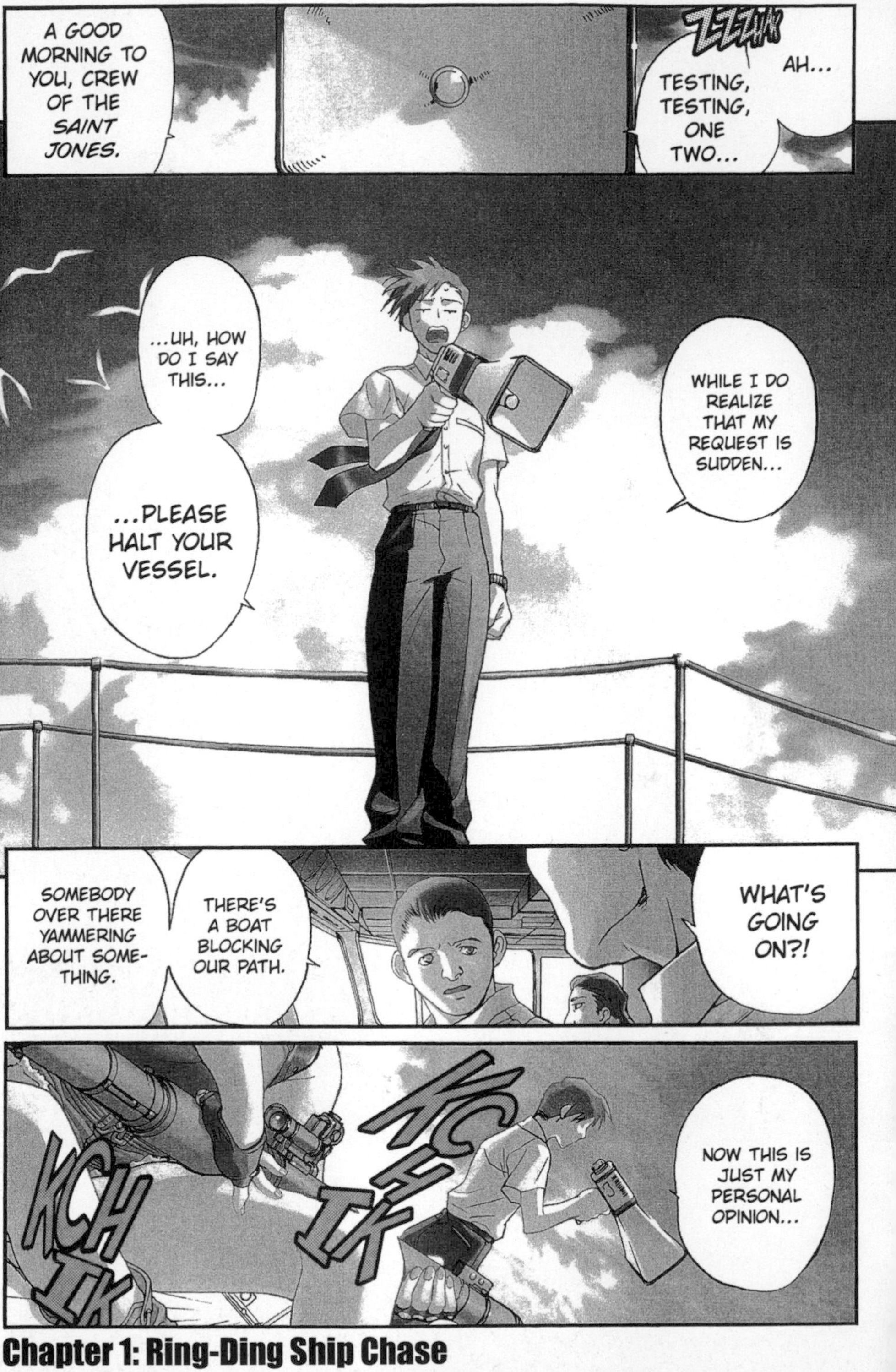
AH...
TESTING, TESTING, ONE TWO...
A GOOD MORNING TO YOU, CREW OF THE *SAINT JONES.*
WHILE I DO REALIZE THAT MY REQUEST IS SUDDEN...
...UH, HOW DO I SAY THIS...
...PLEASE HALT YOUR VESSEL.
WHAT'S GOING ON?!
THERE'S A BOAT BLOCKING OUR PATH.
SOMEBODY OVER THERE YAMMERING ABOUT SOME-THING.
NOW THIS IS JUST MY PERSONAL OPINION...
KCHIK
KCHIK

Chapter 1: Ring-Ding Ship Chase

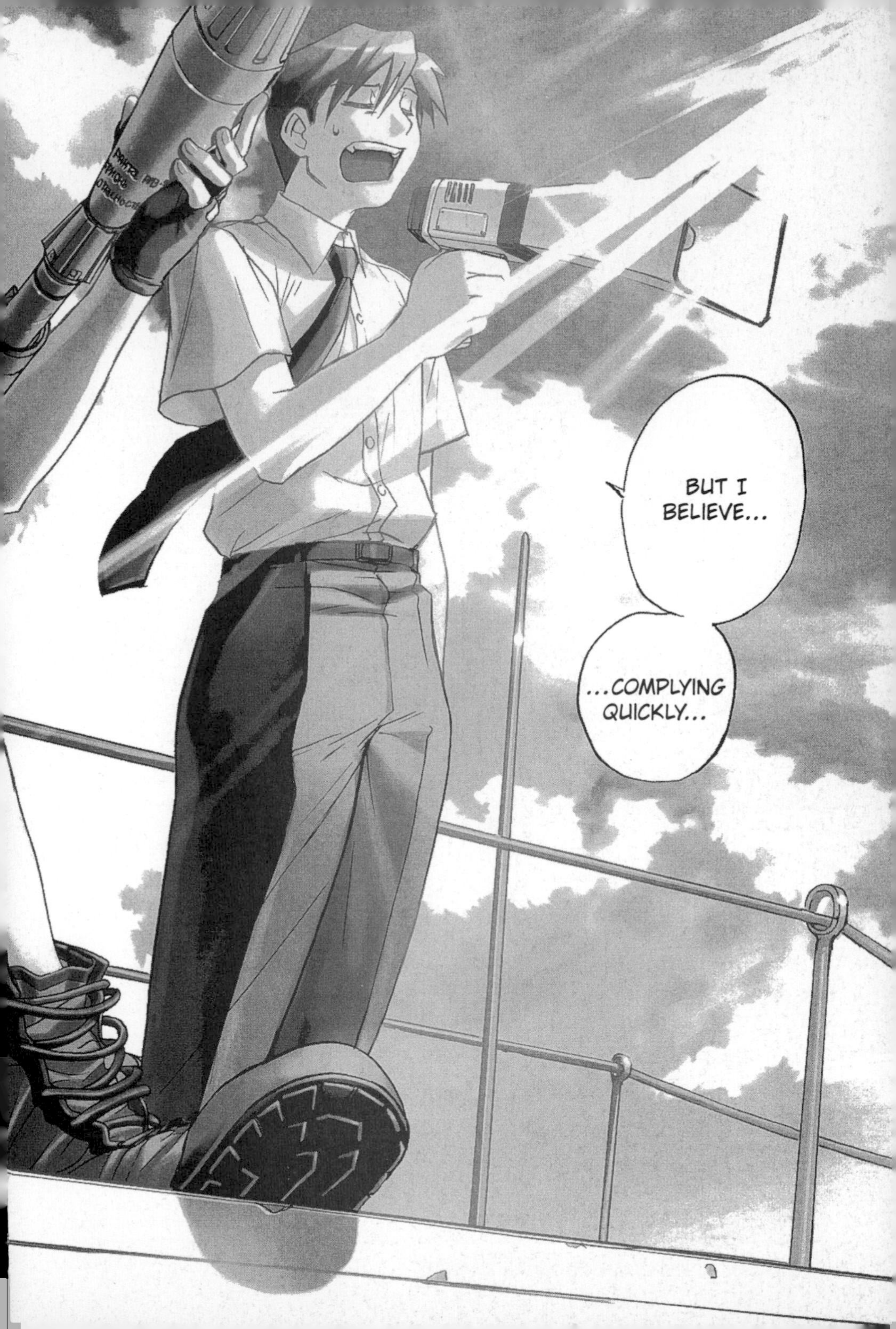
BUT I BELIEVE...
...COMPLYING QUICKLY...

Chapter 1: Ring-Ding Ship Chase

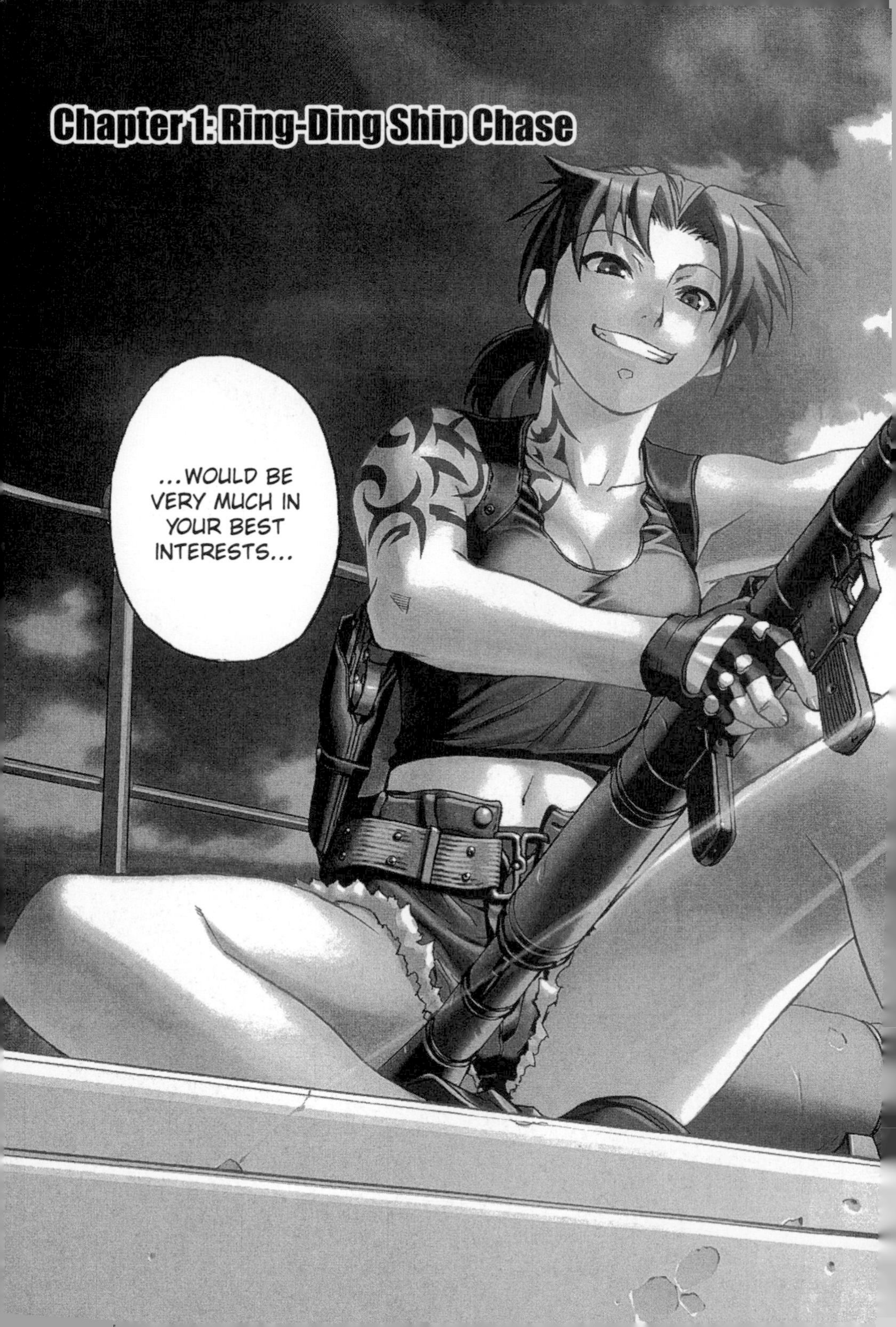
...WOULD BE VERY MUCH IN YOUR BEST INTERESTS...

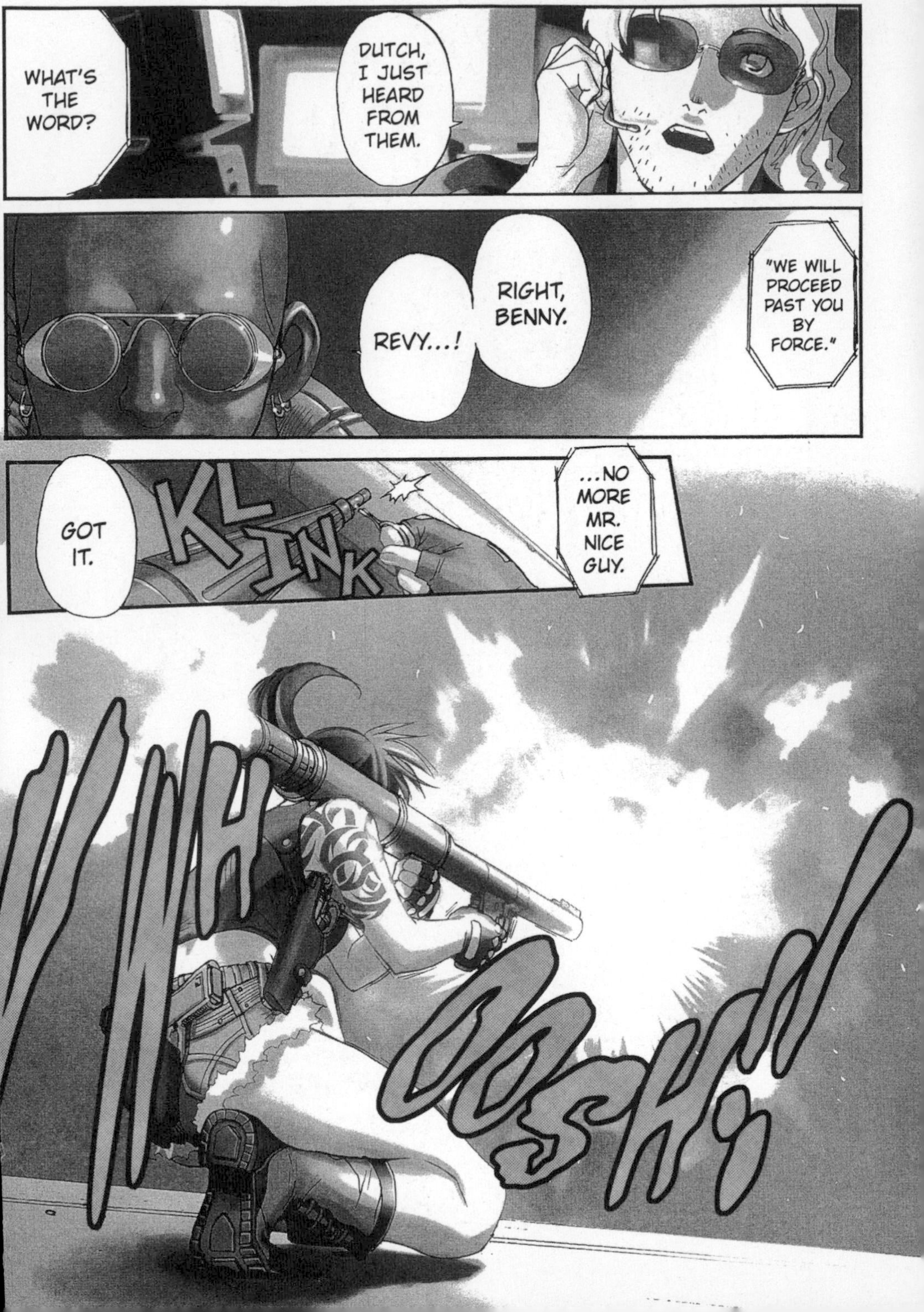
DUTCH, I JUST HEARD FROM THEM.
WHAT'S THE WORD?
"WE WILL PROCEED PAST YOU BY FORCE."
RIGHT, BENNY.
REVY...!
...NO MORE MR. NICE GUY.
KLINK
GOT IT.
WHOOSH!

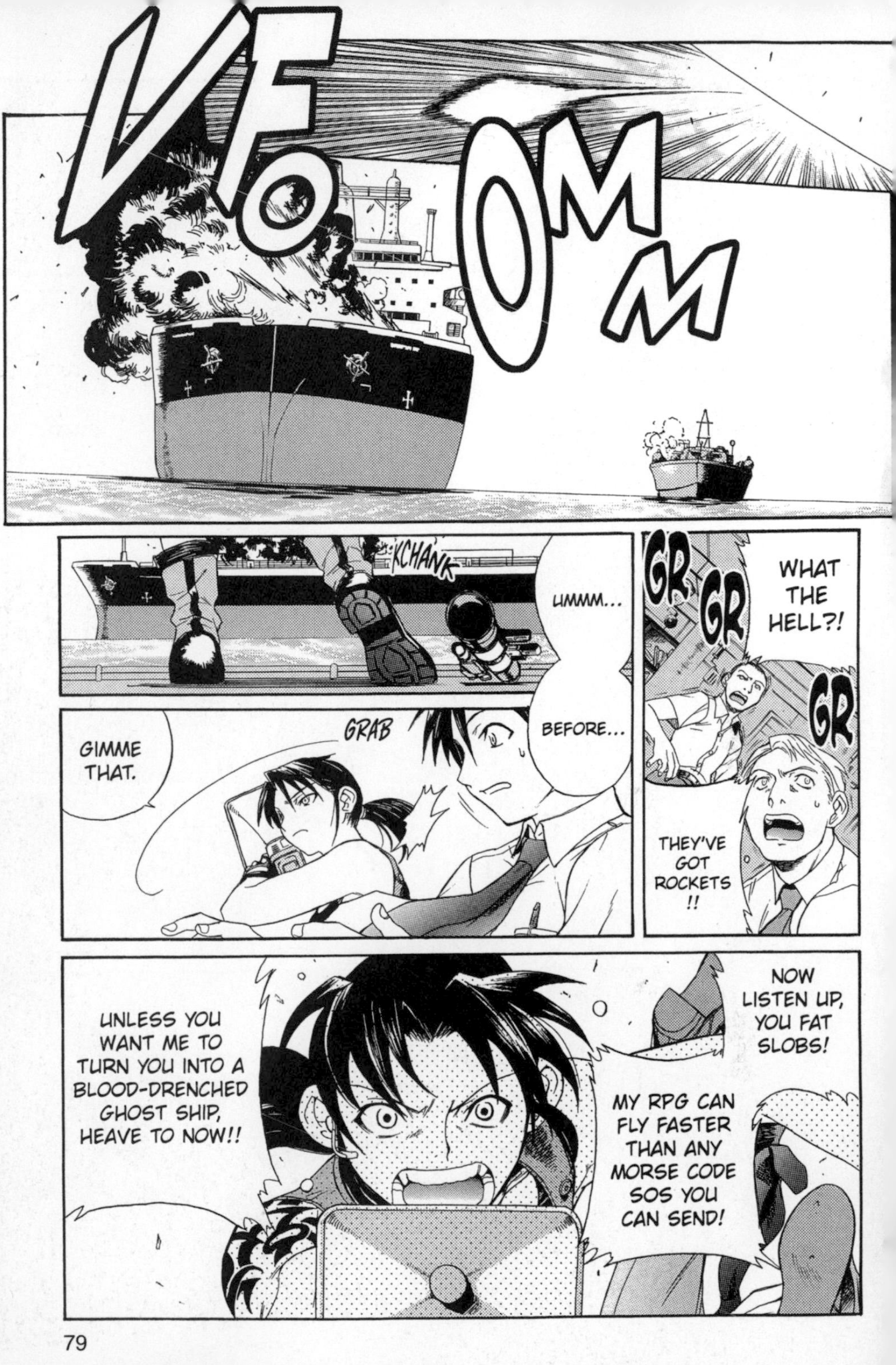
VROOOMM
GR
GR
WHAT THE HELL?!
GR
THEY'VE GOT ROCKETS!!
KCHANK
UMMM...
BEFORE...
GRAB
GIMME THAT.
NOW LISTEN UP, YOU FAT SLOBS!
MY RPG CAN FLY FASTER THAN ANY MORSE CODE SOS YOU CAN SEND!
UNLESS YOU WANT ME TO TURN YOU INTO A BLOOD-DRENCHED GHOST SHIP, HEAVE TO NOW!!

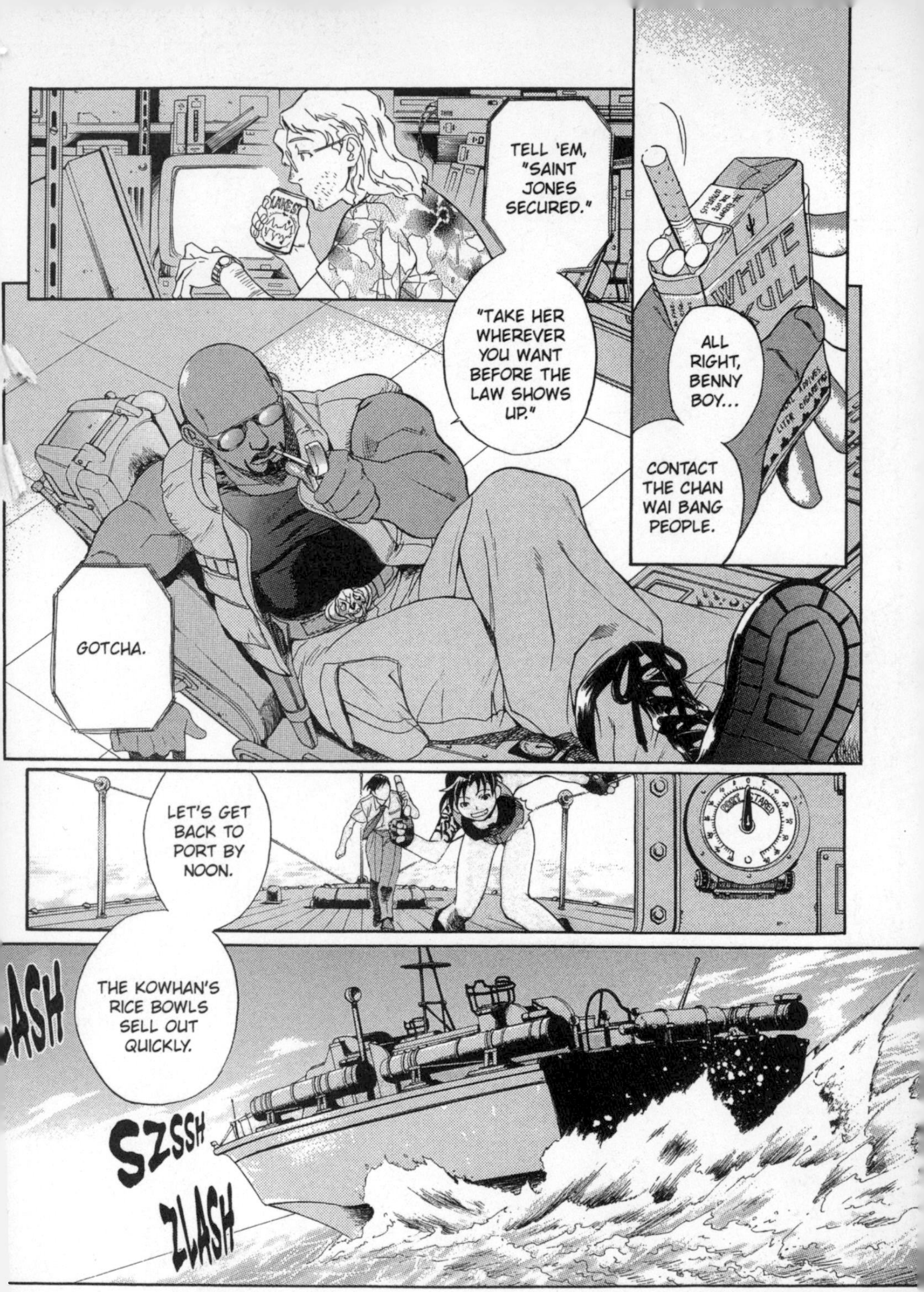
ALL RIGHT, BENNY BOY...
CONTACT THE CHAN WAI BANG PEOPLE.
TELL 'EM, "SAINT JONES SECURED."
"TAKE HER WHEREVER YOU WANT BEFORE THE LAW SHOWS UP."
GOTCHA.
LET'S GET BACK TO PORT BY NOON.
THE KOWHAN'S RICE BOWLS SELL OUT QUICKLY.
LASH
SZSSH
ZLASH

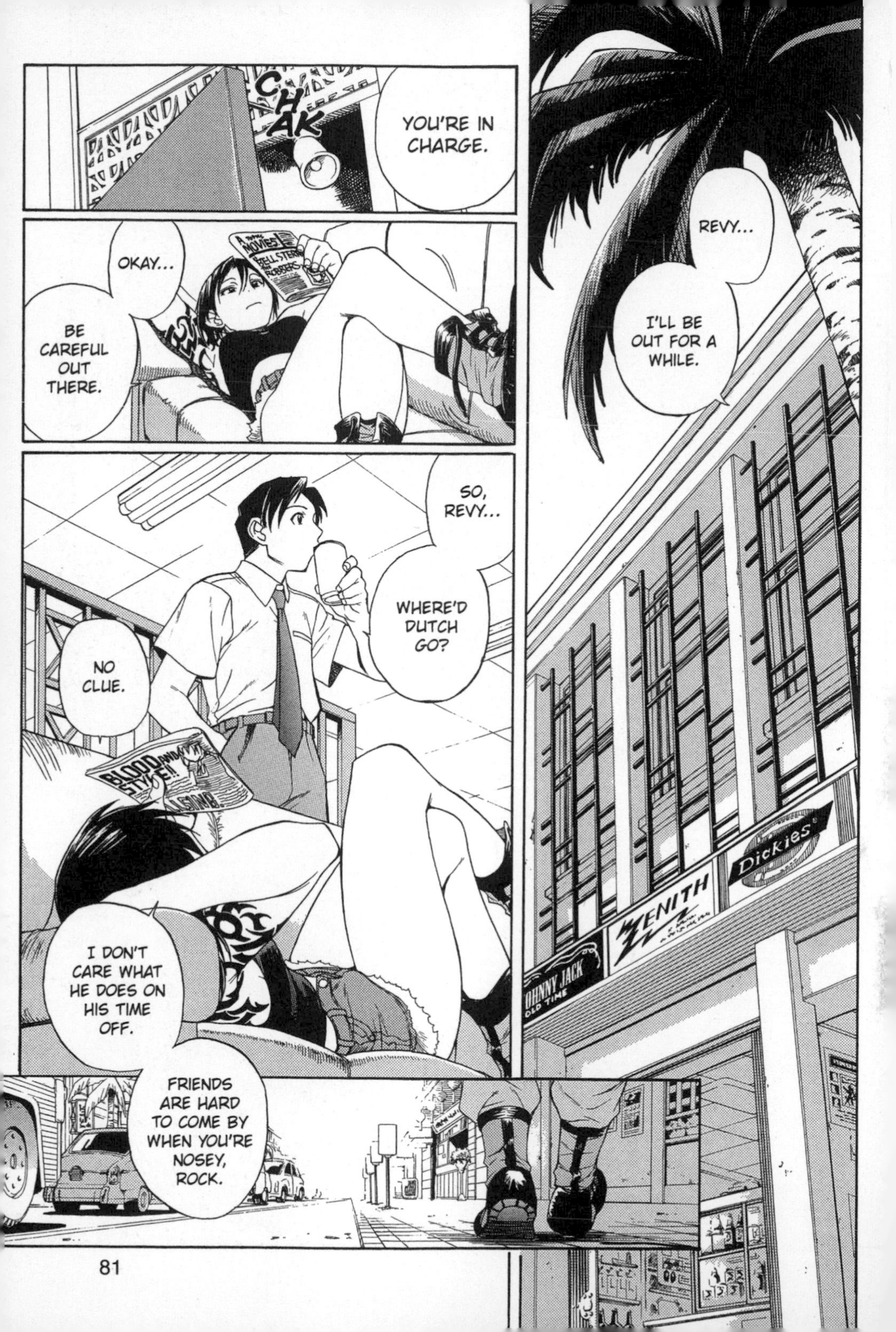
REVY...
I'LL BE OUT FOR A WHILE.
ZENITH
Dickies
OHNNY JACK OLD TIME
CHAK
YOU'RE IN CHARGE.
OKAY...
BE CAREFUL OUT THERE.
SO, REVY...
WHERE'D DUTCH GO?
NO CLUE.
I DON'T CARE WHAT HE DOES ON HIS TIME OFF.
FRIENDS ARE HARD TO COME BY WHEN YOU'RE NOSEY, ROCK.

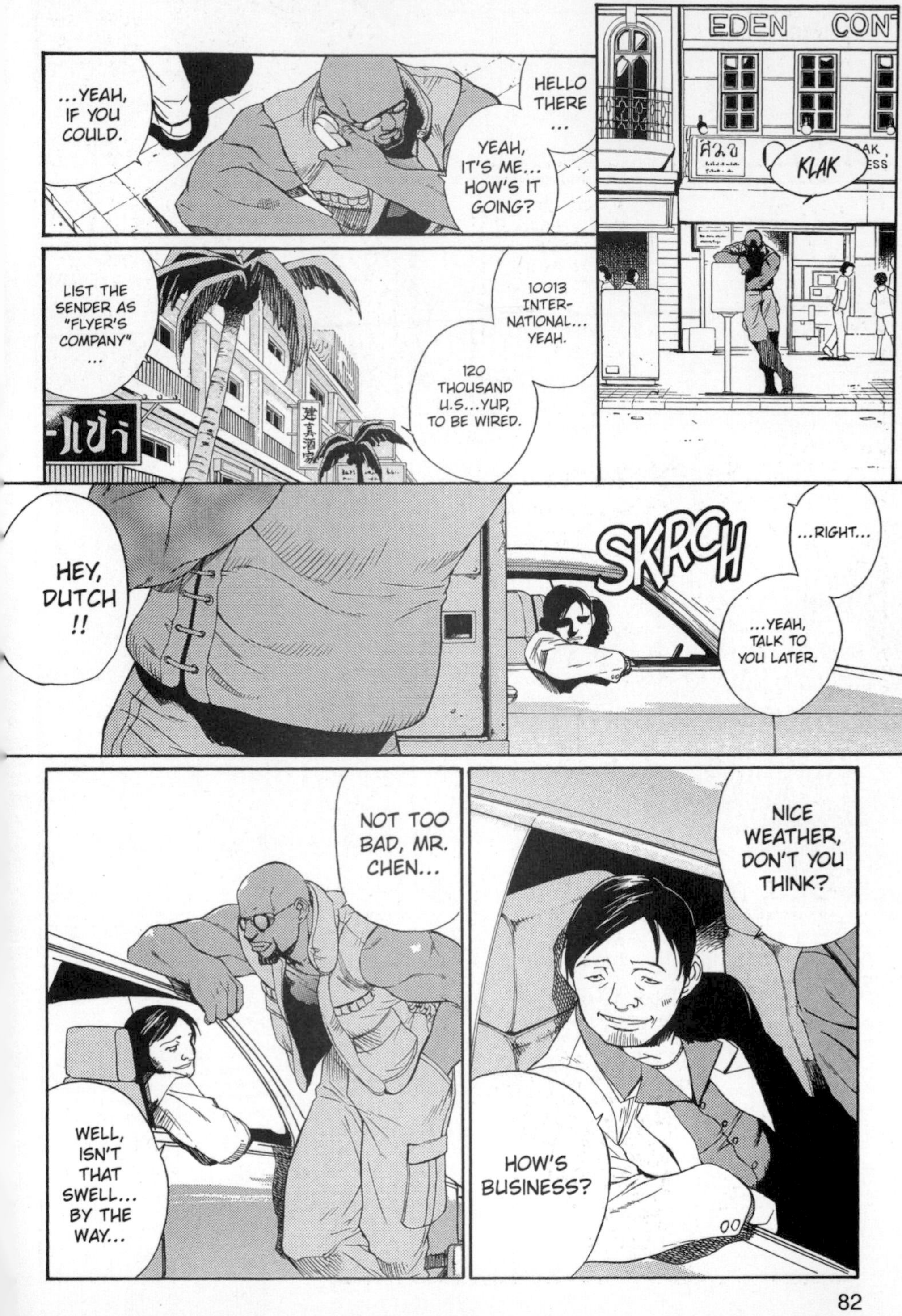
EDEN
KLAK
HELLO THERE ...
YEAH, IT'S ME... HOW'S IT GOING?
...YEAH, IF YOU COULD.
10013 INTERNATIONAL... YEAH.
120 THOUSAND U.S...YUP, TO BE WIRED.
LIST THE SENDER AS "FLYER'S COMPANY" ...
...RIGHT...
...YEAH, TALK TO YOU LATER.
SKRCH
HEY, DUTCH !!
NICE WEATHER, DON'T YOU THINK?
HOW'S BUSINESS?
NOT TOO BAD, MR. CHEN...
WELL, ISN'T THAT SWELL... BY THE WAY...

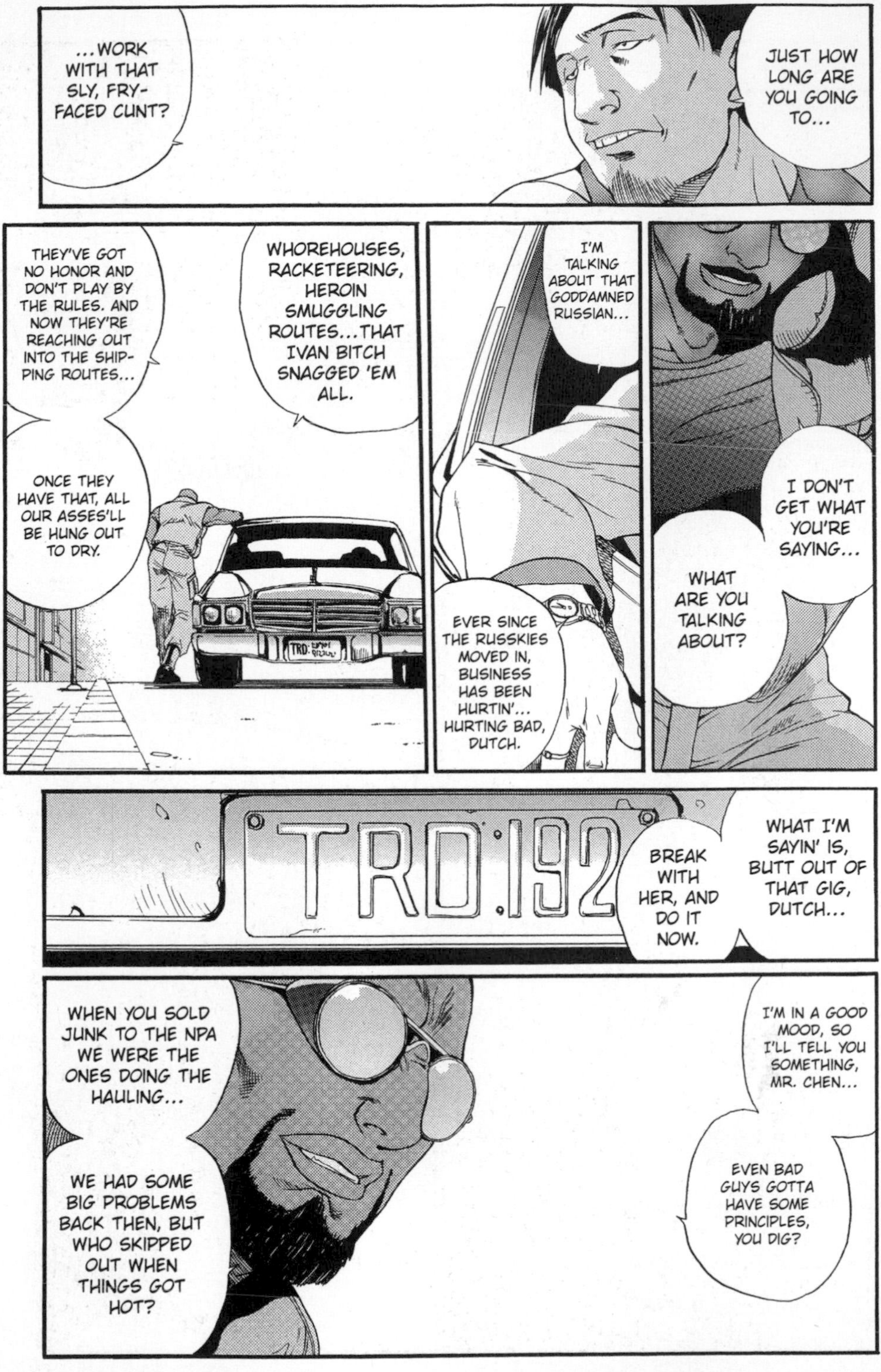
JUST HOW LONG ARE YOU GOING TO...
...WORK WITH THAT SLY, FRY-FACED CUNT?
I DON'T GET WHAT YOU'RE SAYING...
WHAT ARE YOU TALKING ABOUT?
I'M TALKING ABOUT THAT GODDAMNED RUSSIAN...
EVER SINCE THE RUSSKIES MOVED IN, BUSINESS HAS BEEN HURTIN'... HURTING BAD, DUTCH.
WHOREHOUSES, RACKETEERING, HEROIN SMUGGLING ROUTES...THAT IVAN BITCH SNAGGED 'EM ALL.
THEY'VE GOT NO HONOR AND DON'T PLAY BY THE RULES. AND NOW THEY'RE REACHING OUT INTO THE SHIPPING ROUTES...
ONCE THEY HAVE THAT, ALL OUR ASSES'LL BE HUNG OUT TO DRY.
TRD
WHAT I'M SAYIN' IS, BUTT OUT OF THAT GIG, DUTCH...
BREAK WITH HER, AND DO IT NOW.
TRD:192
I'M IN A GOOD MOOD, SO I'LL TELL YOU SOMETHING, MR. CHEN...
EVEN BAD GUYS GOTTA HAVE SOME PRINCIPLES, YOU DIG?
WHEN YOU SOLD JUNK TO THE NPA WE WERE THE ONES DOING THE HAULING...
WE HAD SOME BIG PROBLEMS BACK THEN, BUT WHO SKIPPED OUT WHEN THINGS GOT HOT?

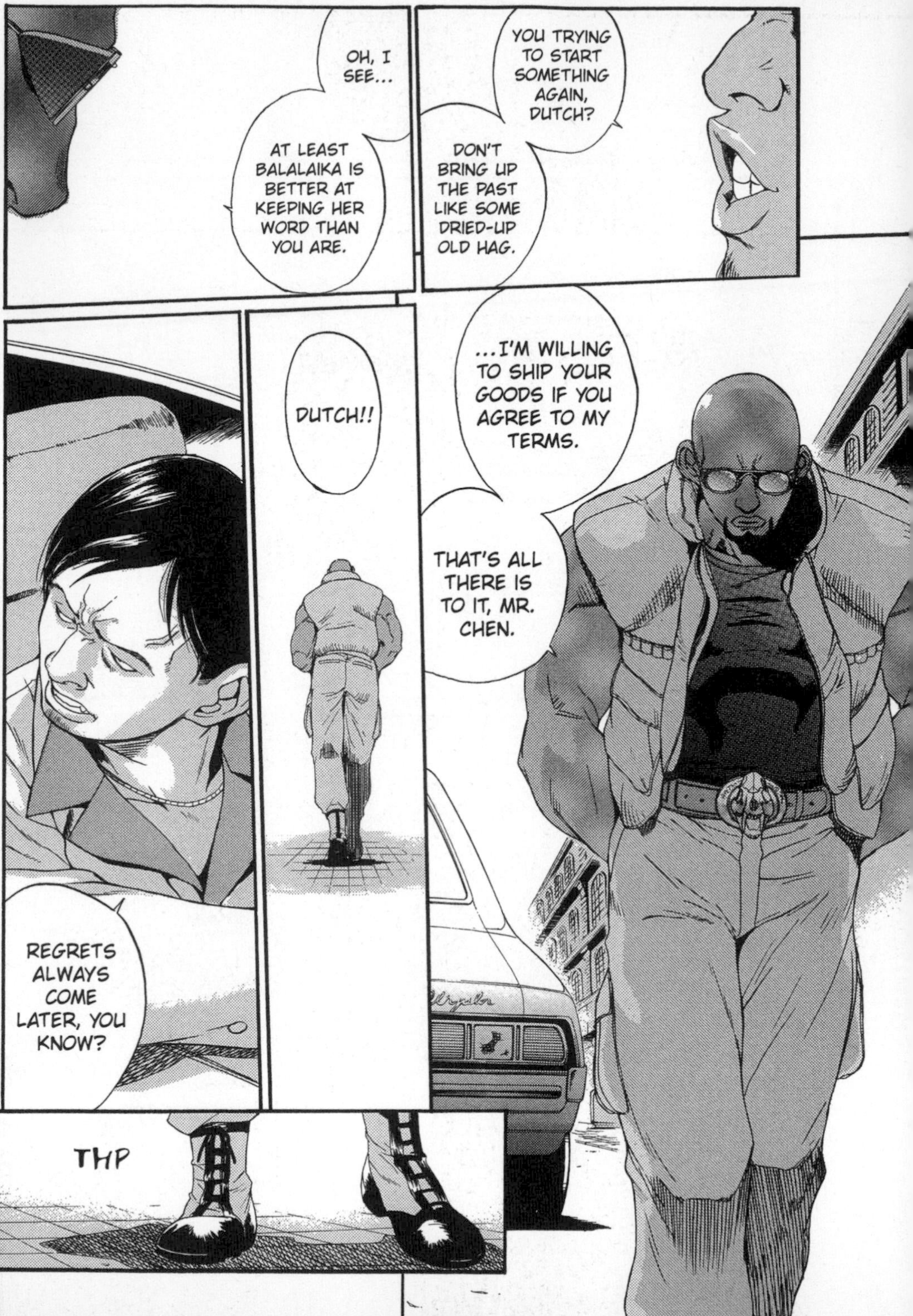
YOU TRYING TO START SOMETHING AGAIN, DUTCH?
DON'T BRING UP THE PAST LIKE SOME DRIED-UP OLD HAG.
OH, I SEE...
AT LEAST BALALAIKA IS BETTER AT KEEPING HER WORD THAN YOU ARE.
...I'M WILLING TO SHIP YOUR GOODS IF YOU AGREE TO MY TERMS.
THAT'S ALL THERE IS TO IT, MR. CHEN.
DUTCH!!
REGRETS ALWAYS COME LATER, YOU KNOW?
THP

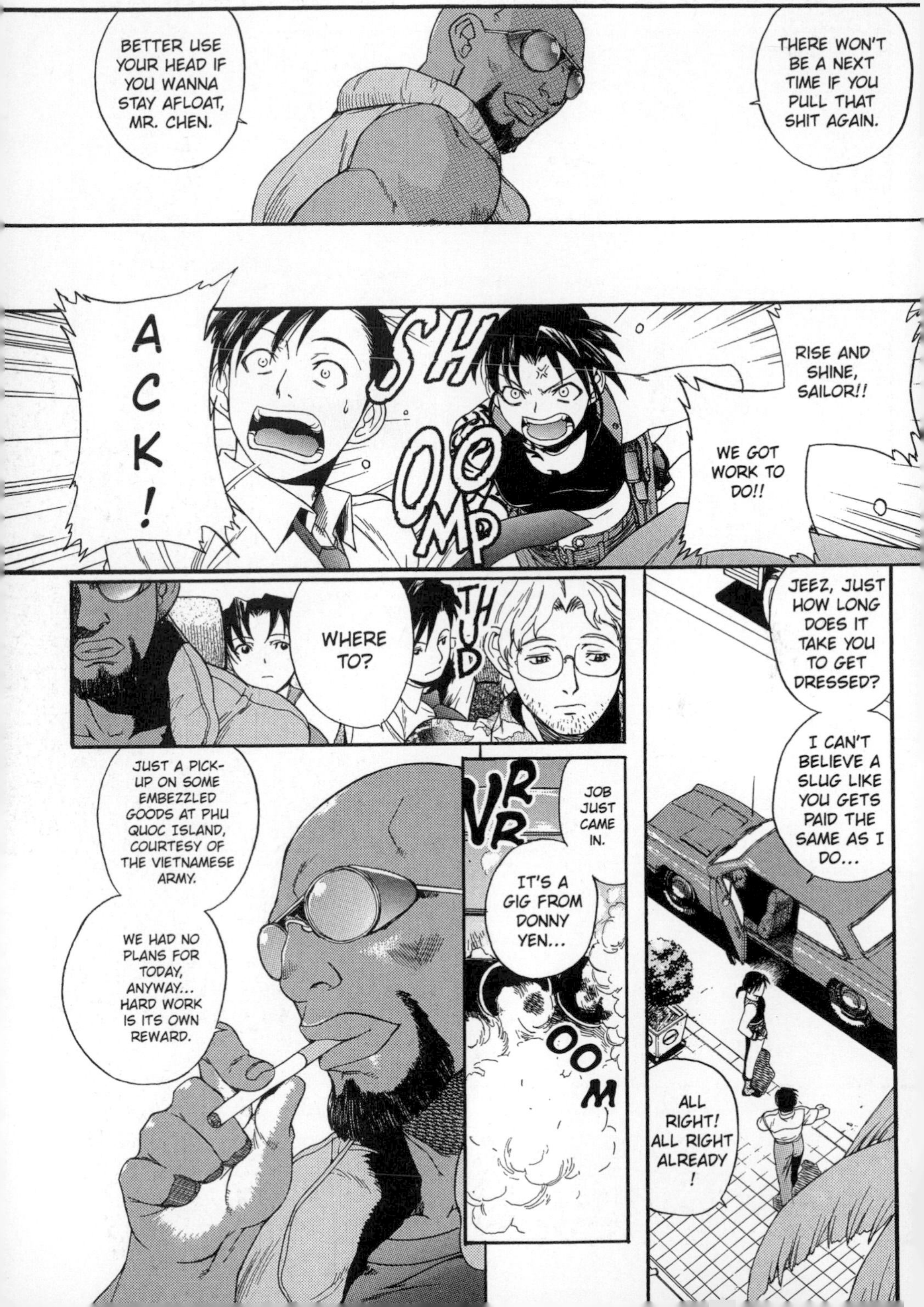
THERE WON'T BE A NEXT TIME IF YOU PULL THAT SHIT AGAIN.
BETTER USE YOUR HEAD IF YOU WANNA STAY AFLOAT, MR. CHEN.
RISE AND SHINE, SAILOR!!
WE GOT WORK TO DO!!
SHOOOMP
ACK!
JEEZ, JUST HOW LONG DOES IT TAKE YOU TO GET DRESSED?
I CAN'T BELIEVE A SLUG LIKE YOU GETS PAID THE SAME AS I DO...
ALL RIGHT! ALL RIGHT ALREADY!
THUD
WHERE TO?
VRR
JOB JUST CAME IN.
IT'S A GIG FROM DONNY YEN...
OOOM
JUST A PICK-UP ON SOME EMBEZZLED GOODS AT PHU QUOC ISLAND, COURTESY OF THE VIETNAMESE ARMY.
WE HAD NO PLANS FOR TODAY, ANYWAY... HARD WORK IS ITS OWN REWARD.

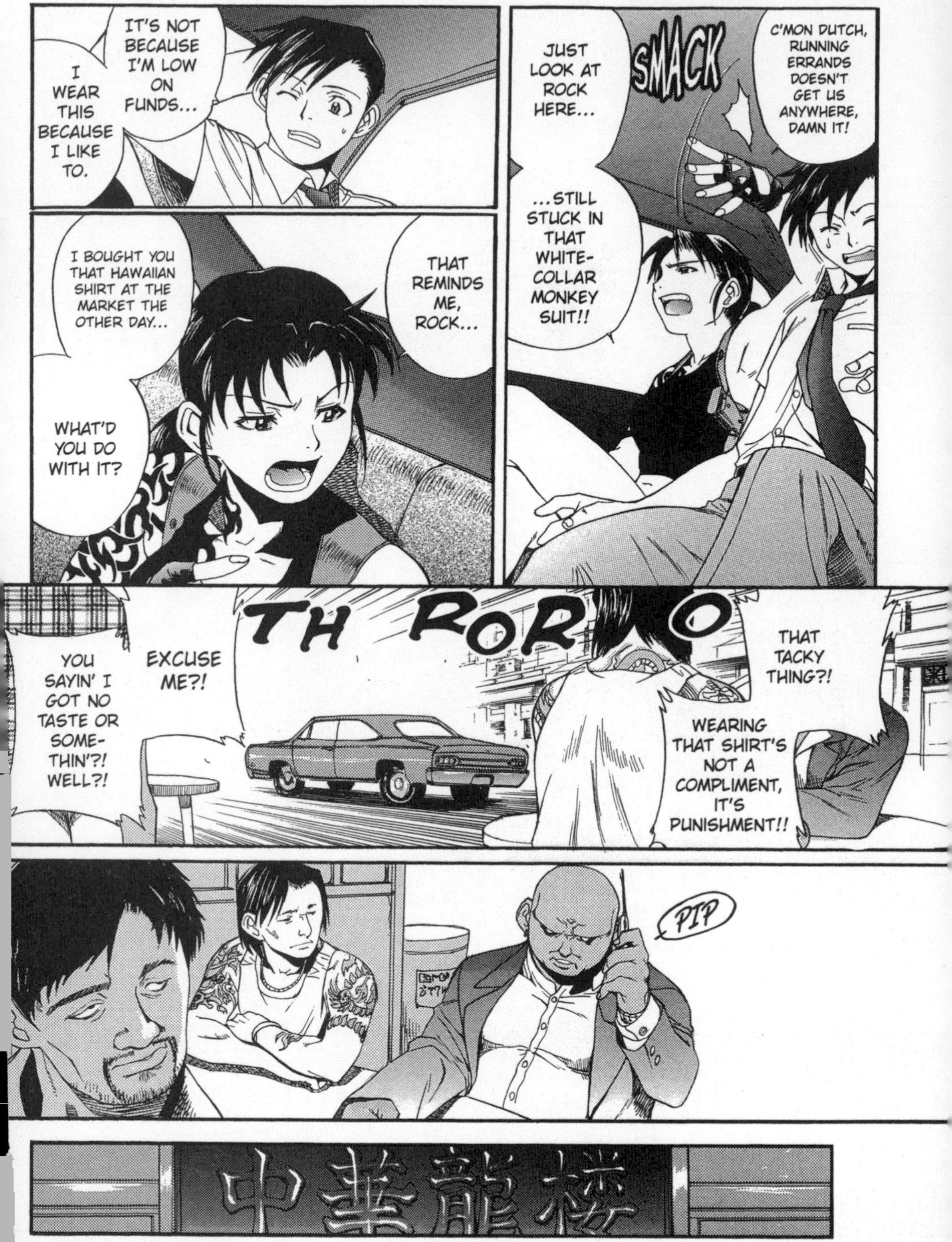
C'MON DUTCH, RUNNING ERRANDS DOESN'T GET US ANYWHERE, DAMN IT!
SMACK
JUST LOOK AT ROCK HERE...
...STILL STUCK IN THAT WHITE-COLLAR MONKEY SUIT!!
IT'S NOT BECAUSE I'M LOW ON FUNDS...
I WEAR THIS BECAUSE I LIKE TO.
THAT REMINDS ME, ROCK...
I BOUGHT YOU THAT HAWAIIAN SHIRT AT THE MARKET THE OTHER DAY...
WHAT'D YOU DO WITH IT?
THAT TACKY THING?!
WEARING THAT SHIRT'S NOT A COMPLIMENT, IT'S PUNISHMENT!!
TH ROR O
EXCUSE ME?!
YOU SAYIN' I GOT NO TASTE OR SOMETHIN'?! WELL?!
PIP
中華龍楼

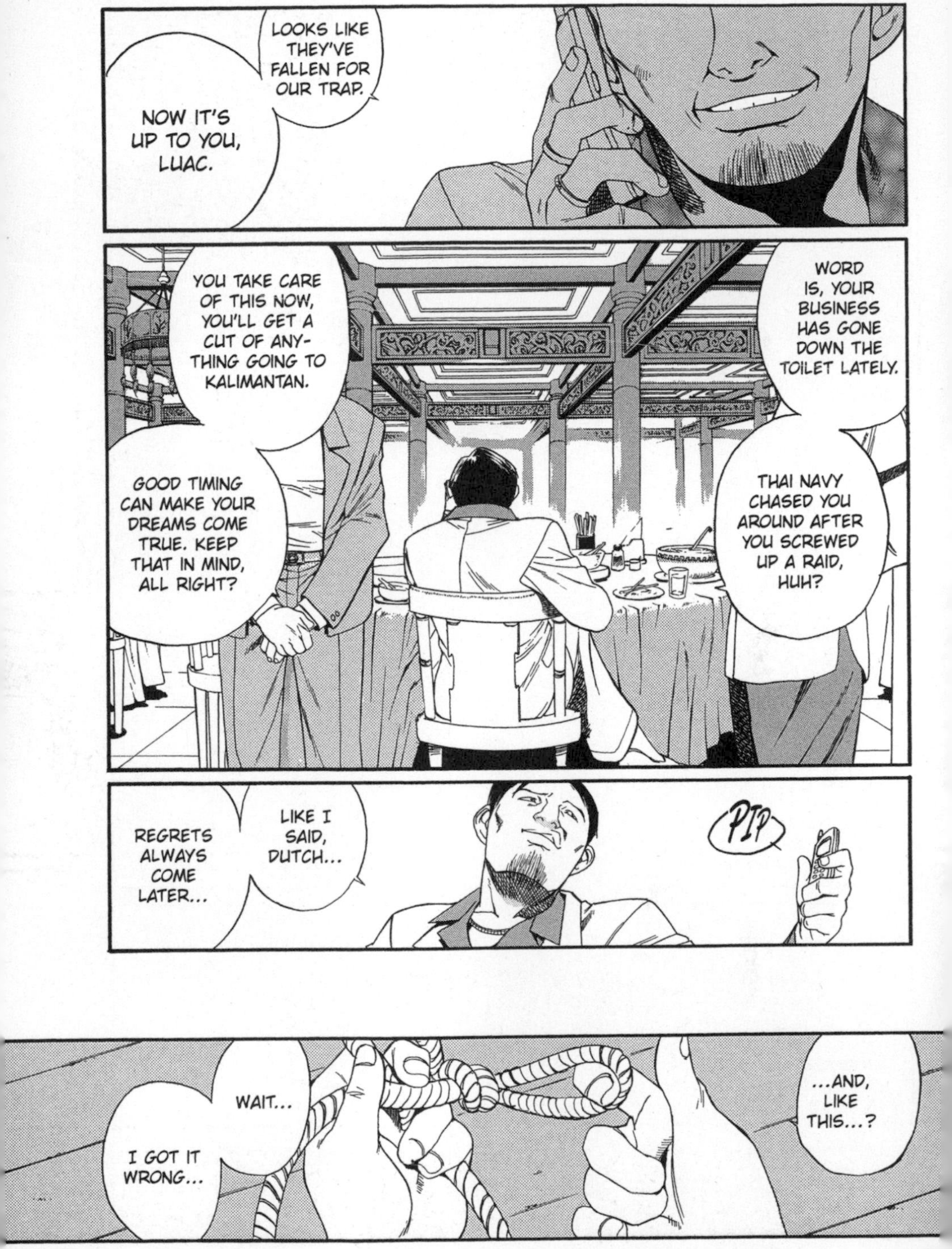
LOOKS LIKE THEY'VE FALLEN FOR OUR TRAP.
NOW IT'S UP TO YOU, LUAC.
WORD IS, YOUR BUSINESS HAS GONE DOWN THE TOILET LATELY.
THAI NAVY CHASED YOU AROUND AFTER YOU SCREWED UP A RAID, HUH?
YOU TAKE CARE OF THIS NOW, YOU'LL GET A CUT OF ANY-THING GOING TO KALIMANTAN.
GOOD TIMING CAN MAKE YOUR DREAMS COME TRUE. KEEP THAT IN MIND, ALL RIGHT?
PIP
LIKE I SAID, DUTCH...
REGRETS ALWAYS COME LATER...
...AND, LIKE THIS...?
WAIT...
I GOT IT WRONG...

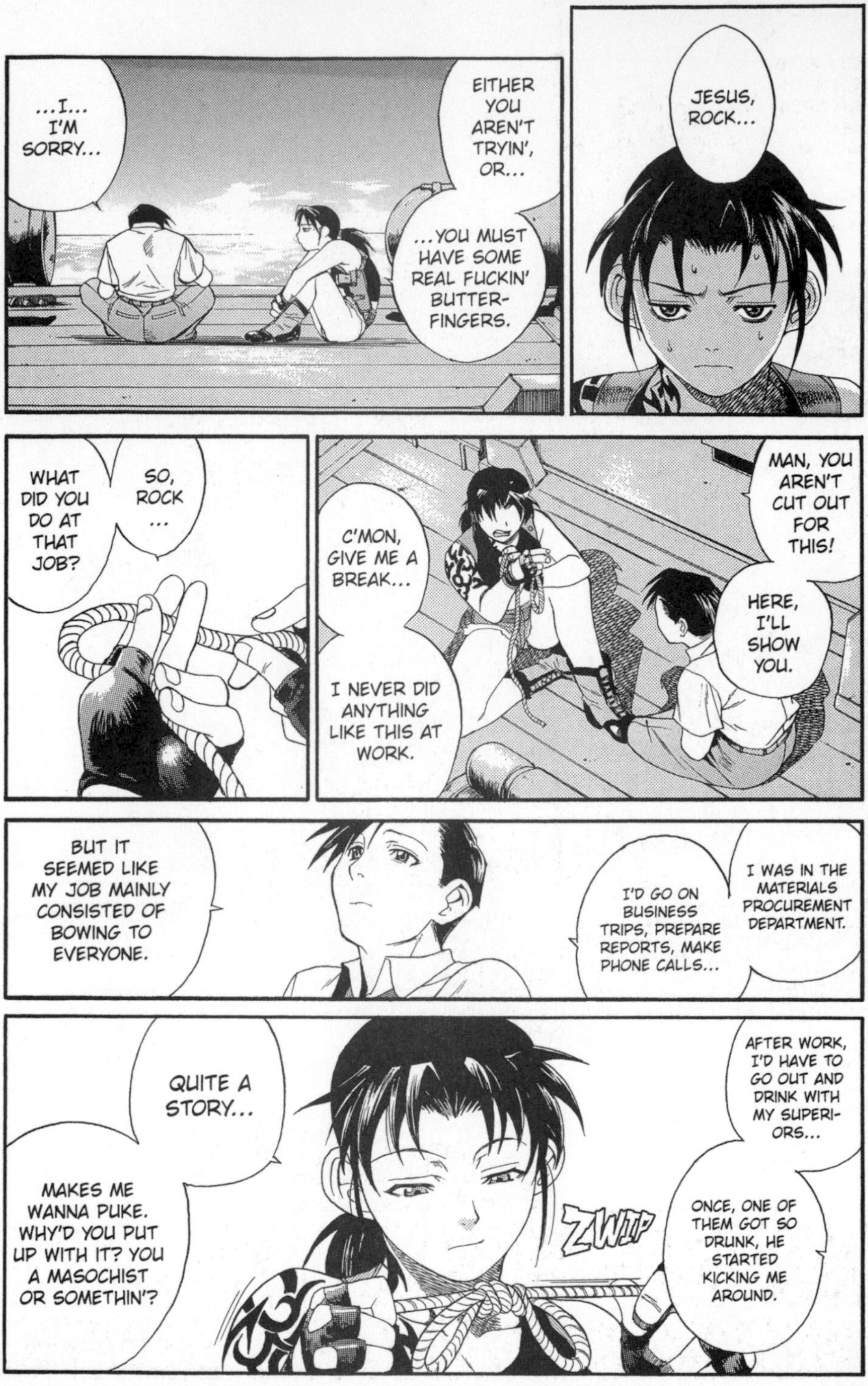
JESUS, ROCK...
EITHER YOU AREN'T TRYIN', OR...
...YOU MUST HAVE SOME REAL FUCKIN' BUTTER-FINGERS.
...I... I'M SORRY...
MAN, YOU AREN'T CUT OUT FOR THIS!
HERE, I'LL SHOW YOU.
C'MON, GIVE ME A BREAK...
I NEVER DID ANYTHING LIKE THIS AT WORK.
SO, ROCK...
WHAT DID YOU DO AT THAT JOB?
I WAS IN THE MATERIALS PROCUREMENT DEPARTMENT.
I'D GO ON BUSINESS TRIPS, PREPARE REPORTS, MAKE PHONE CALLS...
BUT IT SEEMED LIKE MY JOB MAINLY CONSISTED OF BOWING TO EVERYONE.
AFTER WORK, I'D HAVE TO GO OUT AND DRINK WITH MY SUPERI-ORS...
ONCE, ONE OF THEM GOT SO DRUNK, HE STARTED KICKING ME AROUND.
ZWIP
QUITE A STORY...
MAKES ME WANNA PUKE. WHY'D YOU PUT UP WITH IT? YOU A MASOCHIST OR SOMETHIN'?

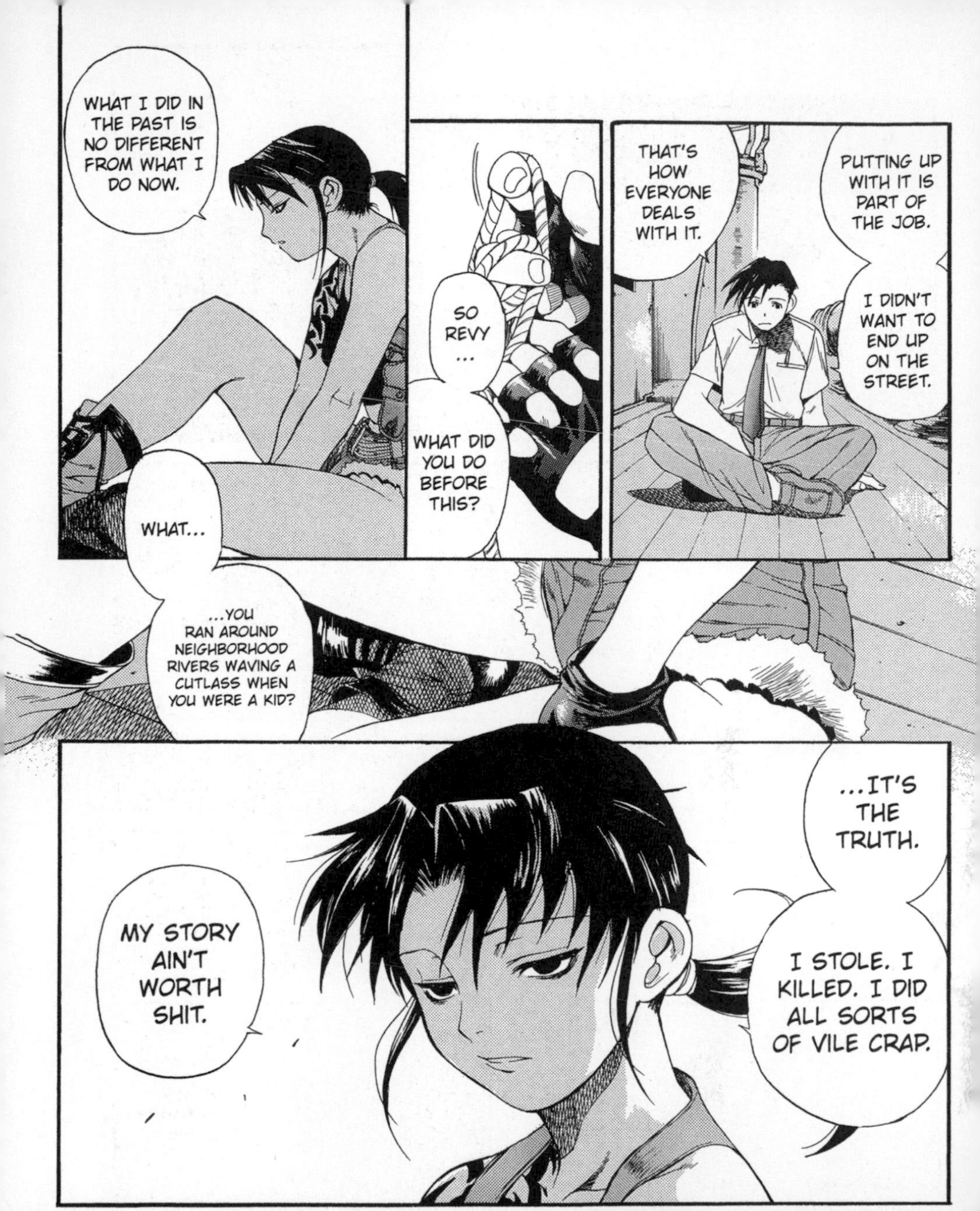
PUTTING UP WITH IT IS PART OF THE JOB.
I DIDN'T WANT TO END UP ON THE STREET.
THAT'S HOW EVERYONE DEALS WITH IT.
SO REVY ...
WHAT DID YOU DO BEFORE THIS?
WHAT I DID IN THE PAST IS NO DIFFERENT FROM WHAT I DO NOW.
WHAT...
...YOU RAN AROUND NEIGHBORHOOD RIVERS WAVING A CUTLASS WHEN YOU WERE A KID?
...IT'S THE TRUTH.
I STOLE. I KILLED. I DID ALL SORTS OF VILE CRAP.
MY STORY AIN'T WORTH SHIT.

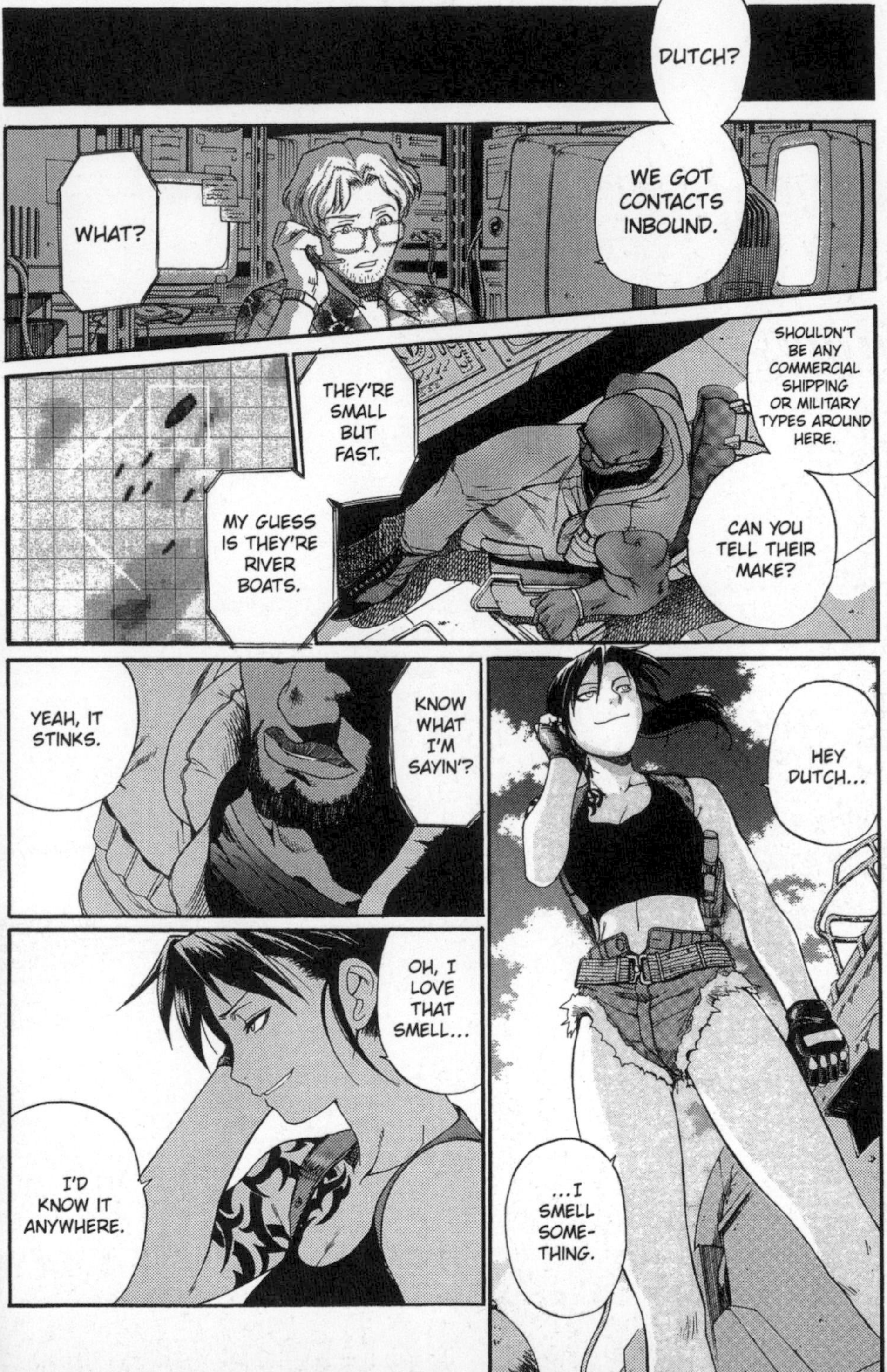
DUTCH?
WE GOT CONTACTS INBOUND.
WHAT?
SHOULDN'T BE ANY COMMERCIAL SHIPPING OR MILITARY TYPES AROUND HERE.
CAN YOU TELL THEIR MAKE?
THEY'RE SMALL BUT FAST.
MY GUESS IS THEY'RE RIVER BOATS.
HEY DUTCH...
...I SMELL SOME-THING.
KNOW WHAT I'M SAYIN'?
YEAH, IT STINKS.
OH, I LOVE THAT SMELL...
I'D KNOW IT ANYWHERE.

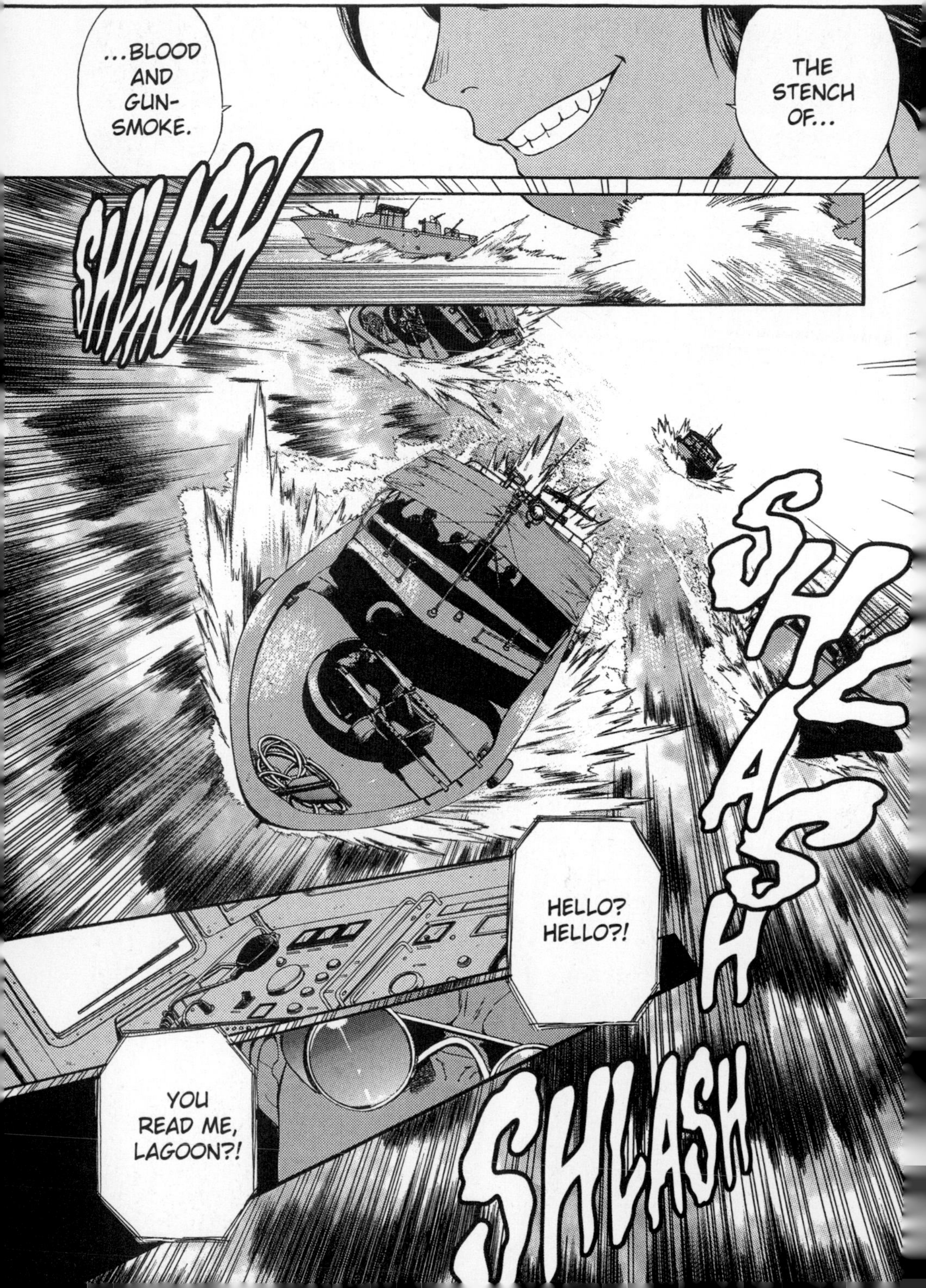
THE STENCH OF...
...BLOOD AND GUN-SMOKE.
SHLASH
SHLASH
HELLO? HELLO?!
YOU READ ME, LAGOON?!
SHLASH

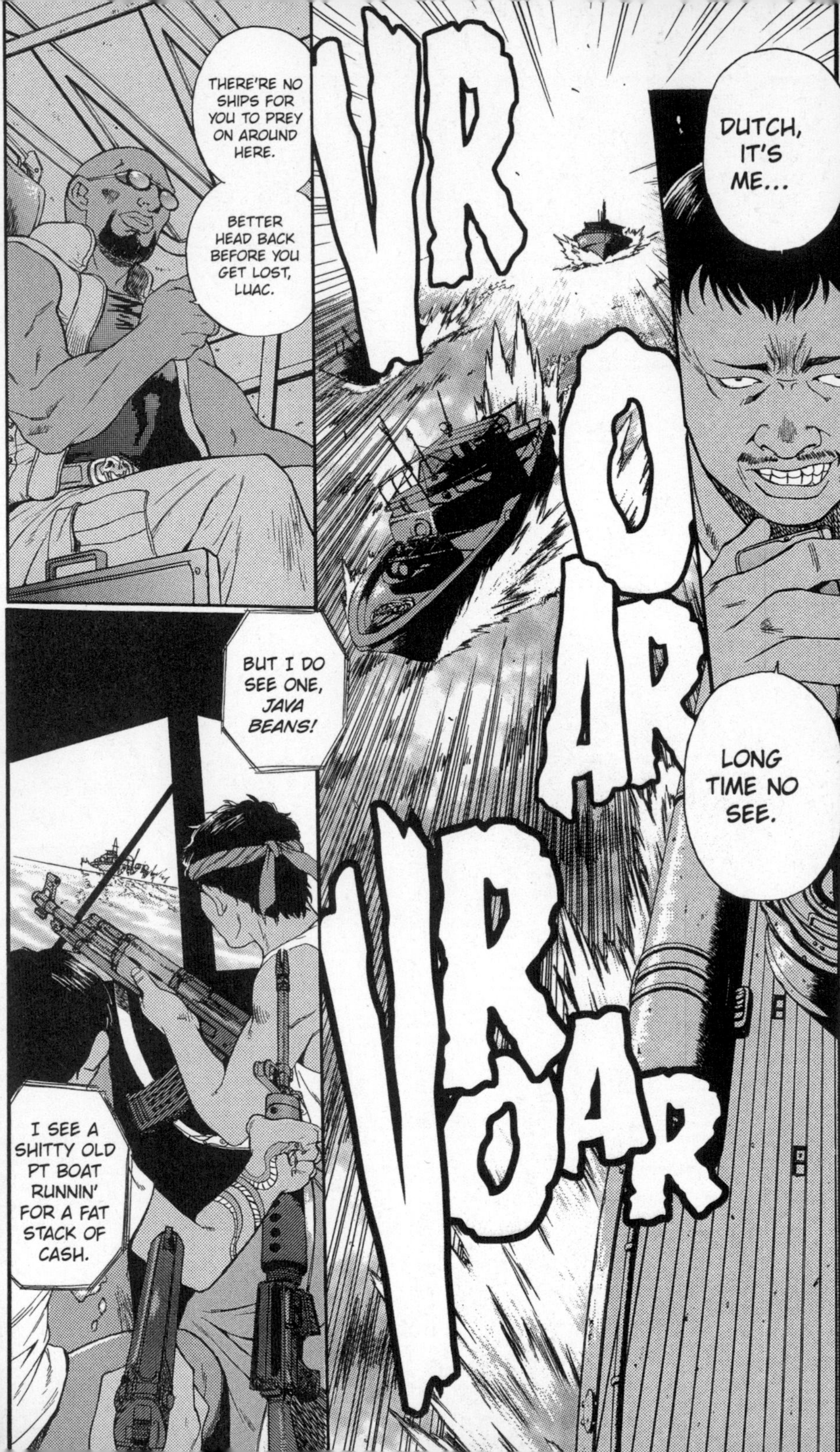
DUTCH, IT'S ME...
VROAR
LONG TIME NO SEE.
VROAR
THERE'RE NO SHIPS FOR YOU TO PREY ON AROUND HERE.
BETTER HEAD BACK BEFORE YOU GET LOST, LUAC.
BUT I DO SEE ONE, *JAVA BEANS!*
I SEE A SHITTY OLD PT BOAT RUNNIN' FOR A FAT STACK OF CASH.

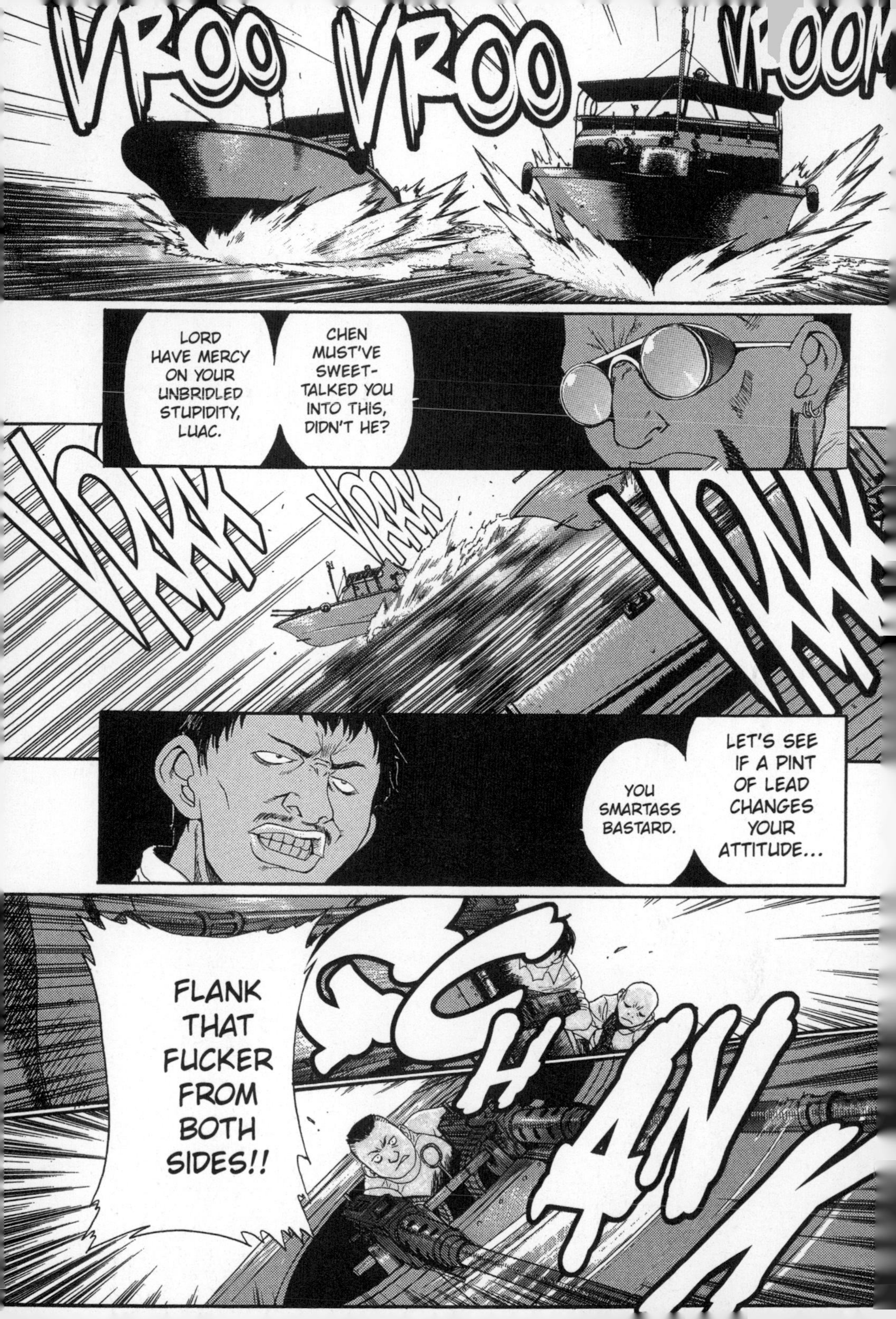
VROO VROO VROOM
CHEN MUST'VE SWEET-TALKED YOU INTO THIS, DIDN'T HE?
LORD HAVE MERCY ON YOUR UNBRIDLED STUPIDITY, LUAC.
LET'S SEE IF A PINT OF LEAD CHANGES YOUR ATTITUDE...
YOU SMARTASS BASTARD.
CHAN
FLANK THAT FUCKER FROM BOTH SIDES!!

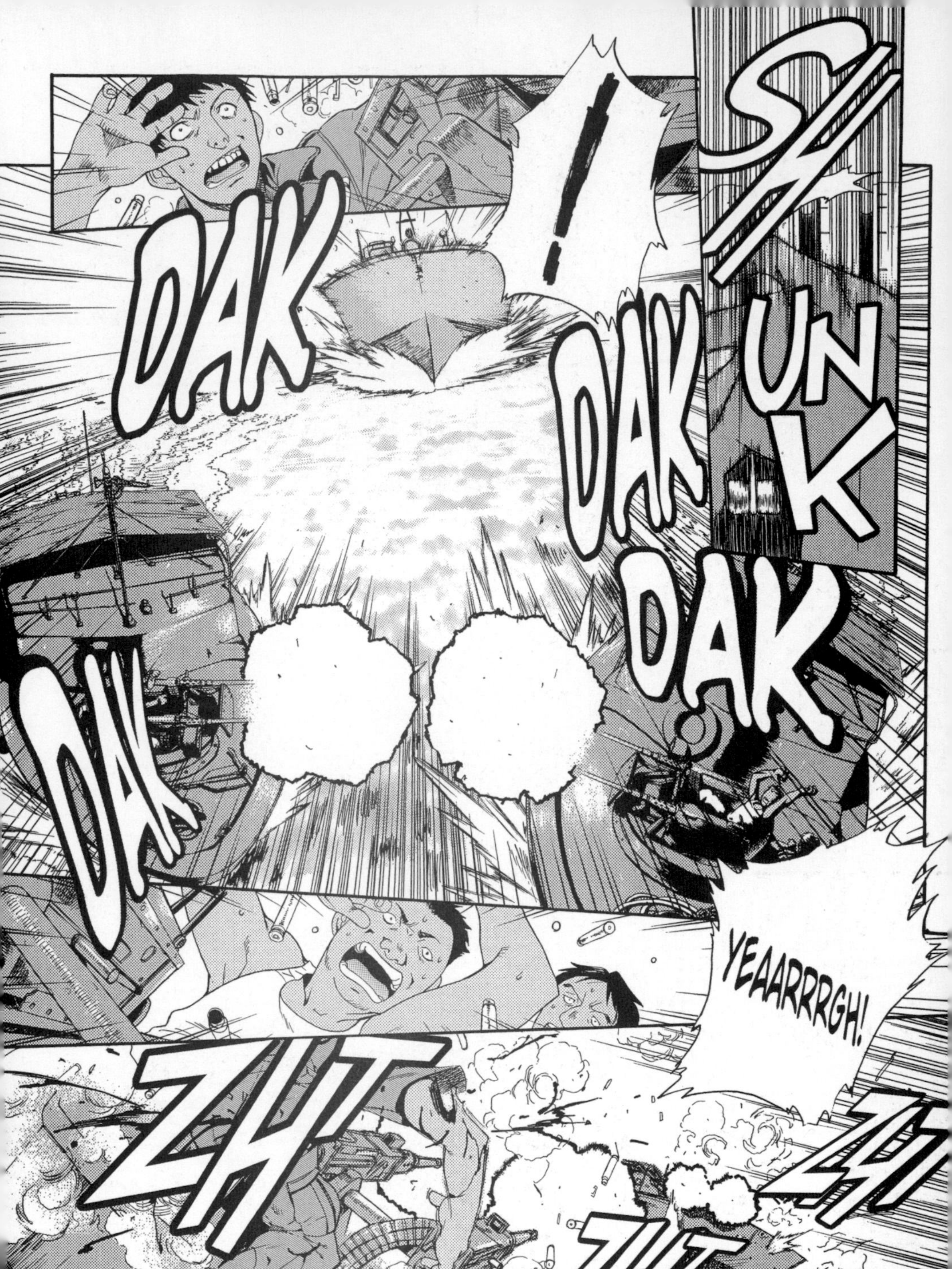
SH
UNK
!
DAK
DAK
DAK
DAK
YEAARRRGH!
ZHT
ZHT
ZHT

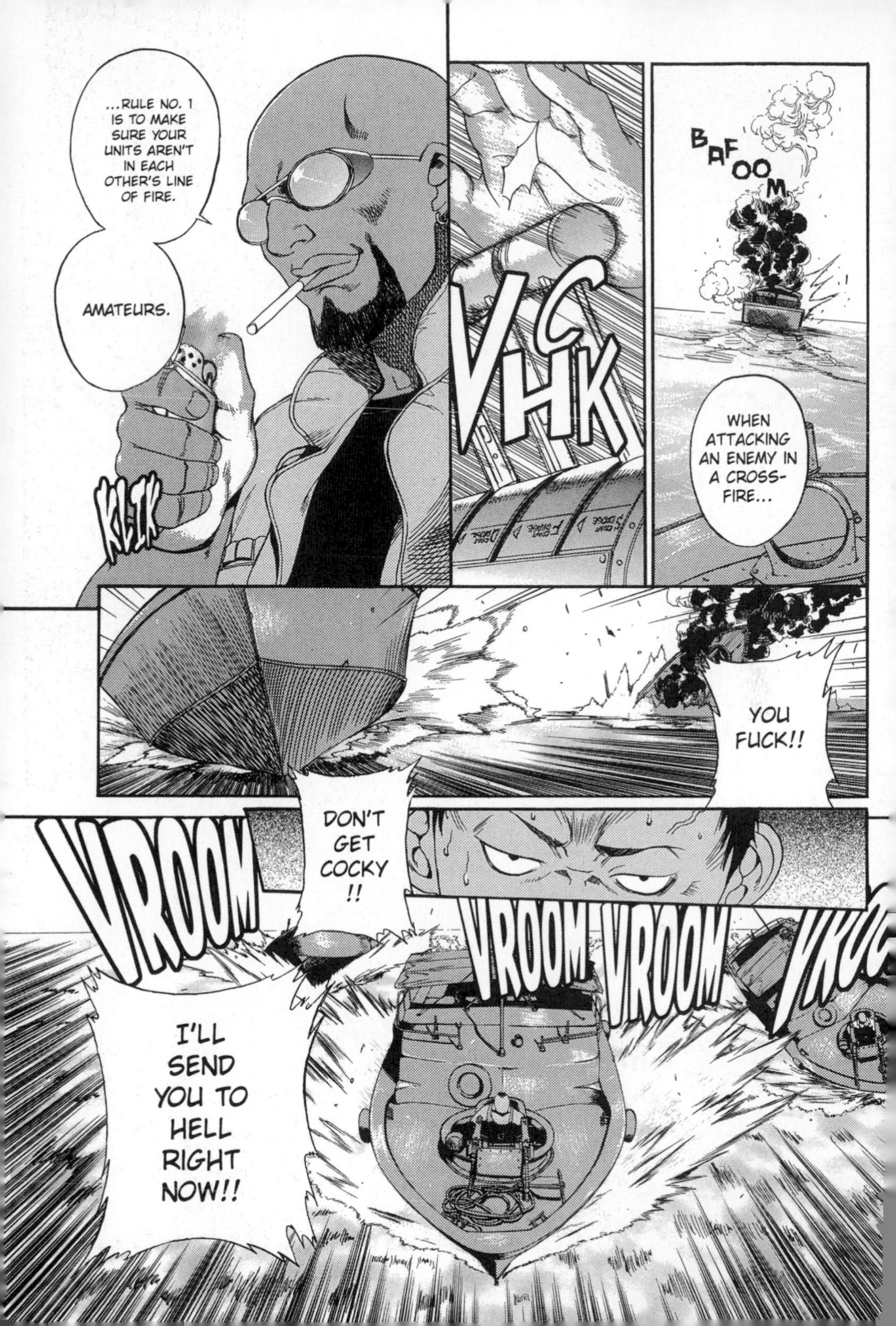
BAFOOM
WHEN ATTACKING AN ENEMY IN A CROSS-FIRE...
VCHK
...RULE NO. 1 IS TO MAKE SURE YOUR UNITS AREN'T IN EACH OTHER'S LINE OF FIRE.
AMATEURS.
KLIK
YOU FUCK!!
DON'T GET COCKY !!
VROOM
VROOM VROOM
I'LL SEND YOU TO HELL RIGHT NOW!!

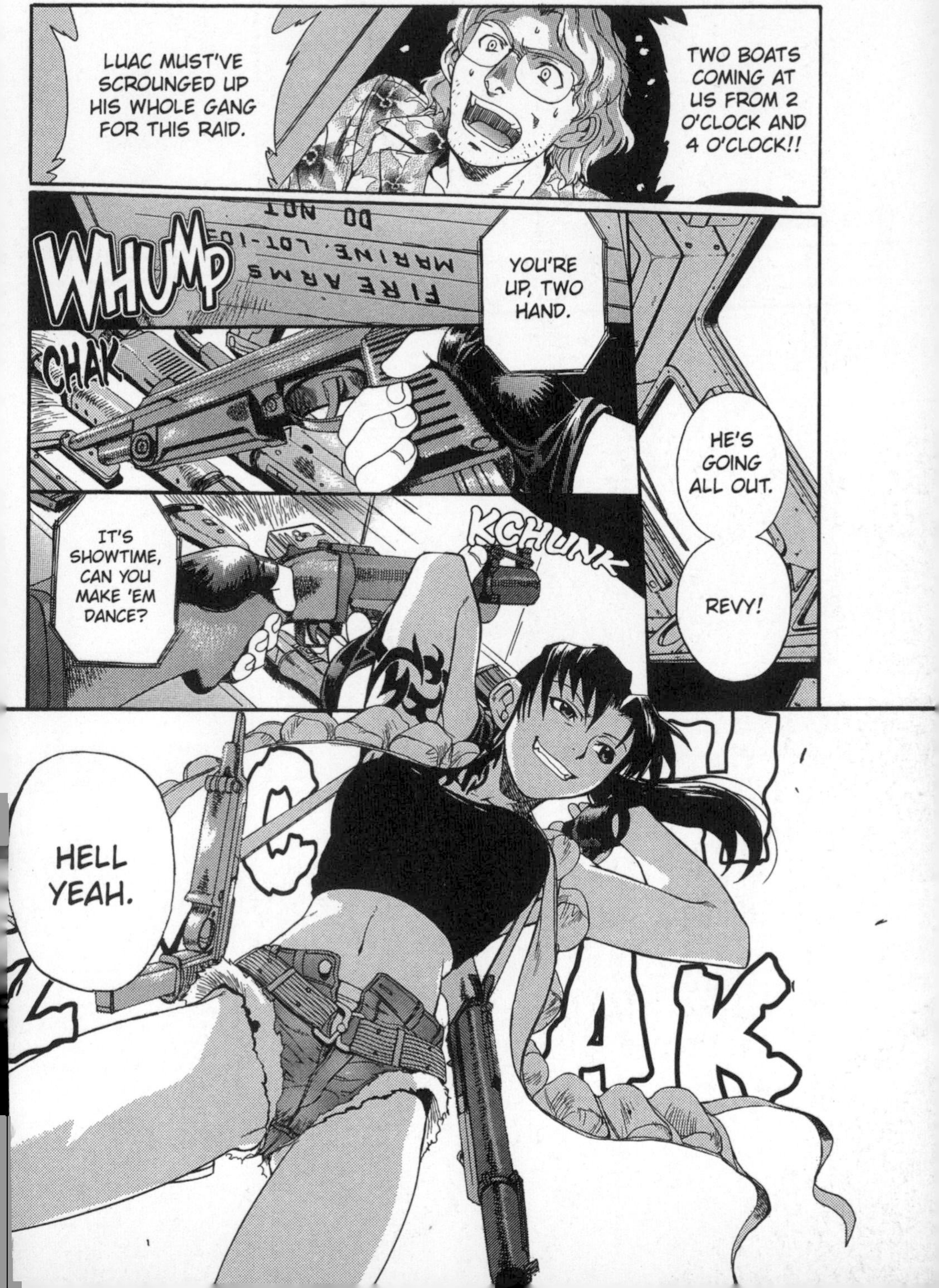
TWO BOATS COMING AT US FROM 2 O'CLOCK AND 4 O'CLOCK!!
LUAC MUST'VE SCROUNGED UP HIS WHOLE GANG FOR THIS RAID.
HE'S GOING ALL OUT.
REVY!
YOU'RE UP, TWO HAND.
WHUMP
CHAK
KCHUNK
IT'S SHOWTIME, CAN YOU MAKE 'EM DANCE?
HELL YEAH.
AK

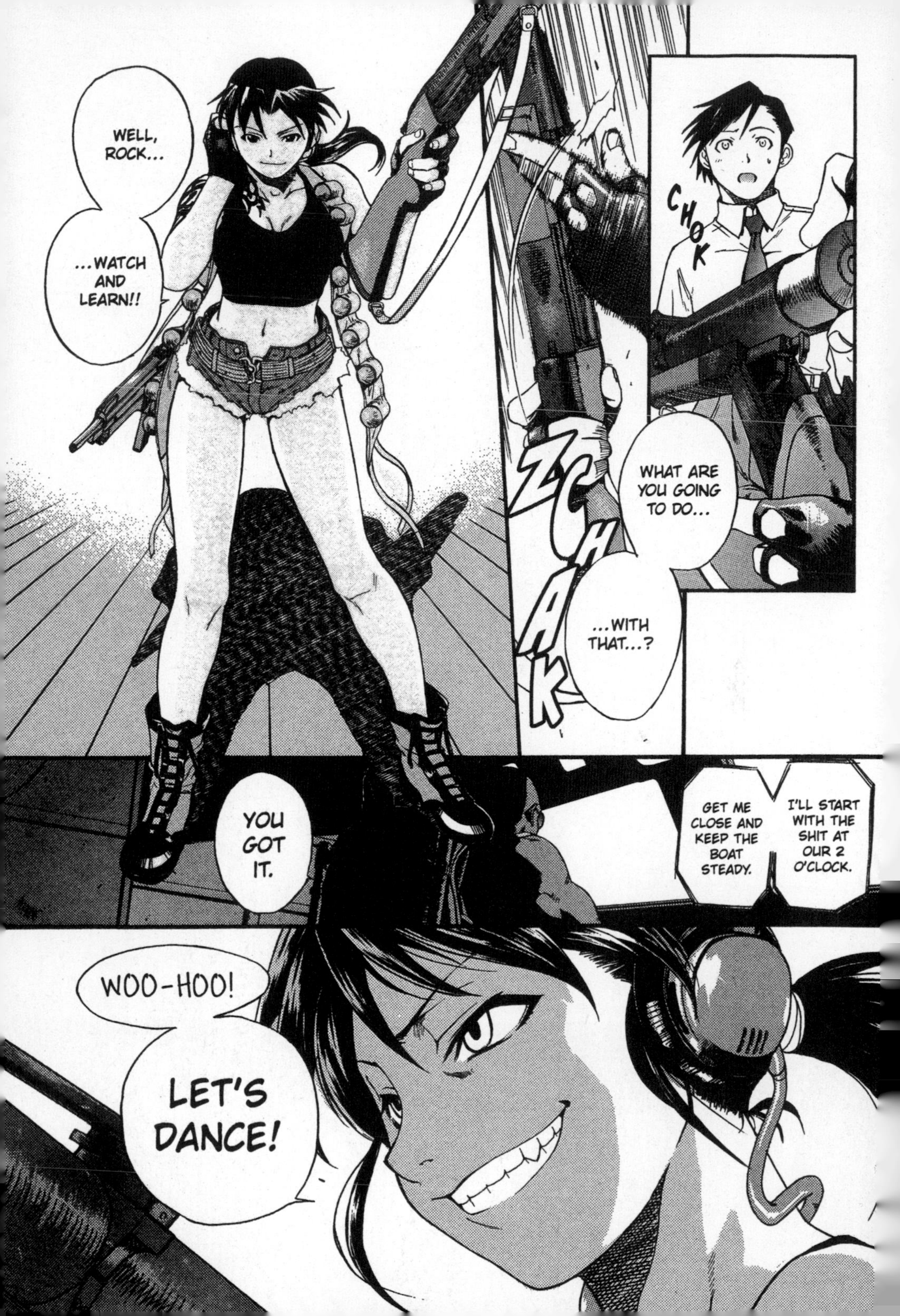
CHOK
ZCHAK
WHAT ARE YOU GOING TO DO...
...WITH THAT...?
WELL, ROCK...
...WATCH AND LEARN!!
I'LL START WITH THE SHIT AT OUR 2 O'CLOCK.
GET ME CLOSE AND KEEP THE BOAT STEADY.
YOU GOT IT.
WOO-HOO!
LET'S DANCE!

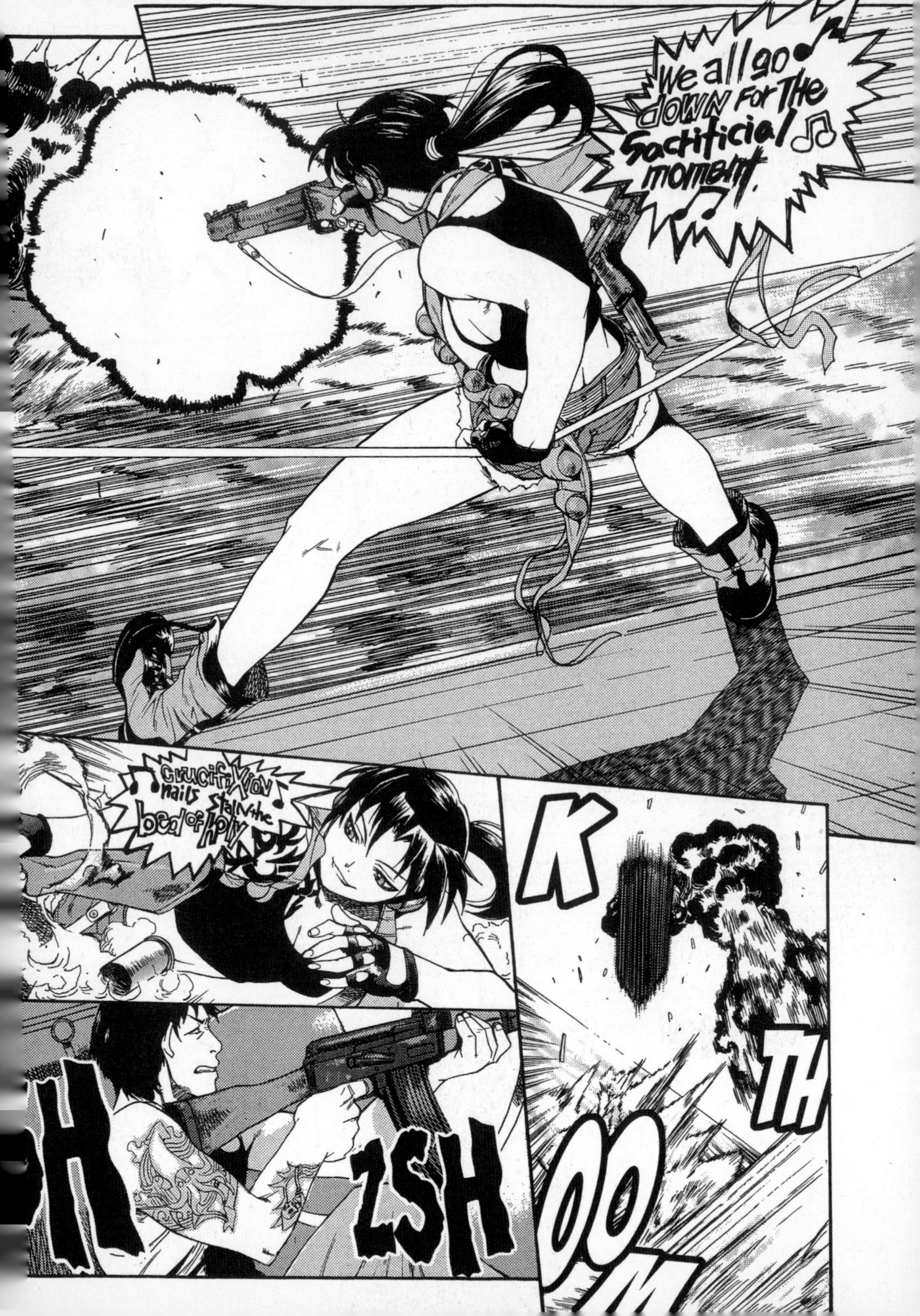
We all go down for the sacrificial moment.
KTHOOM
crucifixion nails stain the bed of holy
SH
ZSH

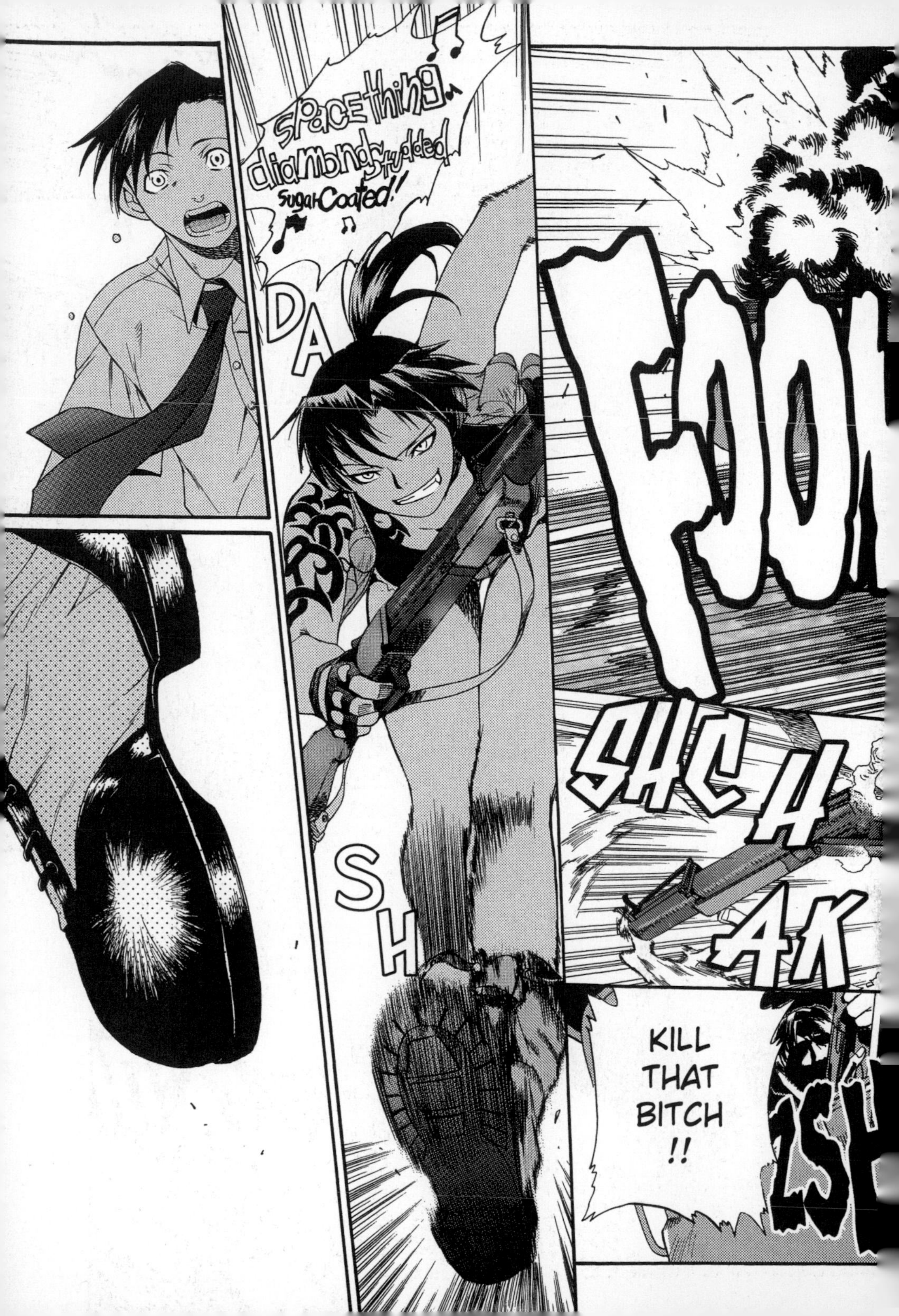

SHCHAK
KILL THAT BITCH!!
Space thing diamond studded Sugar Coated!
DA
SH

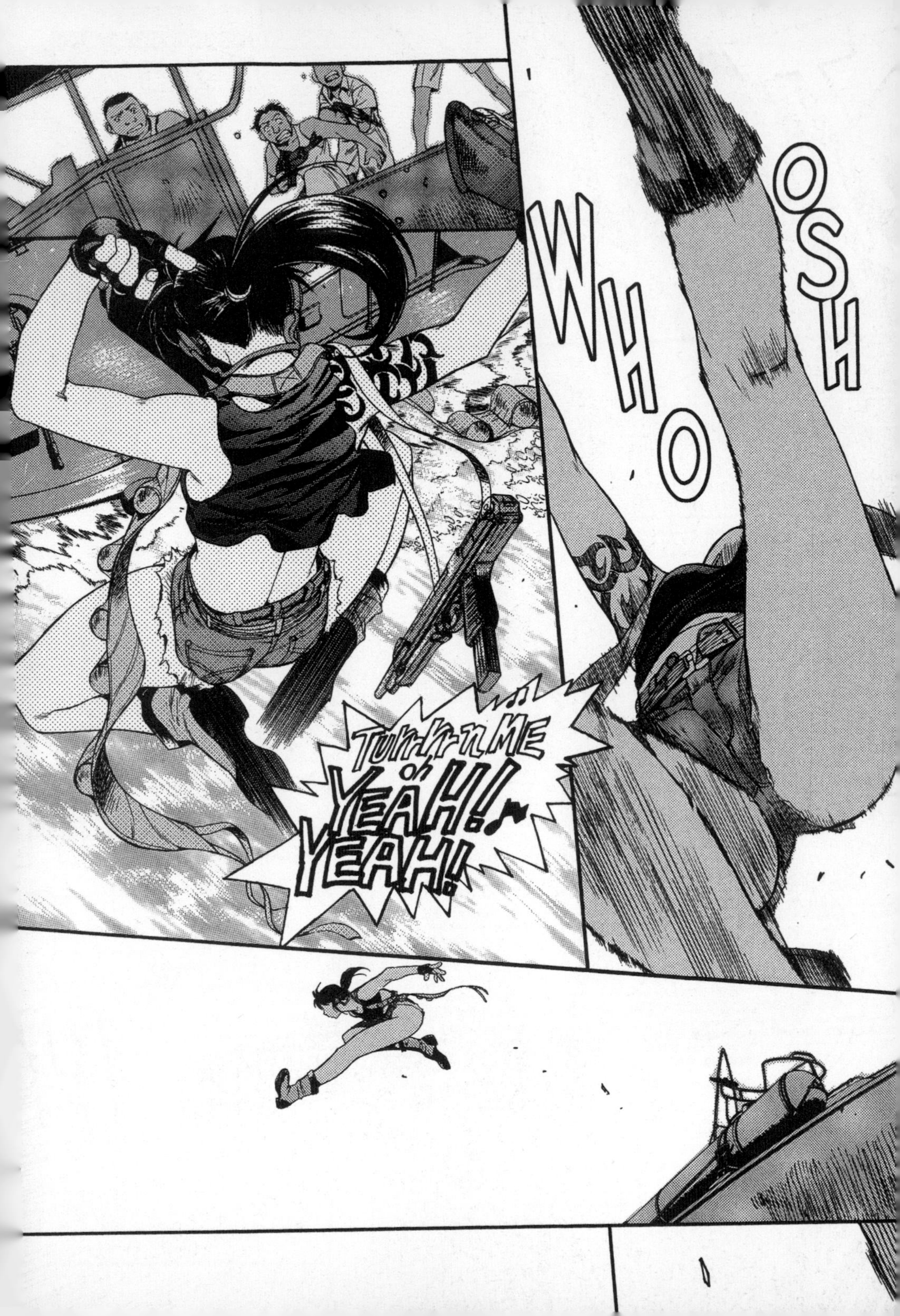
WHOOSH
Turrrn ME oh YEAH! YEAH!

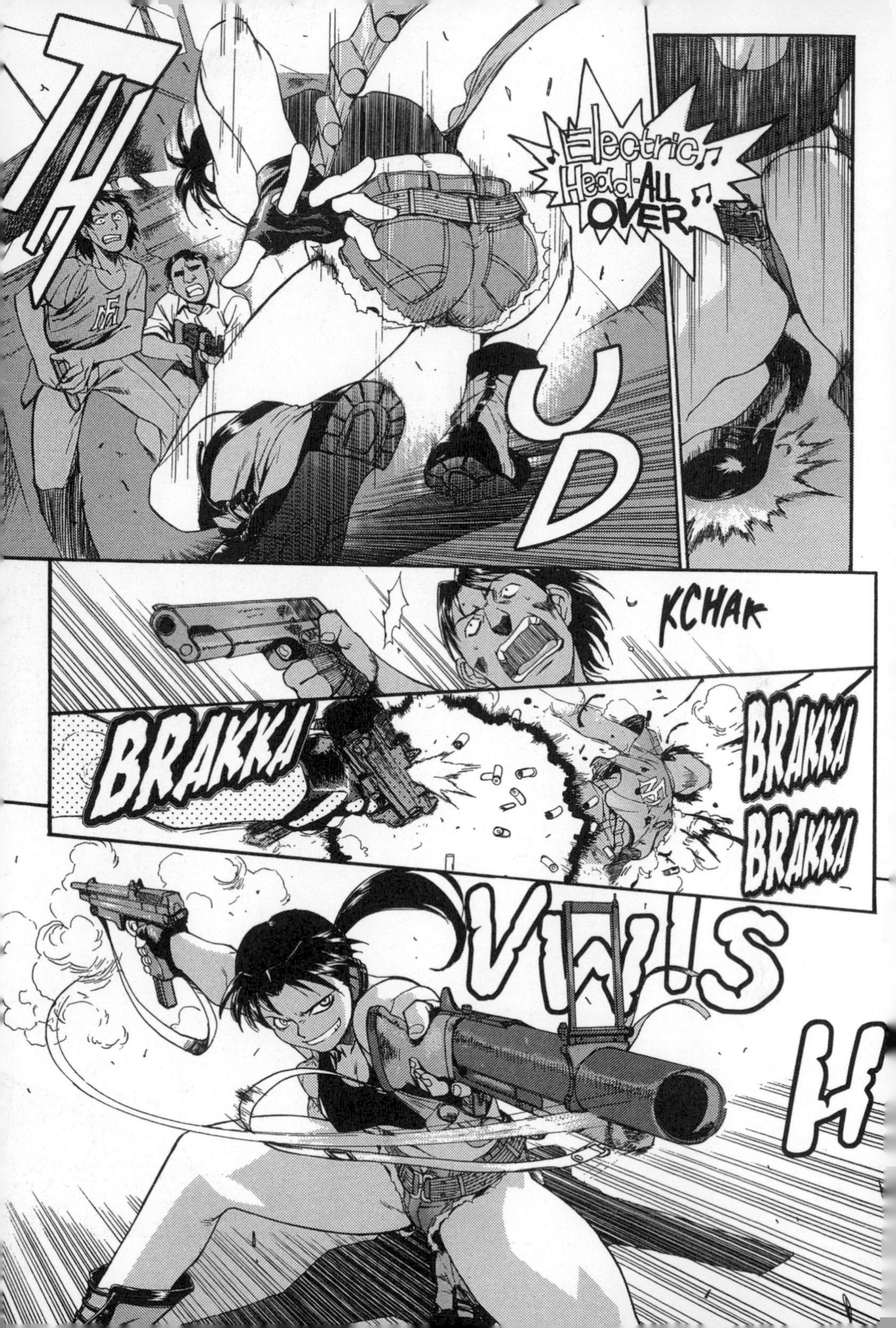

Electric Head-ALL OVER
TH
UD
KCHAK
BRAKKA
BRAKKA
BRAKKA
VWUS
H

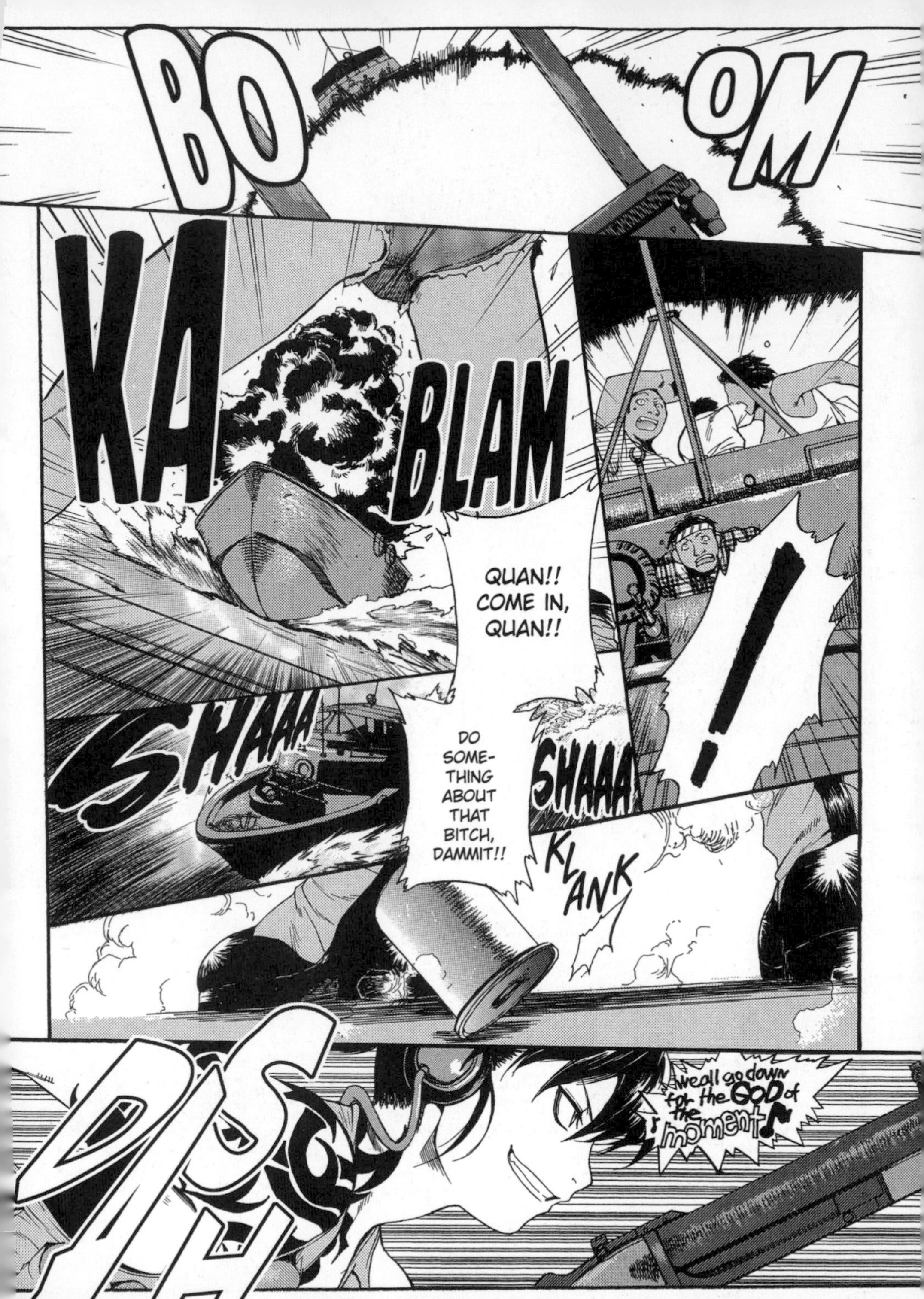
BO OM
!
QUAN!! COME IN, QUAN!!
KA BLAM
DO SOME-THING ABOUT THAT BITCH, DAMMIT!!
SHAAA
SHAAA
KLANK
We all go down for the GOD of the moment!
DASH

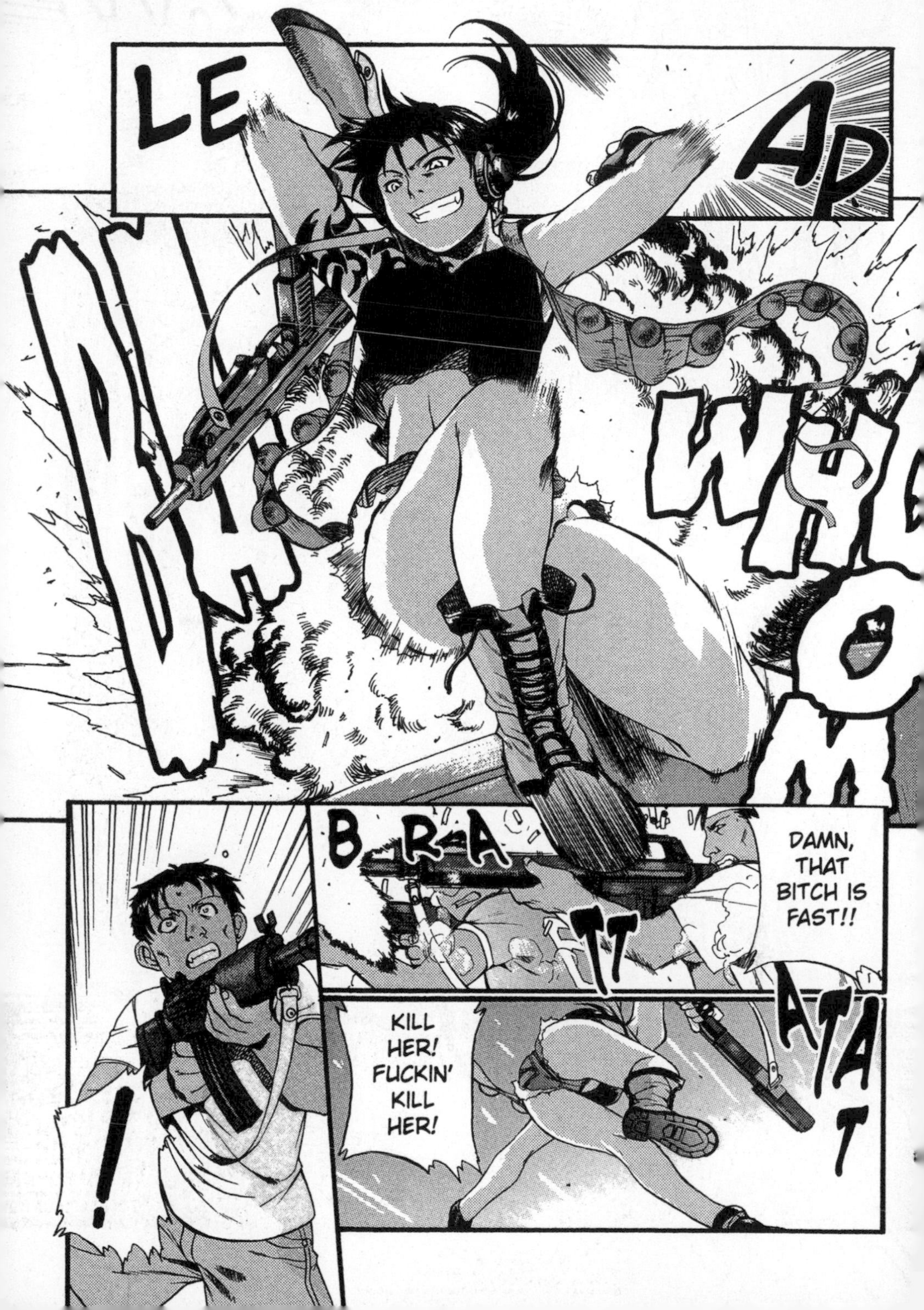

LE
AP
DAMN, THAT BITCH IS FAST!!
B R A
TT
ATAT T
KILL HER! FUCKIN' KILL HER!
!

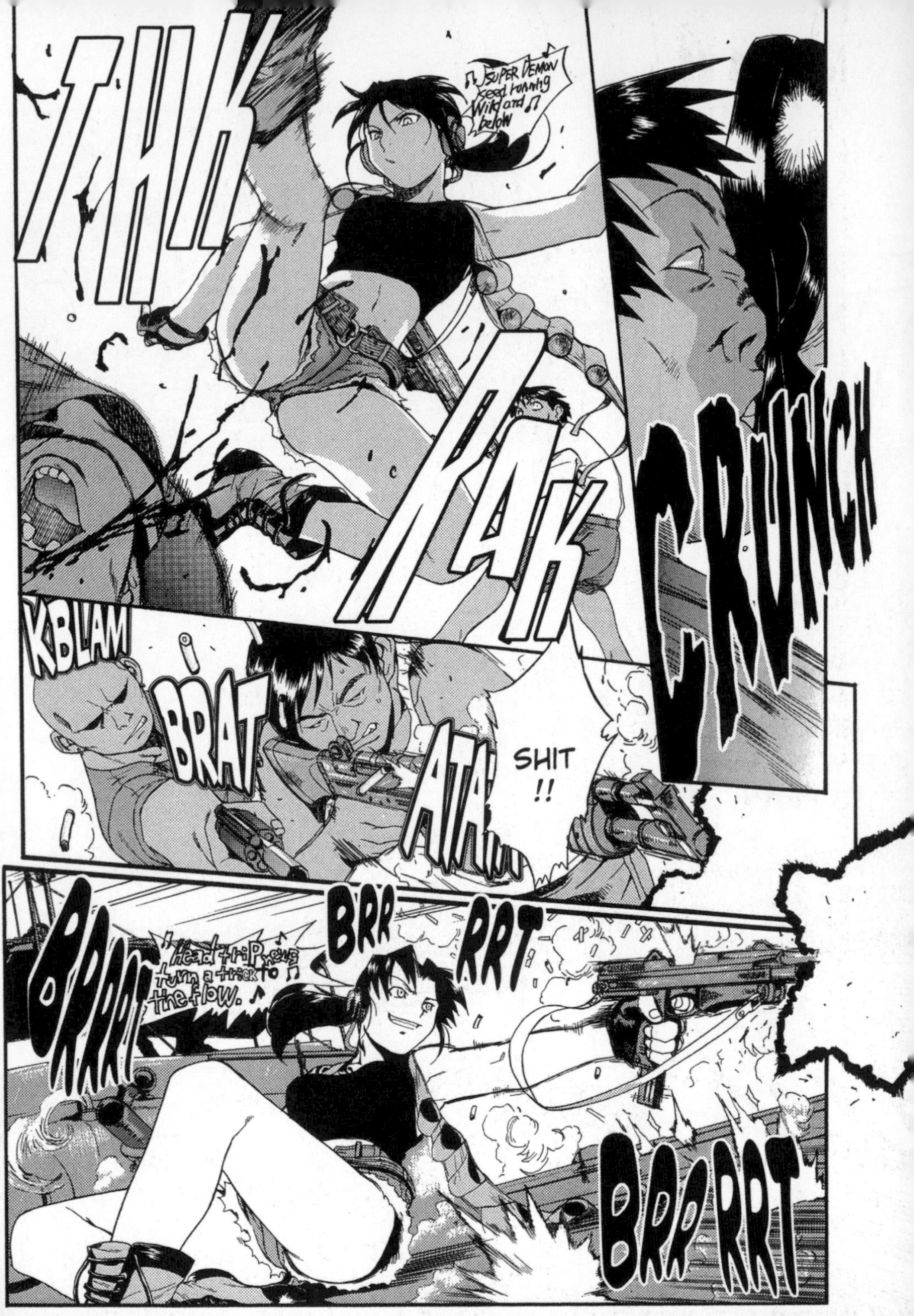
CRUNCH
THK
♫ SUPER DEMON seed running Wild and below ♫
KAK
ATA...
SHIT !!
BRAT
KBLAM
BRR RRT
♪ Head trip news turn a trick to ♫ the flow. ♪
BRRRRT
BRR RRT

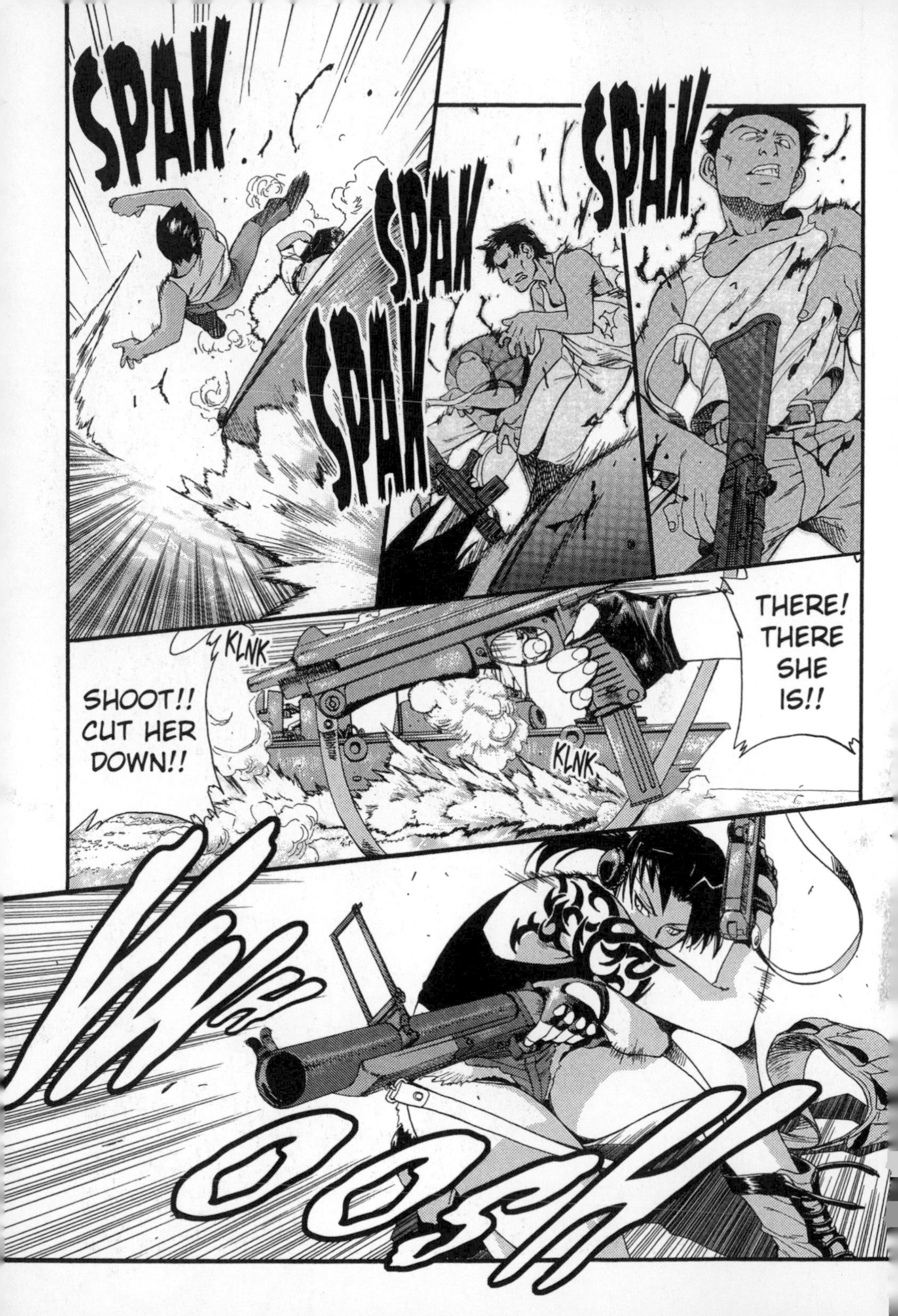
SPAK
SPAK
SPAK
SPAK
THERE! THERE SHE IS!!
KLNK
KLNK
SHOOT!! CUT HER DOWN!!
Whoosh

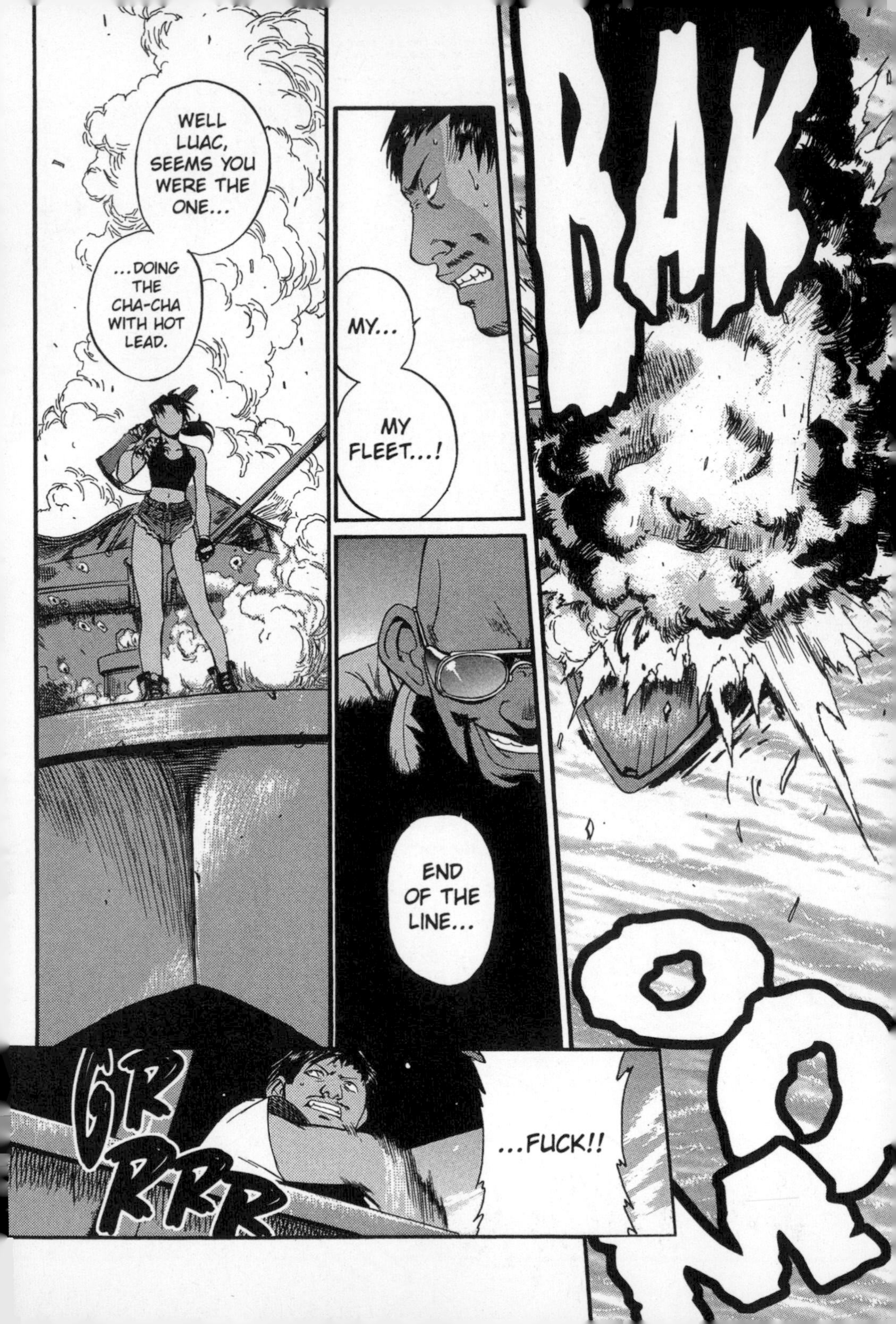
BAKOOM
MY...
MY FLEET...!
END OF THE LINE...
WELL LUAC, SEEMS YOU WERE THE ONE...
...DOING THE CHA-CHA WITH HOT LEAD.
...FUCK!!
GRRRR

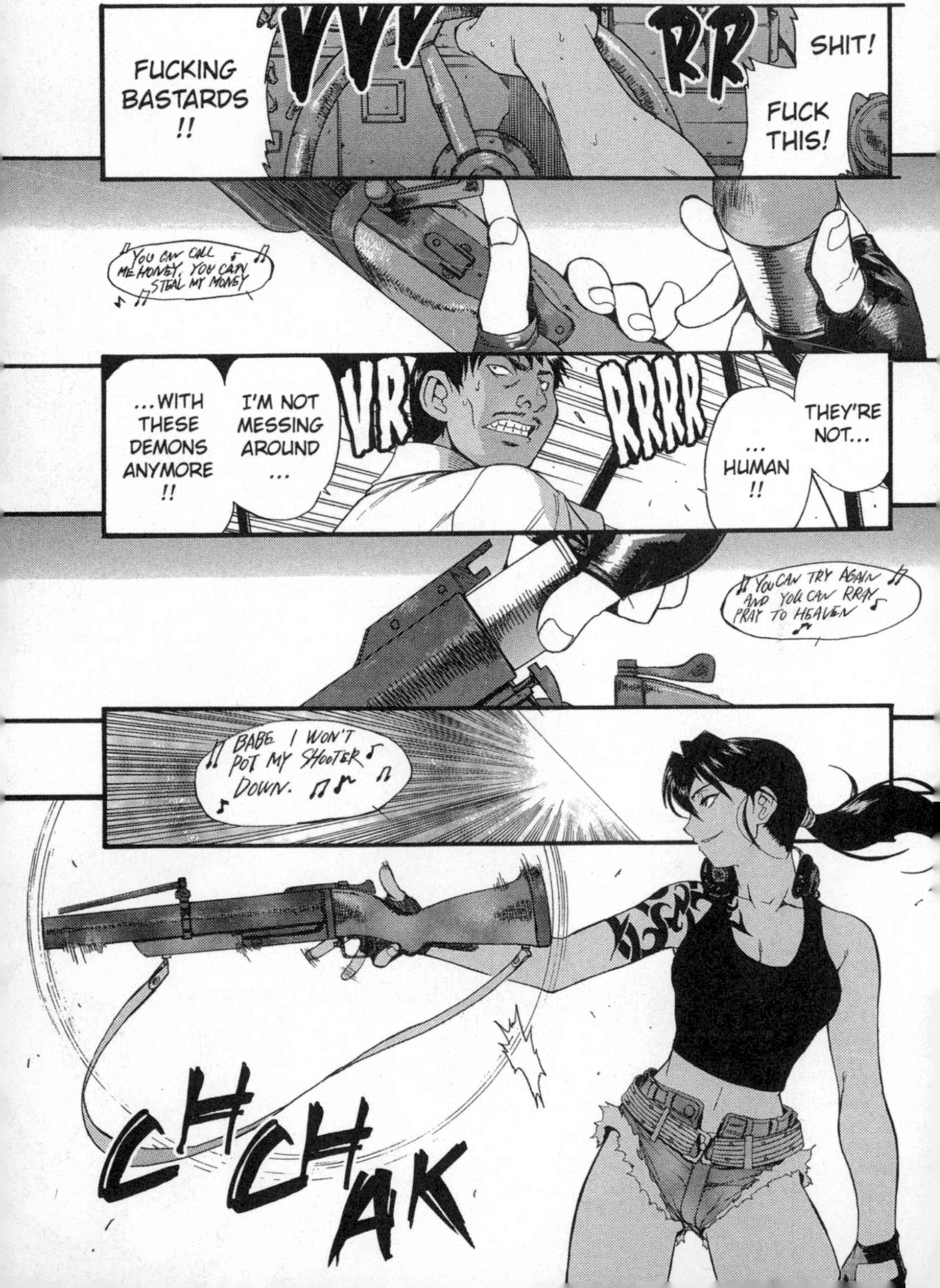
VVVRR
SHIT!
FUCK THIS!
FUCKING BASTARDS !!
YOU CAN CALL ME HONEY, YOU CAN STEAL MY MONEY
VRRRRR
THEY'RE NOT...
...HUMAN !!
I'M NOT MESSING AROUND ...
...WITH THESE DEMONS ANYMORE !!
YOU CAN TRY AGAIN AND YOU CAN PRAY, PRAY TO HEAVEN
BABE I WON'T PUT MY SHOOTER DOWN.
CHCHAK

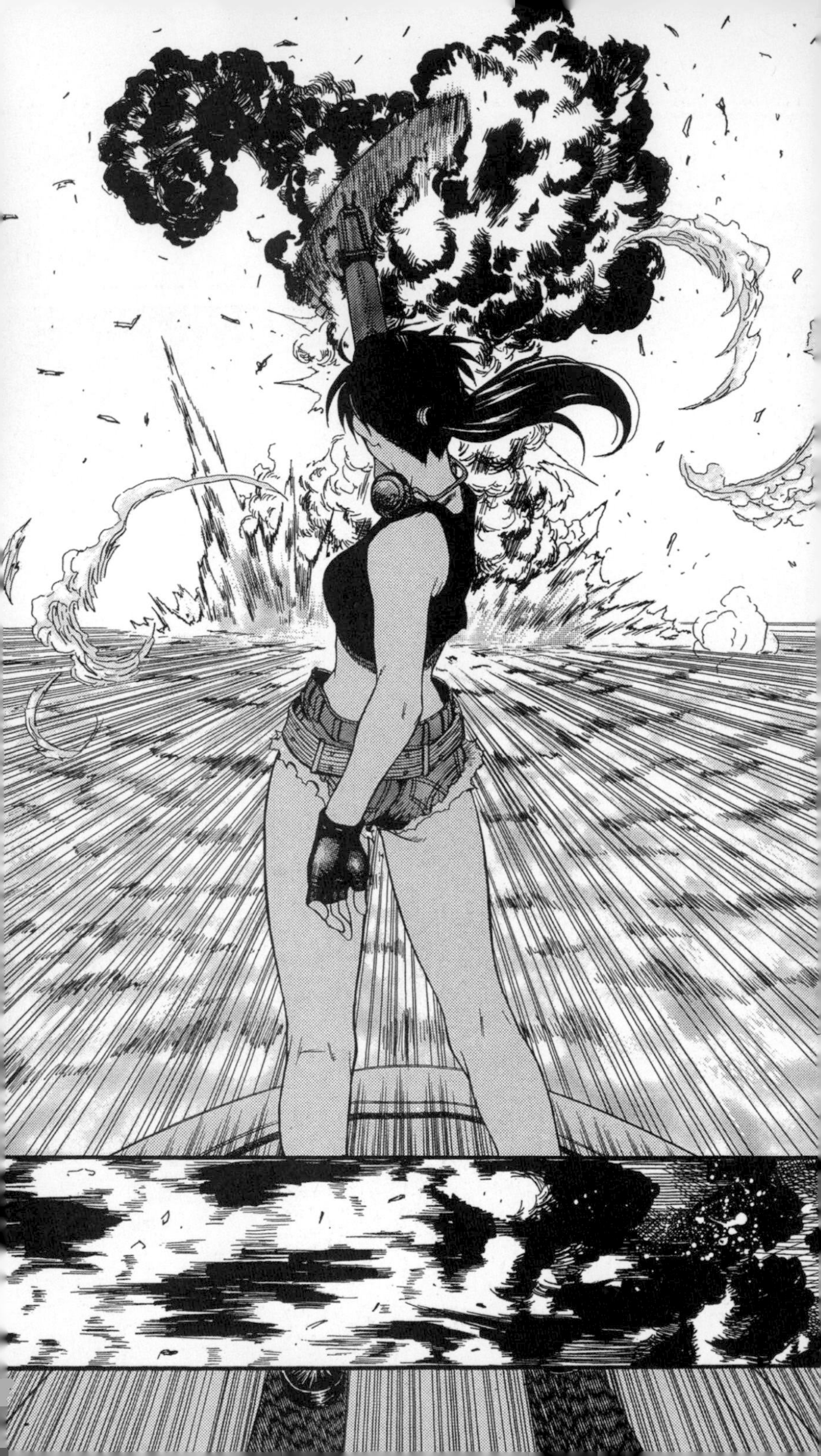

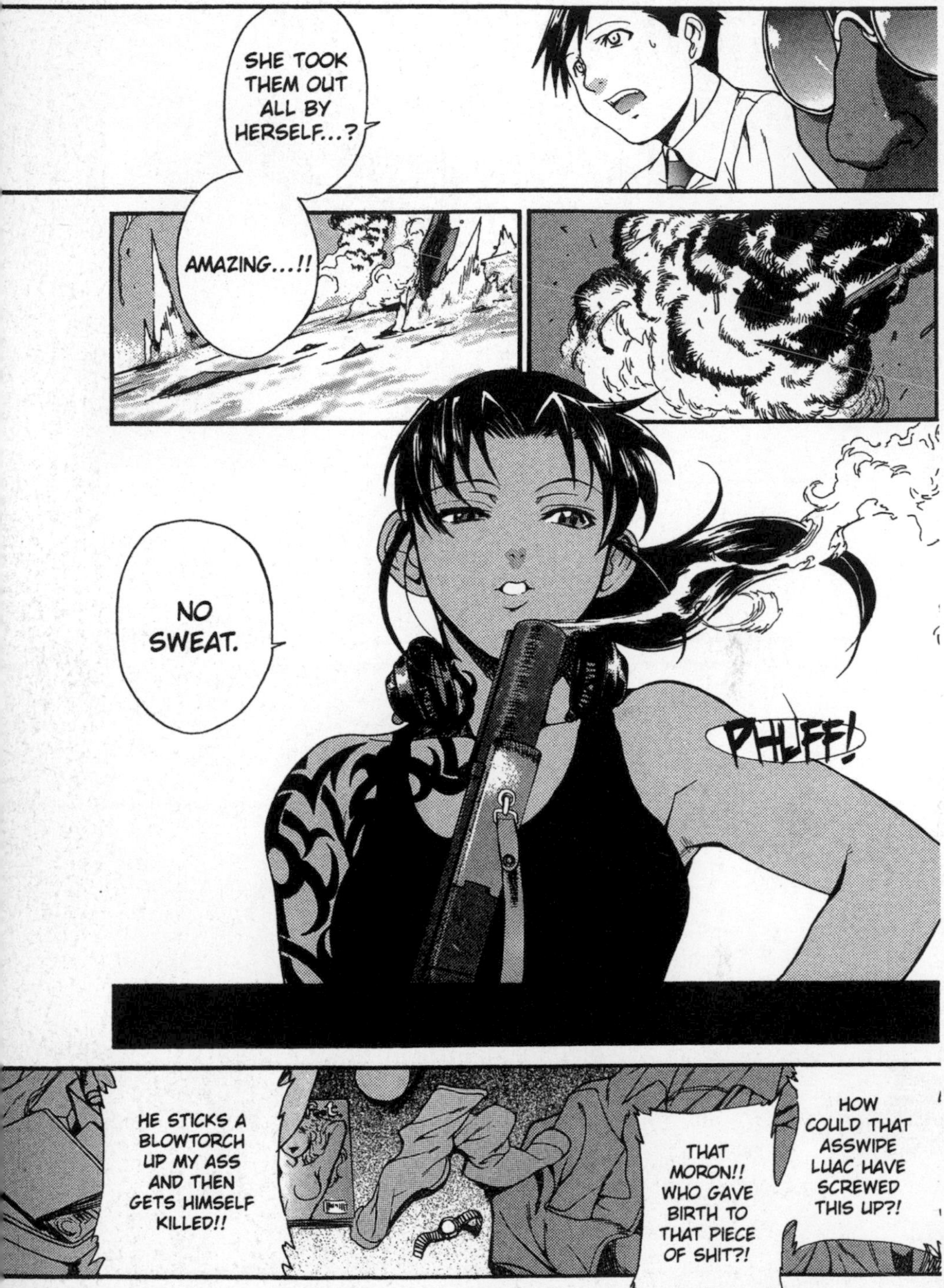
SHE TOOK THEM OUT ALL BY HERSELF...?
AMAZING...!!
NO SWEAT.
PHLFF!
HOW COULD THAT ASSWIPE LUAC HAVE SCREWED THIS UP?!
THAT MORON!! WHO GAVE BIRTH TO THAT PIECE OF SHIT?!
HE STICKS A BLOWTORCH UP MY ASS AND THEN GETS HIMSELF KILLED!!

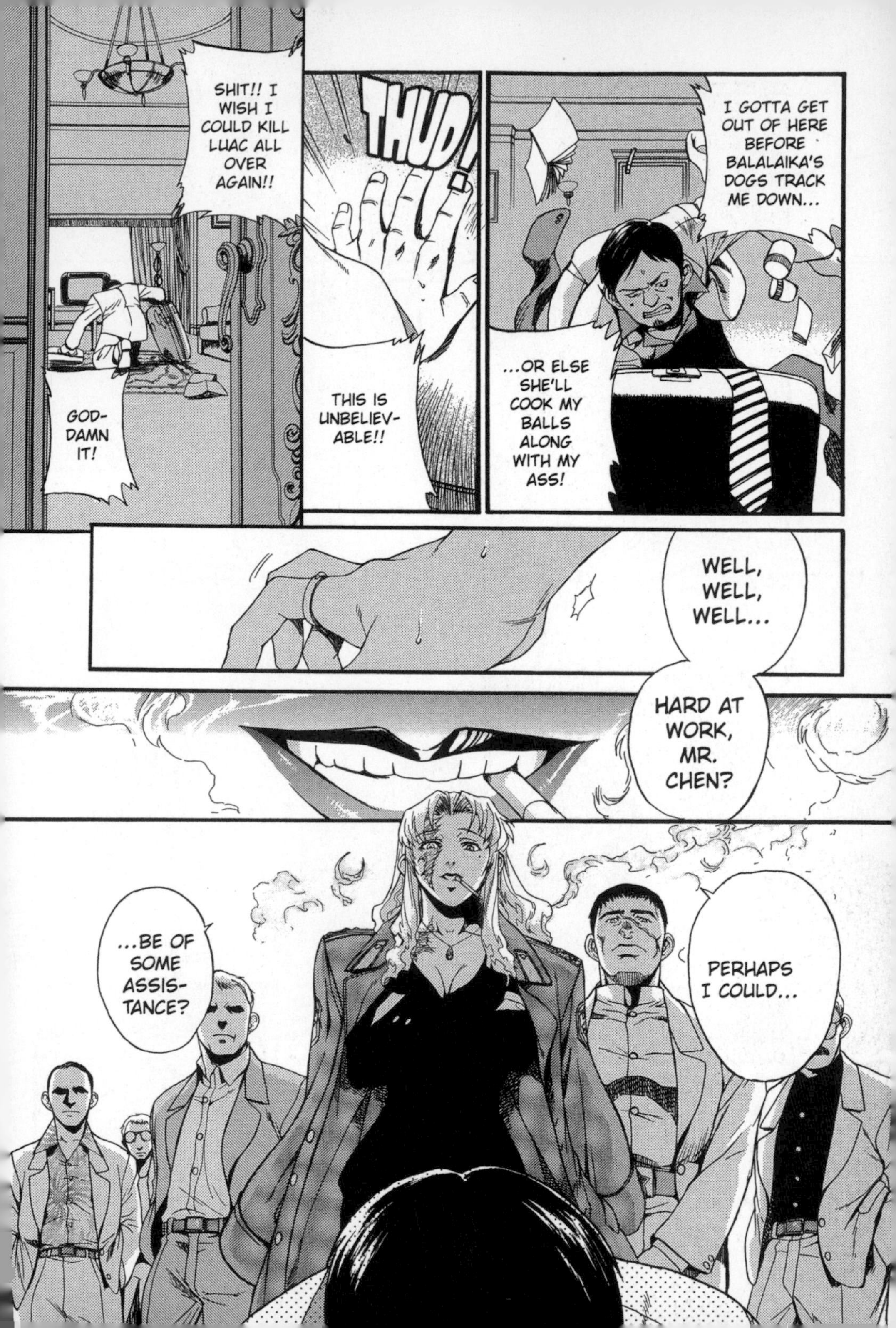
I GOTTA GET OUT OF HERE BEFORE BALALAIKA'S DOGS TRACK ME DOWN...
...OR ELSE SHE'LL COOK MY BALLS ALONG WITH MY ASS!
THUD!
THIS IS UNBELIEV-ABLE!!
SHIT!! I WISH I COULD KILL LUAC ALL OVER AGAIN!!
GOD-DAMN IT!
WELL, WELL, WELL...
HARD AT WORK, MR. CHEN?
PERHAPS I COULD...
...BE OF SOME ASSIS-TANCE?

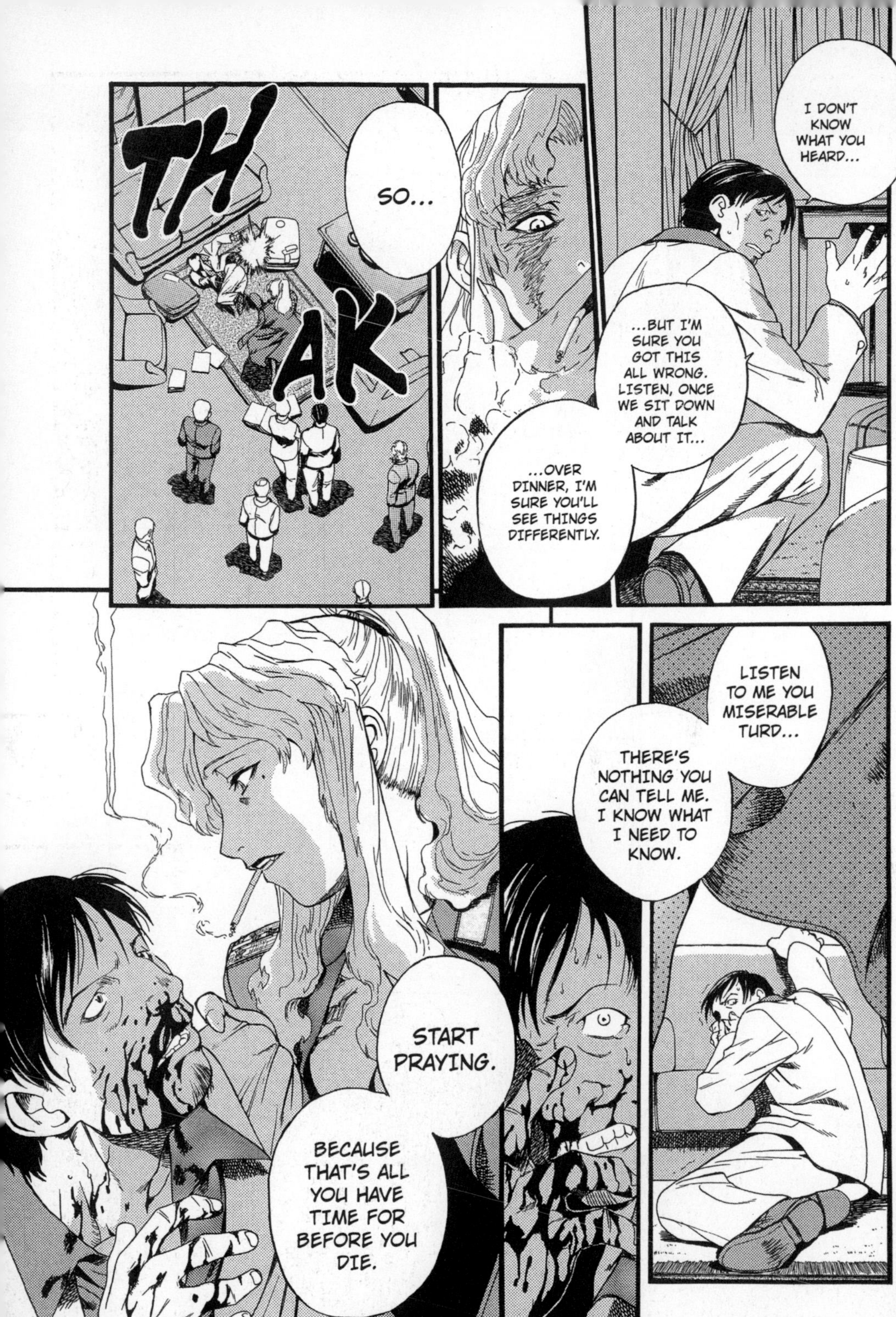
I DON'T KNOW WHAT YOU HEARD...
...BUT I'M SURE YOU GOT THIS ALL WRONG. LISTEN, ONCE WE SIT DOWN AND TALK ABOUT IT...
...OVER DINNER, I'M SURE YOU'LL SEE THINGS DIFFERENTLY.
SO...
THAK
LISTEN TO ME YOU MISERABLE TURD...
THERE'S NOTHING YOU CAN TELL ME. I KNOW WHAT I NEED TO KNOW.
START PRAYING.
BECAUSE THAT'S ALL YOU HAVE TIME FOR BEFORE YOU DIE.

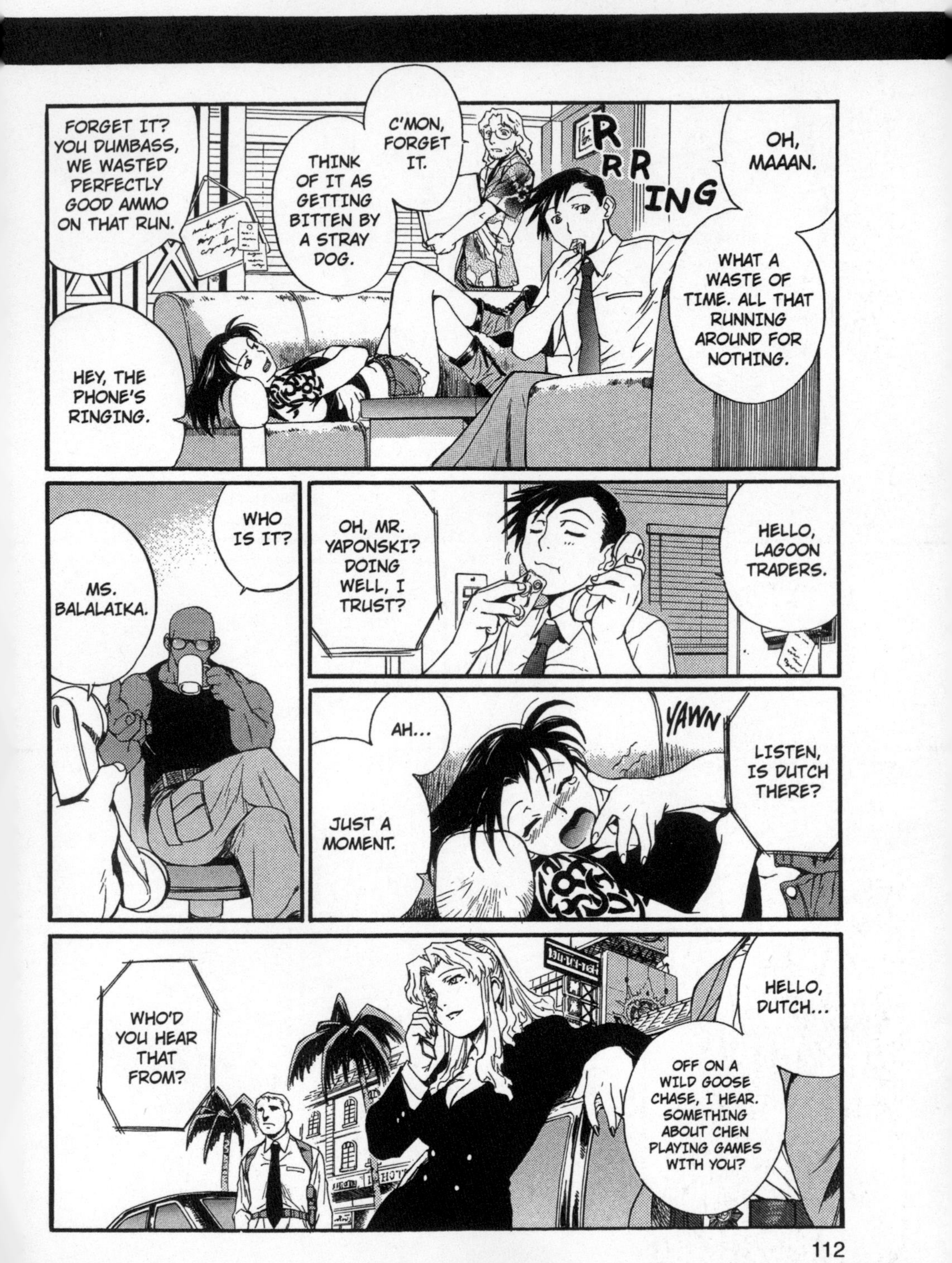
OH, MAAAN.
RRRRING
C'MON, FORGET IT.
WHAT A WASTE OF TIME. ALL THAT RUNNING AROUND FOR NOTHING.
THINK OF IT AS GETTING BITTEN BY A STRAY DOG.
FORGET IT? YOU DUMBASS, WE WASTED PERFECTLY GOOD AMMO ON THAT RUN.
HEY, THE PHONE'S RINGING.
HELLO, LAGOON TRADERS.
OH, MR. YAPONSKI? DOING WELL, I TRUST?
YAWN
LISTEN, IS DUTCH THERE?
AH...
JUST A MOMENT.
WHO IS IT?
MS. BALALAIKA.
HELLO, DUTCH...
OFF ON A WILD GOOSE CHASE, I HEAR. SOMETHING ABOUT CHEN PLAYING GAMES WITH YOU?
WHO'D YOU HEAR THAT FROM?

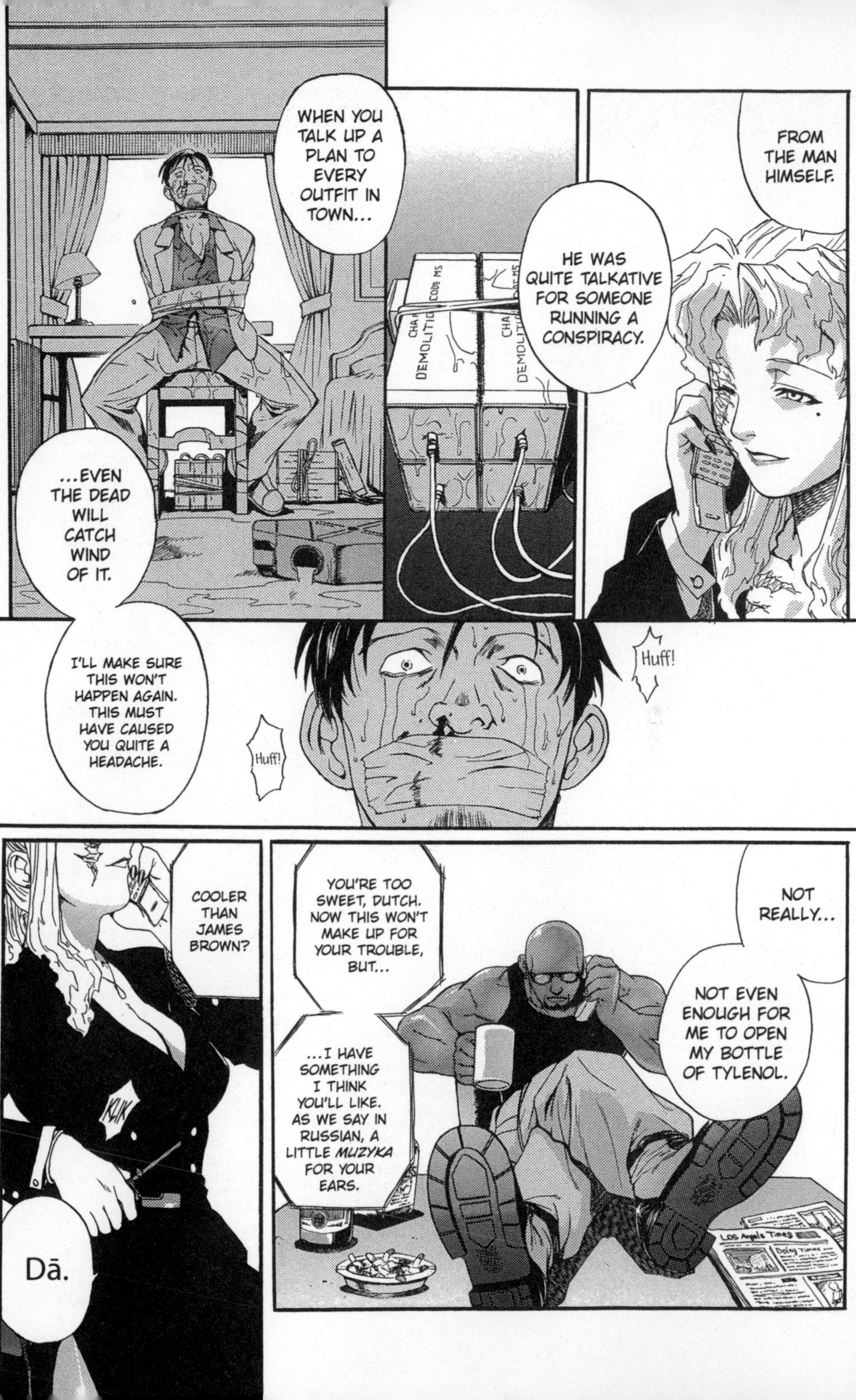
FROM THE MAN HIMSELF.
HE WAS QUITE TALKATIVE FOR SOMEONE RUNNING A CONSPIRACY.
WHEN YOU TALK UP A PLAN TO EVERY OUTFIT IN TOWN...
...EVEN THE DEAD WILL CATCH WIND OF IT.
Huff!
I'LL MAKE SURE THIS WON'T HAPPEN AGAIN. THIS MUST HAVE CAUSED YOU QUITE A HEADACHE.
Huff!
NOT REALLY...
NOT EVEN ENOUGH FOR ME TO OPEN MY BOTTLE OF TYLENOL.
YOU'RE TOO SWEET, DUTCH. NOW THIS WON'T MAKE UP FOR YOUR TROUBLE, BUT...
...I HAVE SOMETHING I THINK YOU'LL LIKE. AS WE SAY IN RUSSIAN, A LITTLE *MUZYKA* FOR YOUR EARS.
LOS Angeles Times
COOLER THAN JAMES BROWN?
KLIK
Dā.

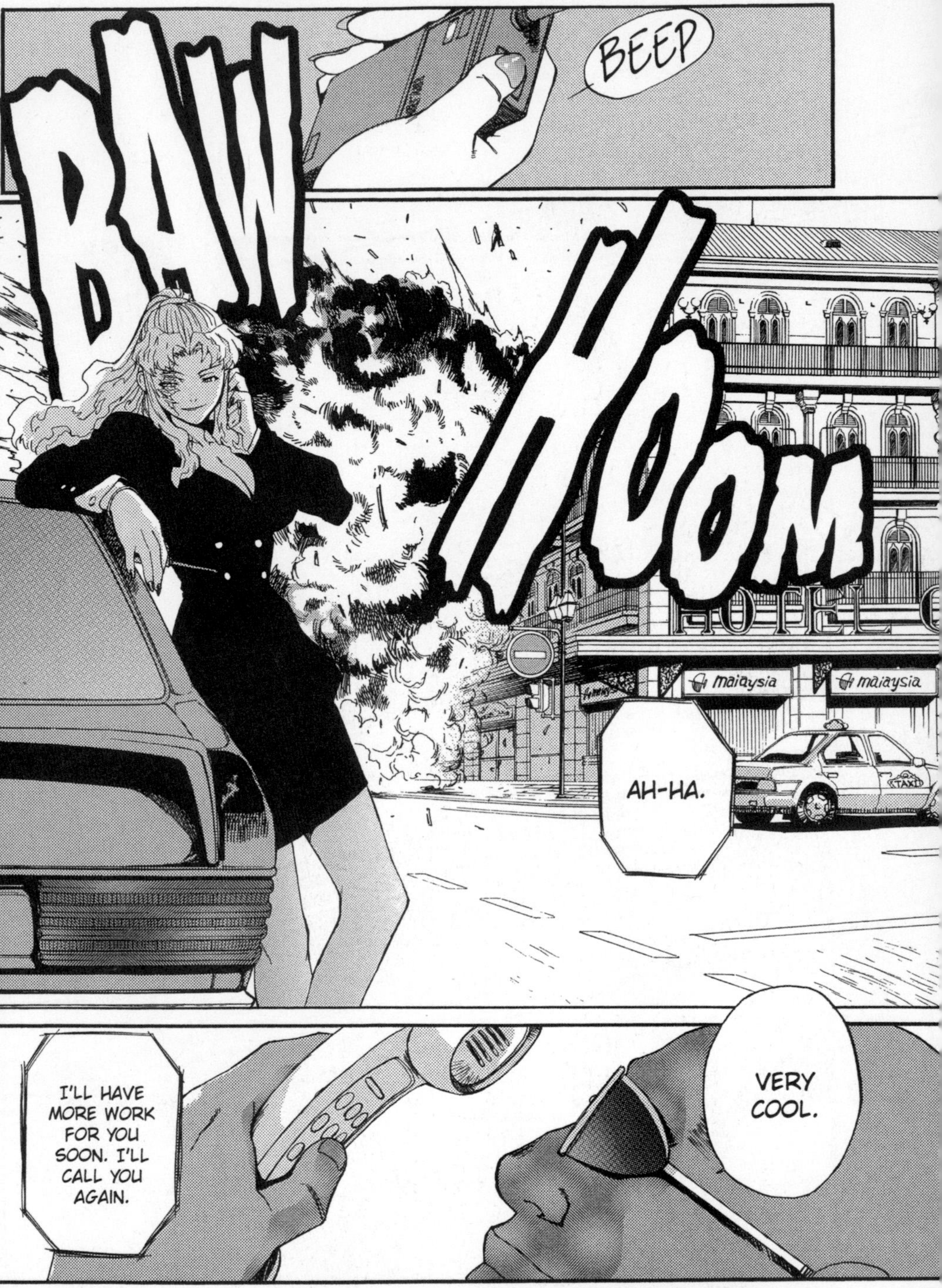
BEEP
BAW
HOOM
HOTEL
malaysia
malaysia
TAXI
AH-HA.
VERY COOL.
I'LL HAVE MORE WORK FOR YOU SOON. I'LL CALL YOU AGAIN.

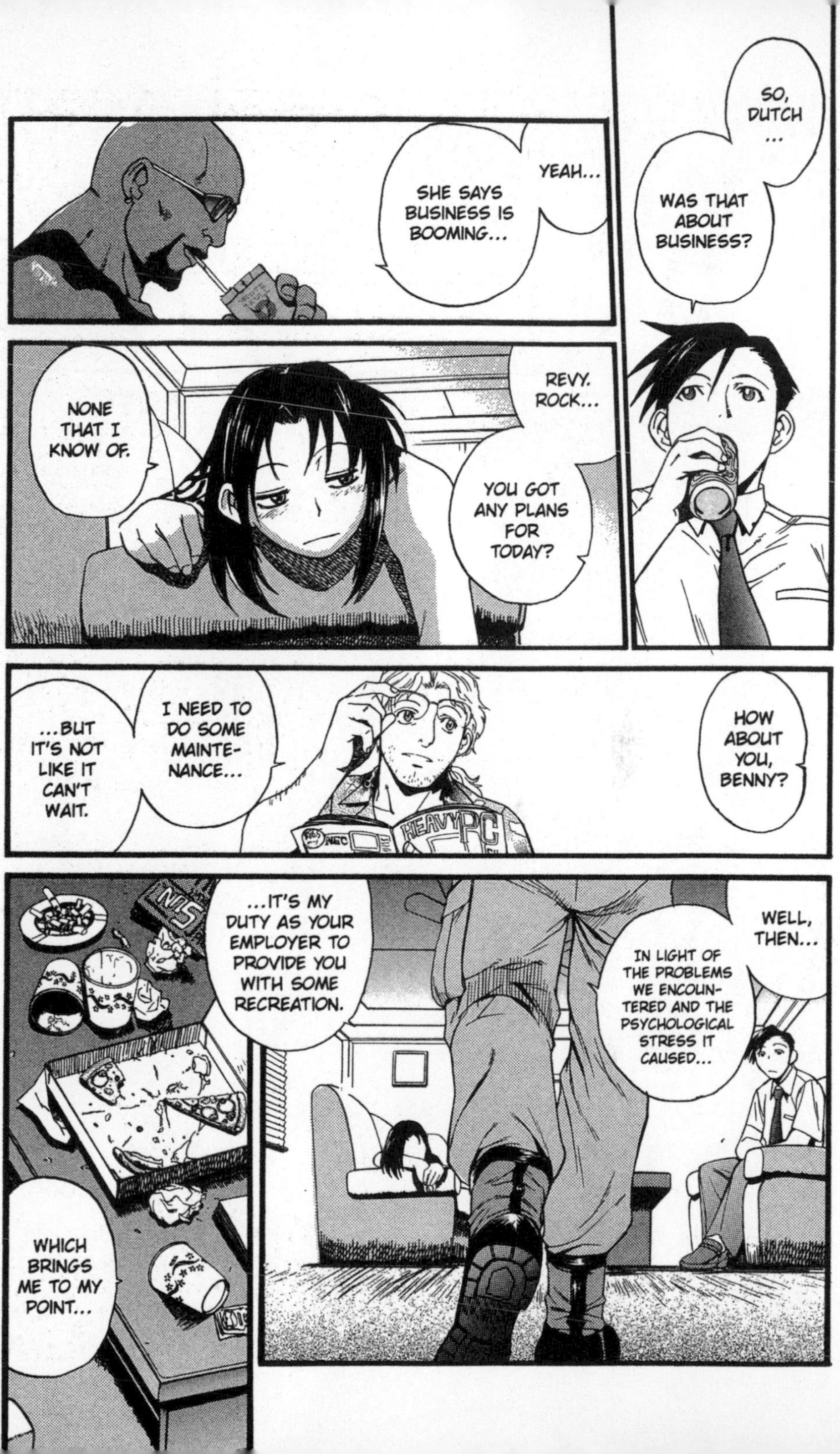
SO, DUTCH ...
WAS THAT ABOUT BUSINESS?
YEAH...
SHE SAYS BUSINESS IS BOOMING...
REVY. ROCK...
YOU GOT ANY PLANS FOR TODAY?
NONE THAT I KNOW OF.
HOW ABOUT YOU, BENNY?
I NEED TO DO SOME MAINTE-NANCE...
...BUT IT'S NOT LIKE IT CAN'T WAIT.
WELL, THEN...
IN LIGHT OF THE PROBLEMS WE ENCOUN-TERED AND THE PSYCHOLOGICAL STRESS IT CAUSED...
...IT'S MY DUTY AS YOUR EMPLOYER TO PROVIDE YOU WITH SOME RECREATION.
WHICH BRINGS ME TO MY POINT...

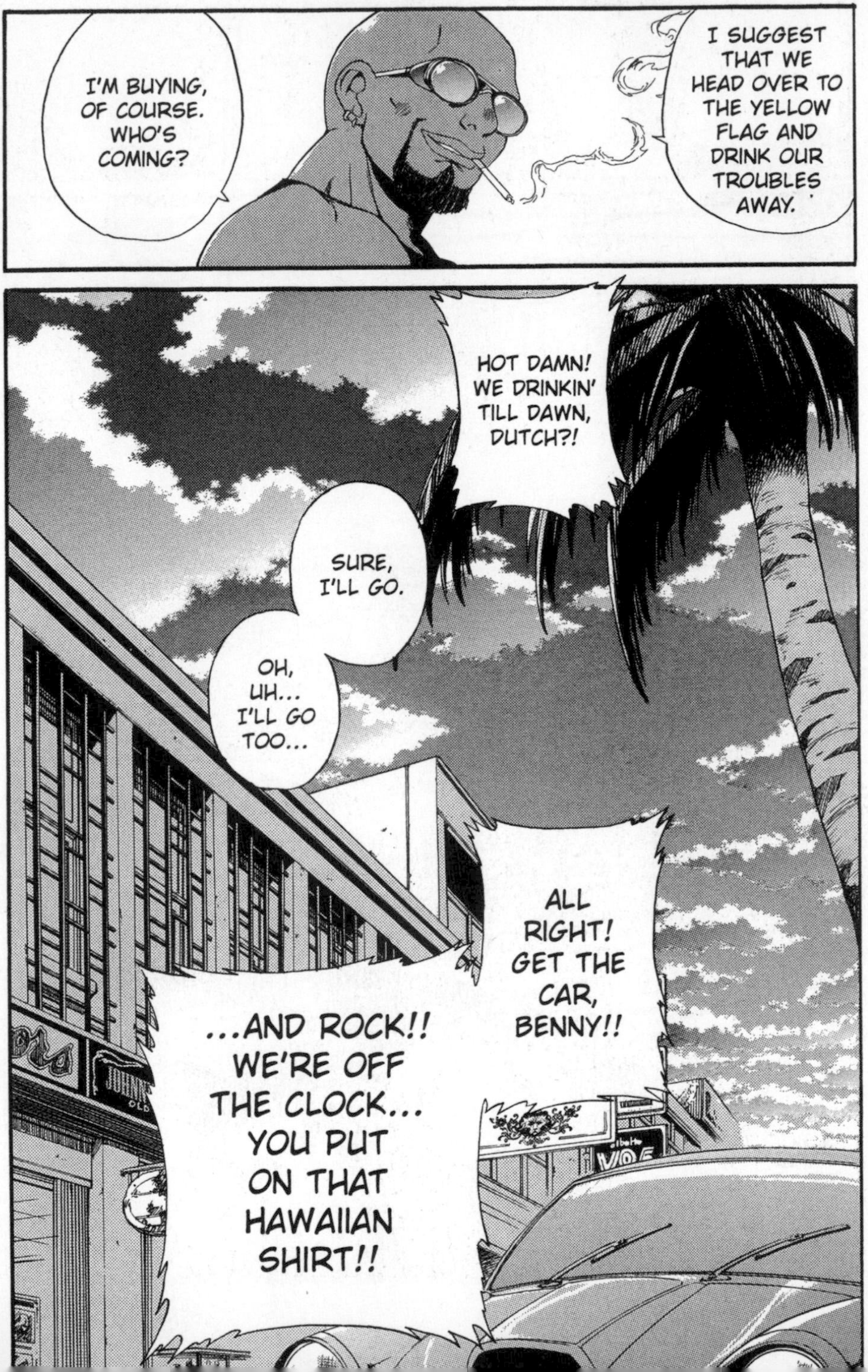
I SUGGEST THAT WE HEAD OVER TO THE YELLOW FLAG AND DRINK OUR TROUBLES AWAY.
I'M BUYING, OF COURSE. WHO'S COMING?
HOT DAMN! WE DRINKIN' TILL DAWN, DUTCH?!
SURE, I'LL GO.
OH, UH... I'LL GO TOO...
ALL RIGHT! GET THE CAR, BENNY!!
...AND ROCK!! WE'RE OFF THE CLOCK... YOU PUT ON THAT HAWAIIAN SHIRT!!

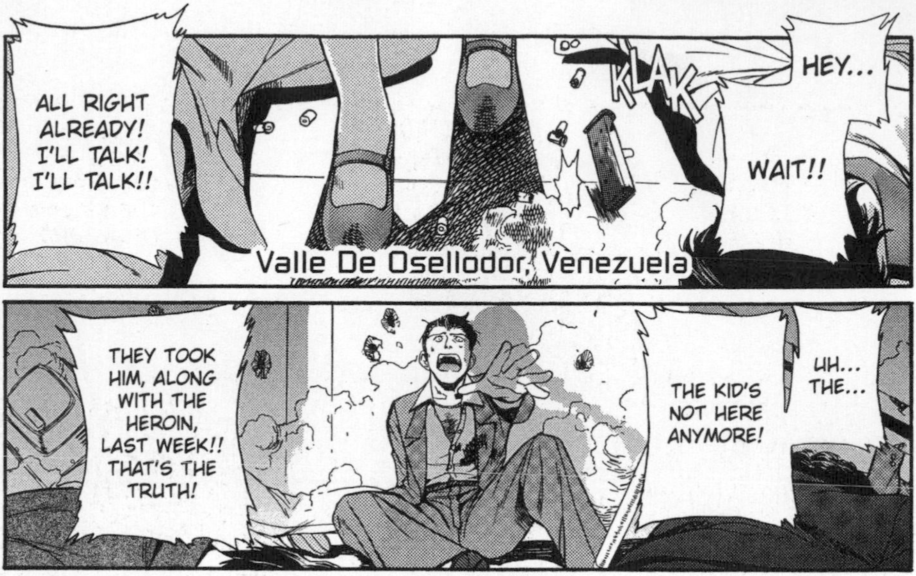
HEY...
WAIT!!
KLAK
ALL RIGHT ALREADY! I'LL TALK! I'LL TALK!!
Valle De Osellodor, Venezuela
UH... THE...
THE KID'S NOT HERE ANYMORE!
THEY TOOK HIM, ALONG WITH THE HEROIN, LAST WEEK!! THAT'S THE TRUTH!

Chapter 2: Rasta Blasta - Part I

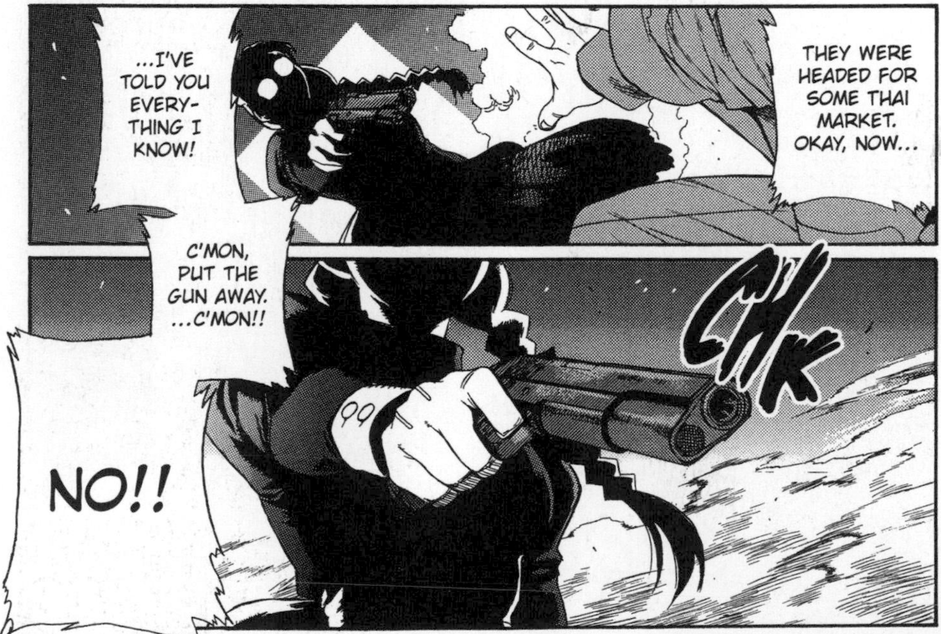
THEY WERE HEADED FOR SOME THAI MARKET. OKAY, NOW...
...I'VE TOLD YOU EVERY-THING I KNOW!
C'MON, PUT THE GUN AWAY. ...C'MON!!
CHK
NO!!

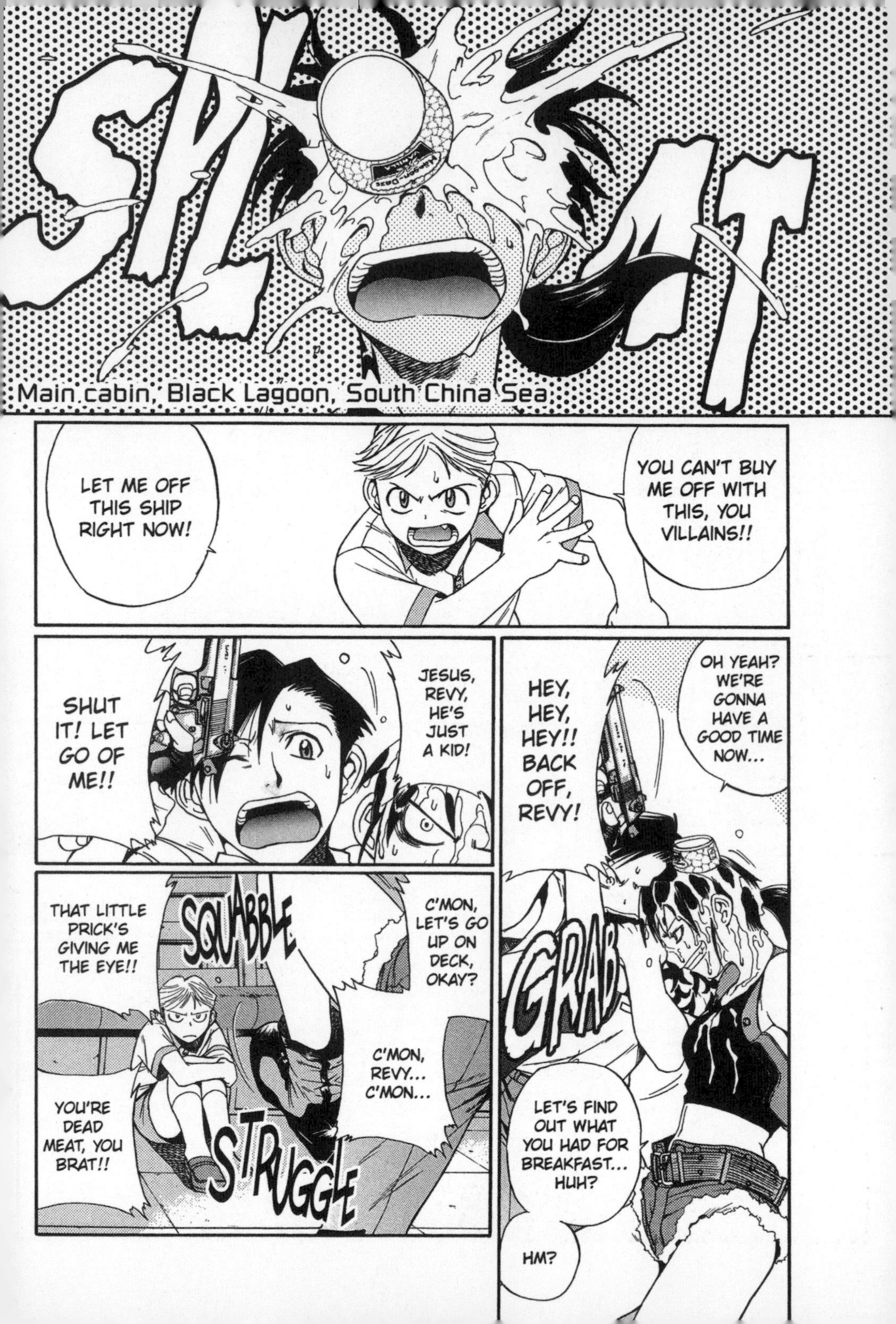
SPLAT
Main cabin, Black Lagoon, South China Sea
YOU CAN'T BUY ME OFF WITH THIS, YOU VILLAINS!!
LET ME OFF THIS SHIP RIGHT NOW!
OH YEAH? WE'RE GONNA HAVE A GOOD TIME NOW...
HEY, HEY, HEY!! BACK OFF, REVY!
GRAB
LET'S FIND OUT WHAT YOU HAD FOR BREAKFAST... HUH?
HM?
JESUS, REVY, HE'S JUST A KID!
SHUT IT! LET GO OF ME!!
C'MON, LET'S GO UP ON DECK, OKAY?
SQUABBLE
THAT LITTLE PRICK'S GIVING ME THE EYE!!
C'MON, REVY... C'MON...
STRUGGLE
YOU'RE DEAD MEAT, YOU BRAT!!

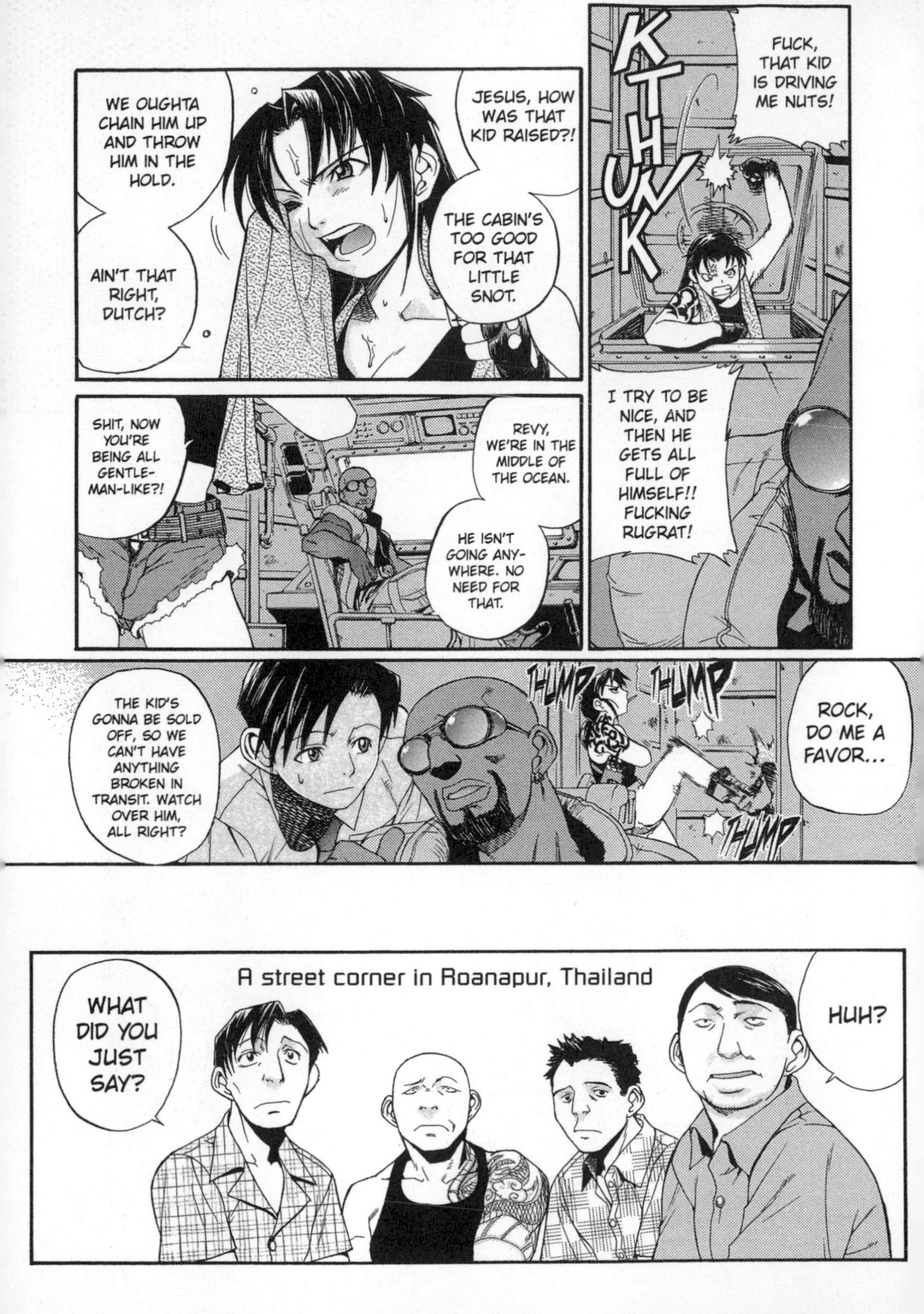
KTHUNK
FUCK, THAT KID IS DRIVING ME NUTS!
I TRY TO BE NICE, AND THEN HE GETS ALL FULL OF HIMSELF!! FUCKING RUGRAT!
JESUS, HOW WAS THAT KID RAISED?!
THE CABIN'S TOO GOOD FOR THAT LITTLE SNOT.
WE OUGHTA CHAIN HIM UP AND THROW HIM IN THE HOLD.
AIN'T THAT RIGHT, DUTCH?
REVY, WE'RE IN THE MIDDLE OF THE OCEAN.
HE ISN'T GOING ANY-WHERE. NO NEED FOR THAT.
SHIT, NOW YOU'RE BEING ALL GENTLE-MAN-LIKE?!
ROCK, DO ME A FAVOR...
THUMP THUMP
THUMP
THE KID'S GONNA BE SOLD OFF, SO WE CAN'T HAVE ANYTHING BROKEN IN TRANSIT. WATCH OVER HIM, ALL RIGHT?
A street corner in Roanapur, Thailand
HUH?
WHAT DID YOU JUST SAY?

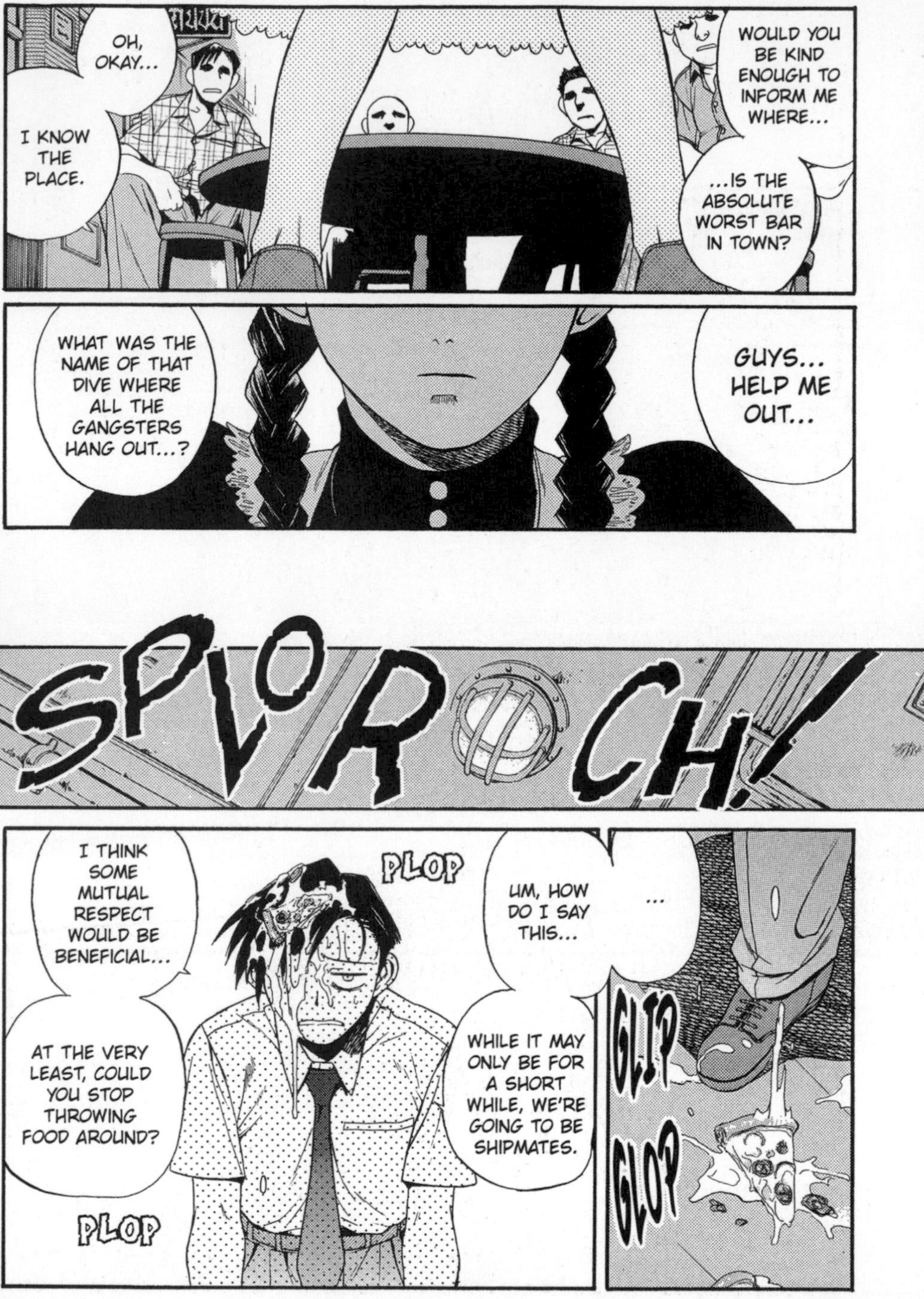
WOULD YOU BE KIND ENOUGH TO INFORM ME WHERE...
...IS THE ABSOLUTE WORST BAR IN TOWN?
OH, OKAY...
I KNOW THE PLACE.
GUYS... HELP ME OUT...
WHAT WAS THE NAME OF THAT DIVE WHERE ALL THE GANGSTERS HANG OUT...?
SPLOR CH!
GLIP
GLOP
...
UM, HOW DO I SAY THIS...
PLOP
I THINK SOME MUTUAL RESPECT WOULD BE BENEFICIAL...
WHILE IT MAY ONLY BE FOR A SHORT WHILE, WE'RE GOING TO BE SHIPMATES.
AT THE VERY LEAST, COULD YOU STOP THROWING FOOD AROUND?
PLOP

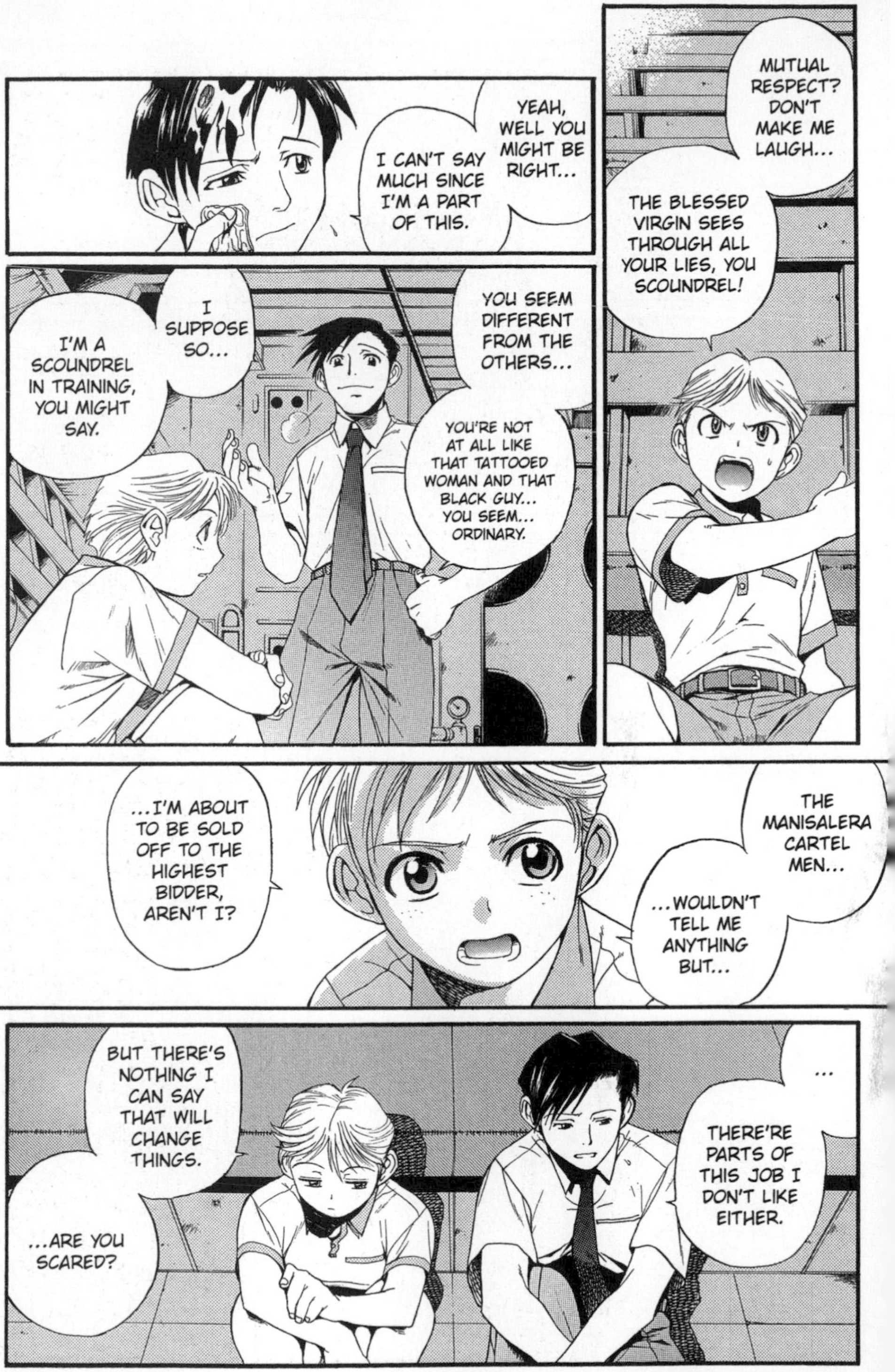
MUTUAL RESPECT? DON'T MAKE ME LAUGH...
THE BLESSED VIRGIN SEES THROUGH ALL YOUR LIES, YOU SCOUNDREL!
YEAH, WELL YOU MIGHT BE RIGHT...
I CAN'T SAY MUCH SINCE I'M A PART OF THIS.
YOU SEEM DIFFERENT FROM THE OTHERS...
YOU'RE NOT AT ALL LIKE THAT TATTOOED WOMAN AND THAT BLACK GUY... YOU SEEM... ORDINARY.
I SUPPOSE SO...
I'M A SCOUNDREL IN TRAINING, YOU MIGHT SAY.
THE MANISALERA CARTEL MEN...
...WOULDN'T TELL ME ANYTHING BUT...
...I'M ABOUT TO BE SOLD OFF TO THE HIGHEST BIDDER, AREN'T I?
...
THERE'RE PARTS OF THIS JOB I DON'T LIKE EITHER.
BUT THERE'S NOTHING I CAN SAY THAT WILL CHANGE THINGS.
...ARE YOU SCARED?

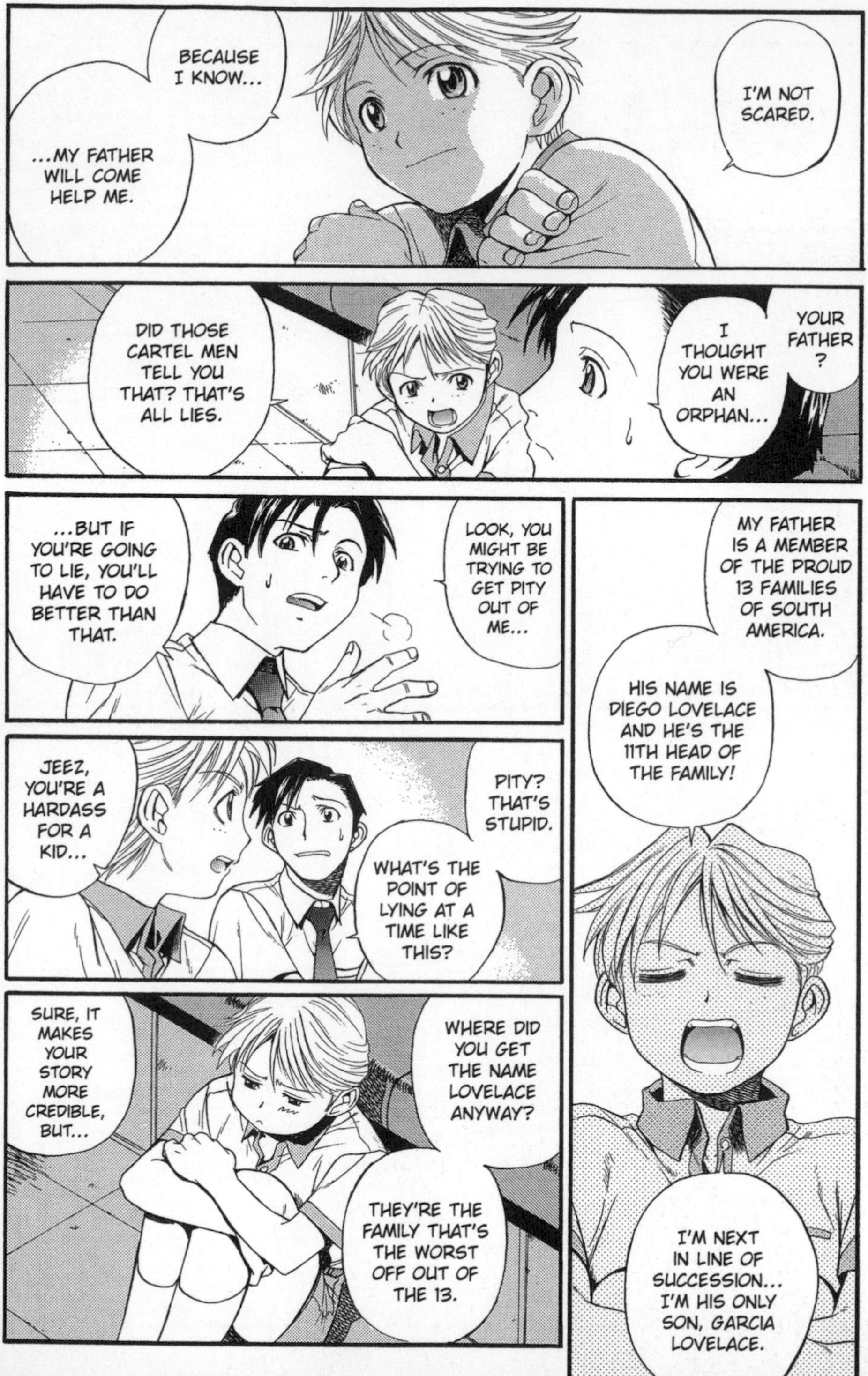
I'M NOT SCARED.
BECAUSE I KNOW...
...MY FATHER WILL COME HELP ME.
YOUR FATHER?
I THOUGHT YOU WERE AN ORPHAN...
DID THOSE CARTEL MEN TELL YOU THAT? THAT'S ALL LIES.
MY FATHER IS A MEMBER OF THE PROUD 13 FAMILIES OF SOUTH AMERICA.
HIS NAME IS DIEGO LOVELACE AND HE'S THE 11TH HEAD OF THE FAMILY!
I'M NEXT IN LINE OF SUCCESSION... I'M HIS ONLY SON, GARCIA LOVELACE.
LOOK, YOU MIGHT BE TRYING TO GET PITY OUT OF ME...
...BUT IF YOU'RE GOING TO LIE, YOU'LL HAVE TO DO BETTER THAN THAT.
PITY? THAT'S STUPID.
WHAT'S THE POINT OF LYING AT A TIME LIKE THIS?
JEEZ, YOU'RE A HARDASS FOR A KID...
WHERE DID YOU GET THE NAME LOVELACE ANYWAY?
THEY'RE THE FAMILY THAT'S THE WORST OFF OUT OF THE 13.
SURE, IT MAKES YOUR STORY MORE CREDIBLE, BUT...

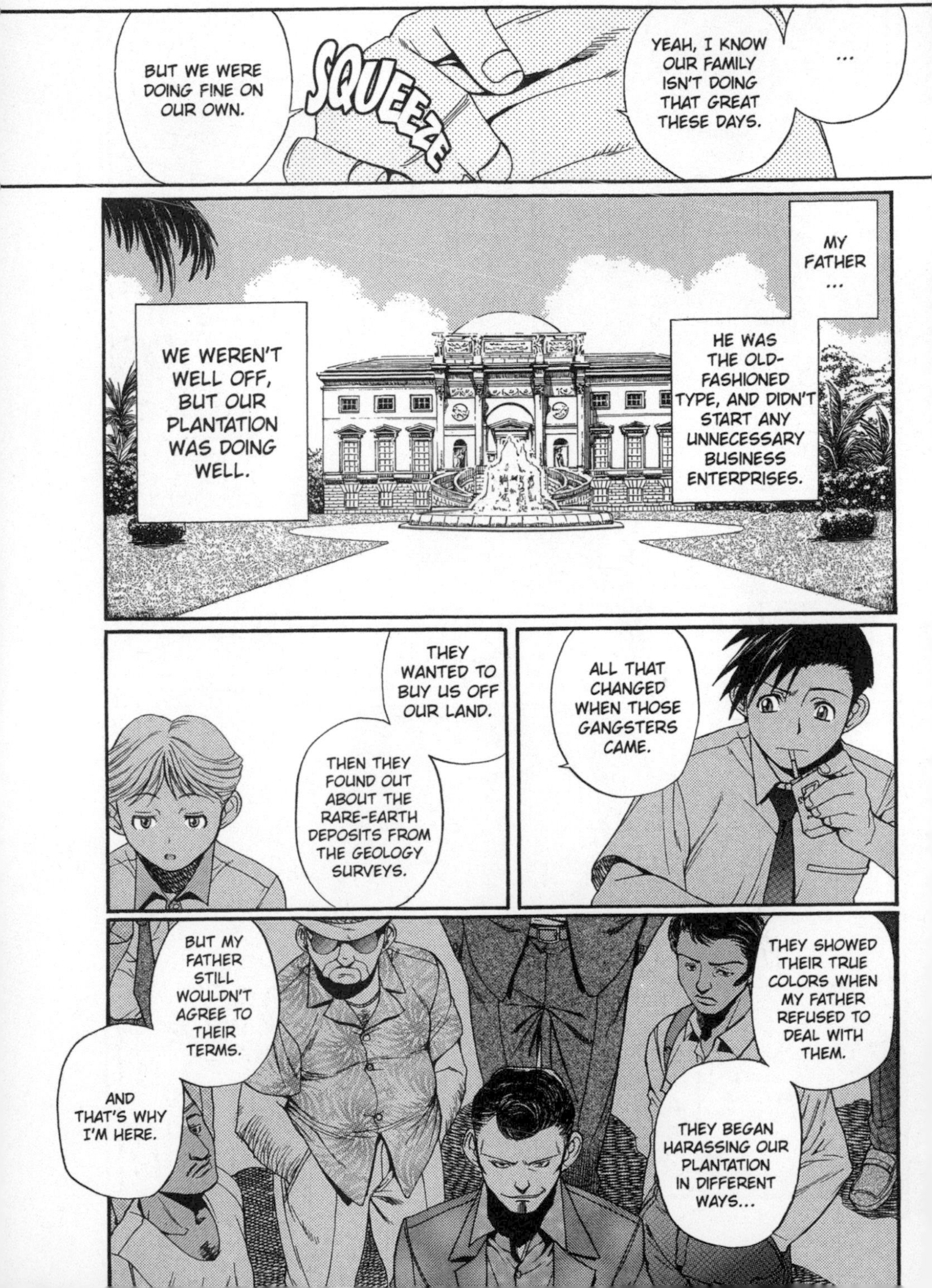
...
YEAH, I KNOW OUR FAMILY ISN'T DOING THAT GREAT THESE DAYS.
SQUEEEZE
BUT WE WERE DOING FINE ON OUR OWN.
MY FATHER ...
HE WAS THE OLD-FASHIONED TYPE, AND DIDN'T START ANY UNNECESSARY BUSINESS ENTERPRISES.
WE WEREN'T WELL OFF, BUT OUR PLANTATION WAS DOING WELL.
ALL THAT CHANGED WHEN THOSE GANGSTERS CAME.
THEY WANTED TO BUY US OFF OUR LAND.
THEN THEY FOUND OUT ABOUT THE RARE-EARTH DEPOSITS FROM THE GEOLOGY SURVEYS.
THEY SHOWED THEIR TRUE COLORS WHEN MY FATHER REFUSED TO DEAL WITH THEM.
THEY BEGAN HARASSING OUR PLANTATION IN DIFFERENT WAYS...
BUT MY FATHER STILL WOULDN'T AGREE TO THEIR TERMS.
AND THAT'S WHY I'M HERE.

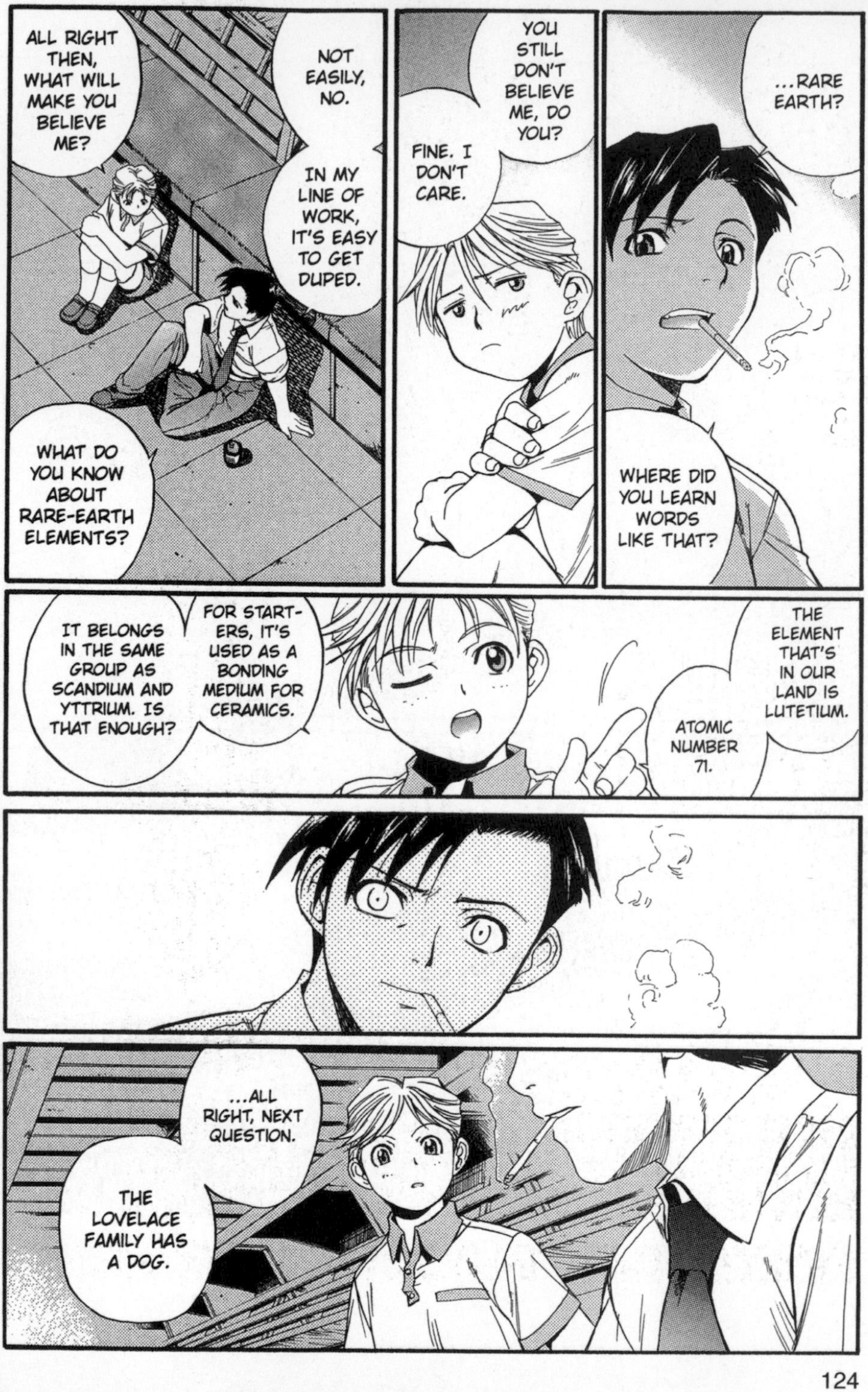
...RARE EARTH?
WHERE DID YOU LEARN WORDS LIKE THAT?
YOU STILL DON'T BELIEVE ME, DO YOU?
FINE. I DON'T CARE.
NOT EASILY, NO.
IN MY LINE OF WORK, IT'S EASY TO GET DUPED.
ALL RIGHT THEN, WHAT WILL MAKE YOU BELIEVE ME?
WHAT DO YOU KNOW ABOUT RARE-EARTH ELEMENTS?
THE ELEMENT THAT'S IN OUR LAND IS LUTETIUM.
ATOMIC NUMBER 71.
FOR STARTERS, IT'S USED AS A BONDING MEDIUM FOR CERAMICS.
IT BELONGS IN THE SAME GROUP AS SCANDIUM AND YTTRIUM. IS THAT ENOUGH?
...ALL RIGHT, NEXT QUESTION.
THE LOVELACE FAMILY HAS A DOG.

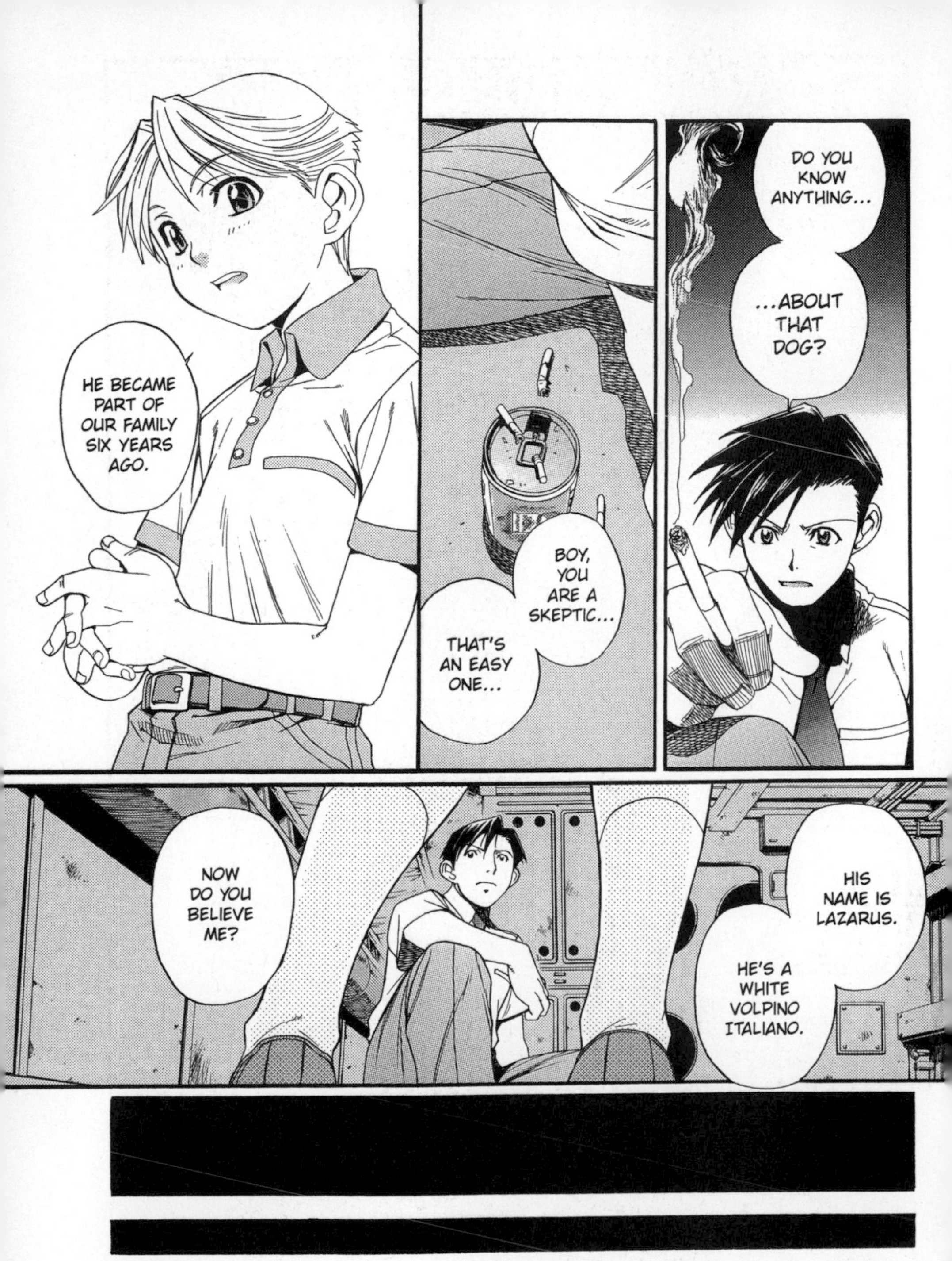
DO YOU KNOW ANYTHING...
...ABOUT THAT DOG?
BOY, YOU ARE A SKEPTIC...
THAT'S AN EASY ONE...
HE BECAME PART OF OUR FAMILY SIX YEARS AGO.
HIS NAME IS LAZARUS.
HE'S A WHITE VOLPINO ITALIANO.
NOW DO YOU BELIEVE ME?

[redacted]

[redacted]

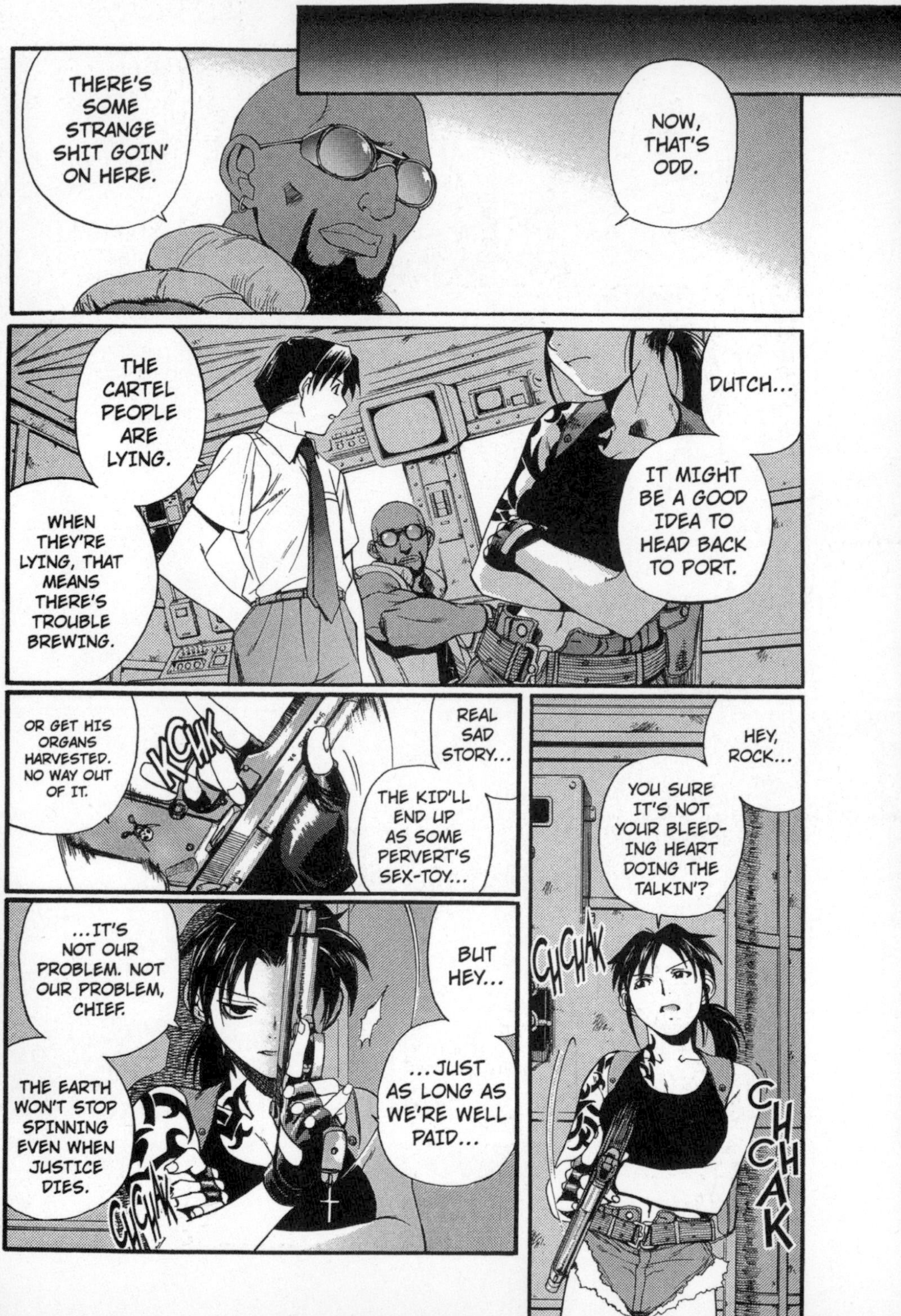
NOW, THAT'S ODD.
THERE'S SOME STRANGE SHIT GOIN' ON HERE.
DUTCH...
IT MIGHT BE A GOOD IDEA TO HEAD BACK TO PORT.
THE CARTEL PEOPLE ARE LYING.
WHEN THEY'RE LYING, THAT MEANS THERE'S TROUBLE BREWING.
HEY, ROCK...
YOU SURE IT'S NOT YOUR BLEEDING HEART DOING THE TALKIN'?
CHCHAK
CHCHAK
REAL SAD STORY...
THE KID'LL END UP AS SOME PERVERT'S SEX-TOY...
OR GET HIS ORGANS HARVESTED. NO WAY OUT OF IT.
KCHK
BUT HEY...
...JUST AS LONG AS WE'RE WELL PAID...
...IT'S NOT OUR PROBLEM. NOT OUR PROBLEM, CHIEF.
THE EARTH WON'T STOP SPINNING EVEN WHEN JUSTICE DIES.
CHCHAK

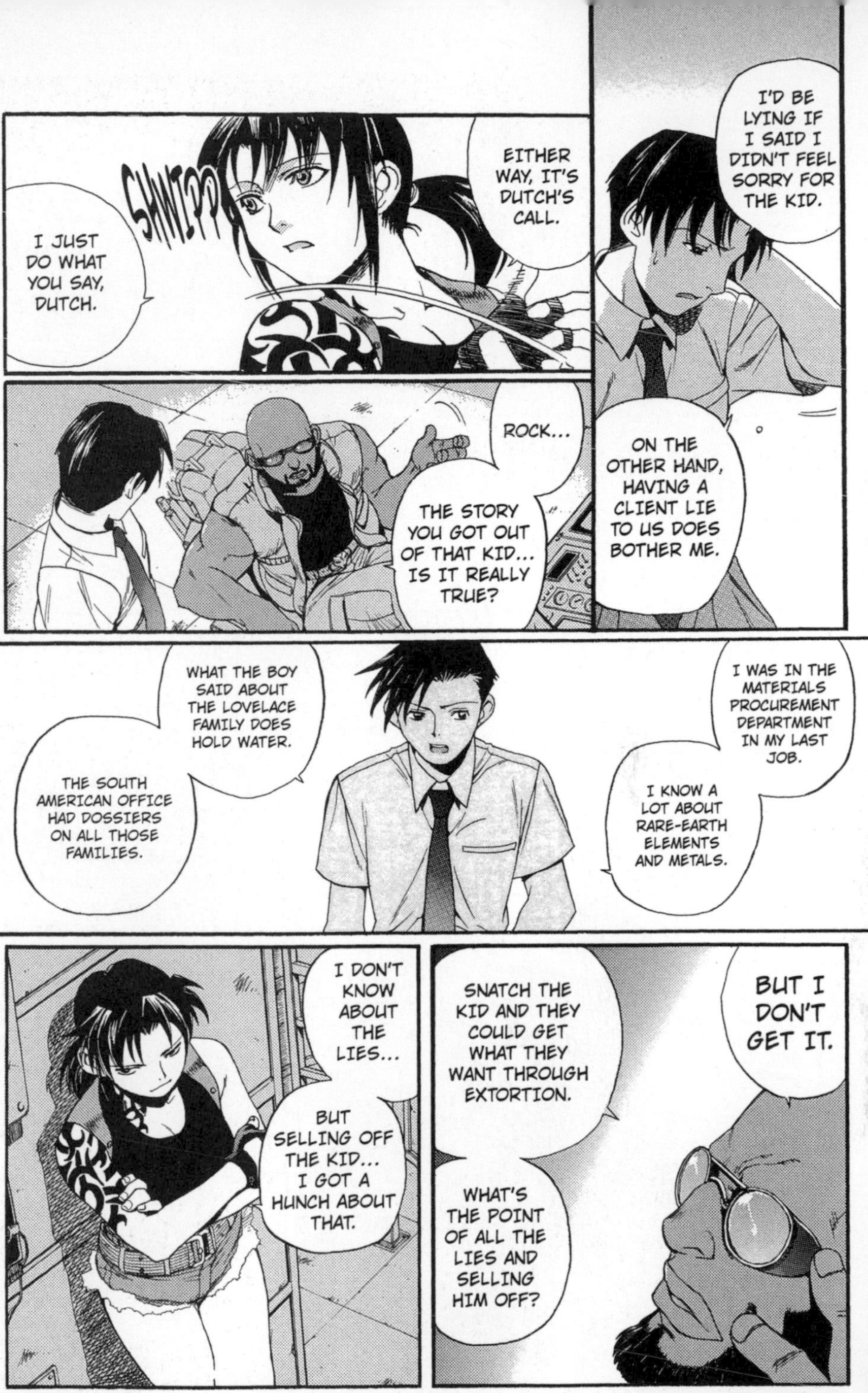
I'D BE LYING IF I SAID I DIDN'T FEEL SORRY FOR THE KID.
ON THE OTHER HAND, HAVING A CLIENT LIE TO US DOES BOTHER ME.
EITHER WAY, IT'S DUTCH'S CALL.
SHWIP
I JUST DO WHAT YOU SAY, DUTCH.
ROCK...
THE STORY YOU GOT OUT OF THAT KID... IS IT REALLY TRUE?
I WAS IN THE MATERIALS PROCUREMENT DEPARTMENT IN MY LAST JOB.
I KNOW A LOT ABOUT RARE-EARTH ELEMENTS AND METALS.
WHAT THE BOY SAID ABOUT THE LOVELACE FAMILY DOES HOLD WATER.
THE SOUTH AMERICAN OFFICE HAD DOSSIERS ON ALL THOSE FAMILIES.
BUT I DON'T GET IT.
SNATCH THE KID AND THEY COULD GET WHAT THEY WANT THROUGH EXTORTION.
WHAT'S THE POINT OF ALL THE LIES AND SELLING HIM OFF?
I DON'T KNOW ABOUT THE LIES...
BUT SELLING OFF THE KID... I GOT A HUNCH ABOUT THAT.

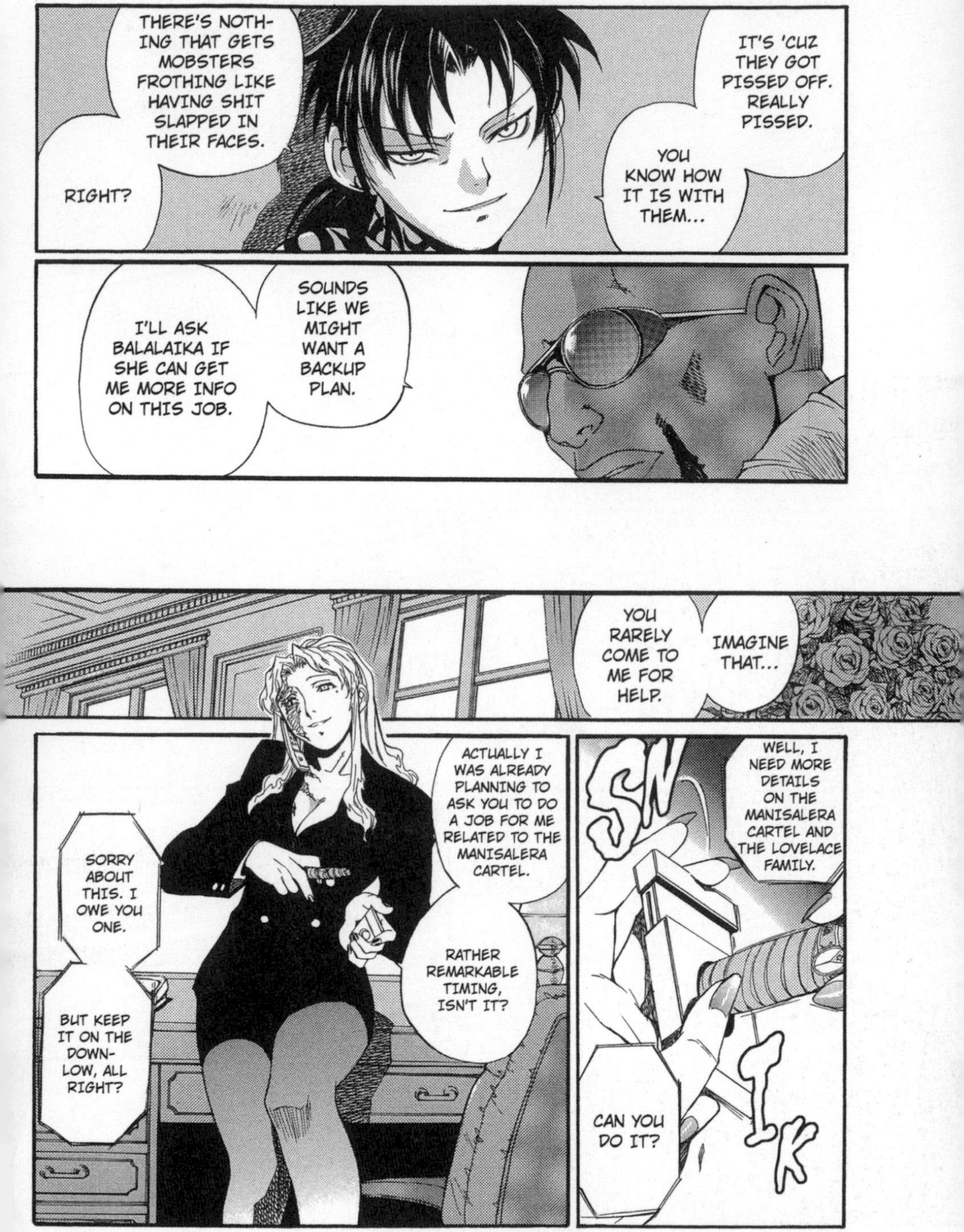
IT'S 'CUZ THEY GOT PISSED OFF. REALLY PISSED.
YOU KNOW HOW IT IS WITH THEM...
THERE'S NOTHING THAT GETS MOBSTERS FROTHING LIKE HAVING SHIT SLAPPED IN THEIR FACES.
RIGHT?
SOUNDS LIKE WE MIGHT WANT A BACKUP PLAN.
I'LL ASK BALALAIKA IF SHE CAN GET ME MORE INFO ON THIS JOB.
IMAGINE THAT...
YOU RARELY COME TO ME FOR HELP.
WELL, I NEED MORE DETAILS ON THE MANISALERA CARTEL AND THE LOVELACE FAMILY.
SNIK
CAN YOU DO IT?
ACTUALLY I WAS ALREADY PLANNING TO ASK YOU TO DO A JOB FOR ME RELATED TO THE MANISALERA CARTEL.
RATHER REMARKABLE TIMING, ISN'T IT?
SORRY ABOUT THIS. I OWE YOU ONE.
BUT KEEP IT ON THE DOWN-LOW, ALL RIGHT?

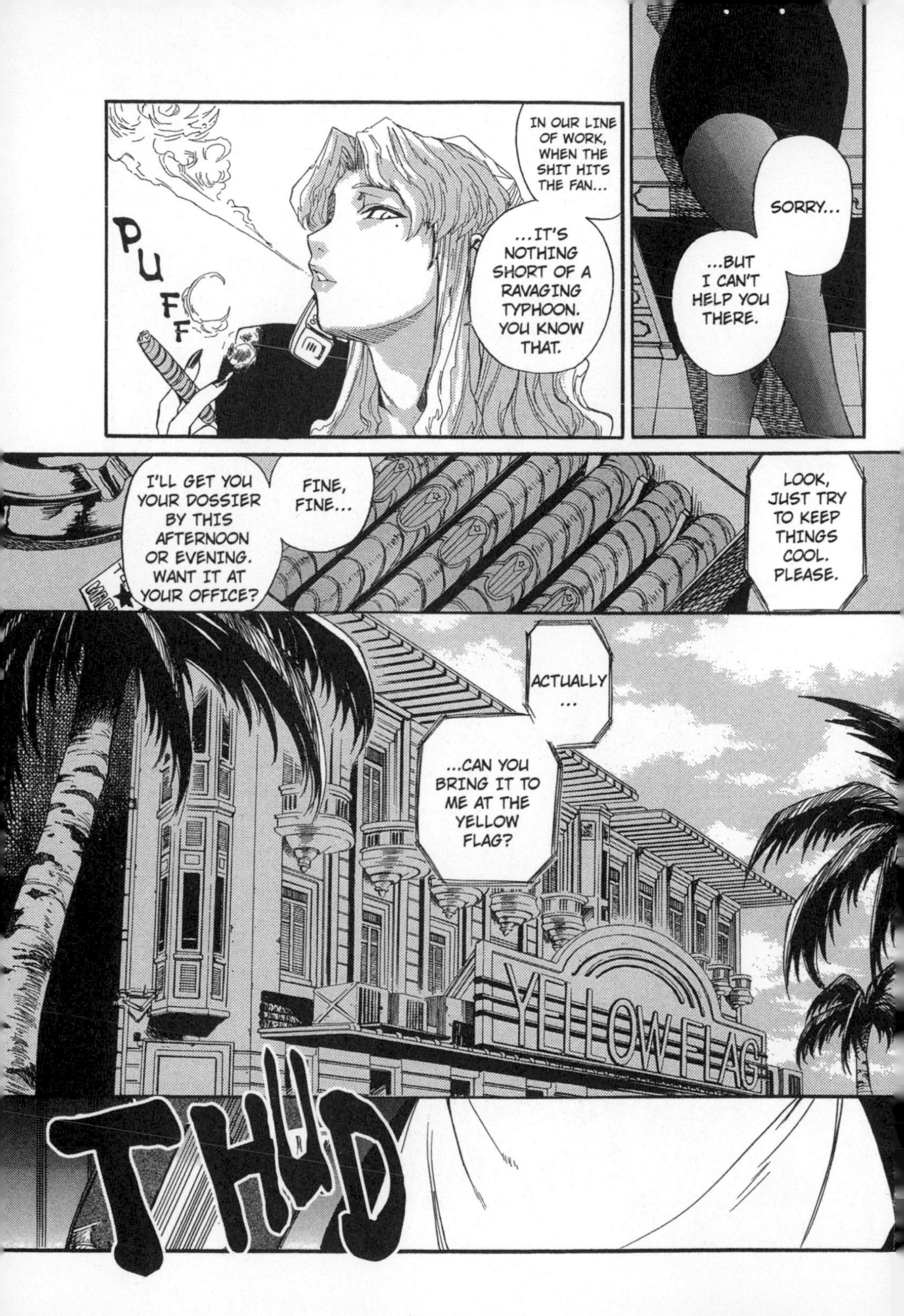
SORRY...
...BUT I CAN'T HELP YOU THERE.
IN OUR LINE OF WORK, WHEN THE SHIT HITS THE FAN...
...IT'S NOTHING SHORT OF A RAVAGING TYPHOON. YOU KNOW THAT.
PUFF
LOOK, JUST TRY TO KEEP THINGS COOL. PLEASE.
FINE, FINE...
I'LL GET YOU YOUR DOSSIER BY THIS AFTERNOON OR EVENING. WANT IT AT YOUR OFFICE?
ACTUALLY...
...CAN YOU BRING IT TO ME AT THE YELLOW FLAG?
YELLOW FLAG
THUD

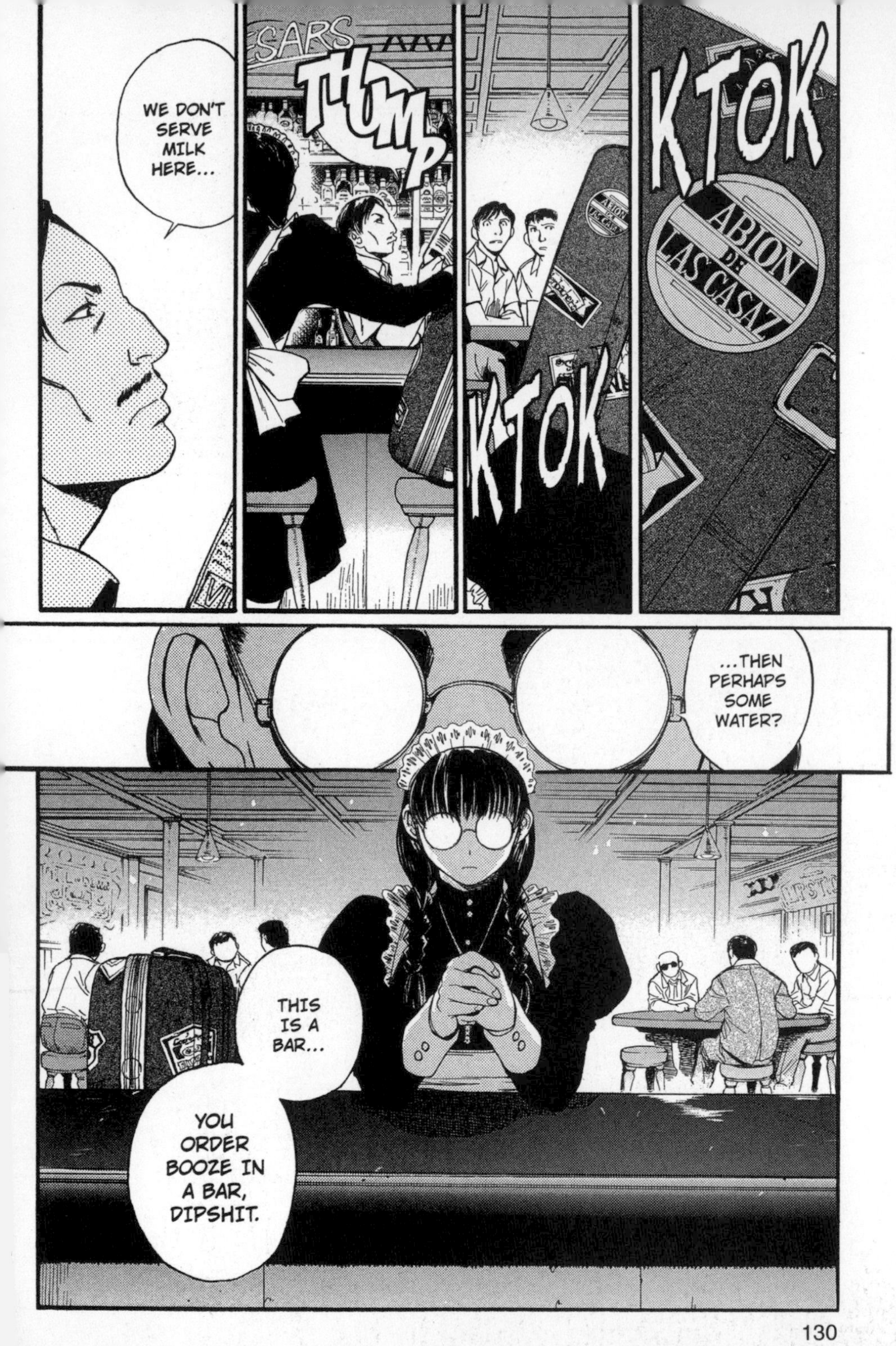
KTOK
ABION DE LAS CASAZ
KTOK
THUMP
WE DON'T SERVE MILK HERE...
...THEN PERHAPS SOME WATER?
THIS IS A BAR...
YOU ORDER BOOZE IN A BAR, DIPSHIT.

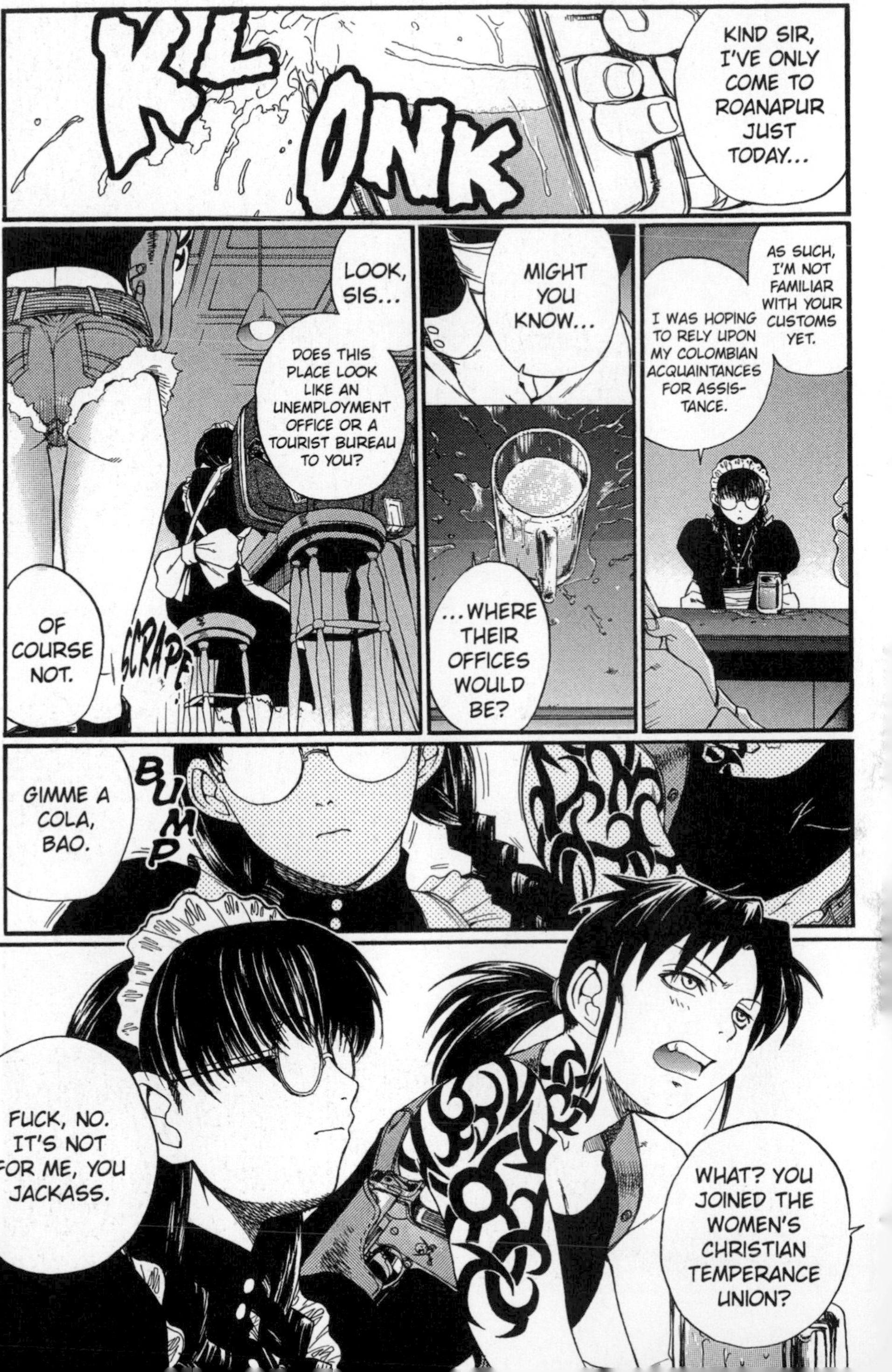
KIND SIR, I'VE ONLY COME TO ROANAPUR JUST TODAY...
KL
ONK
AS SUCH, I'M NOT FAMILIAR WITH YOUR CUSTOMS YET.
I WAS HOPING TO RELY UPON MY COLOMBIAN ACQUAINTANCES FOR ASSISTANCE.
MIGHT YOU KNOW...
...WHERE THEIR OFFICES WOULD BE?
LOOK, SIS...
DOES THIS PLACE LOOK LIKE AN UNEMPLOYMENT OFFICE OR A TOURIST BUREAU TO YOU?
OF COURSE NOT.
SCRAPE
BUMP
GIMME A COLA, BAO.
WHAT? YOU JOINED THE WOMEN'S CHRISTIAN TEMPERANCE UNION?
FUCK, NO. IT'S NOT FOR ME, YOU JACKASS.

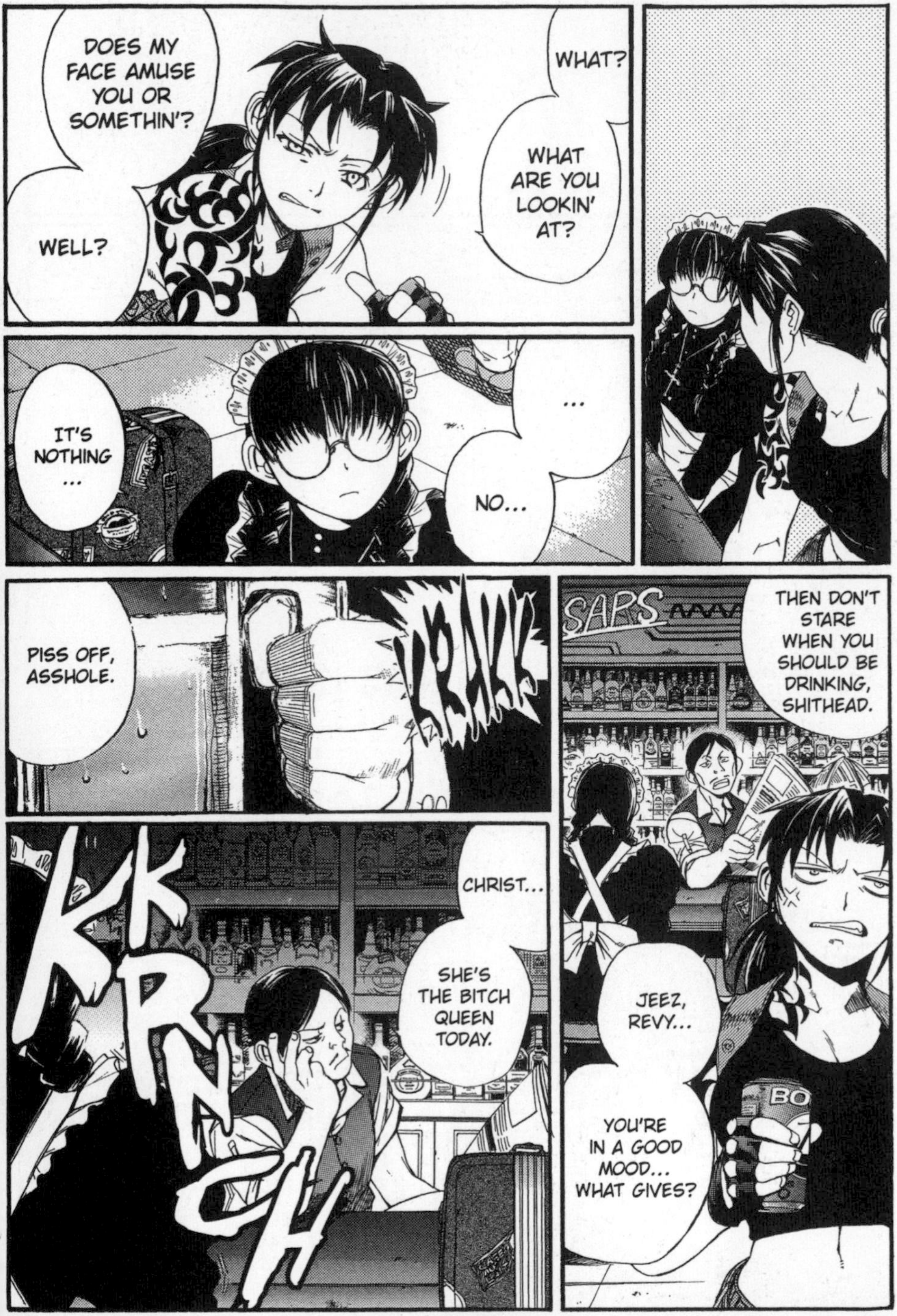
WHAT?
WHAT ARE YOU LOOKIN' AT?
DOES MY FACE AMUSE YOU OR SOMETHIN'?
WELL?
...
NO...
IT'S NOTHING ...
THEN DON'T STARE WHEN YOU SHOULD BE DRINKING, SHITHEAD.
SARS
JEEZ, REVY...
YOU'RE IN A GOOD MOOD... WHAT GIVES?
KRAKK
PISS OFF, ASSHOLE.
CHRIST...
SHE'S THE BITCH QUEEN TODAY.
KKRNCH

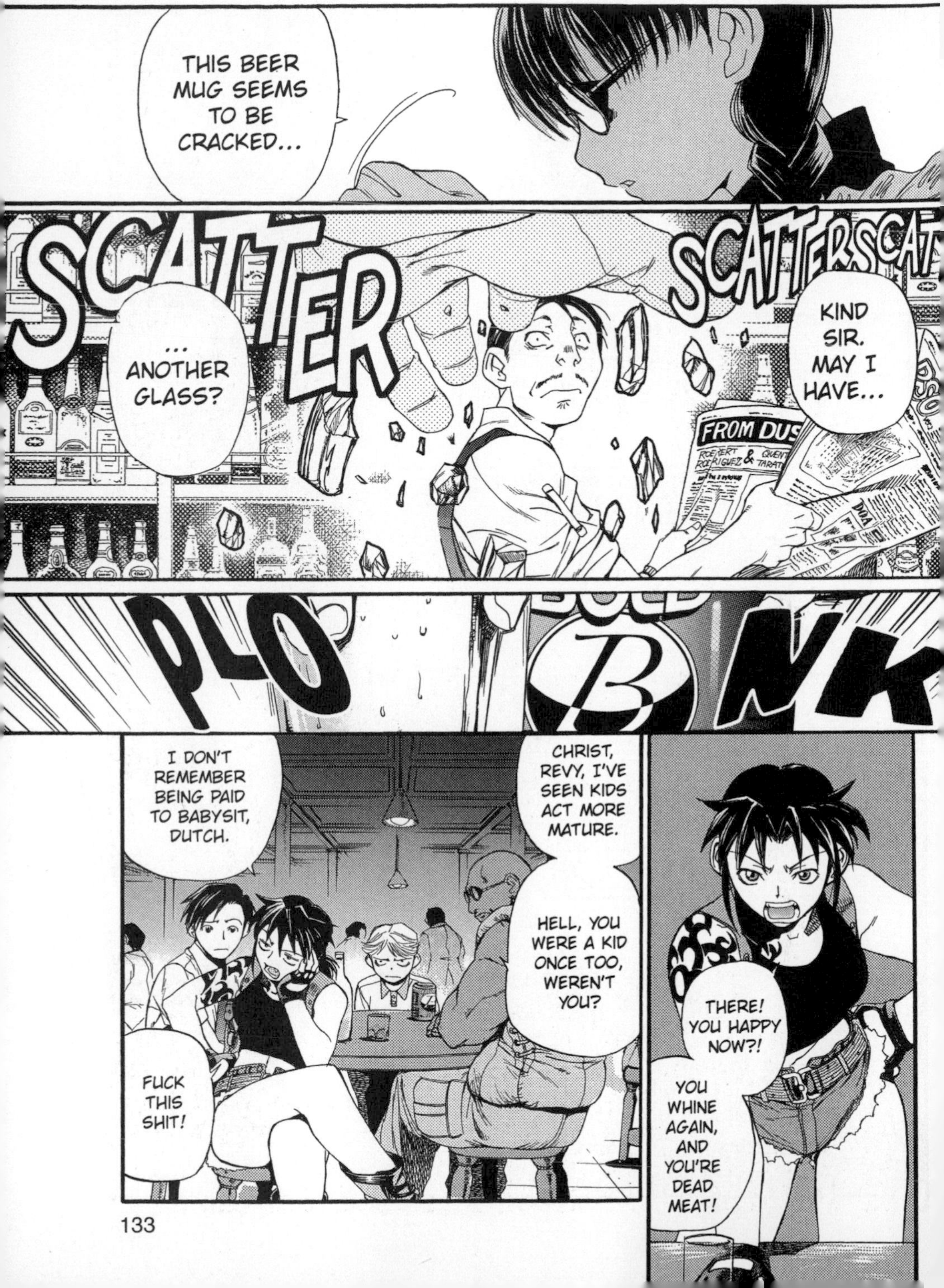
THIS BEER MUG SEEMS TO BE CRACKED...
SCATTERSCAT
KIND SIR. MAY I HAVE...
... ANOTHER GLASS?
SCATTER
PLO
NK
THERE! YOU HAPPY NOW?!
YOU WHINE AGAIN, AND YOU'RE DEAD MEAT!
CHRIST, REVY, I'VE SEEN KIDS ACT MORE MATURE.
HELL, YOU WERE A KID ONCE TOO, WEREN'T YOU?
I DON'T REMEMBER BEING PAID TO BABYSIT, DUTCH.
FUCK THIS SHIT!

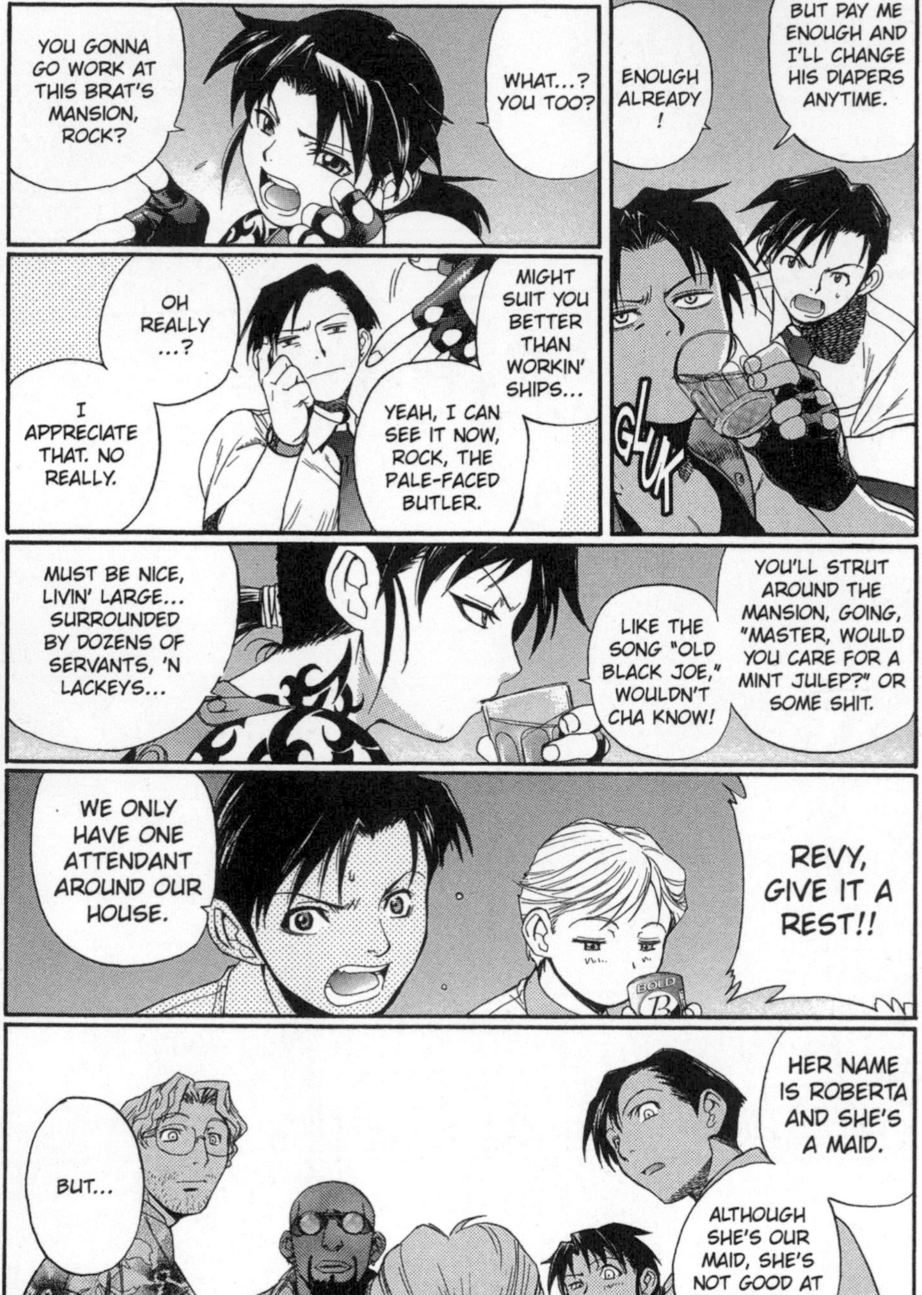
BUT PAY ME ENOUGH AND I'LL CHANGE HIS DIAPERS ANYTIME.
ENOUGH ALREADY!
GLUK
WHAT...? YOU TOO?
YOU GONNA GO WORK AT THIS BRAT'S MANSION, ROCK?
MIGHT SUIT YOU BETTER THAN WORKIN' SHIPS...
YEAH, I CAN SEE IT NOW, ROCK, THE PALE-FACED BUTLER.
OH REALLY ...?
I APPRECIATE THAT. NO REALLY.
YOU'LL STRUT AROUND THE MANSION, GOING, "MASTER, WOULD YOU CARE FOR A MINT JULEP?" OR SOME SHIT.
LIKE THE SONG "OLD BLACK JOE," WOULDN'T CHA KNOW!
MUST BE NICE, LIVIN' LARGE... SURROUNDED BY DOZENS OF SERVANTS, 'N LACKEYS...
REVY, GIVE IT A REST!!
WE ONLY HAVE ONE ATTENDANT AROUND OUR HOUSE.
HER NAME IS ROBERTA AND SHE'S A MAID.
ALTHOUGH SHE'S OUR MAID, SHE'S NOT GOOD AT COOKING OR CLEANING.
BUT...

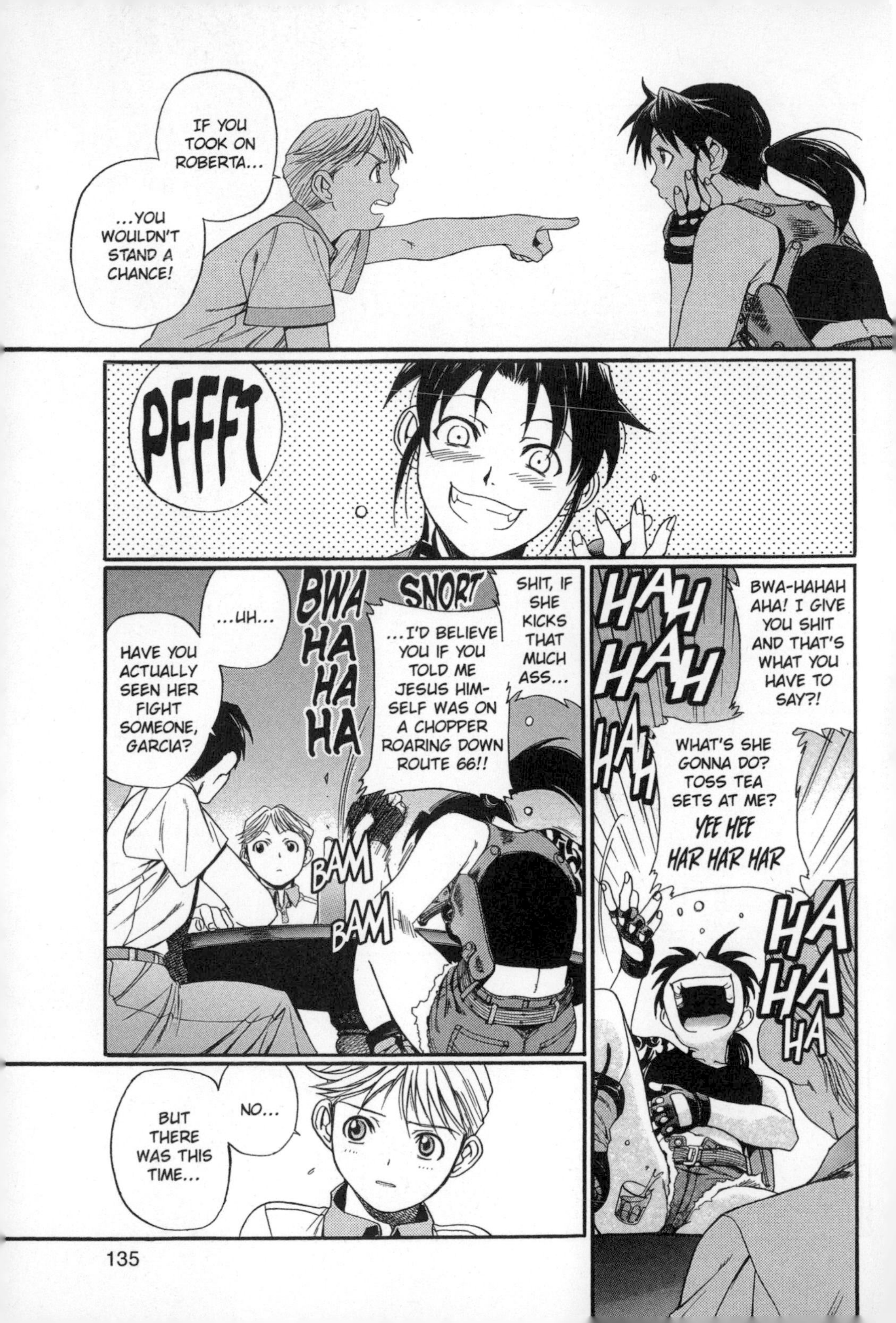

IF YOU TOOK ON ROBERTA...
...YOU WOULDN'T STAND A CHANCE!
PFFFT
BWA-HAHAH AHA! I GIVE YOU SHIT AND THAT'S WHAT YOU HAVE TO SAY?!
HAH HAH HAH HAH
WHAT'S SHE GONNA DO? TOSS TEA SETS AT ME?
YEE HEE HAR HAR HAR
HA HA HA HA HA
SHIT, IF SHE KICKS THAT MUCH ASS...
SNORT
...I'D BELIEVE YOU IF YOU TOLD ME JESUS HIM-SELF WAS ON A CHOPPER ROARING DOWN ROUTE 66!!
BWA HA HA HA HA
...UH...
HAVE YOU ACTUALLY SEEN HER FIGHT SOMEONE, GARCIA?
BAM
BAM
NO...
BUT THERE WAS THIS TIME...

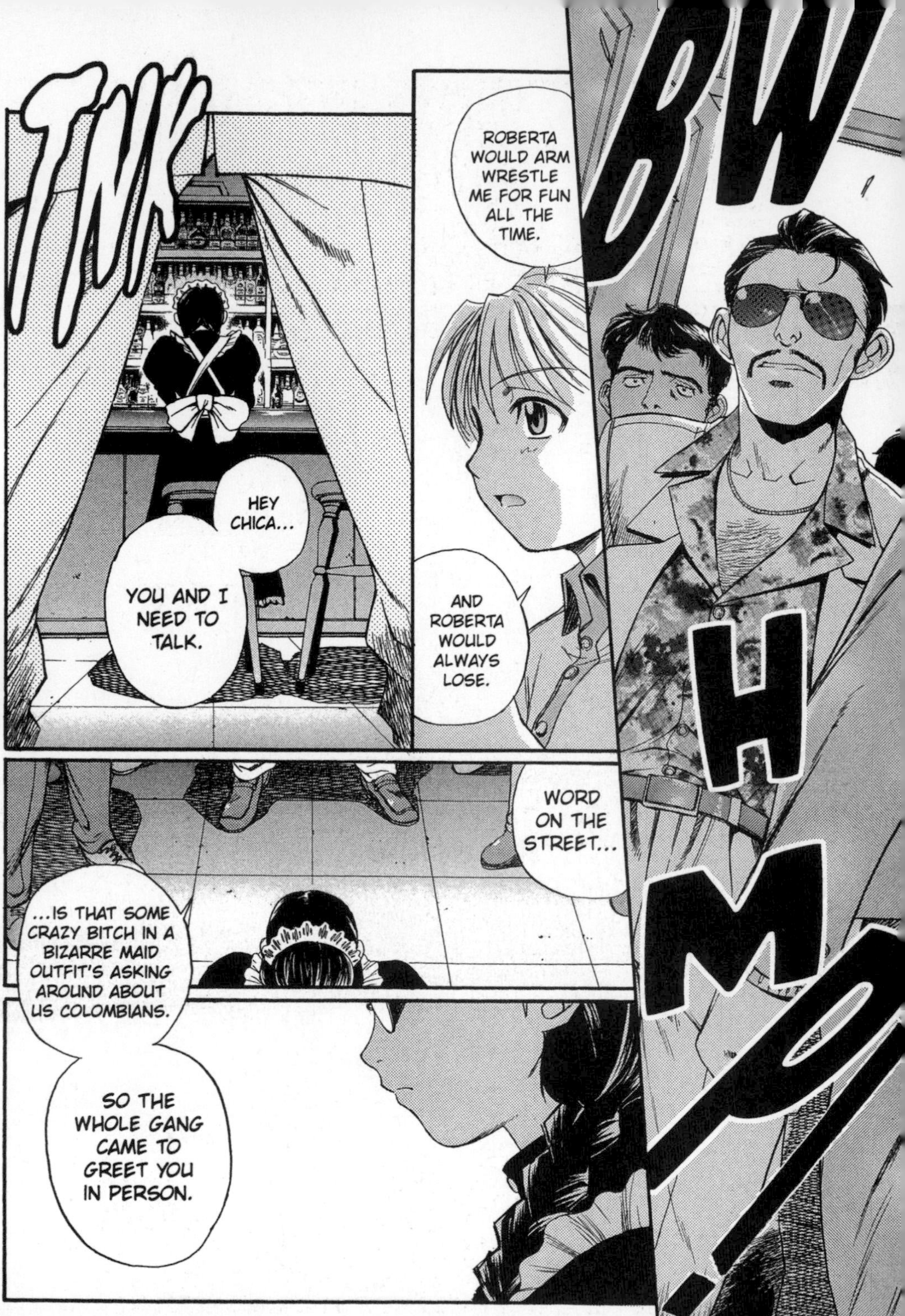
BWHM
ROBERTA WOULD ARM WRESTLE ME FOR FUN ALL THE TIME.
AND ROBERTA WOULD ALWAYS LOSE.
TINK
HEY CHICA...
YOU AND I NEED TO TALK.
WORD ON THE STREET...
...IS THAT SOME CRAZY BITCH IN A BIZARRE MAID OUTFIT'S ASKING AROUND ABOUT US COLOMBIANS.
SO THE WHOLE GANG CAME TO GREET YOU IN PERSON.

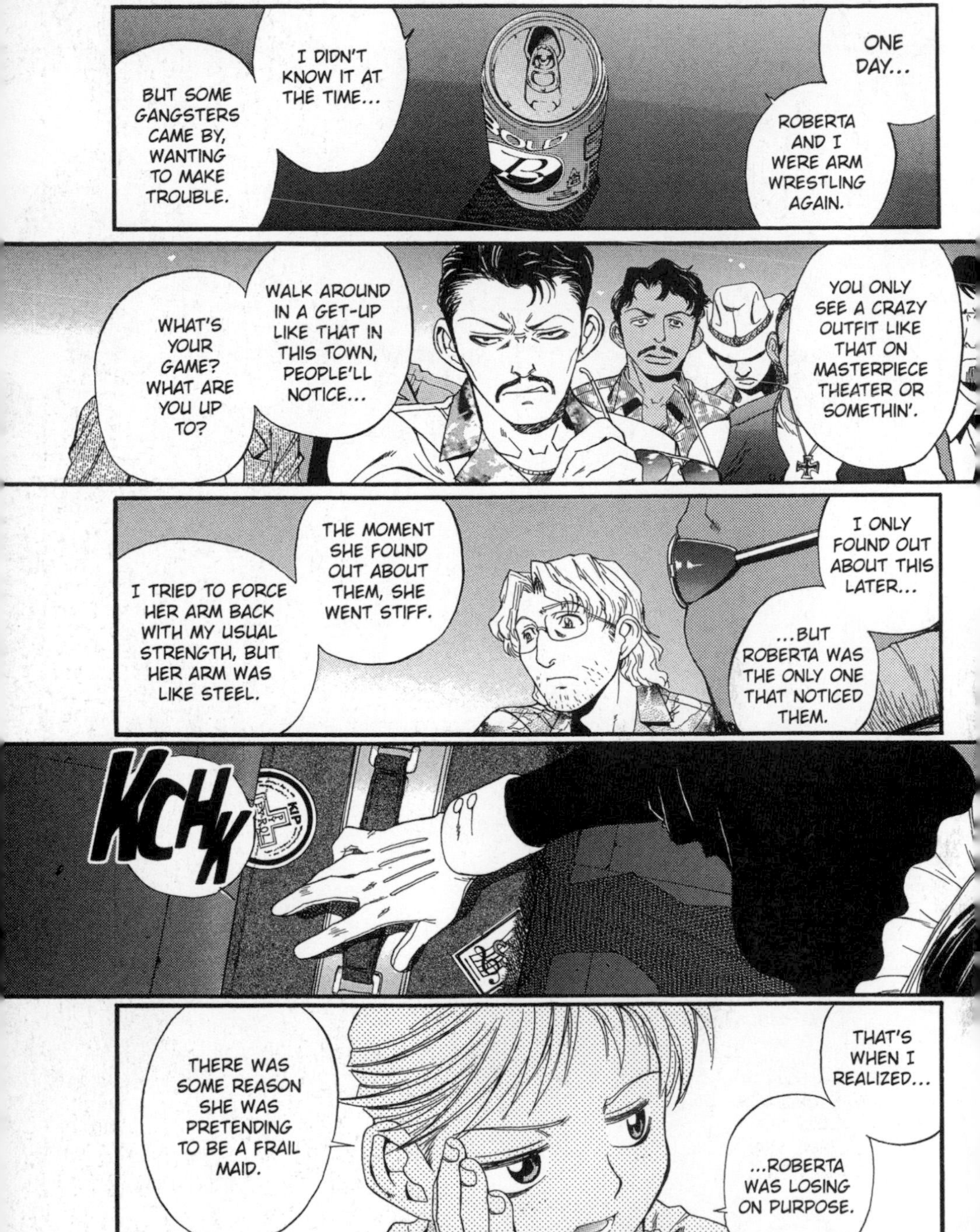
ONE DAY...
ROBERTA AND I WERE ARM WRESTLING AGAIN.
I DIDN'T KNOW IT AT THE TIME...
BUT SOME GANGSTERS CAME BY, WANTING TO MAKE TROUBLE.
YOU ONLY SEE A CRAZY OUTFIT LIKE THAT ON MASTERPIECE THEATER OR SOMETHIN'.
WALK AROUND IN A GET-UP LIKE THAT IN THIS TOWN, PEOPLE'LL NOTICE...
WHAT'S YOUR GAME? WHAT ARE YOU UP TO?
I ONLY FOUND OUT ABOUT THIS LATER...
...BUT ROBERTA WAS THE ONLY ONE THAT NOTICED THEM.
THE MOMENT SHE FOUND OUT ABOUT THEM, SHE WENT STIFF.
I TRIED TO FORCE HER ARM BACK WITH MY USUAL STRENGTH, BUT HER ARM WAS LIKE STEEL.
KCHK
THAT'S WHEN I REALIZED...
...ROBERTA WAS LOSING ON PURPOSE.
THERE WAS SOME REASON SHE WAS PRETENDING TO BE A FRAIL MAID.

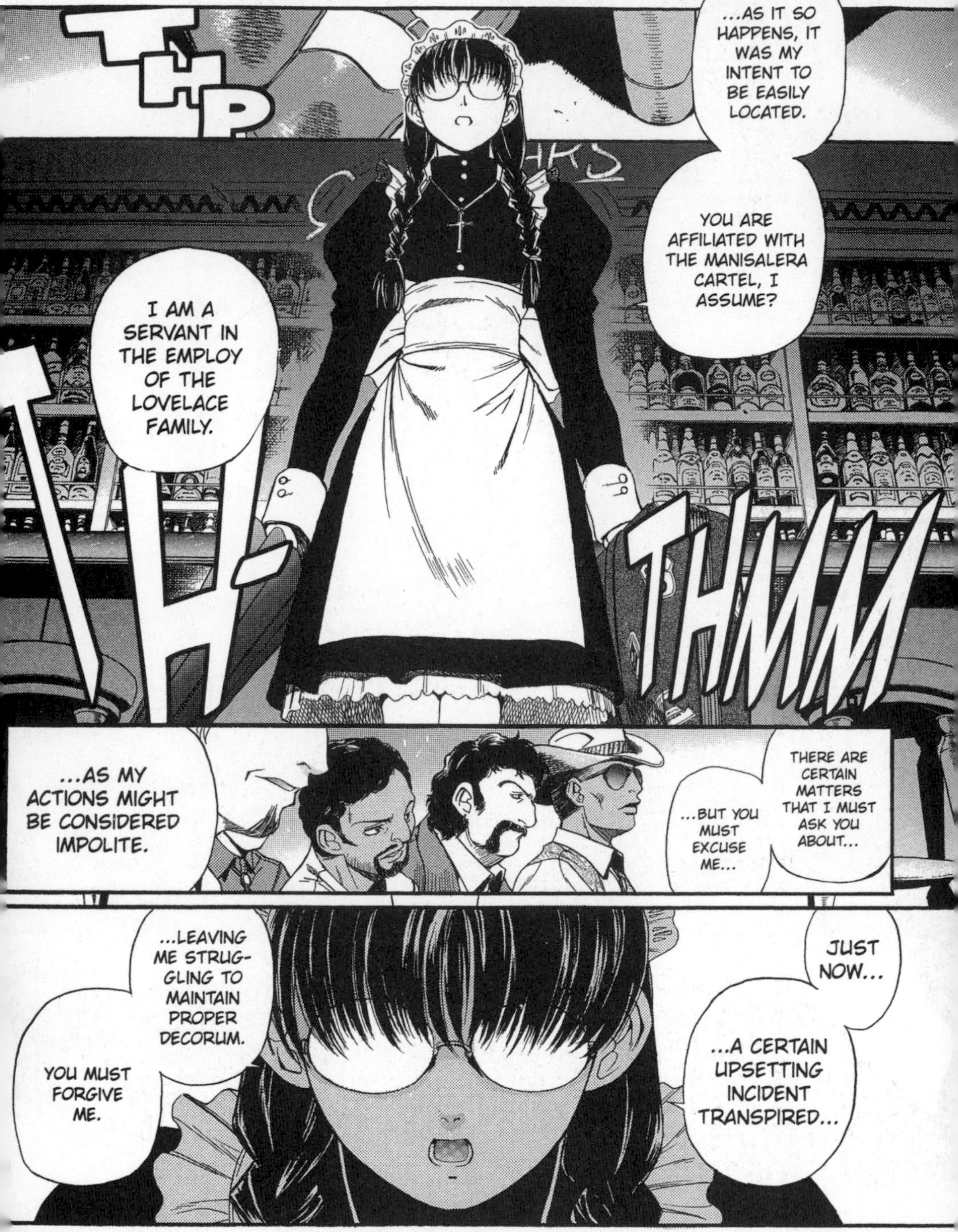
THP
...AS IT SO HAPPENS, IT WAS MY INTENT TO BE EASILY LOCATED.
YOU ARE AFFILIATED WITH THE MANISALERA CARTEL, I ASSUME?
I AM A SERVANT IN THE EMPLOY OF THE LOVELACE FAMILY.
THMM
THERE ARE CERTAIN MATTERS THAT I MUST ASK YOU ABOUT...
...BUT YOU MUST EXCUSE ME...
...AS MY ACTIONS MIGHT BE CONSIDERED IMPOLITE.
JUST NOW...
...A CERTAIN UPSETTING INCIDENT TRANSPIRED...
...LEAVING ME STRUG-GLING TO MAINTAIN PROPER DECORUM.
YOU MUST FORGIVE ME.

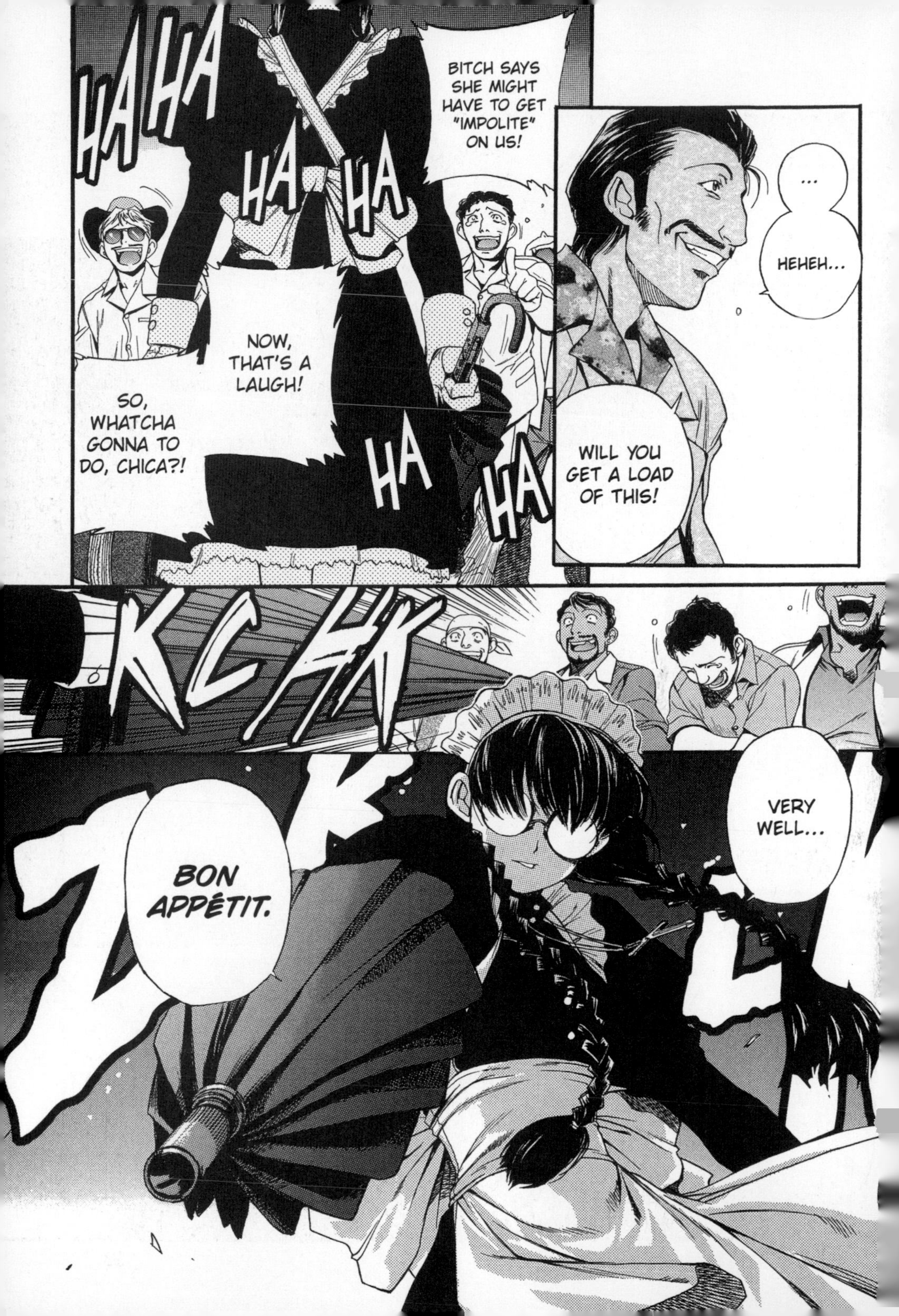
...
HEHEH...
WILL YOU GET A LOAD OF THIS!
BITCH SAYS SHE MIGHT HAVE TO GET "IMPOLITE" ON US!
HA HA HA
HA HA
NOW, THAT'S A LAUGH!
SO, WHATCHA GONNA TO DO, CHICA?!
HA HA
KCHK
VERY WELL...
BON APPÊTIT.

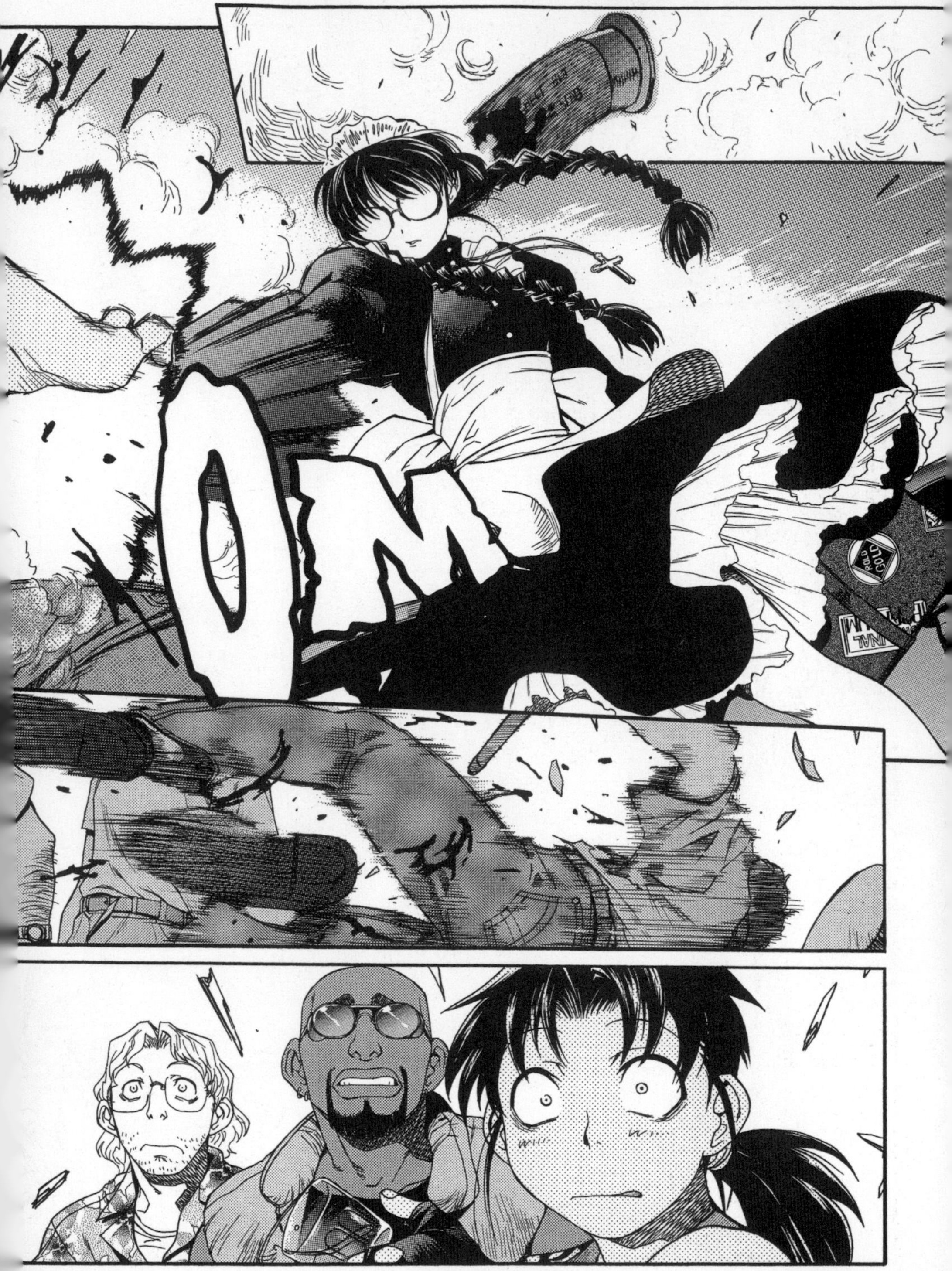
OM

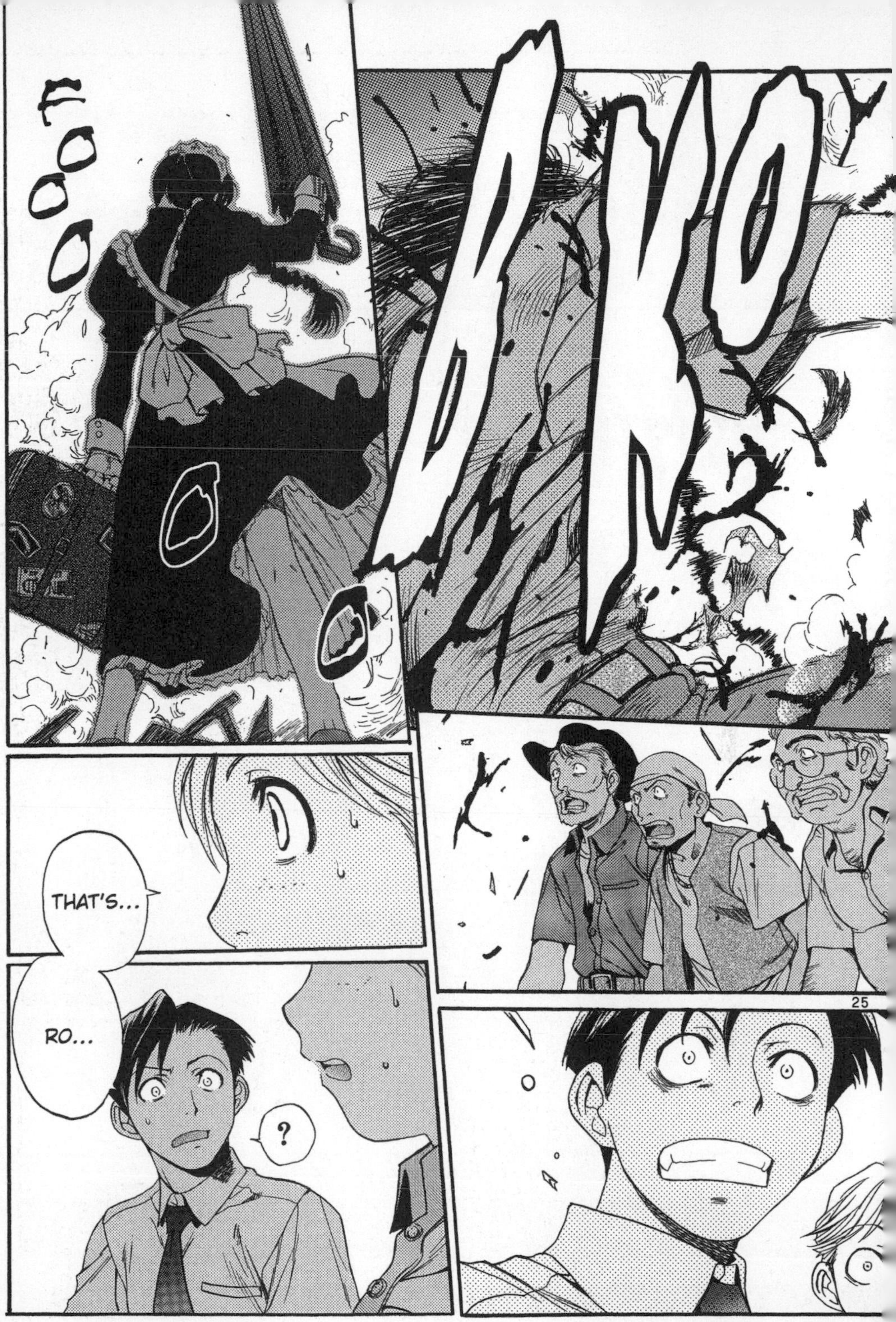
DKO
FOOO
THAT'S...
RO...
?
25

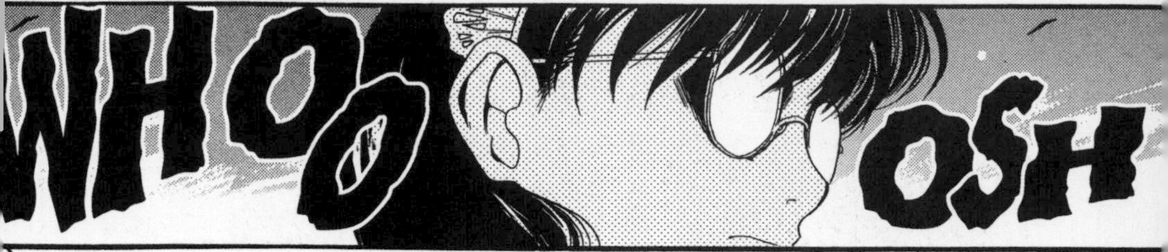
WHOO
OSH

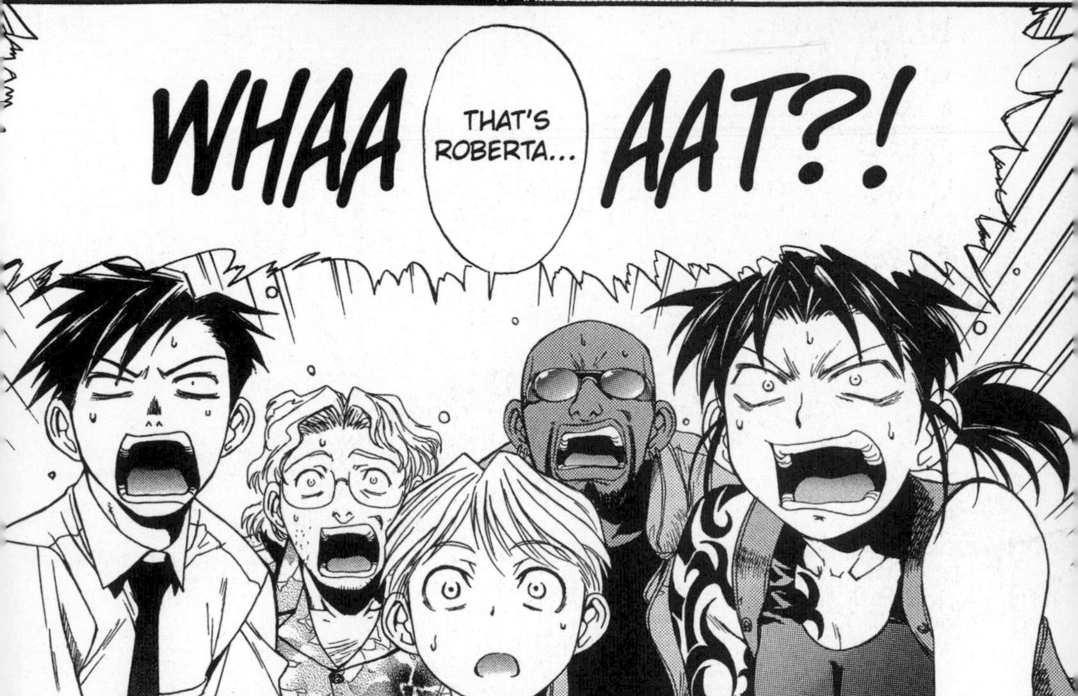
THAT'S ROBERTA...
WHAA
AAT?!

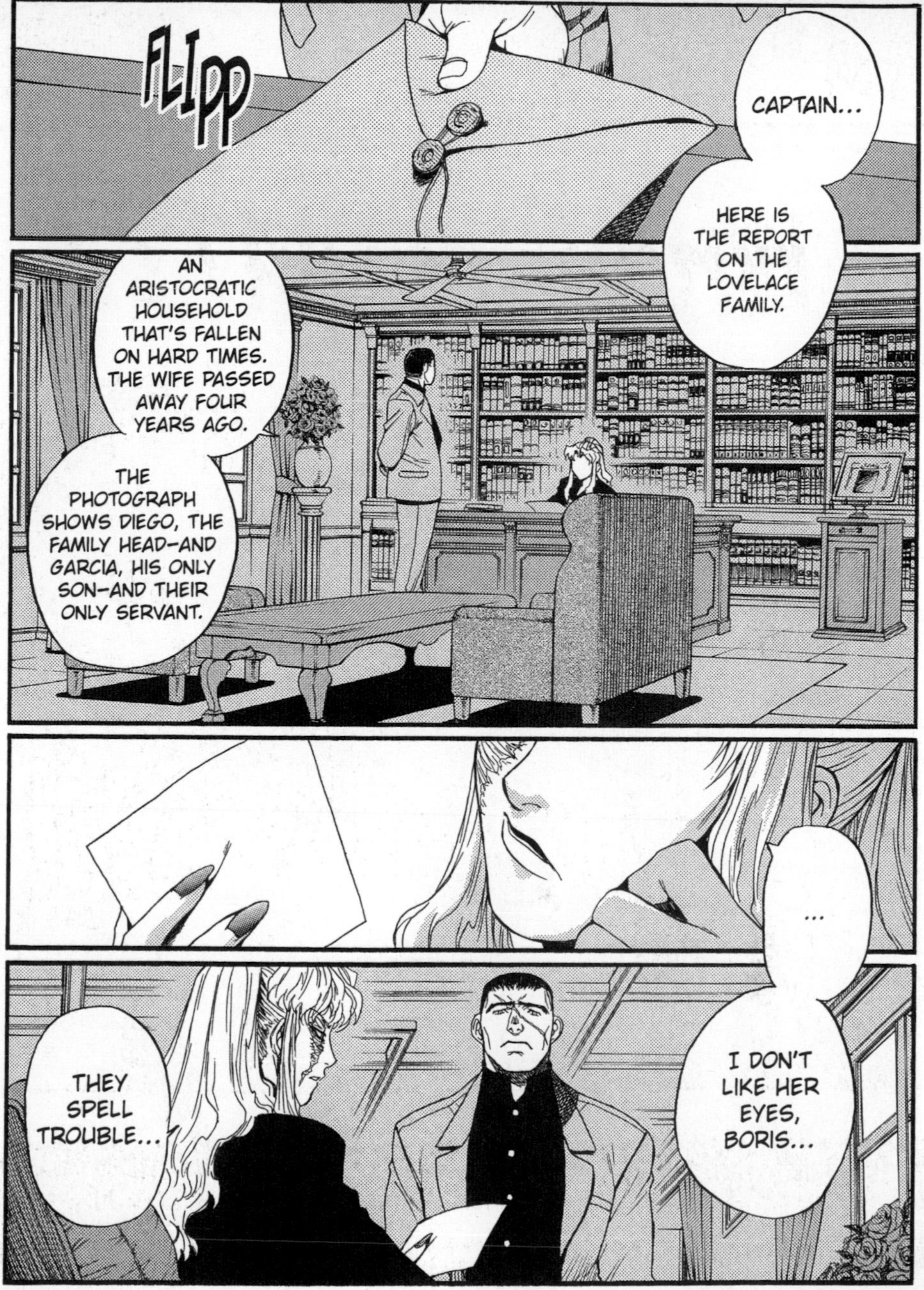
CAPTAIN...
FLIPP
HERE IS THE REPORT ON THE LOVELACE FAMILY.
AN ARISTOCRATIC HOUSEHOLD THAT'S FALLEN ON HARD TIMES. THE WIFE PASSED AWAY FOUR YEARS AGO.
THE PHOTOGRAPH SHOWS DIEGO, THE FAMILY HEAD—AND GARCIA, HIS ONLY SON—AND THEIR ONLY SERVANT.
...
I DON'T LIKE HER EYES, BORIS...
THEY SPELL TROUBLE...

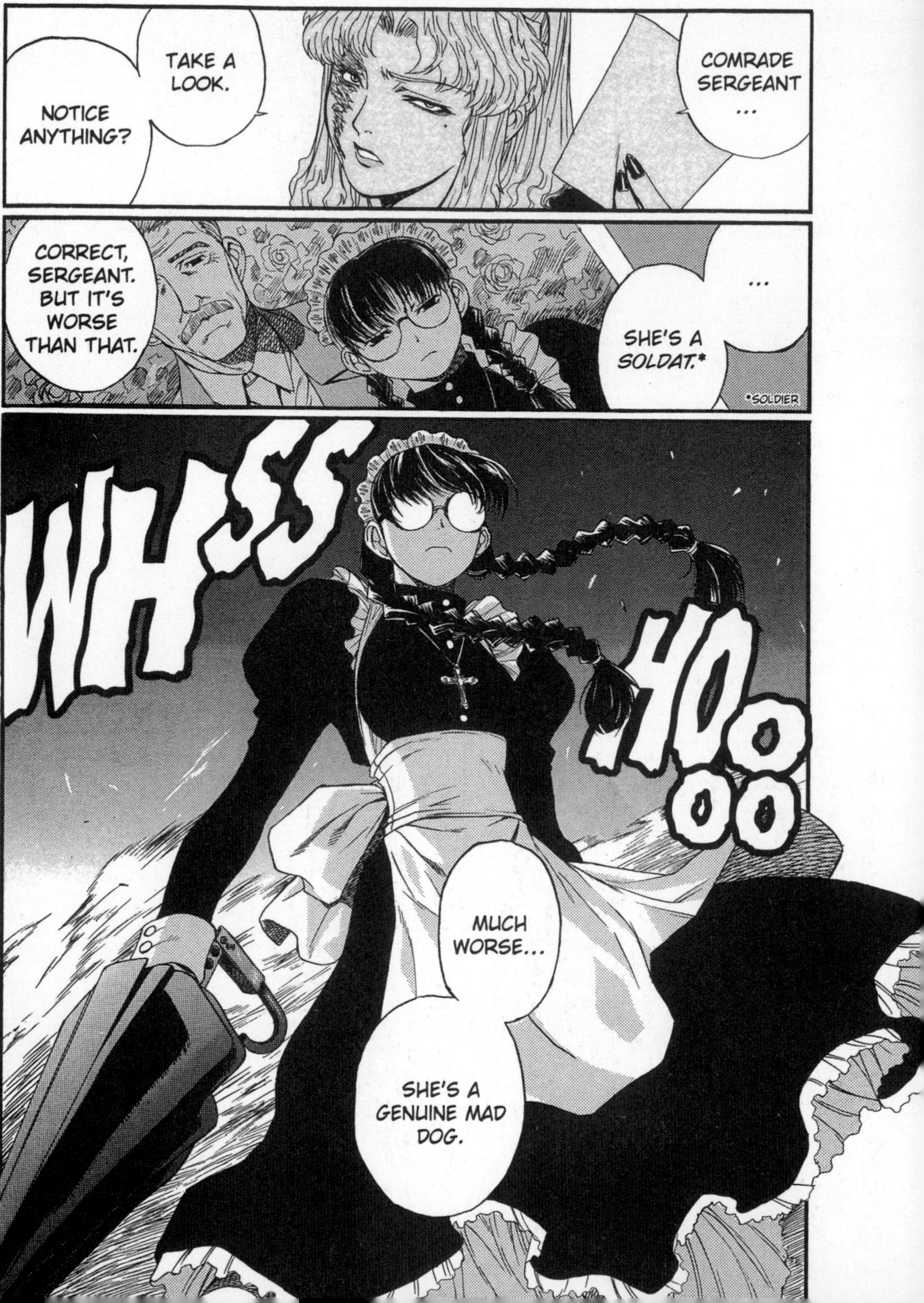
COMRADE SERGEANT ...
TAKE A LOOK.
NOTICE ANYTHING?
...
SHE'S A SOLDAT.*
*SOLDIER
CORRECT, SERGEANT. BUT IT'S WORSE THAN THAT.
WHSS
HOOOO
MUCH WORSE...
SHE'S A GENUINE MAD DOG.

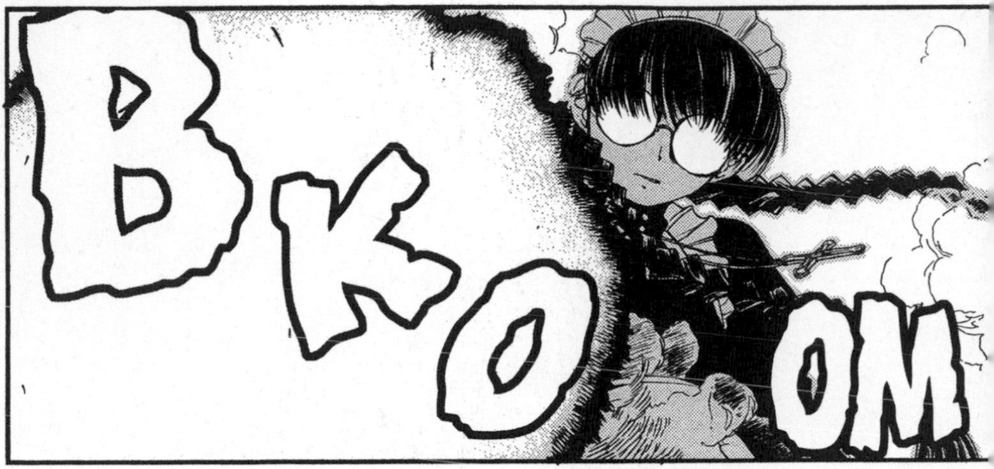
BKOOM

Chapter 3: Rasta Blasta - Part II

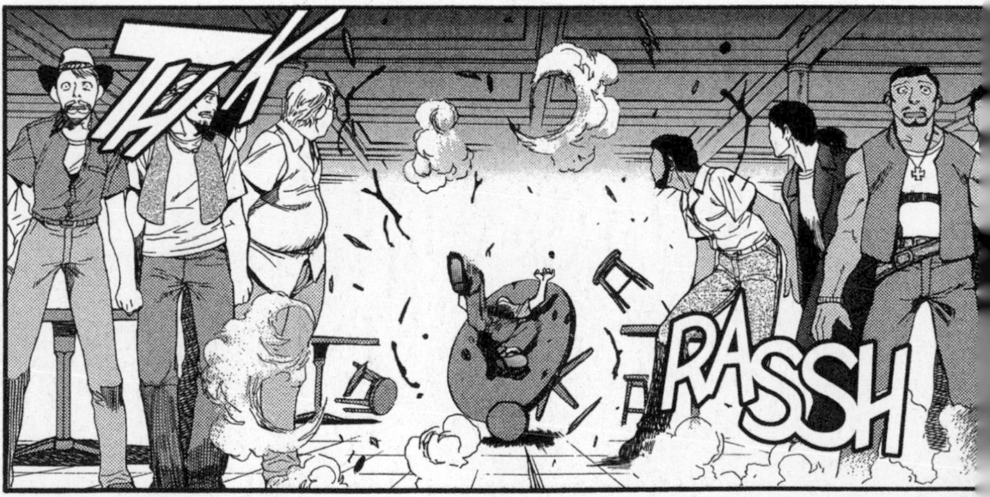
THK
RASSH

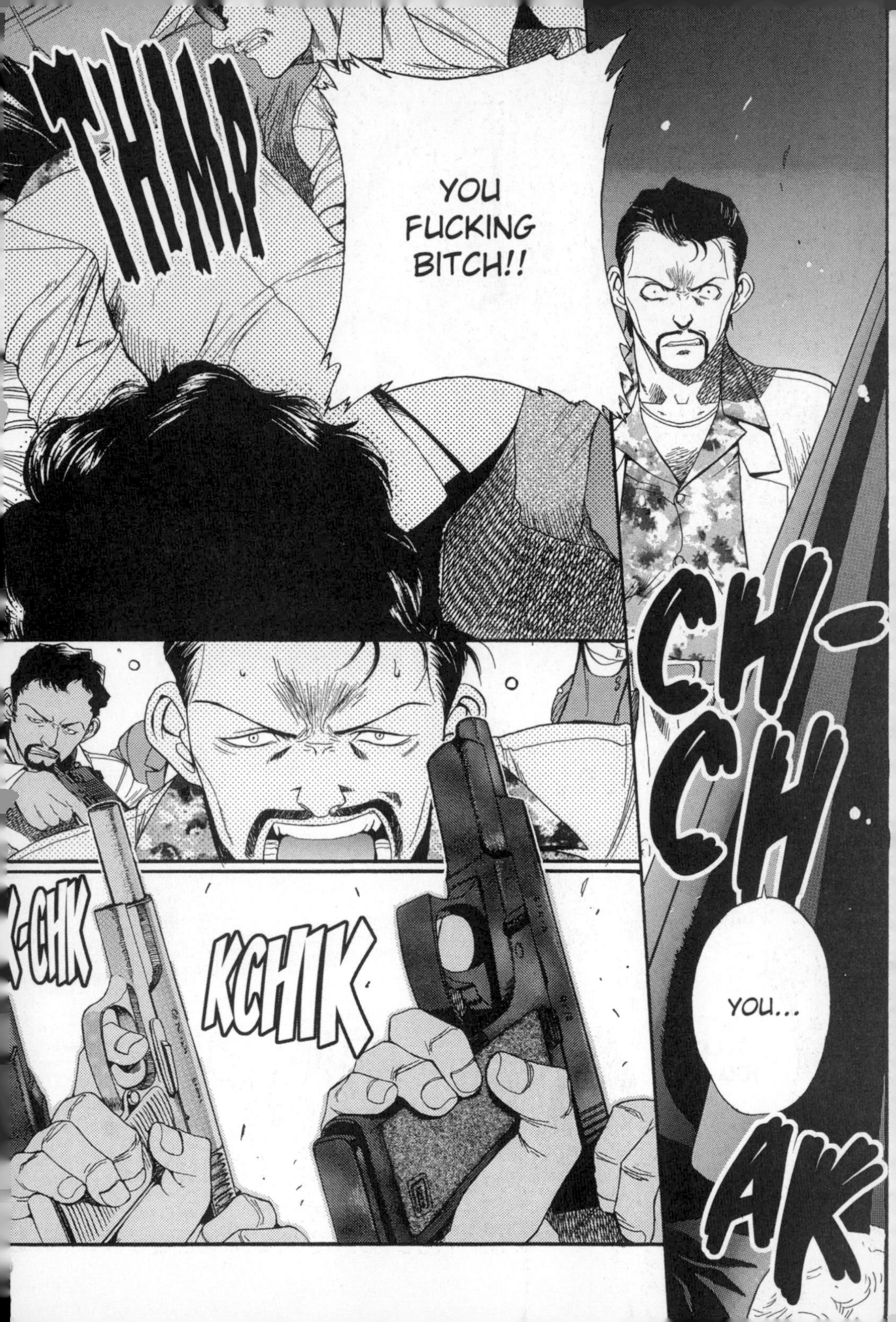
THMP
YOU FUCKING BITCH!!
CH-CH-
AK
YOU...
KCHIK
-CHIK

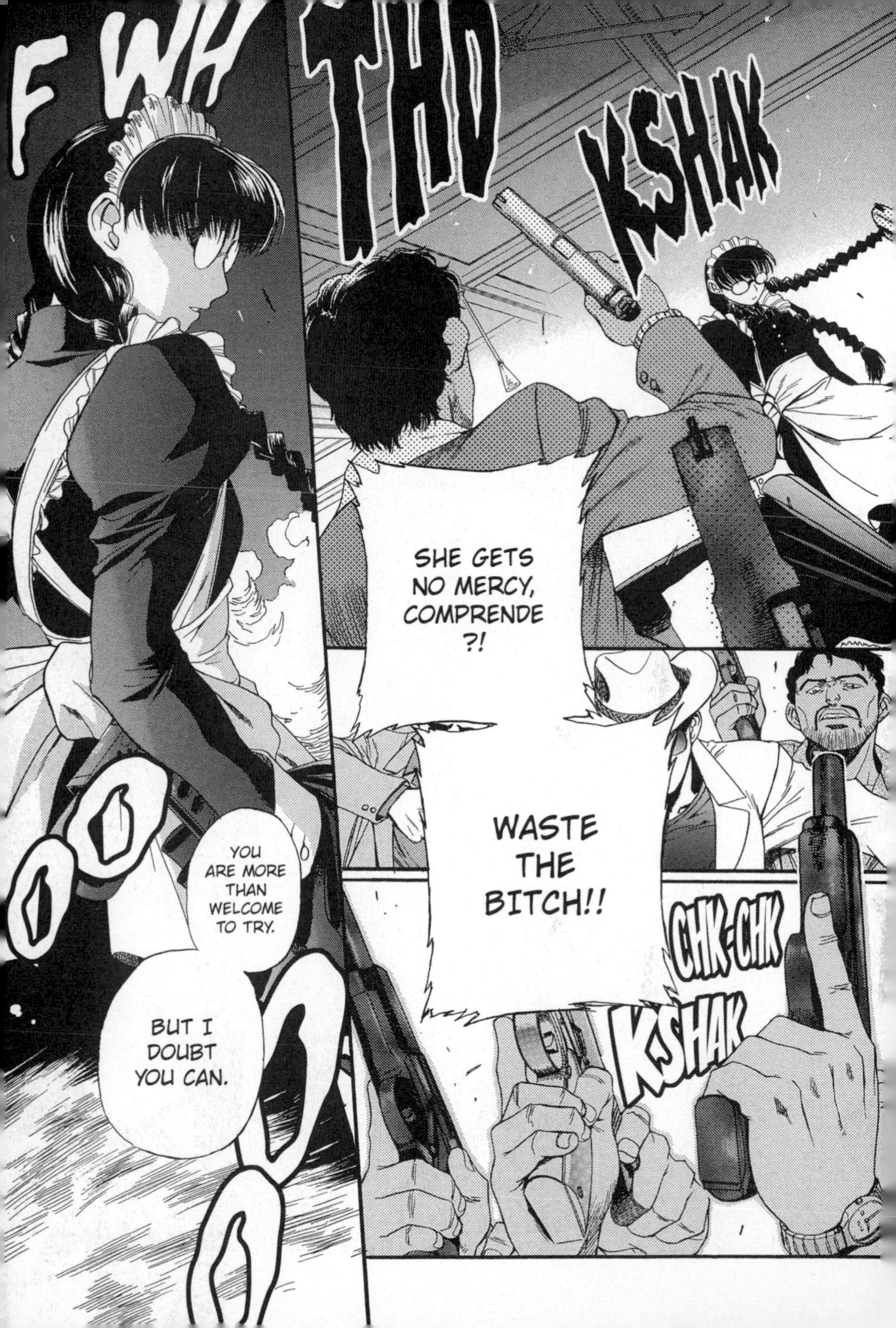
KSHAK
THD
SHE GETS NO MERCY, COMPRENDE ?!
WASTE THE BITCH!!
CHK-CHK
KSHAK
F WH
YOU ARE MORE THAN WELCOME TO TRY.
BUT I DOUBT YOU CAN.

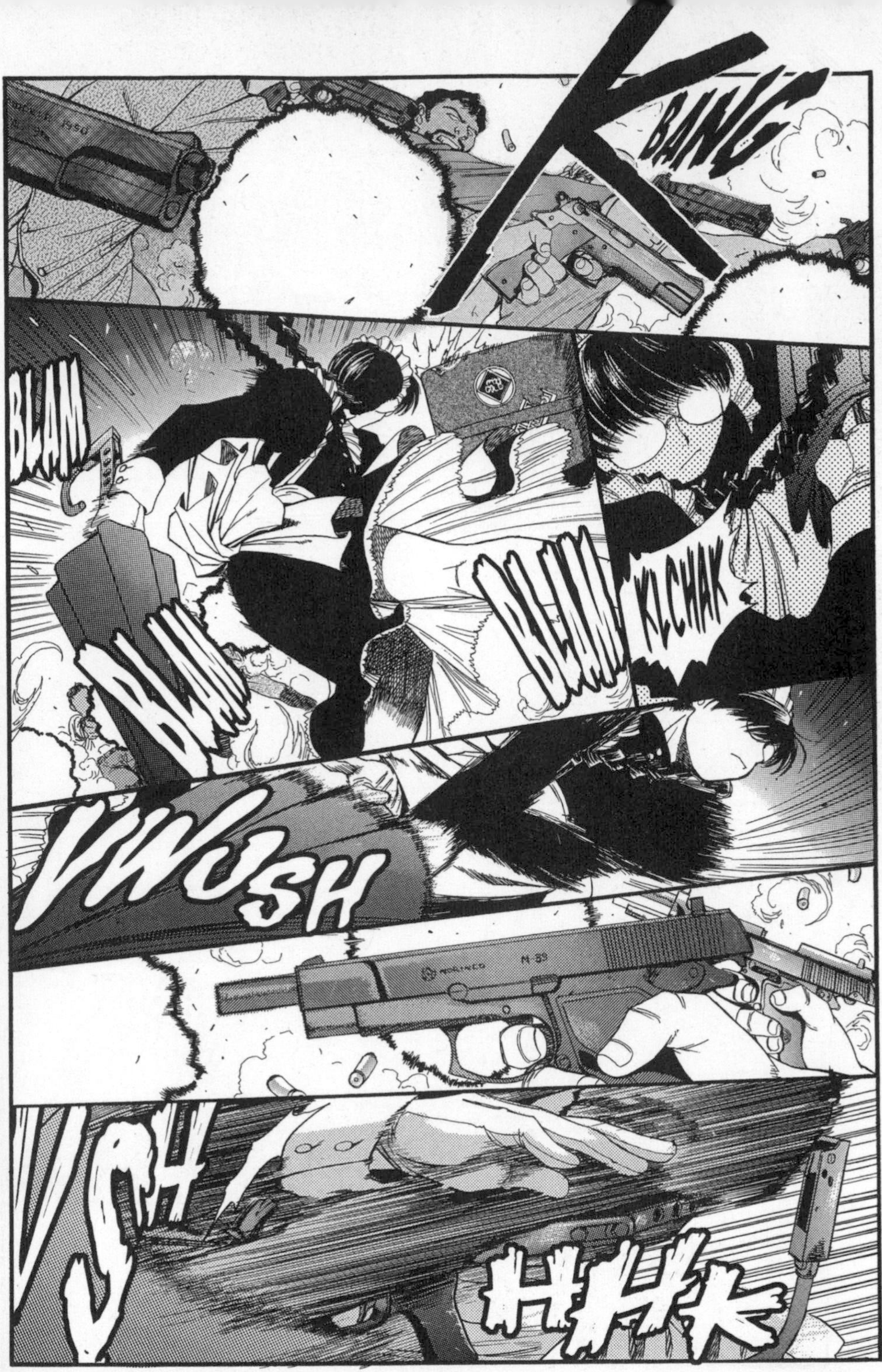
KBANG
KLCHAK
BLAM
BLAM
BLAM
VWUSH
HHK
VSH

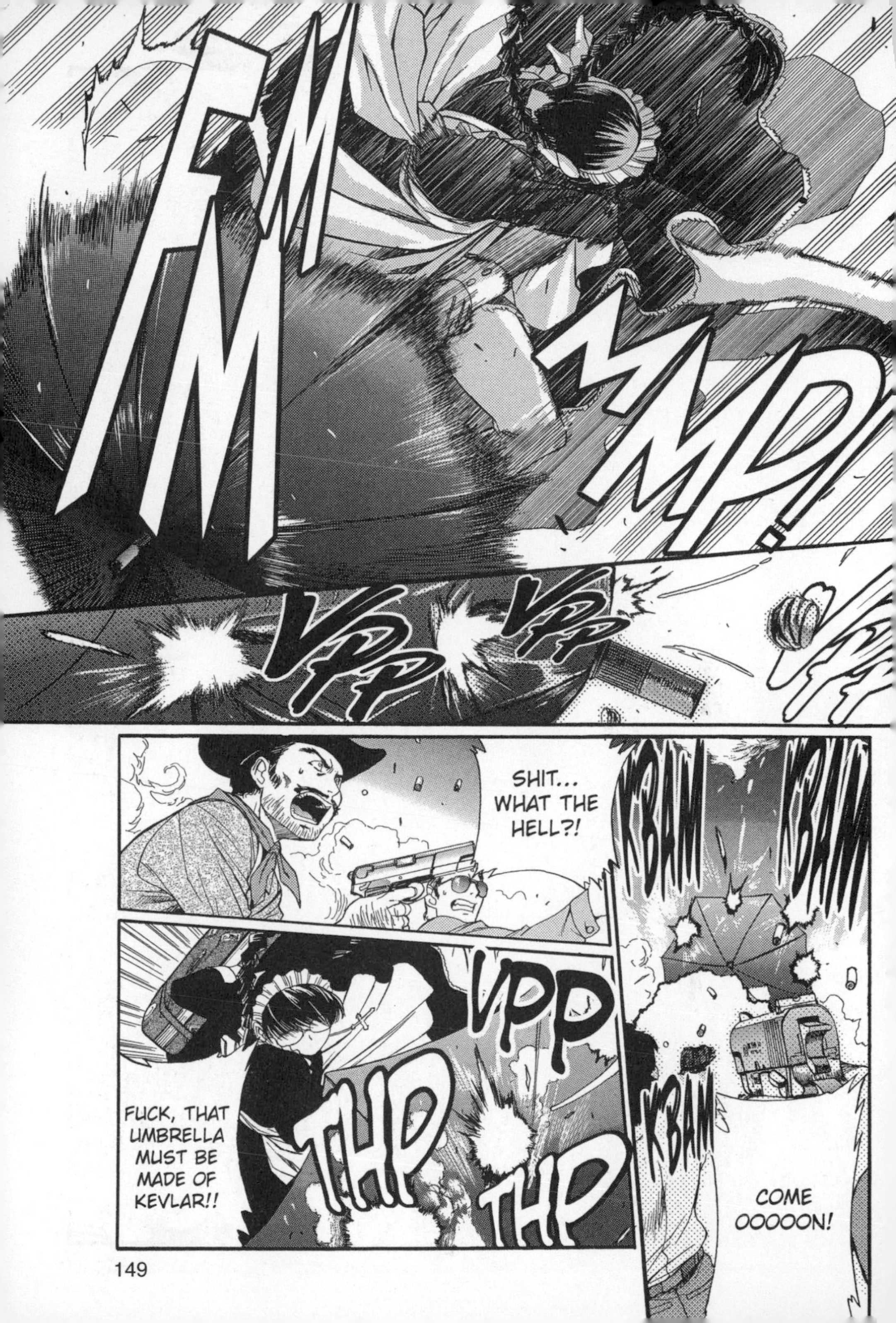
FMMMMP!
VPP
VPP
KBAM
KBAM
KBAM
COME OOOOON!
SHIT... WHAT THE HELL?!
VPP
THP
THP
FUCK, THAT UMBRELLA MUST BE MADE OF KEVLAR!!

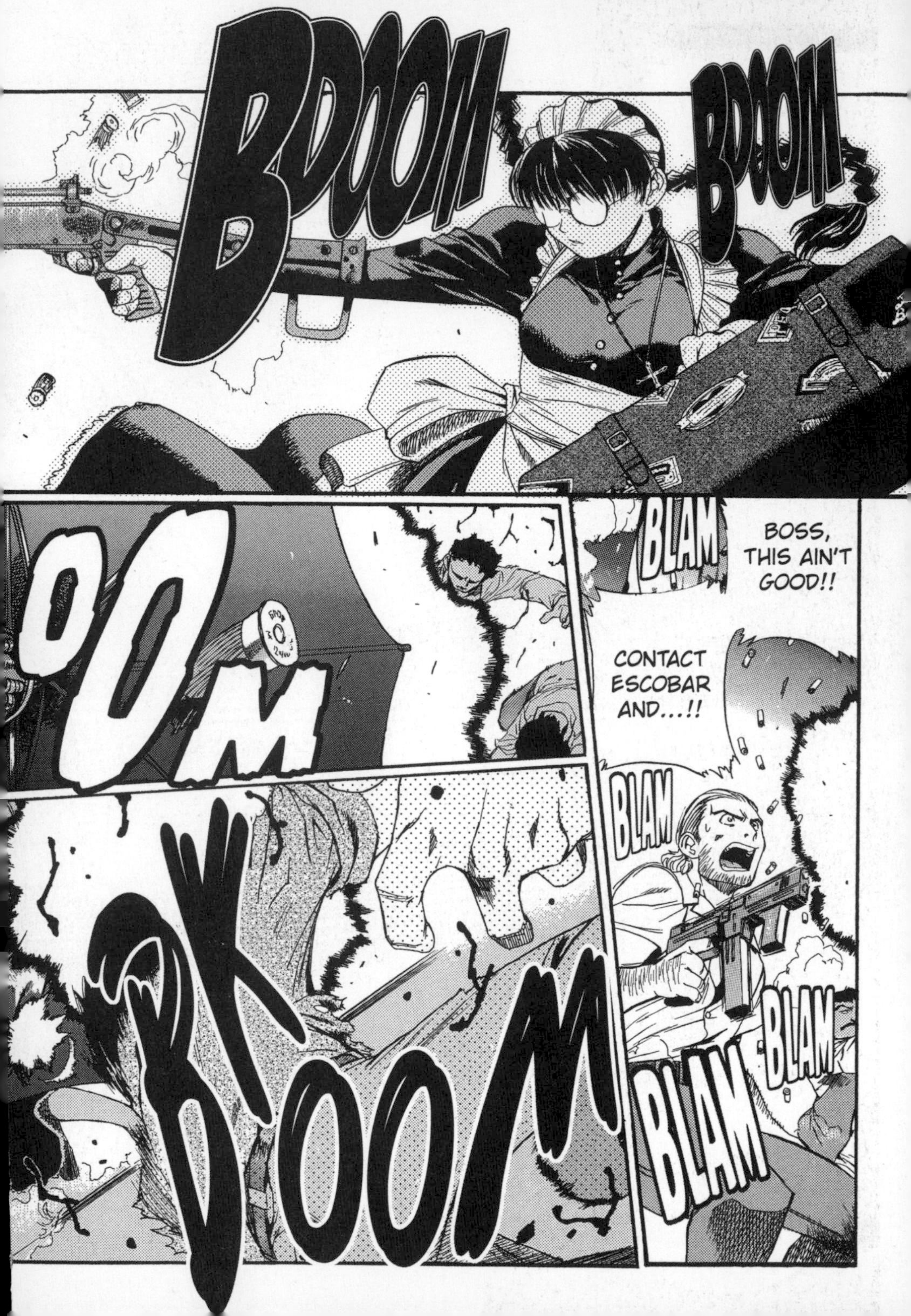
BDOOM
BDOOM
BLAM
BOSS, THIS AIN'T GOOD!!
CONTACT ESCOBAR AND...!!
BLAM
BLAM
BLAM
BLAM
OOM
BOOM

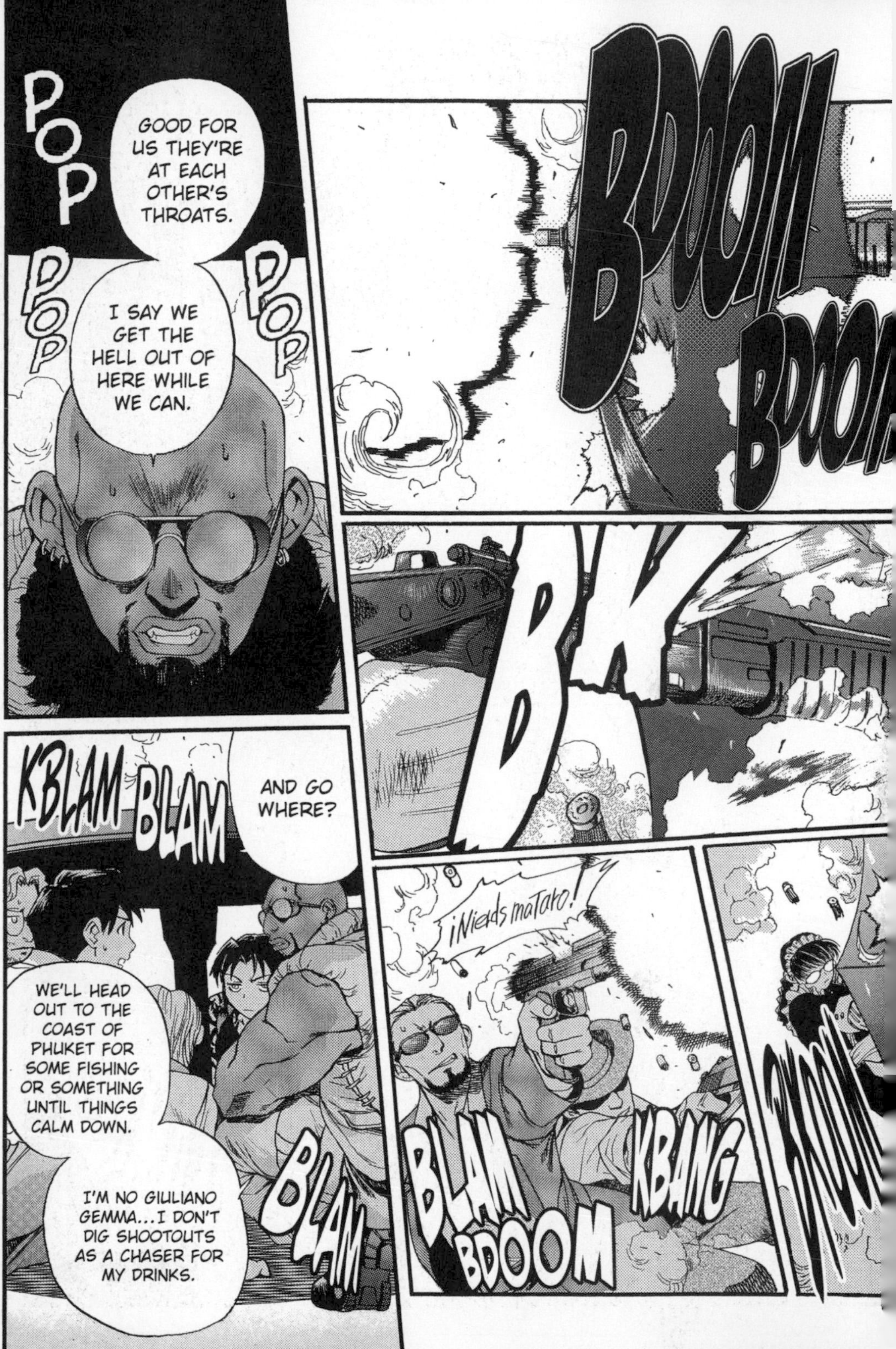
BDOOM
BDOOM
BK
POP
POP
POP
POP
GOOD FOR US THEY'RE AT EACH OTHER'S THROATS.
I SAY WE GET THE HELL OUT OF HERE WHILE WE CAN.
¡Nieads mataro!
KBANG
BLAM
BDOOM
KBLAM
BLAM
AND GO WHERE?
WE'LL HEAD OUT TO THE COAST OF PHUKET FOR SOME FISHING OR SOMETHING UNTIL THINGS CALM DOWN.
BLAM
BLAM
I'M NO GIULIANO GEMMA...I DON'T DIG SHOOTOUTS AS A CHASER FOR MY DRINKS.

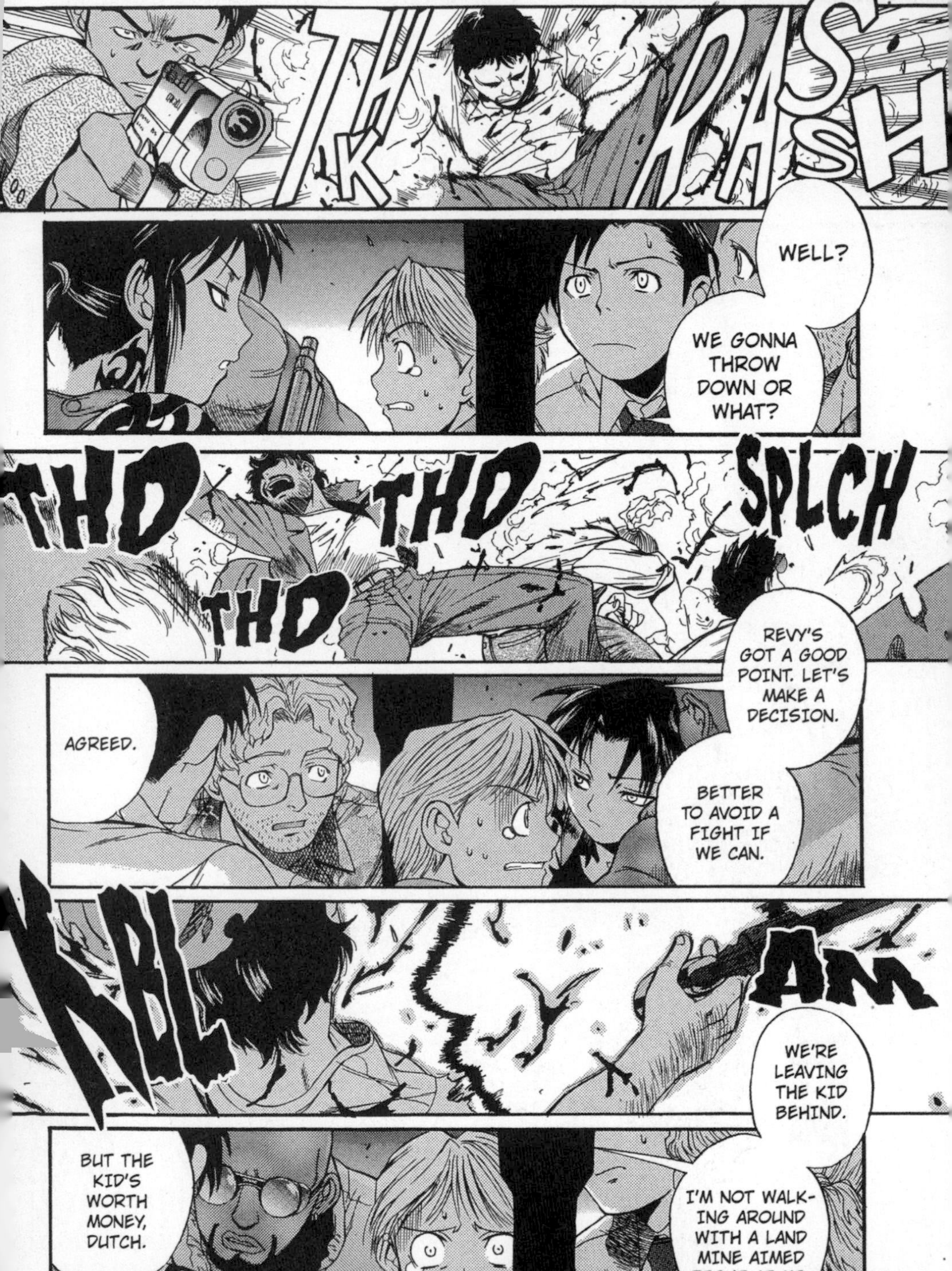
RASH
THK
WELL?
WE GONNA THROW DOWN OR WHAT?
SPLCH
THD
THD
THD
REVY'S GOT A GOOD POINT. LET'S MAKE A DECISION.
BETTER TO AVOID A FIGHT IF WE CAN.
AGREED.
BLAM
WE'RE LEAVING THE KID BEHIND.
I'M NOT WALK-ING AROUND WITH A LAND MINE AIMED RIGHT AT ME.
BUT THE KID'S WORTH MONEY, DUTCH.

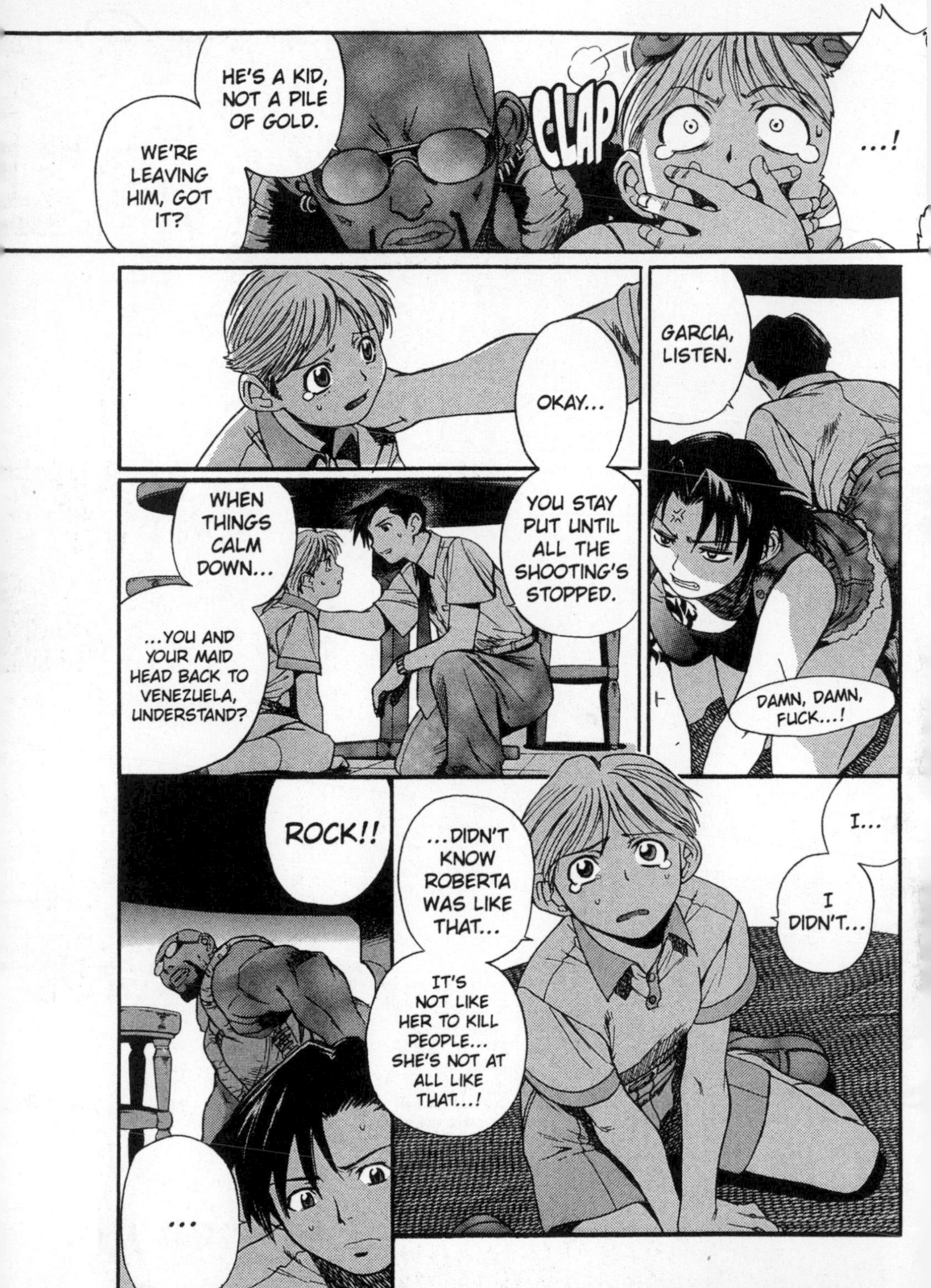
...!
CLAP
HE'S A KID, NOT A PILE OF GOLD.
WE'RE LEAVING HIM, GOT IT?
GARCIA, LISTEN.
DAMN, DAMN, FUCK...!
OKAY...
YOU STAY PUT UNTIL ALL THE SHOOTING'S STOPPED.
WHEN THINGS CALM DOWN...
...YOU AND YOUR MAID HEAD BACK TO VENEZUELA, UNDERSTAND?
I...
I DIDN'T...
...DIDN'T KNOW ROBERTA WAS LIKE THAT...
IT'S NOT LIKE HER TO KILL PEOPLE... SHE'S NOT AT ALL LIKE THAT...!
ROCK!!
...

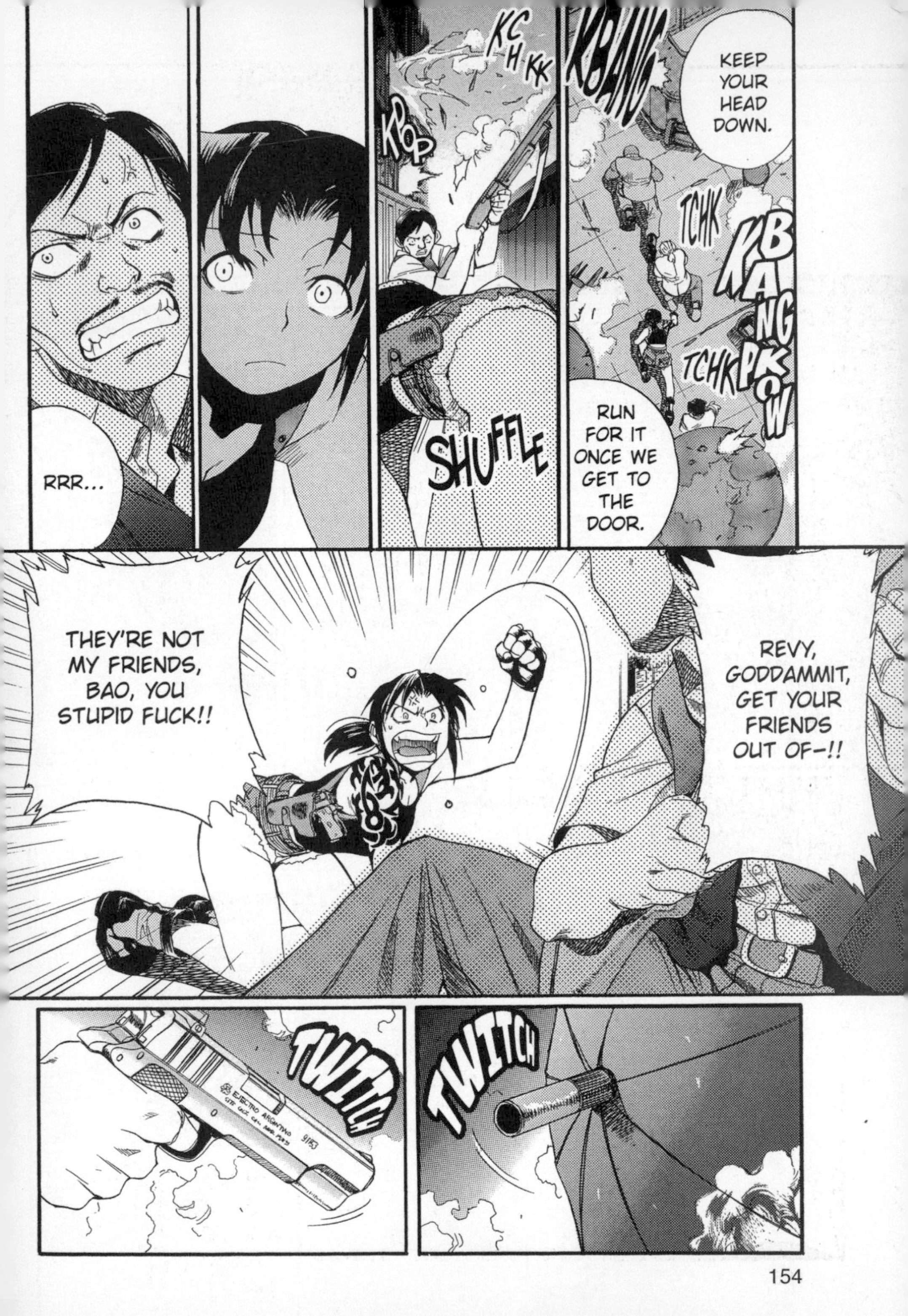
KBANG
KEEP YOUR HEAD DOWN.
TCHK
KBANG
TCHK
PKOW
RUN FOR IT ONCE WE GET TO THE DOOR.
KCH HKK
KROP
SHUFFLE
RRR...
REVY, GODDAMMIT, GET YOUR FRIENDS OUT OF-!!
THEY'RE NOT MY FRIENDS, BAO, YOU STUPID FUCK!!
TWITCH
TWITCH

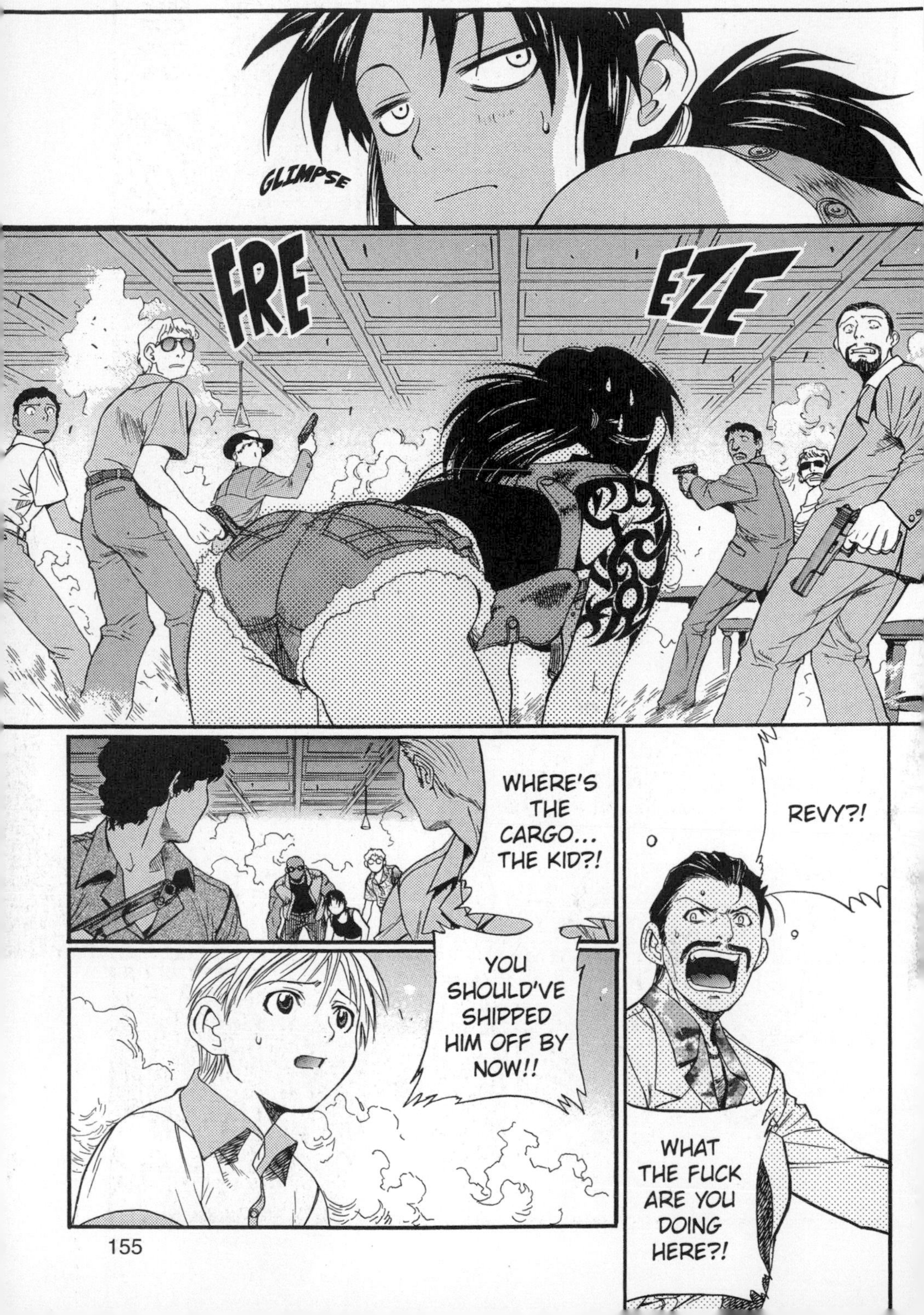
GLIMPSE
FRE
EZE
REVY?!
WHAT THE FUCK ARE YOU DOING HERE?!
WHERE'S THE CARGO... THE KID?!
YOU SHOULD'VE SHIPPED HIM OFF BY NOW!!

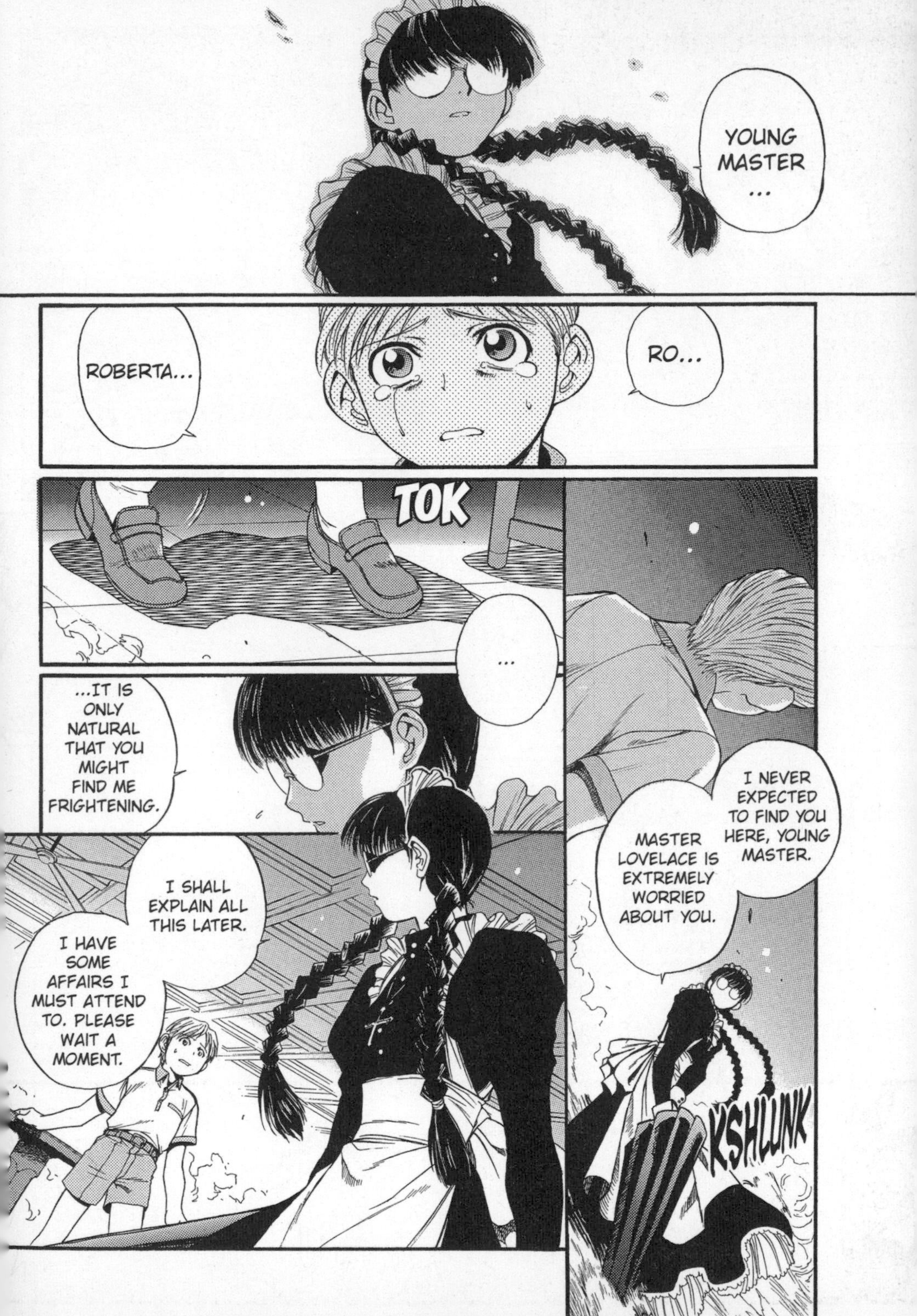
YOUNG MASTER ...
RO...
ROBERTA...
I NEVER EXPECTED TO FIND YOU HERE, YOUNG MASTER.
MASTER LOVELACE IS EXTREMELY WORRIED ABOUT YOU.
KSHLUNK
TOK
...
...IT IS ONLY NATURAL THAT YOU MIGHT FIND ME FRIGHTENING.
I SHALL EXPLAIN ALL THIS LATER.
I HAVE SOME AFFAIRS I MUST ATTEND TO. PLEASE WAIT A MOMENT.

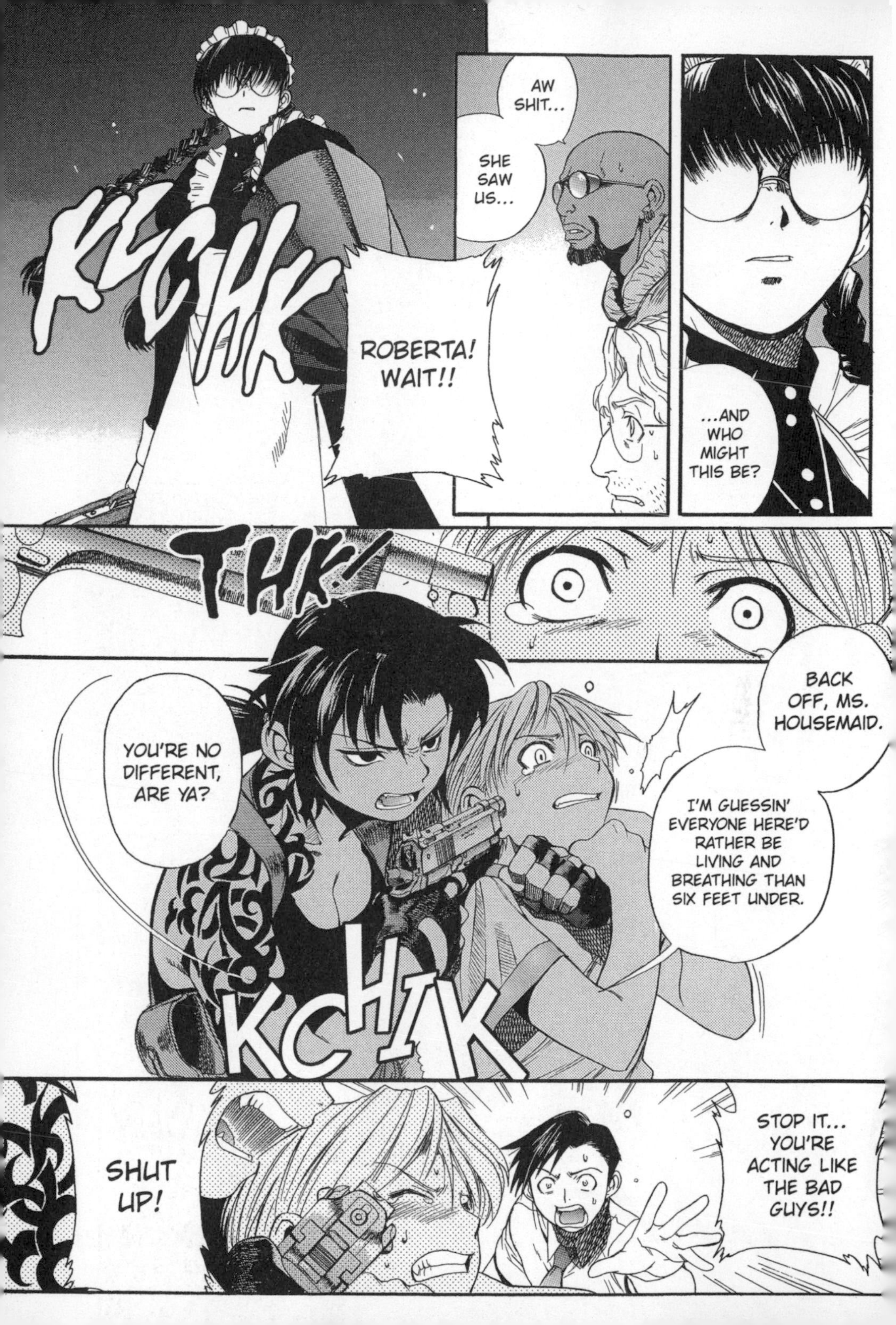
...AND WHO MIGHT THIS BE?
AW SHIT...
SHE SAW US...
ROBERTA! WAIT!!
KCHK
THK!
BACK OFF, MS. HOUSEMAID.
I'M GUESSIN' EVERYONE HERE'D RATHER BE LIVING AND BREATHING THAN SIX FEET UNDER.
YOU'RE NO DIFFERENT, ARE YA?
KCHIK
STOP IT... YOU'RE ACTING LIKE THE BAD GUYS!!
SHUT UP!

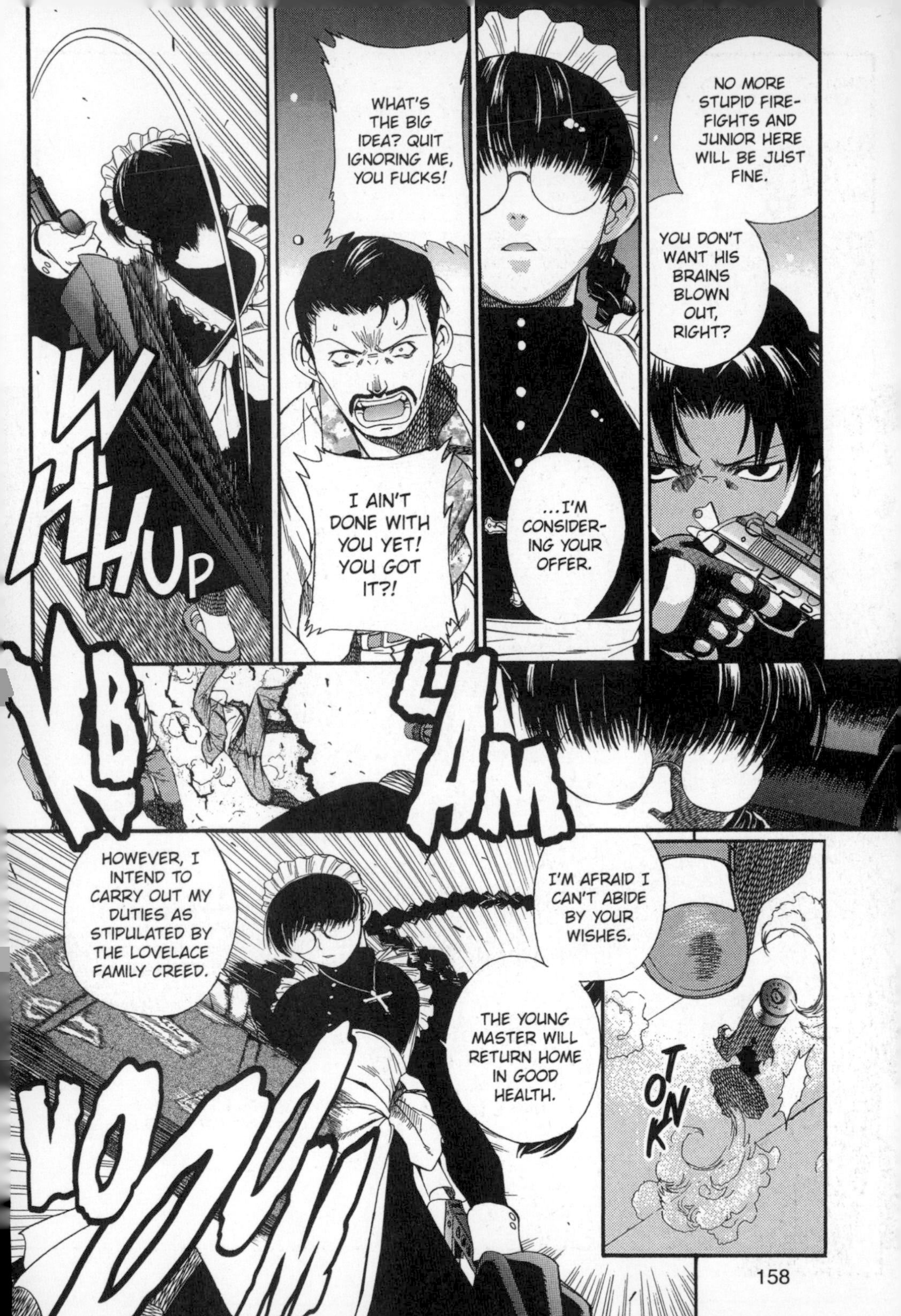
NO MORE STUPID FIRE-FIGHTS AND JUNIOR HERE WILL BE JUST FINE.
YOU DON'T WANT HIS BRAINS BLOWN OUT, RIGHT?
...I'M CONSIDERING YOUR OFFER.
WHAT'S THE BIG IDEA? QUIT IGNORING ME, YOU FUCKS!
I AIN'T DONE WITH YOU YET! YOU GOT IT?!
WHHUP
KBLAM
TONK
I'M AFRAID I CAN'T ABIDE BY YOUR WISHES.
THE YOUNG MASTER WILL RETURN HOME IN GOOD HEALTH.
HOWEVER, I INTEND TO CARRY OUT MY DUTIES AS STIPULATED BY THE LOVELACE FAMILY CREED.
VOOM

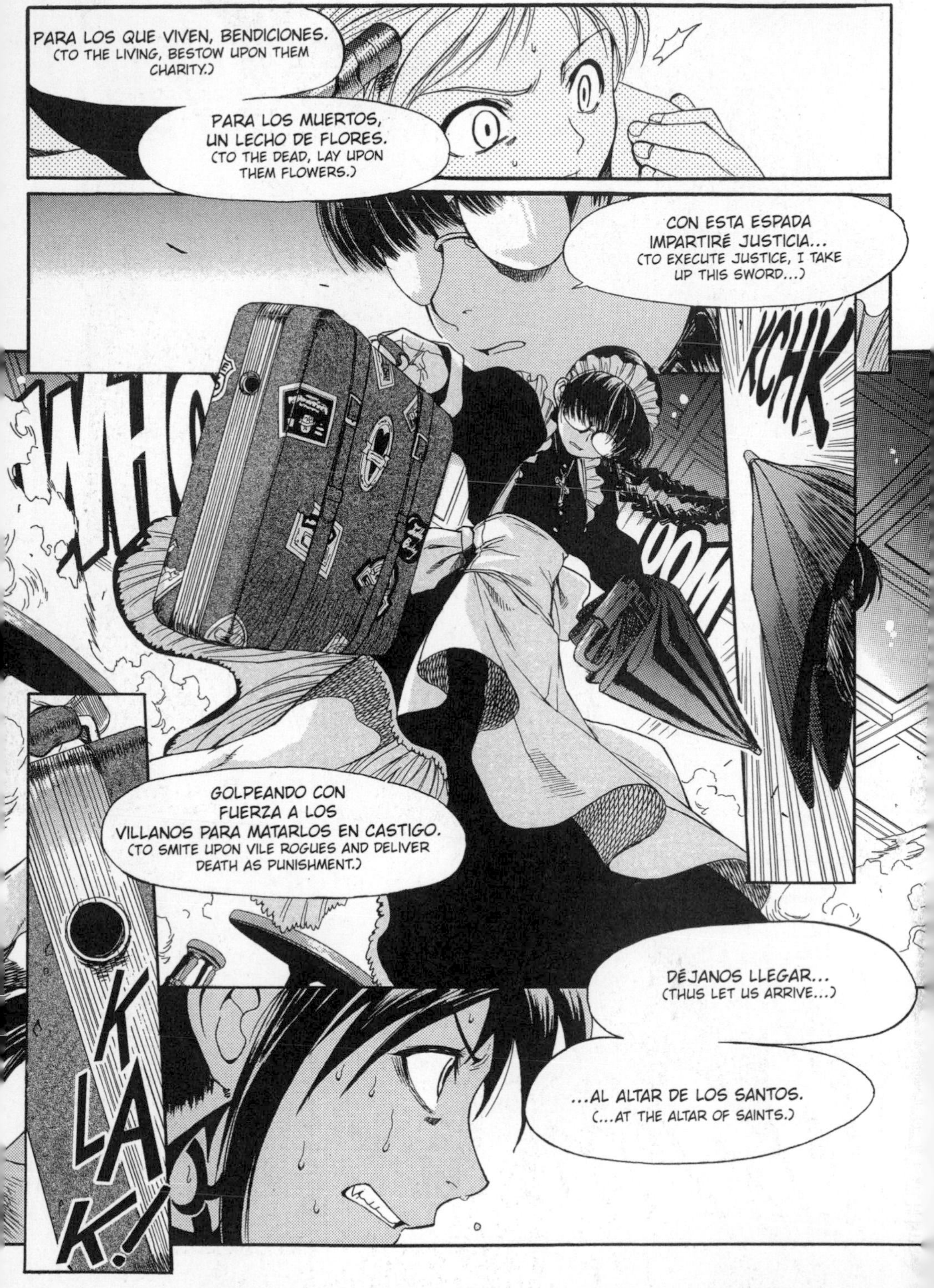
PARA LOS QUE VIVEN, BENDICIONES.
(TO THE LIVING, BESTOW UPON THEM CHARITY.)
PARA LOS MUERTOS, UN LECHO DE FLORES.
(TO THE DEAD, LAY UPON THEM FLOWERS.)
CON ESTA ESPADA IMPARTIRÉ JUSTICIA...
(TO EXECUTE JUSTICE, I TAKE UP THIS SWORD...)
KCHK
GOLPEANDO CON FUERZA A LOS VILLANOS PARA MATARLOS EN CASTIGO.
(TO SMITE UPON VILE ROGUES AND DELIVER DEATH AS PUNISHMENT.)
DÉJANOS LLEGAR...
(THUS LET US ARRIVE...)
...AL ALTAR DE LOS SANTOS.
(...AT THE ALTAR OF SAINTS.)
KLAK!

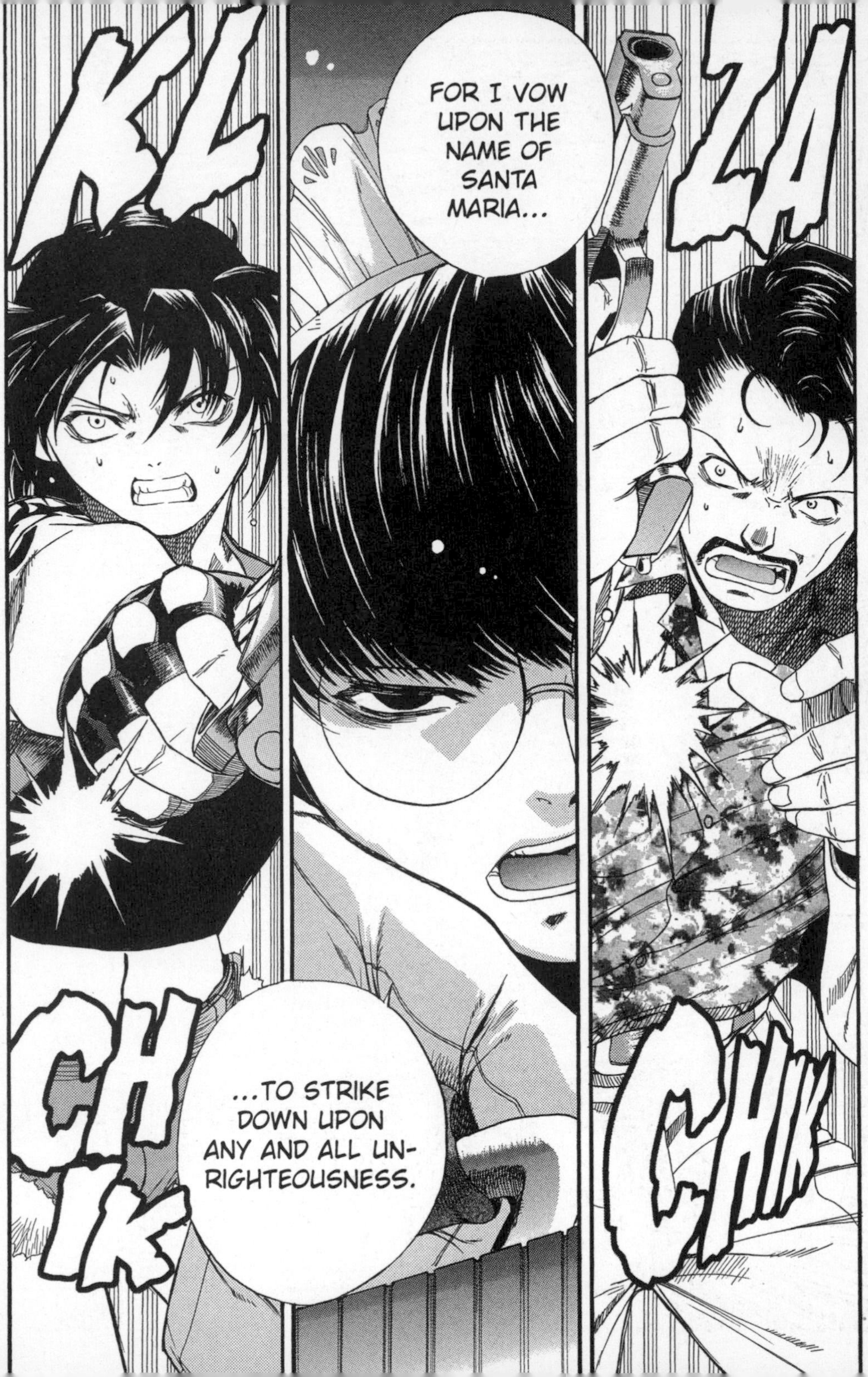
ZA
CHIK
FOR I VOW UPON THE NAME OF SANTA MARIA...
...TO STRIKE DOWN UPON ANY AND ALL UN-RIGHTEOUSNESS.
KL
CHK

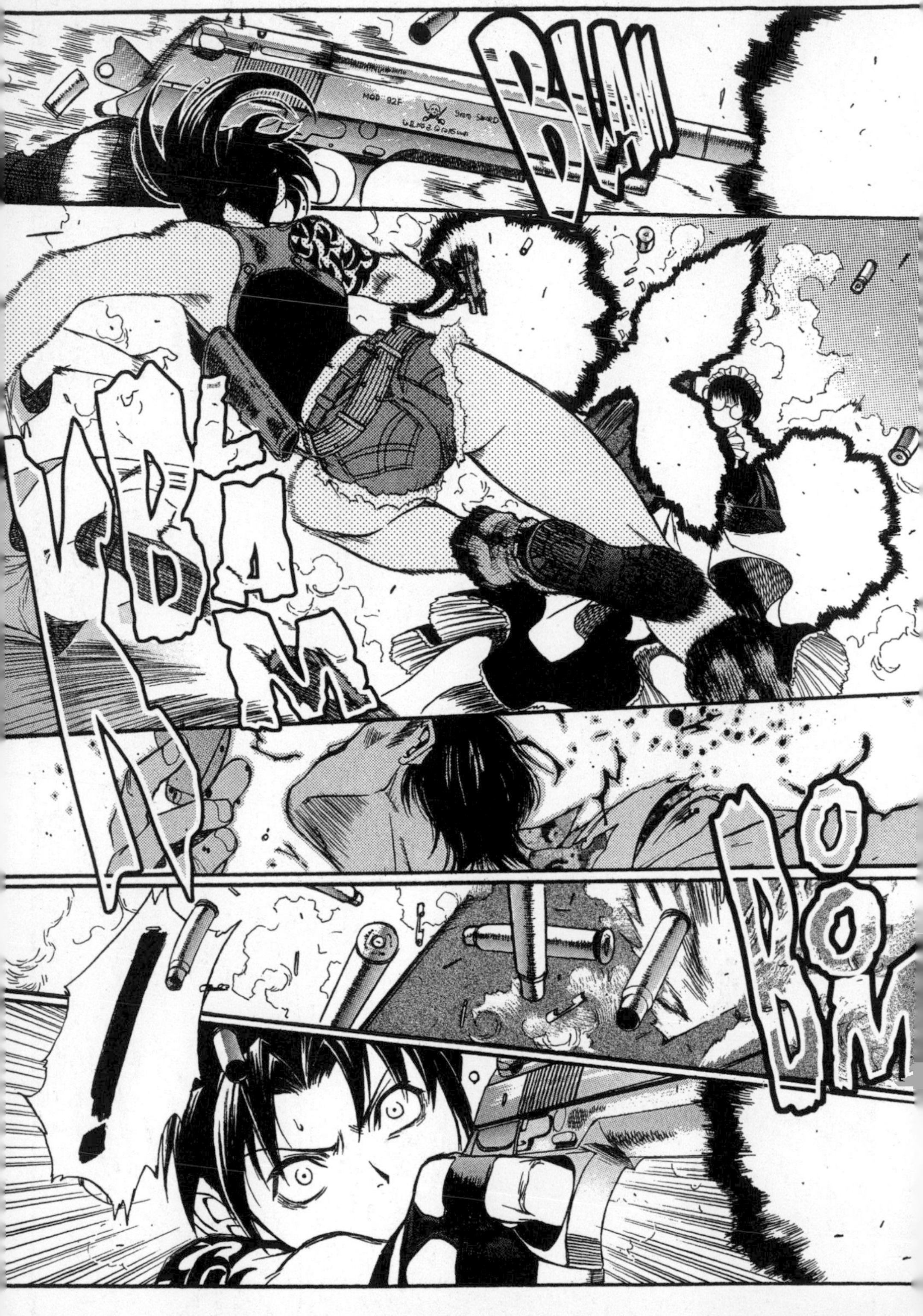
BLAM
MOD 92F
BLAM
BOOM
!

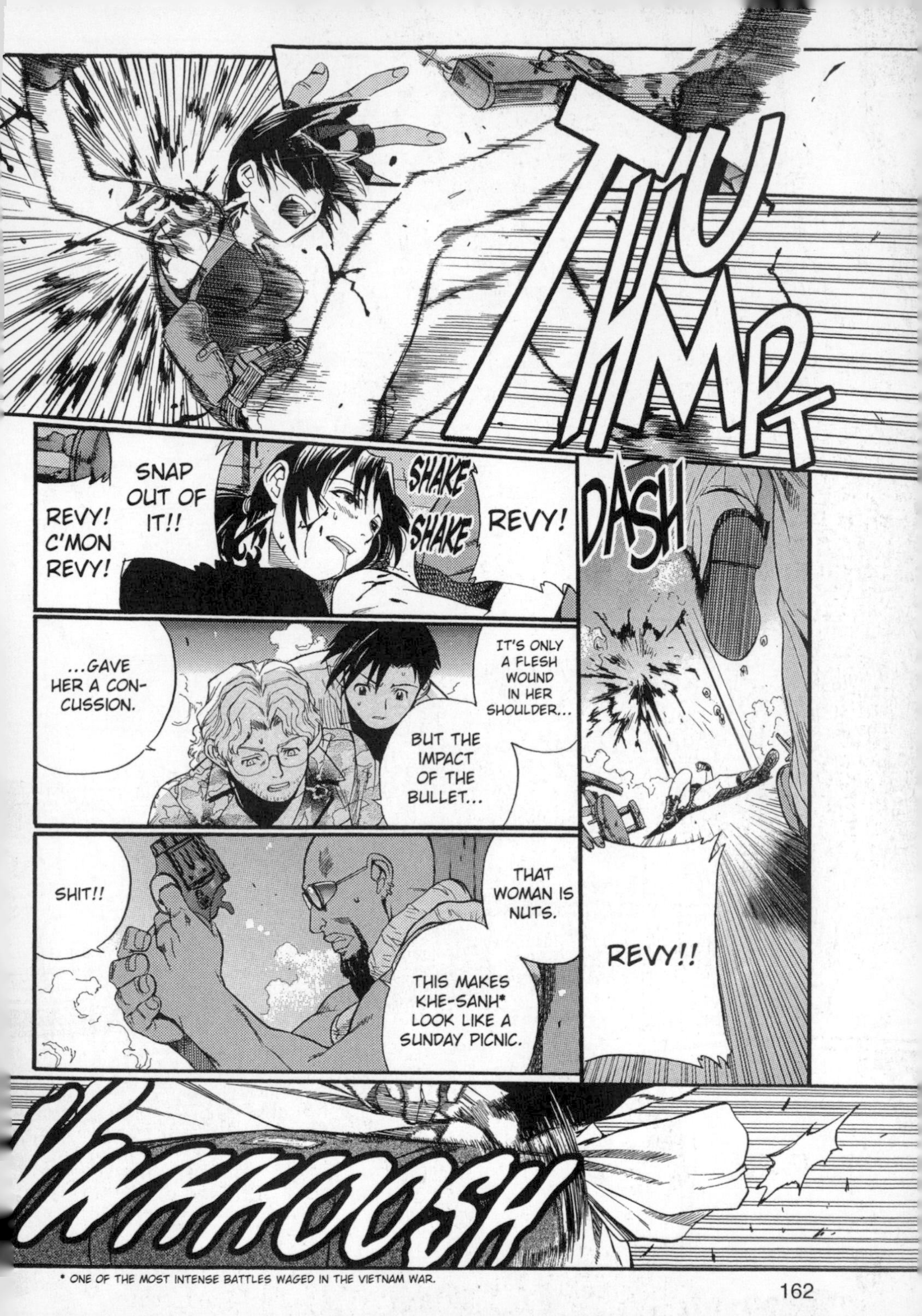
THUMP
DASH
REVY!!
REVY!
SHAKE
SHAKE
SNAP OUT OF IT!!
REVY! C'MON REVY!
IT'S ONLY A FLESH WOUND IN HER SHOULDER...
BUT THE IMPACT OF THE BULLET...
...GAVE HER A CONCUSSION.
THAT WOMAN IS NUTS.
THIS MAKES KHE-SANH* LOOK LIKE A SUNDAY PICNIC.
SHIT!!
WHOOSH

* ONE OF THE MOST INTENSE BATTLES WAGED IN THE VIETNAM WAR.

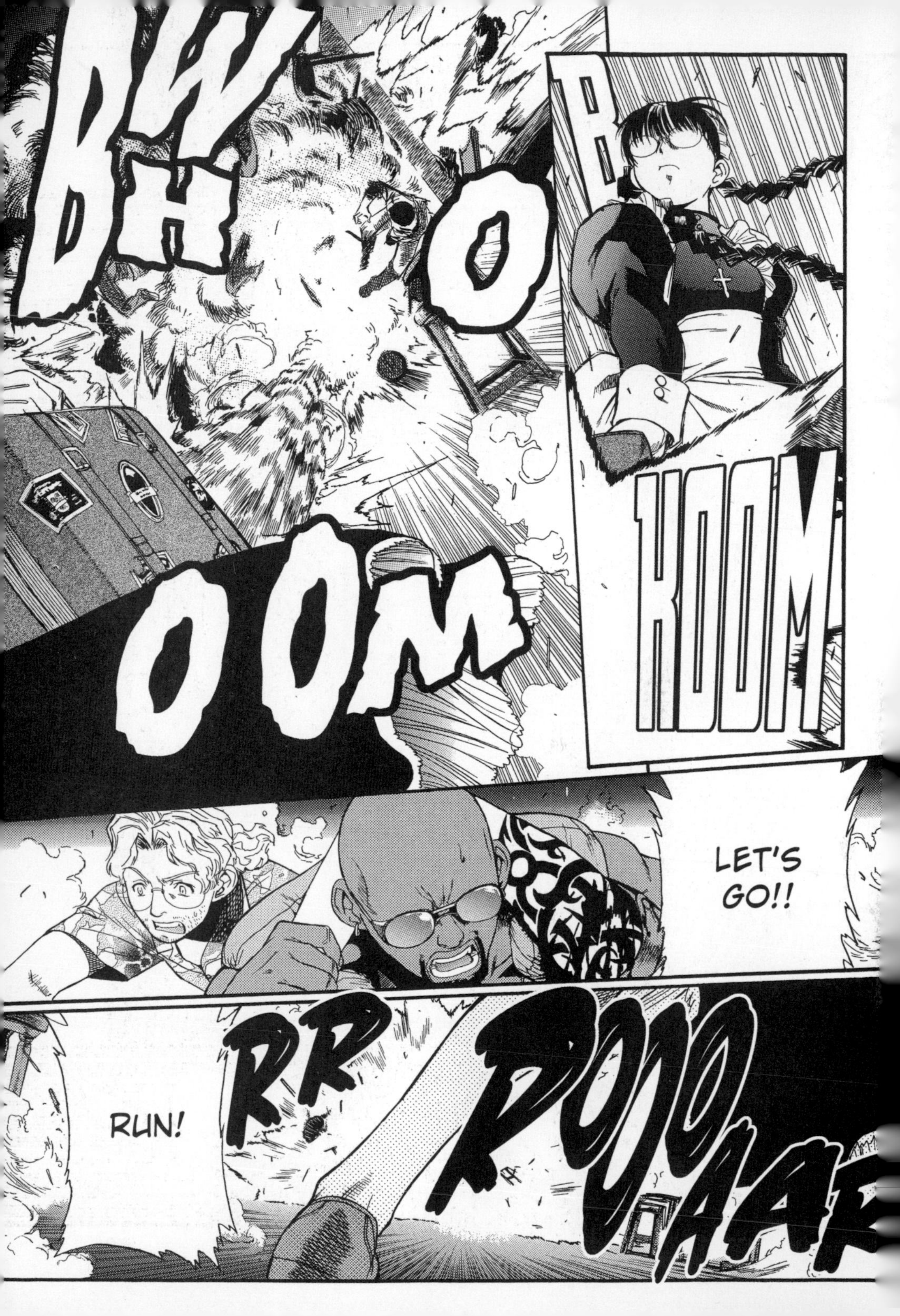
LET'S GO!!
RUN!

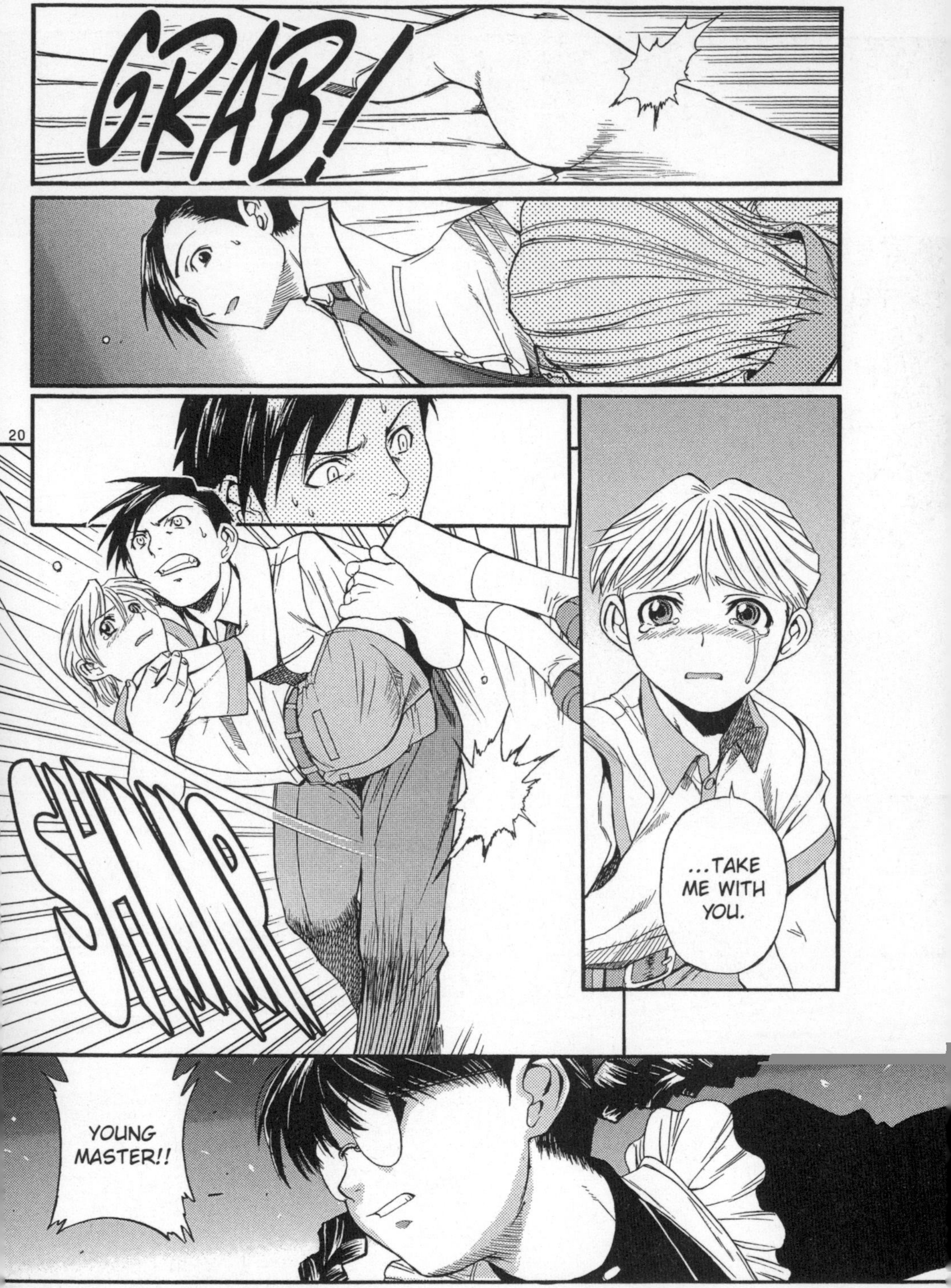
GRAB!
...TAKE ME WITH YOU.
YOUNG MASTER!!

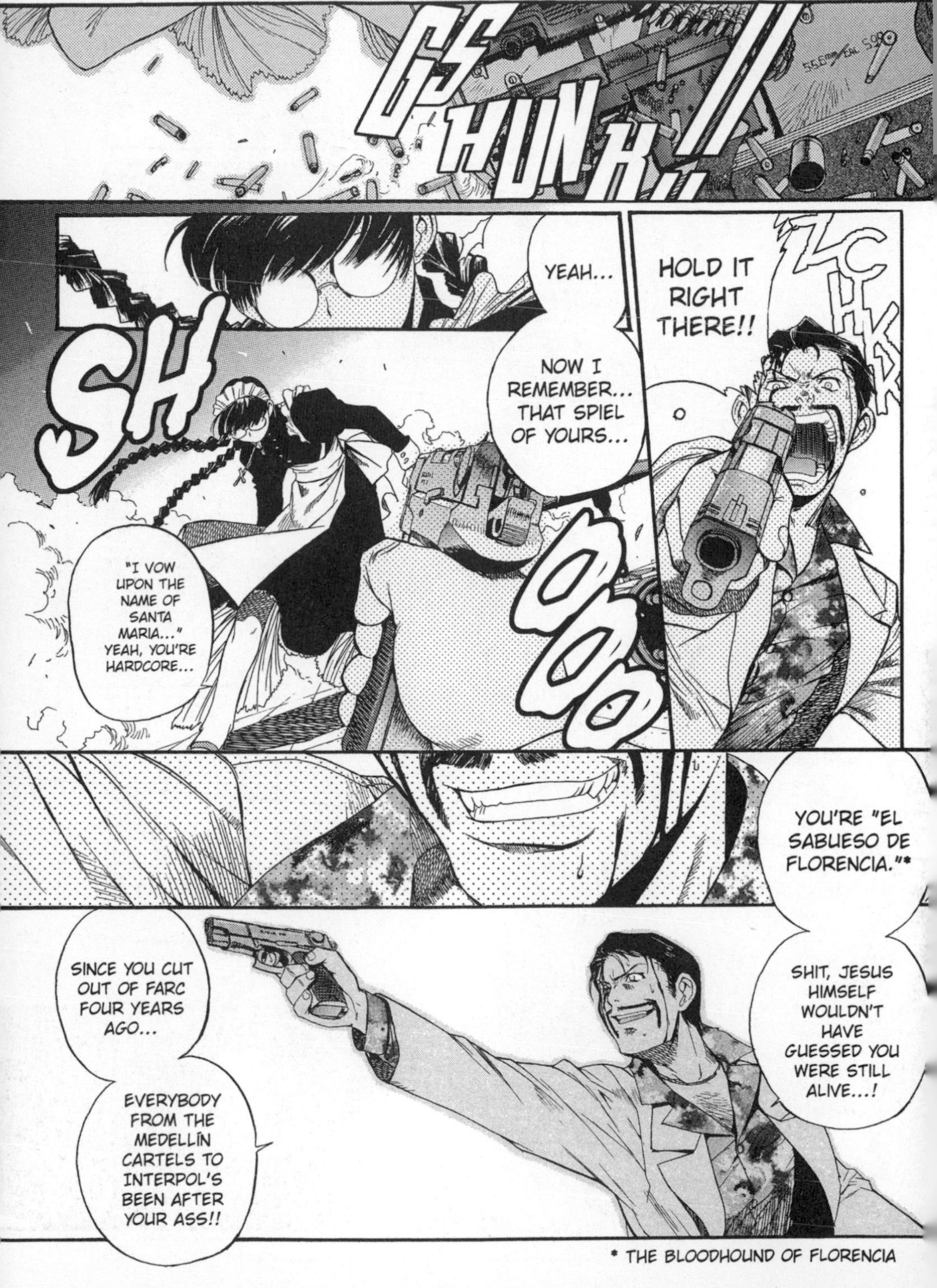
GSHUNK!!
ZCHKK
HOLD IT RIGHT THERE!!
YEAH...
NOW I REMEMBER... THAT SPIEL OF YOURS...
SH
DOOOO
"I VOW UPON THE NAME OF SANTA MARIA..." YEAH, YOU'RE HARDCORE...
YOU'RE "EL SABUESO DE FLORENCIA."*
SHIT, JESUS HIMSELF WOULDN'T HAVE GUESSED YOU WERE STILL ALIVE...!
SINCE YOU CUT OUT OF FARC FOUR YEARS AGO...
EVERYBODY FROM THE MEDELLÍN CARTELS TO INTERPOL'S BEEN AFTER YOUR ASS!!

* THE BLOODHOUND OF FLORENCIA

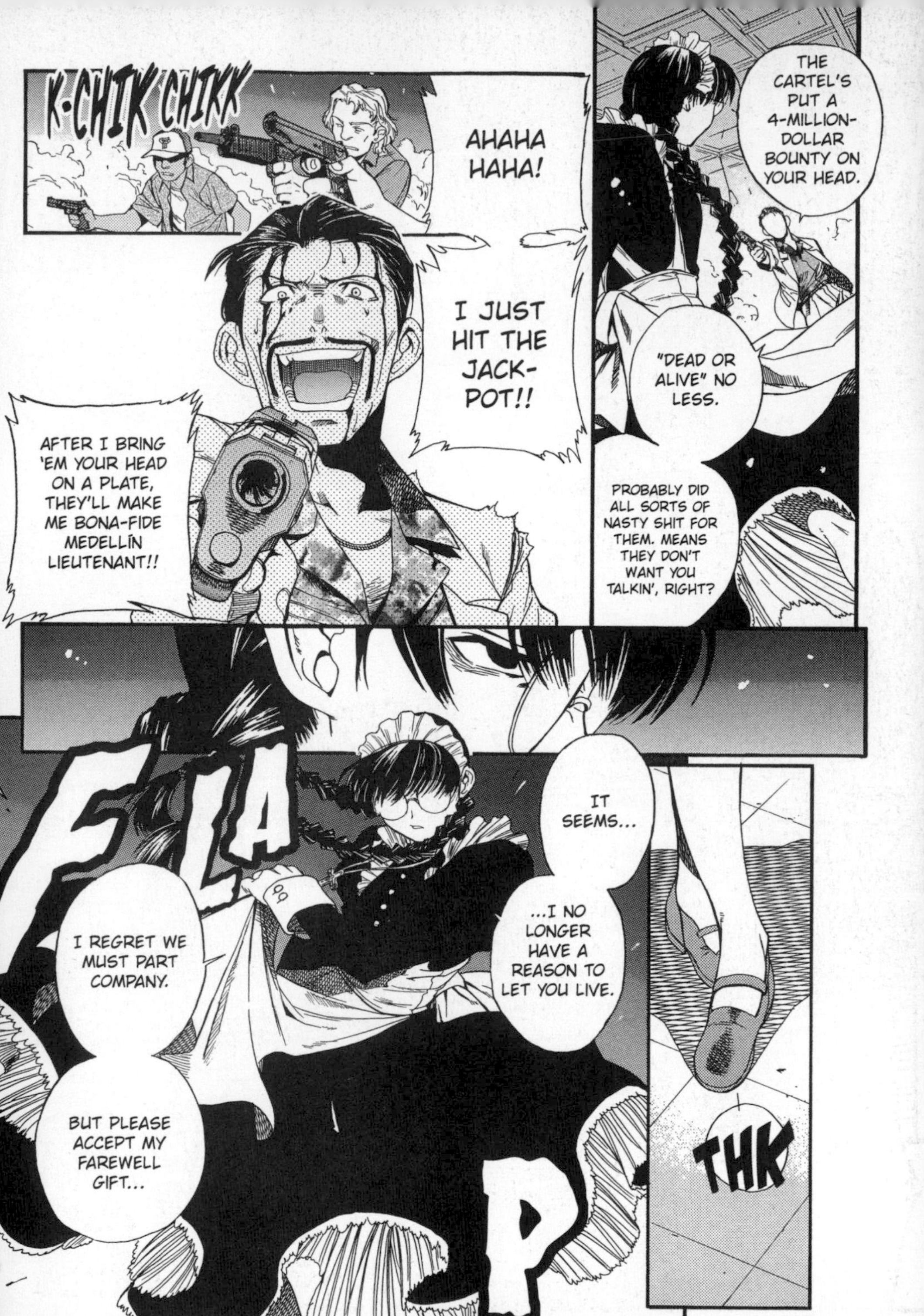
THE CARTEL'S PUT A 4-MILLION-DOLLAR BOUNTY ON YOUR HEAD.
"DEAD OR ALIVE" NO LESS.
PROBABLY DID ALL SORTS OF NASTY SHIT FOR THEM. MEANS THEY DON'T WANT YOU TALKIN', RIGHT?
K-CHIK CHIKK
AHAHA HAHA!
I JUST HIT THE JACK-POT!!
AFTER I BRING 'EM YOUR HEAD ON A PLATE, THEY'LL MAKE ME BONA-FIDE MEDELLÍN LIEUTENANT!!
THK
IT SEEMS...
...I NO LONGER HAVE A REASON TO LET YOU LIVE.
I REGRET WE MUST PART COMPANY.
BUT PLEASE ACCEPT MY FAREWELL GIFT...
SLA
P

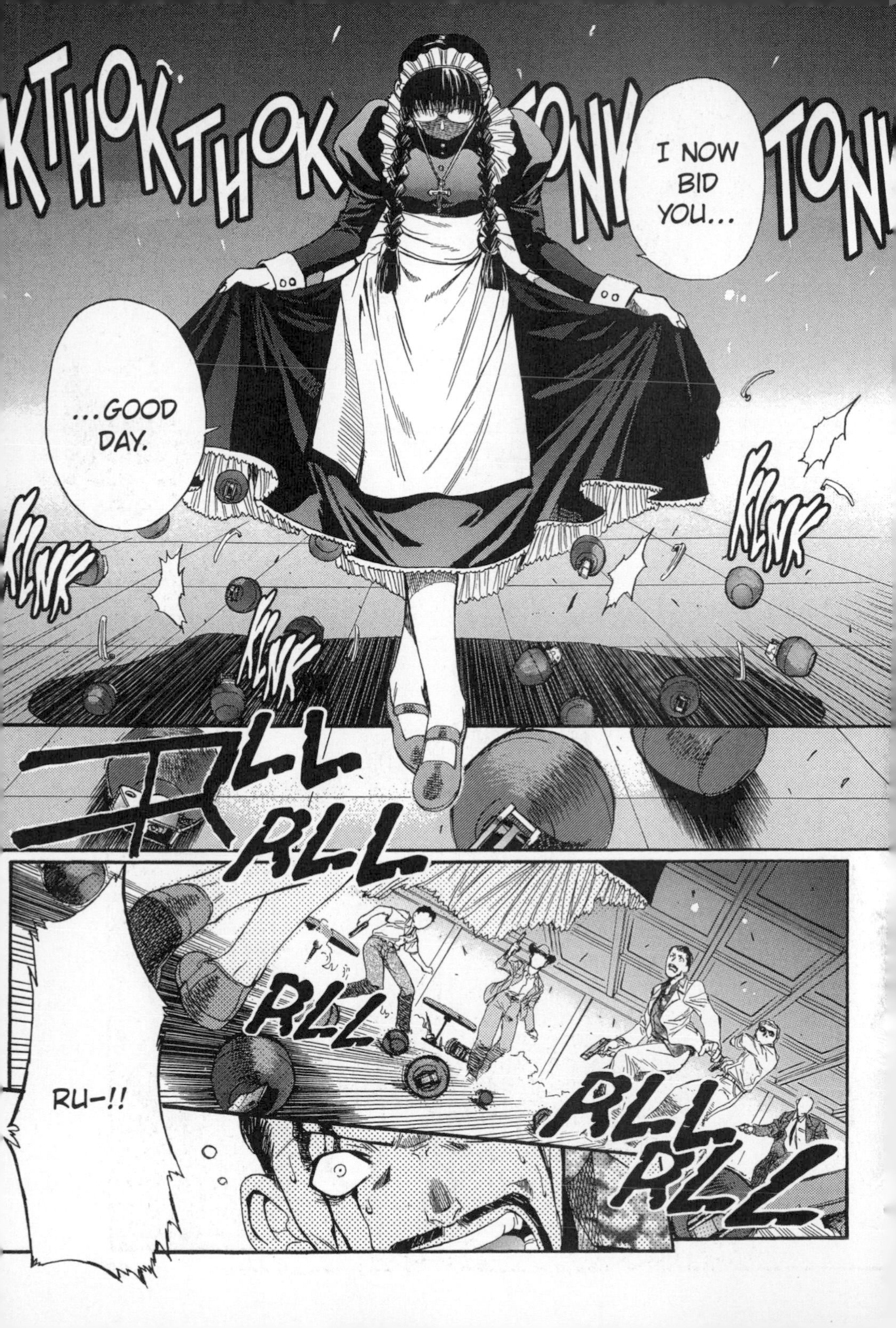
TONK TONK
I NOW BID YOU...
KTHOK KTHOK
...GOOD DAY.
KLNK
KLNK
KLNK
RLL RLL
RLL
RLL RLL
RU-!!

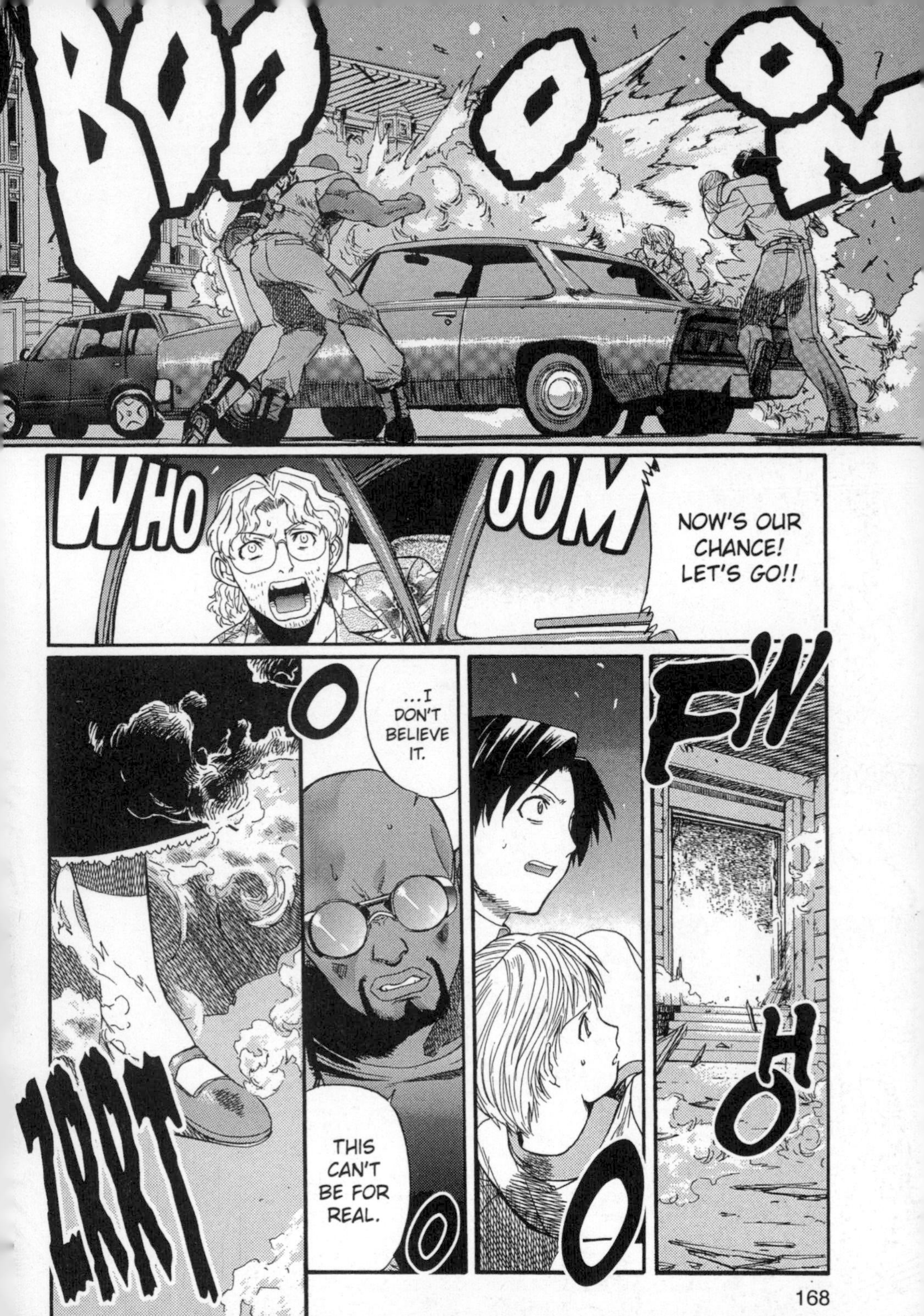
BOOOOM
WHOOOM
NOW'S OUR CHANCE! LET'S GO!!
FW
O
H
O
O
O
...I DON'T BELIEVE IT.
THIS CAN'T BE FOR REAL.
ZRRT

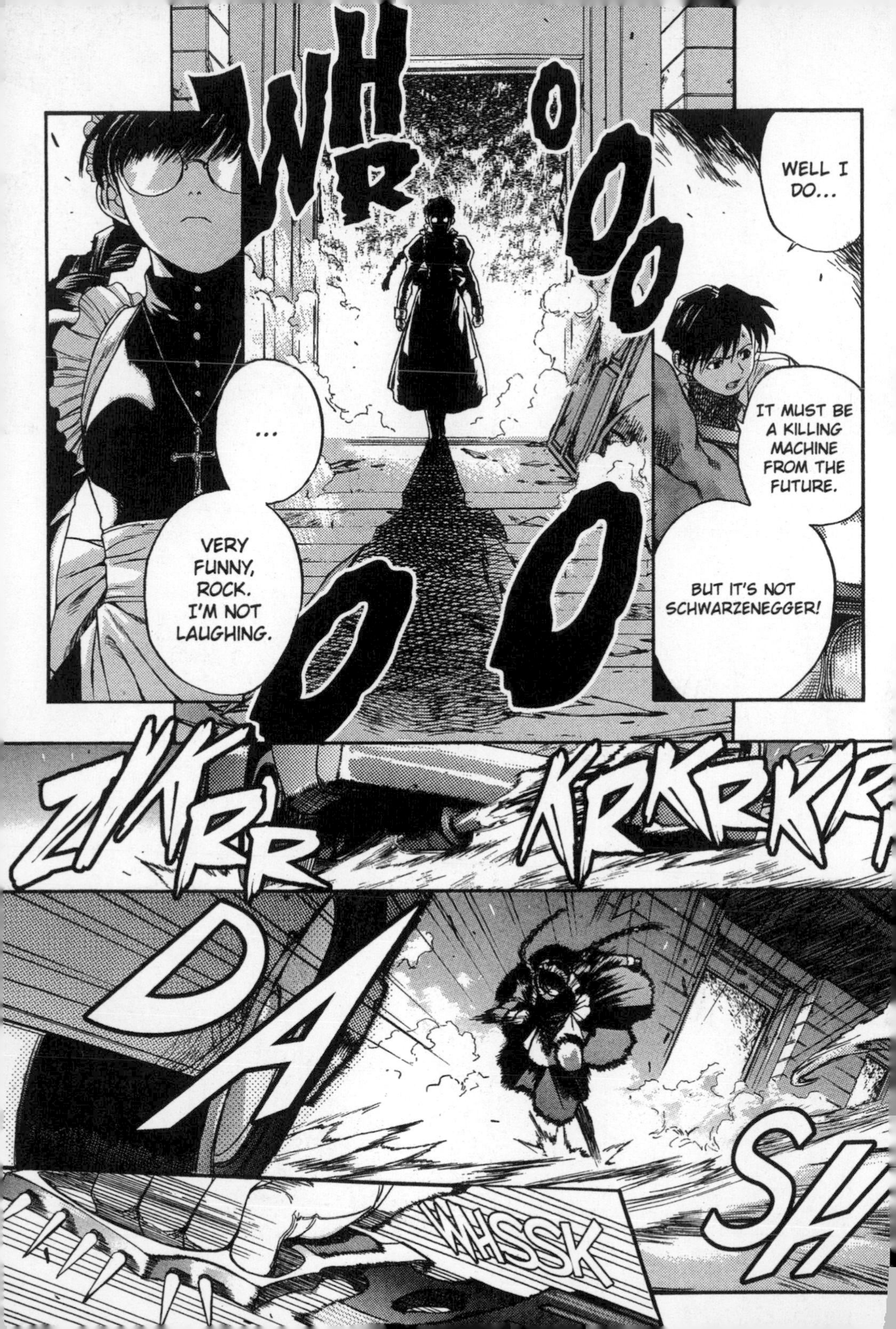

WELL I DO...
IT MUST BE A KILLING MACHINE FROM THE FUTURE.
BUT IT'S NOT SCHWARZENEGGER!
WHROOOOO
...
VERY FUNNY, ROCK. I'M NOT LAUGHING.
KRKRKR
ZKRR
DASH
WHSSK

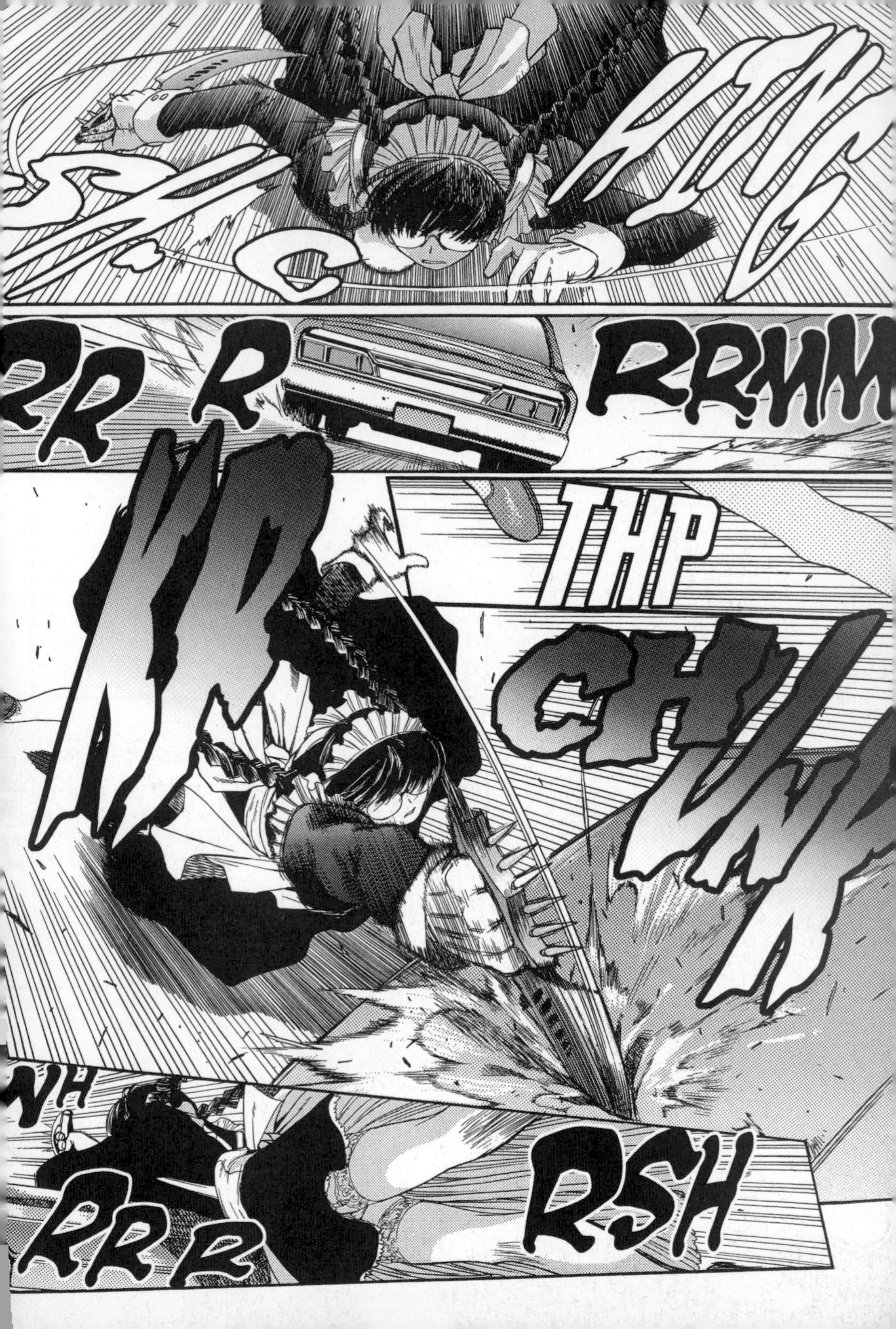
RRUM
RR R
THP
CH
RSH
RRR

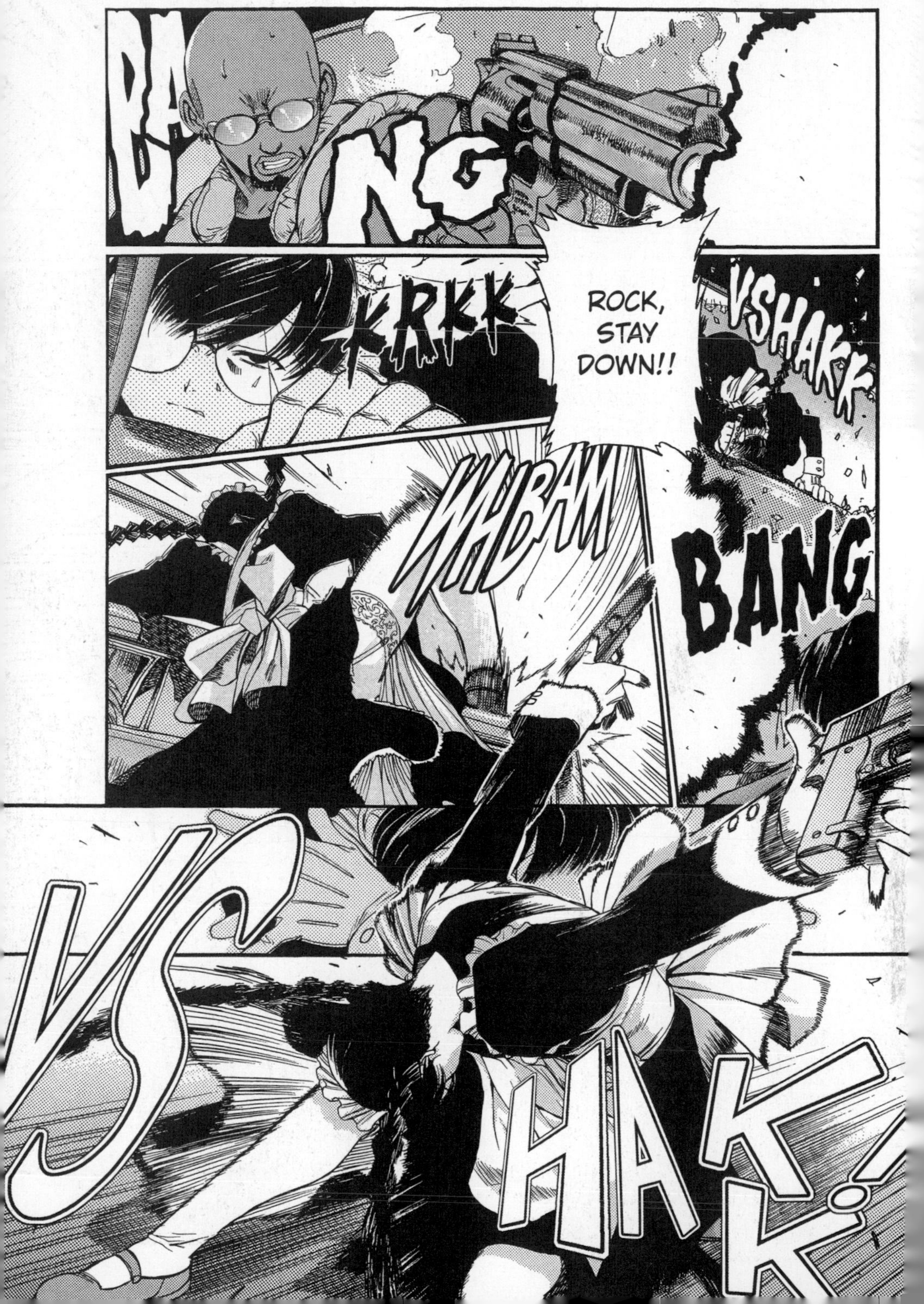
BANG
VSHAKK
ROCK, STAY DOWN!!
KRKK
BANG
WHBAM
VSHAKK

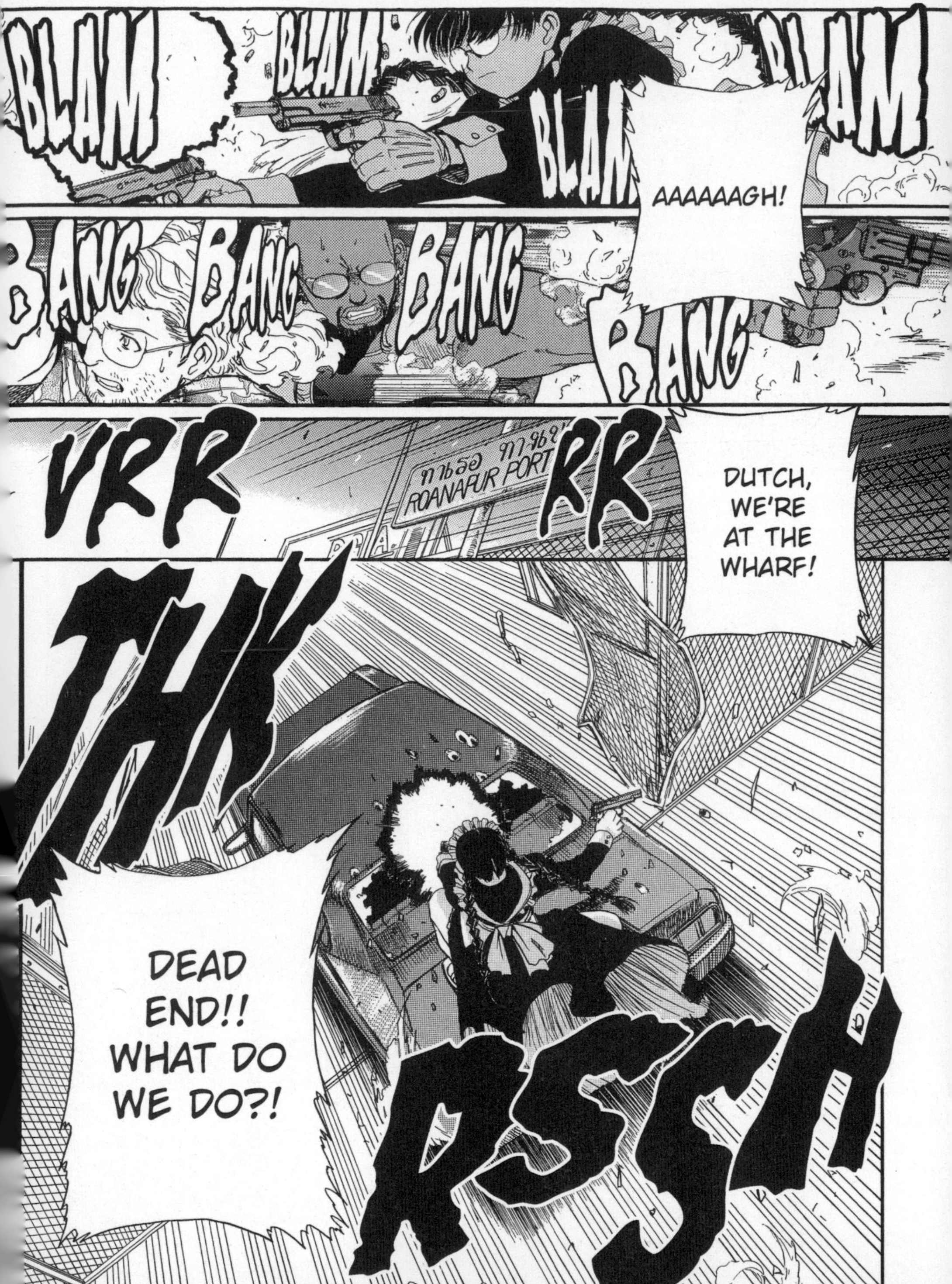
BLAM
AAAAAAGH!
BLAM
BLAM
BLAM
BLAM
BANG
BANG
BANG
BANG
DUTCH, WE'RE AT THE WHARF!
RR
ROANAPUR PORT
VRR
THK
RSSH
DEAD END!! WHAT DO WE DO?!

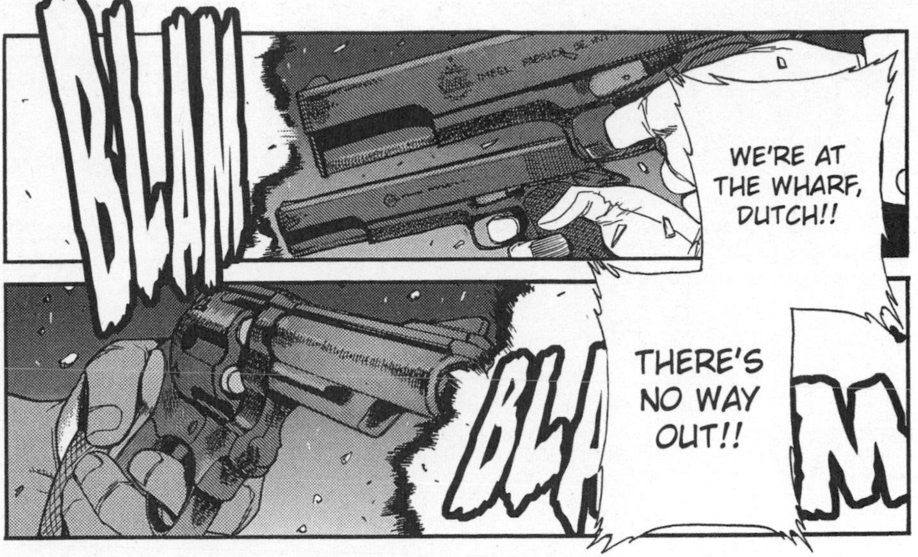
WE'RE AT THE WHARF, DUTCH!!
BLAM
THERE'S NO WAY OUT!!
BLAM

Chapter 4: Rasta Blasta - Part III

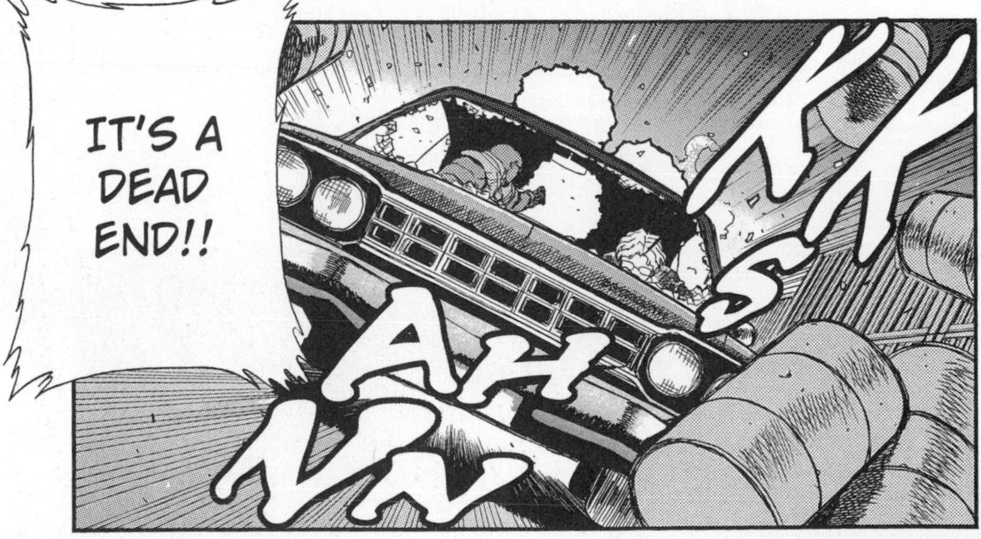
IT'S A DEAD END!!

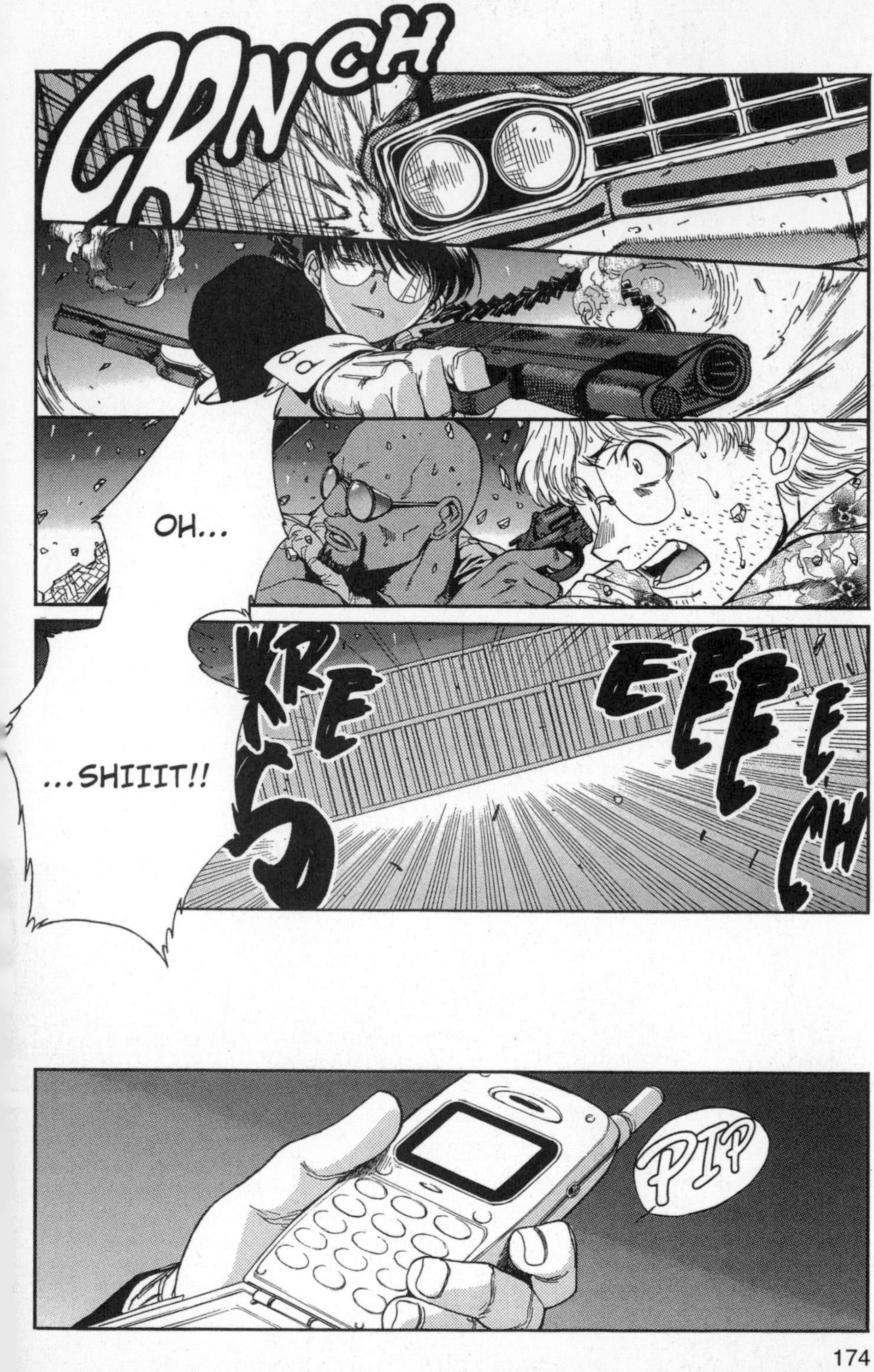
CRNCH
OH...
...SHIIIT!!
KREEEEECH
PIP

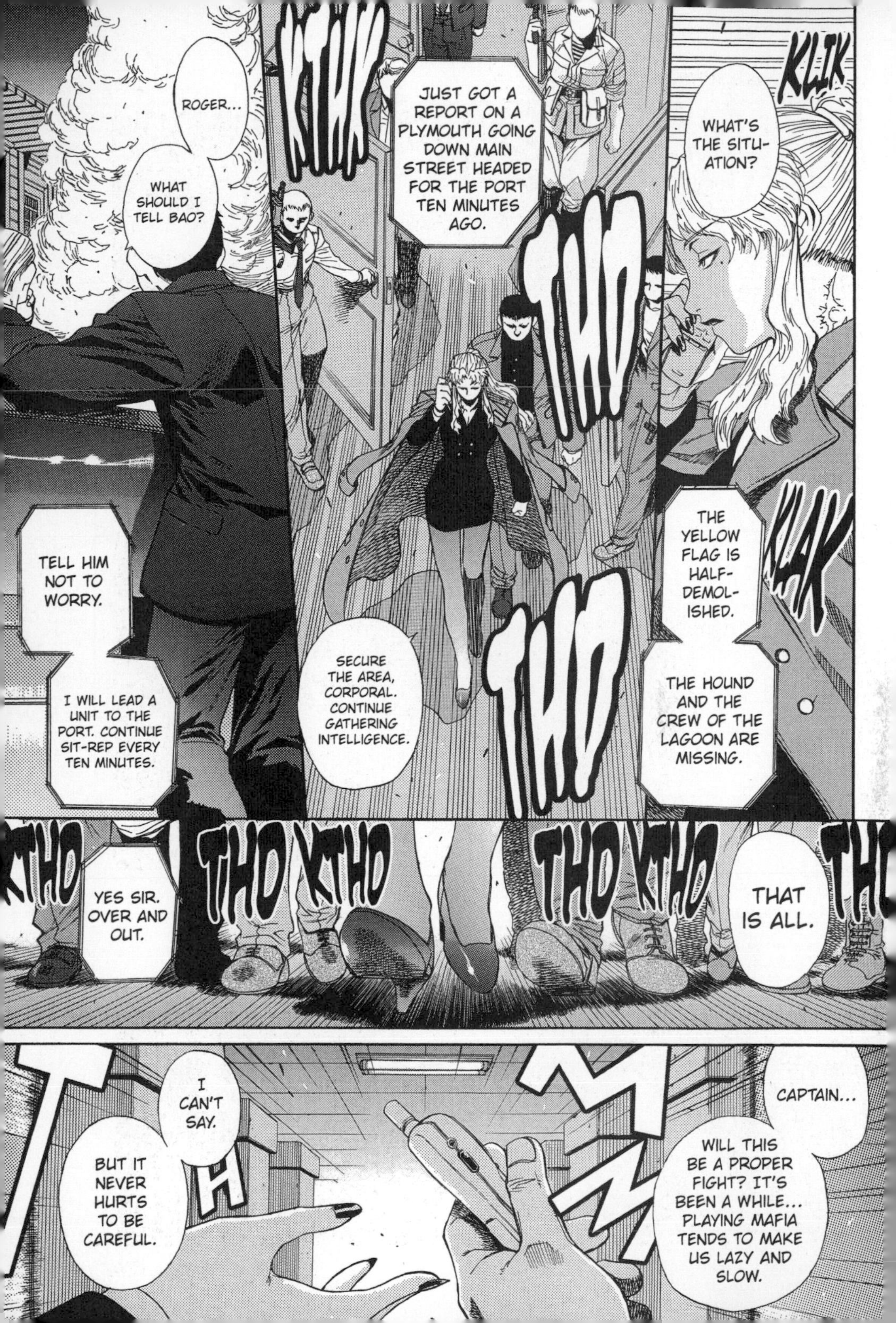
KLIK
WHAT'S THE SITUATION?
KLAK
THE YELLOW FLAG IS HALF-DEMOLISHED.
THE HOUND AND THE CREW OF THE LAGOON ARE MISSING.
JUST GOT A REPORT ON A PLYMOUTH GOING DOWN MAIN STREET HEADED FOR THE PORT TEN MINUTES AGO.
THO
THO
SECURE THE AREA, CORPORAL. CONTINUE GATHERING INTELLIGENCE.
ROGER...
WHAT SHOULD I TELL BAO?
TELL HIM NOT TO WORRY.
I WILL LEAD A UNIT TO THE PORT. CONTINUE SIT-REP EVERY TEN MINUTES.
THAT IS ALL.
THO KTHO
THO KTHO
YES SIR. OVER AND OUT.
KTHO
CAPTAIN...
WILL THIS BE A PROPER FIGHT? IT'S BEEN A WHILE... PLAYING MAFIA TENDS TO MAKE US LAZY AND SLOW.
I CAN'T SAY.
BUT IT NEVER HURTS TO BE CAREFUL.

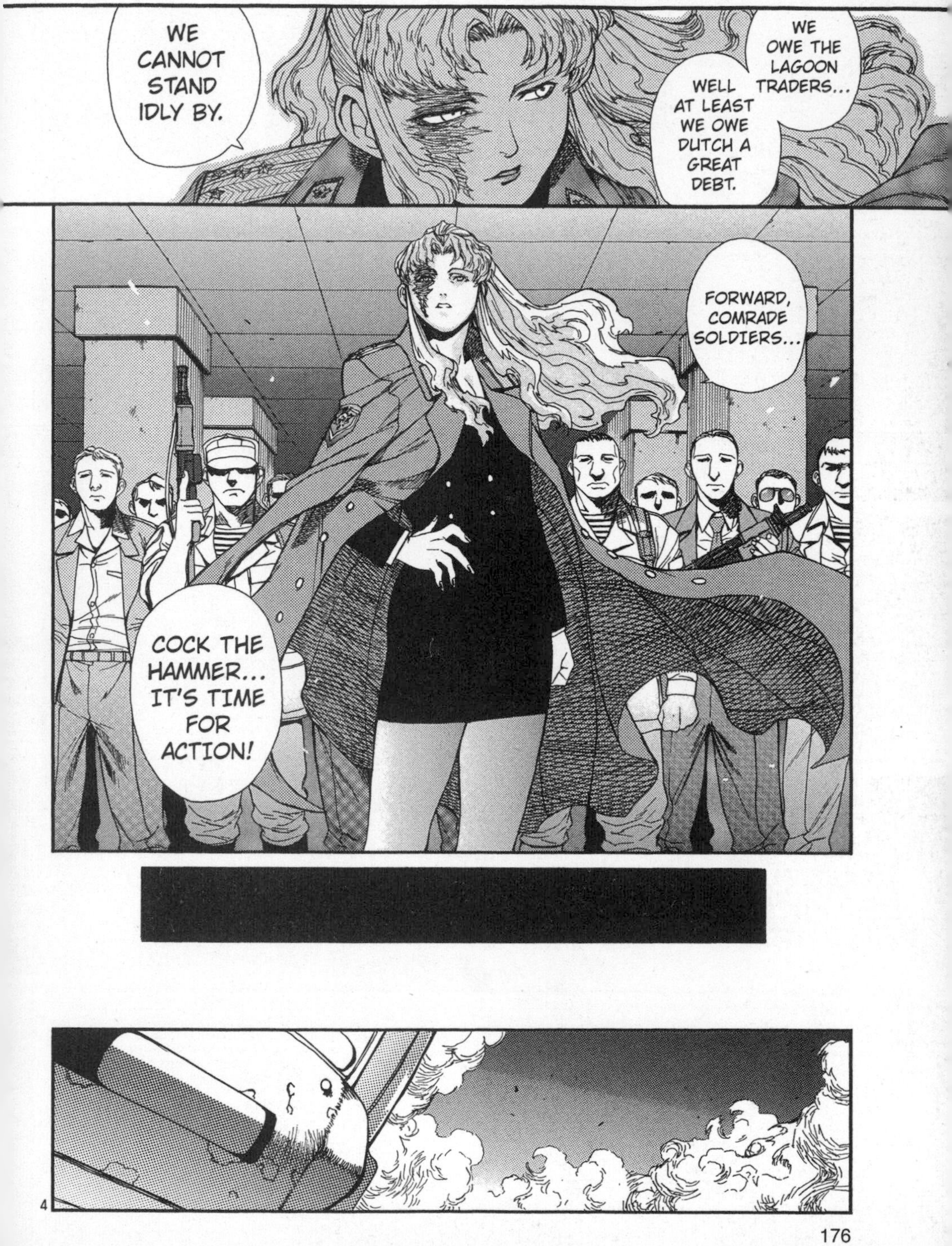
WE OWE THE LAGOON TRADERS...
WELL AT LEAST WE OWE DUTCH A GREAT DEBT.
WE CANNOT STAND IDLY BY.
FORWARD, COMRADE SOLDIERS...
COCK THE HAMMER... IT'S TIME FOR ACTION!

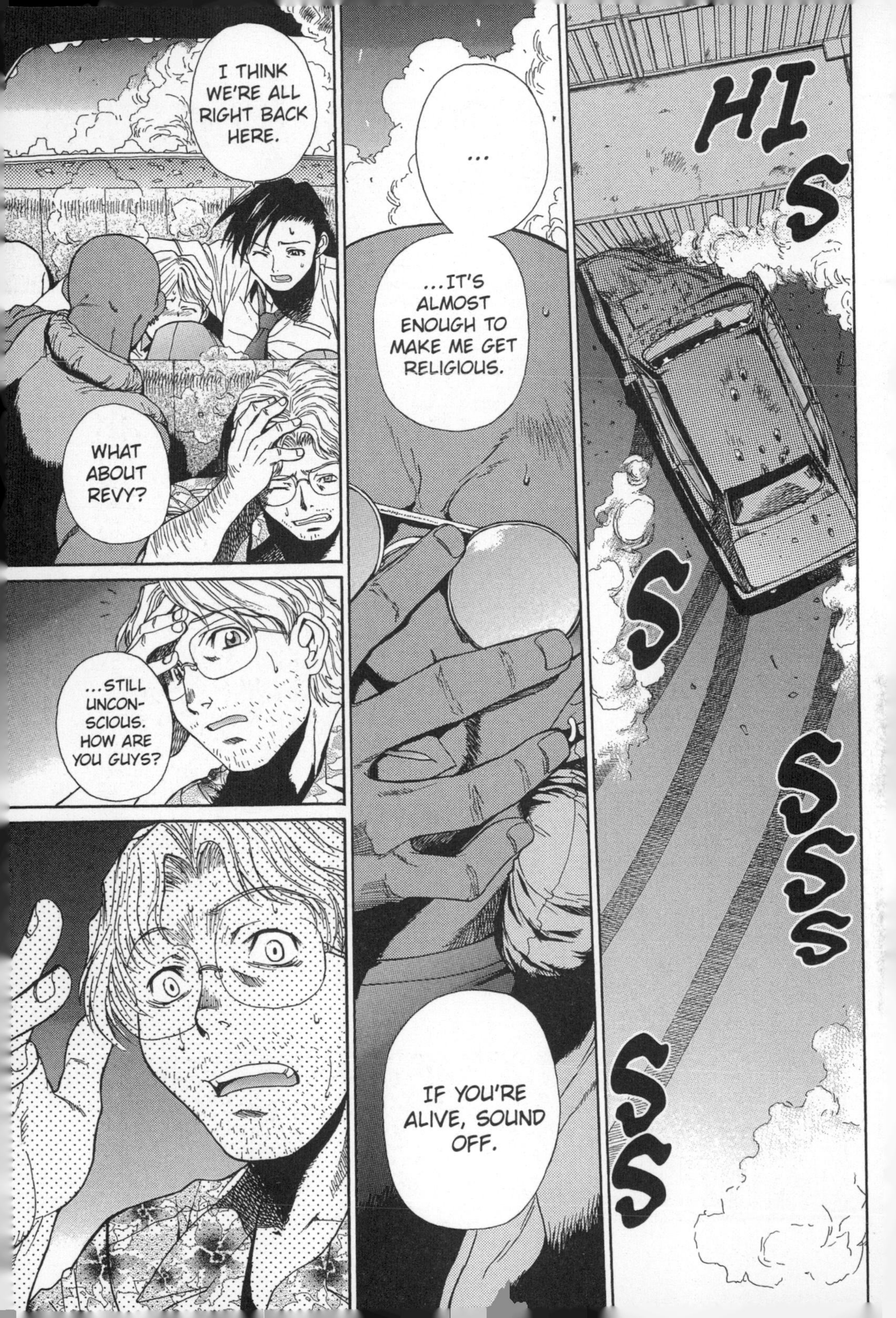

HISSSSSSSS
...
...IT'S ALMOST ENOUGH TO MAKE ME GET RELIGIOUS.
IF YOU'RE ALIVE, SOUND OFF.
I THINK WE'RE ALL RIGHT BACK HERE.
WHAT ABOUT REVY?
...STILL UNCONSCIOUS. HOW ARE YOU GUYS?

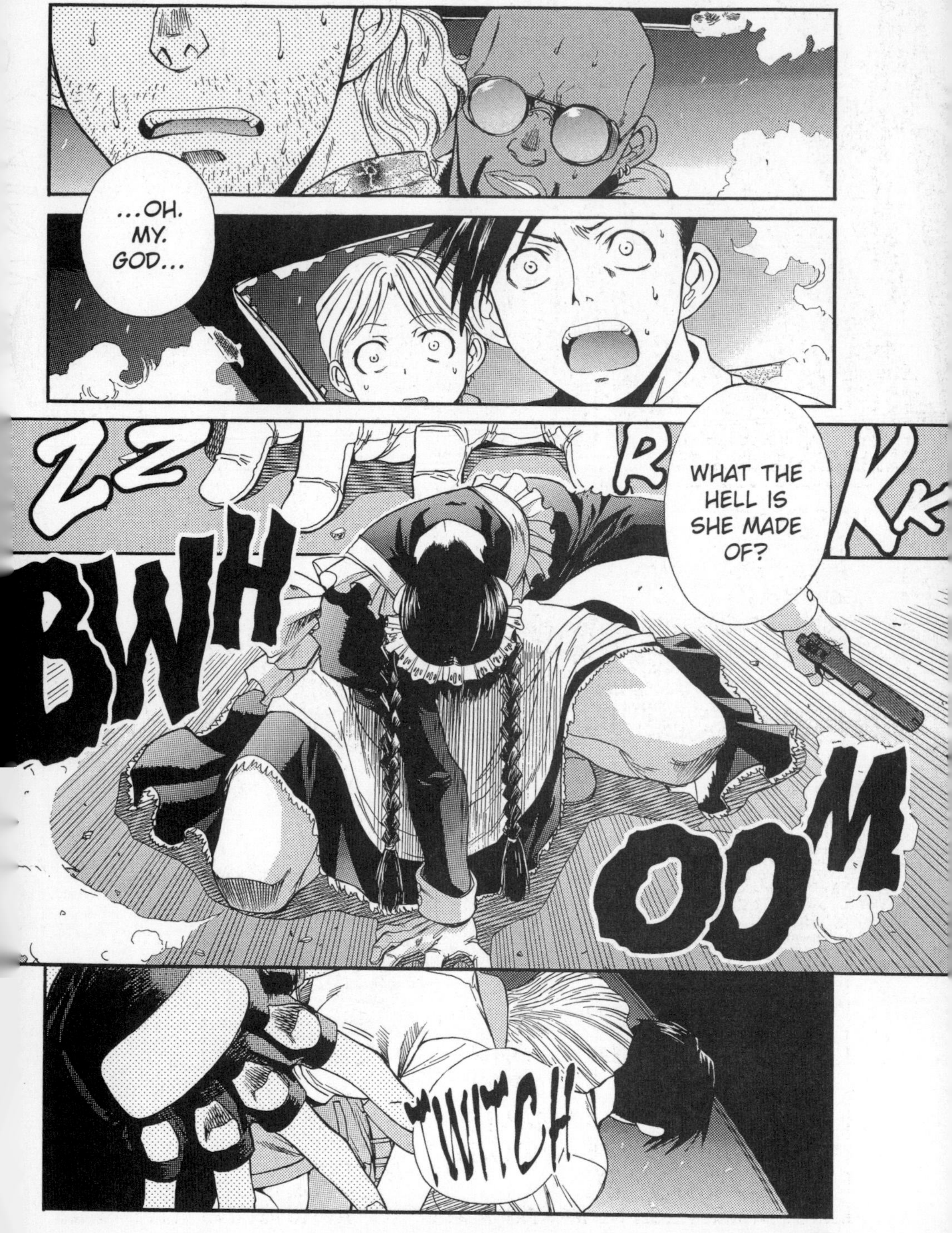
...OH. MY. GOD...
ZZRKK
WHAT THE HELL IS SHE MADE OF?
BWHOOM
TWITCH

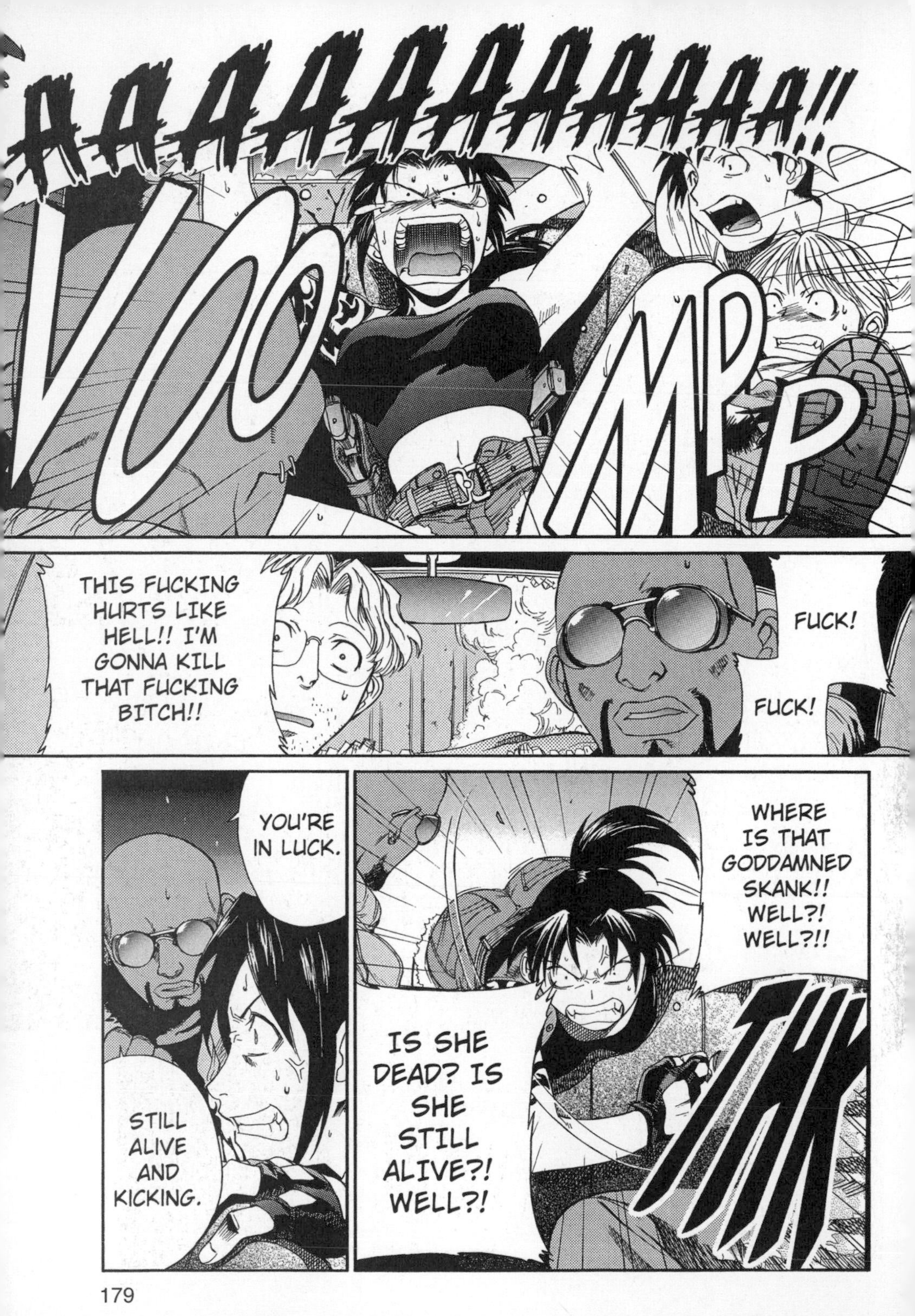
AAAAAAAAAAAA!!
VOOMPP
FUCK!
FUCK!
THIS FUCKING HURTS LIKE HELL!! I'M GONNA KILL THAT FUCKING BITCH!!
WHERE IS THAT GODDAMNED SKANK!! WELL?! WELL?!!
IS SHE DEAD? IS SHE STILL ALIVE?! WELL?!
THK
YOU'RE IN LUCK.
STILL ALIVE AND KICKING.

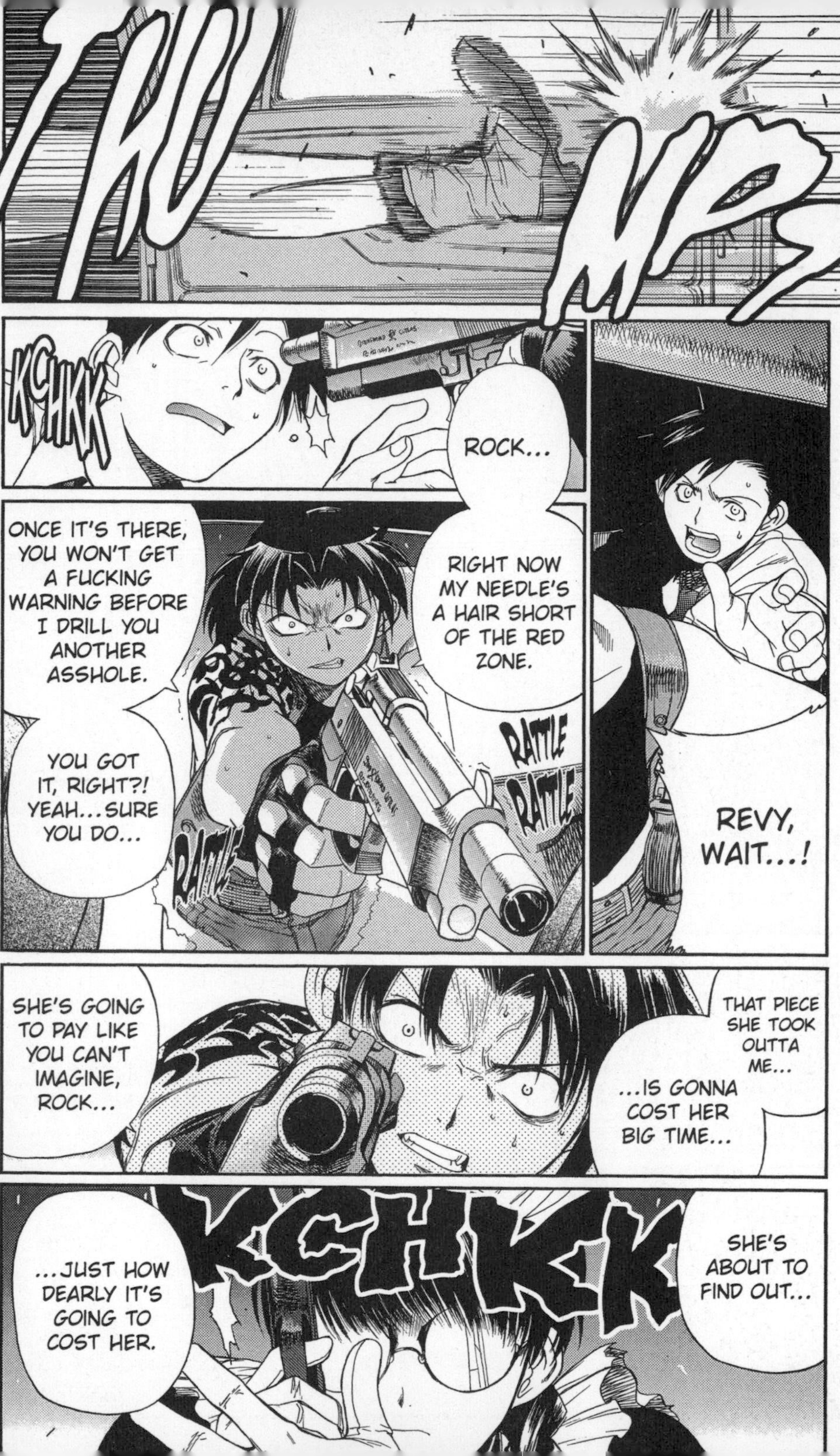
THRO
MP
REVY, WAIT...!
KCHKK
ROCK...
RIGHT NOW MY NEEDLE'S A HAIR SHORT OF THE RED ZONE.
ONCE IT'S THERE, YOU WON'T GET A FUCKING WARNING BEFORE I DRILL YOU ANOTHER ASSHOLE.
RATTLE
RATTLE
YOU GOT IT, RIGHT?! YEAH...SURE YOU DO...
RATTLE
THAT PIECE SHE TOOK OUTTA ME...
...IS GONNA COST HER BIG TIME...
SHE'S GOING TO PAY LIKE YOU CAN'T IMAGINE, ROCK...
SHE'S ABOUT TO FIND OUT...
KCHKK
...JUST HOW DEARLY IT'S GOING TO COST HER.

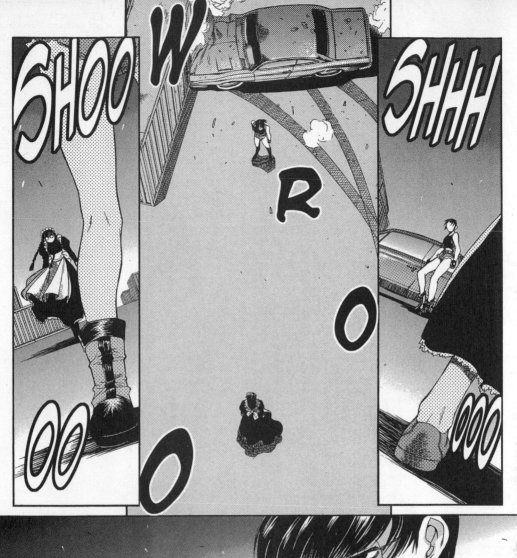

GO AHEAD, SEÑORITA. DRAW.

WHAT'S WRONG? YOU GOT THE SHAKES?

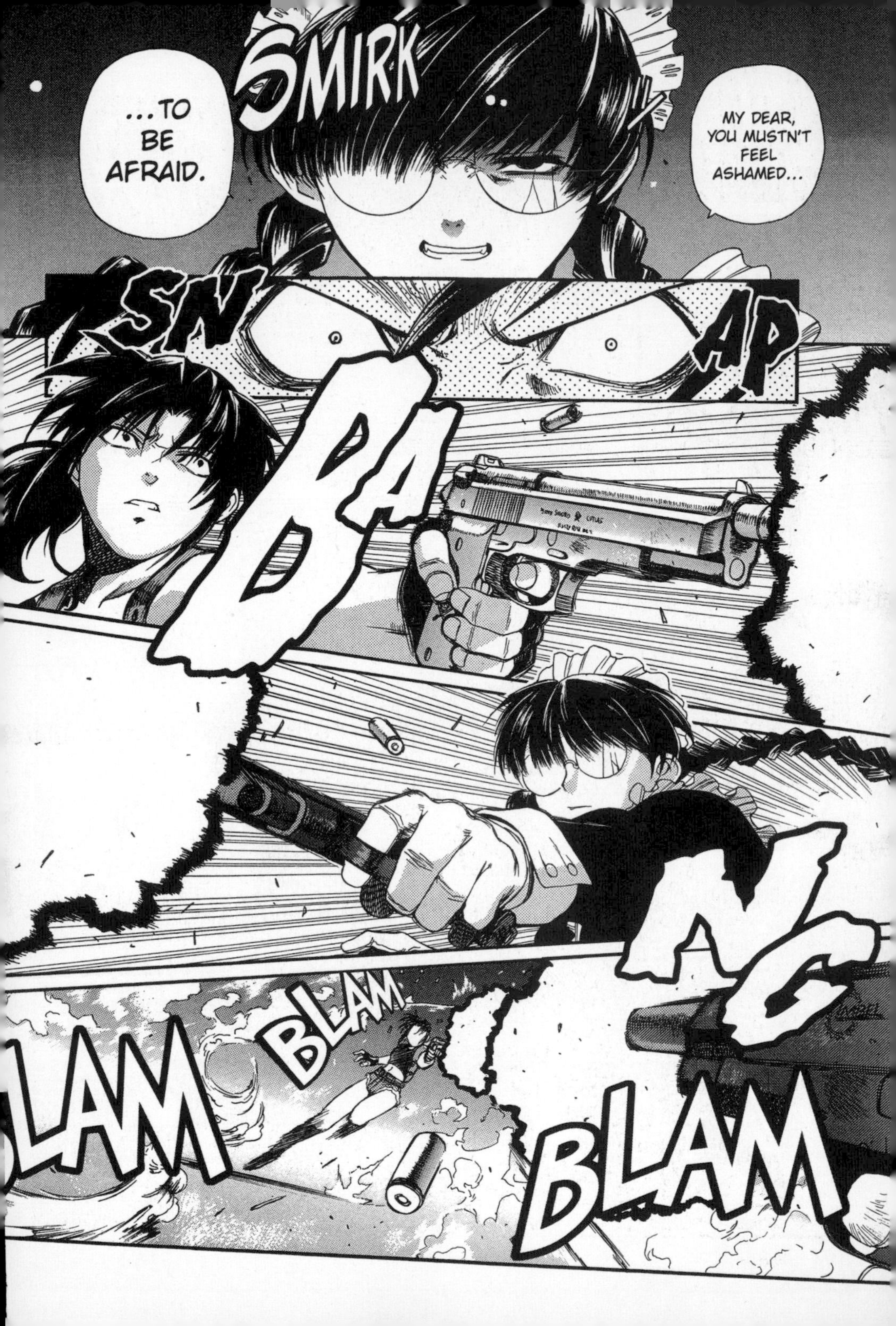
MY DEAR, YOU MUSTN'T FEEL ASHAMED...
SMIRK
...TO BE AFRAID.
SNAP
BANG
BLAM
BLAM
BLAM

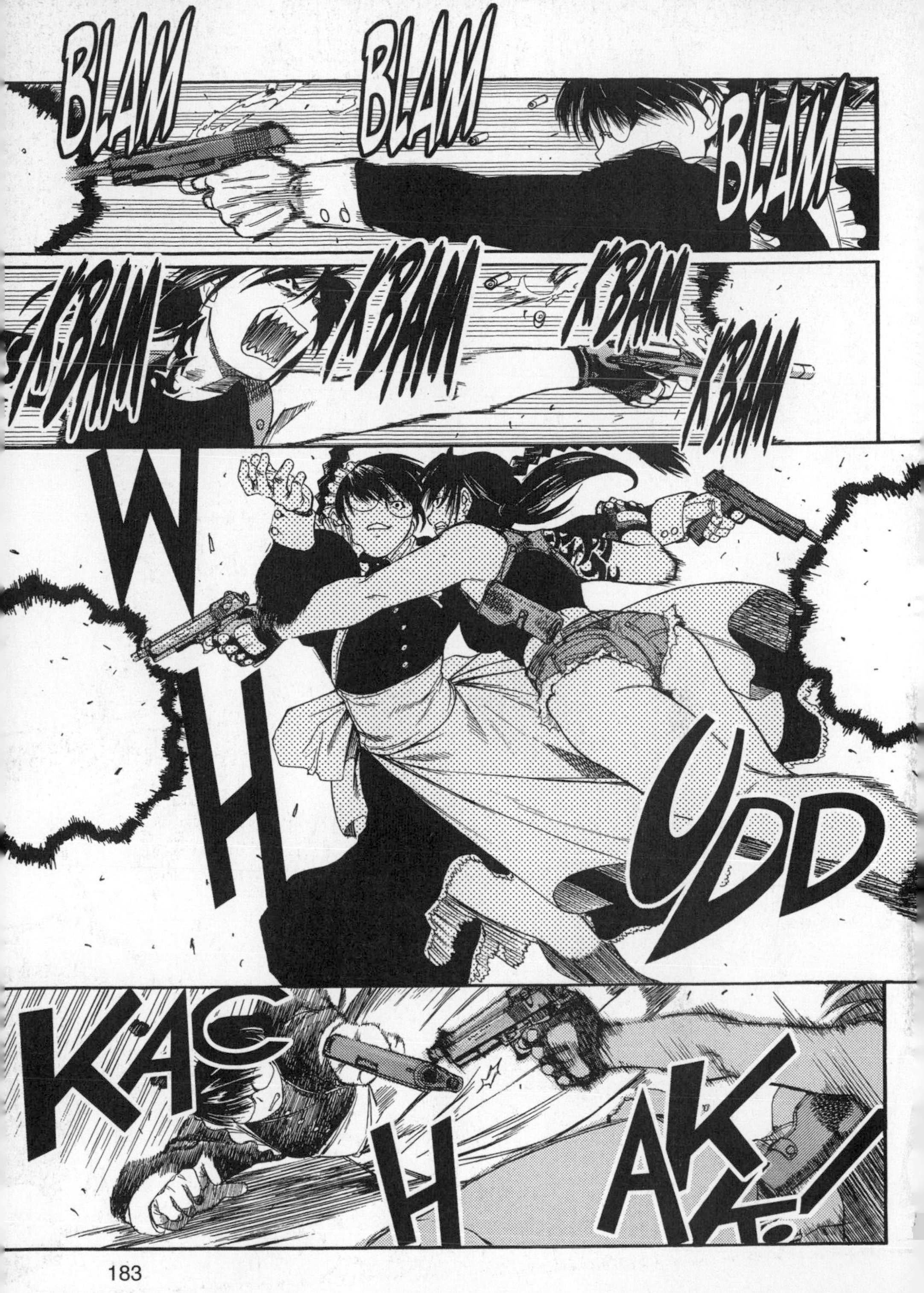
BLAM
BLAM
BLAM
KBAM
KBAM
KBAM
KBAM
WHUDD
KACHAK!

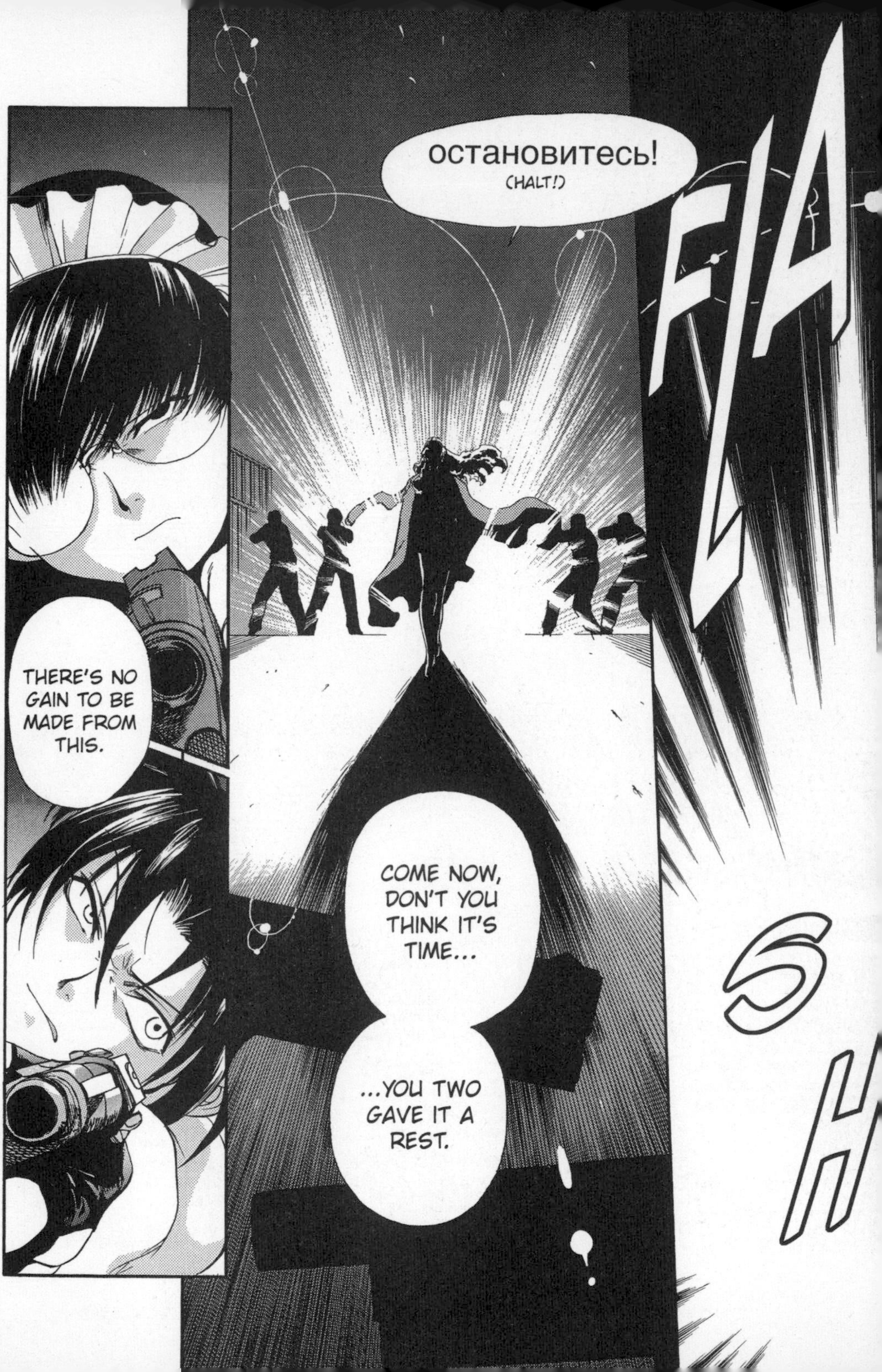
остановитесь!
(HALT!)
FLASH
COME NOW, DON'T YOU THINK IT'S TIME...
...YOU TWO GAVE IT A REST.
THERE'S NO GAIN TO BE MADE FROM THIS.

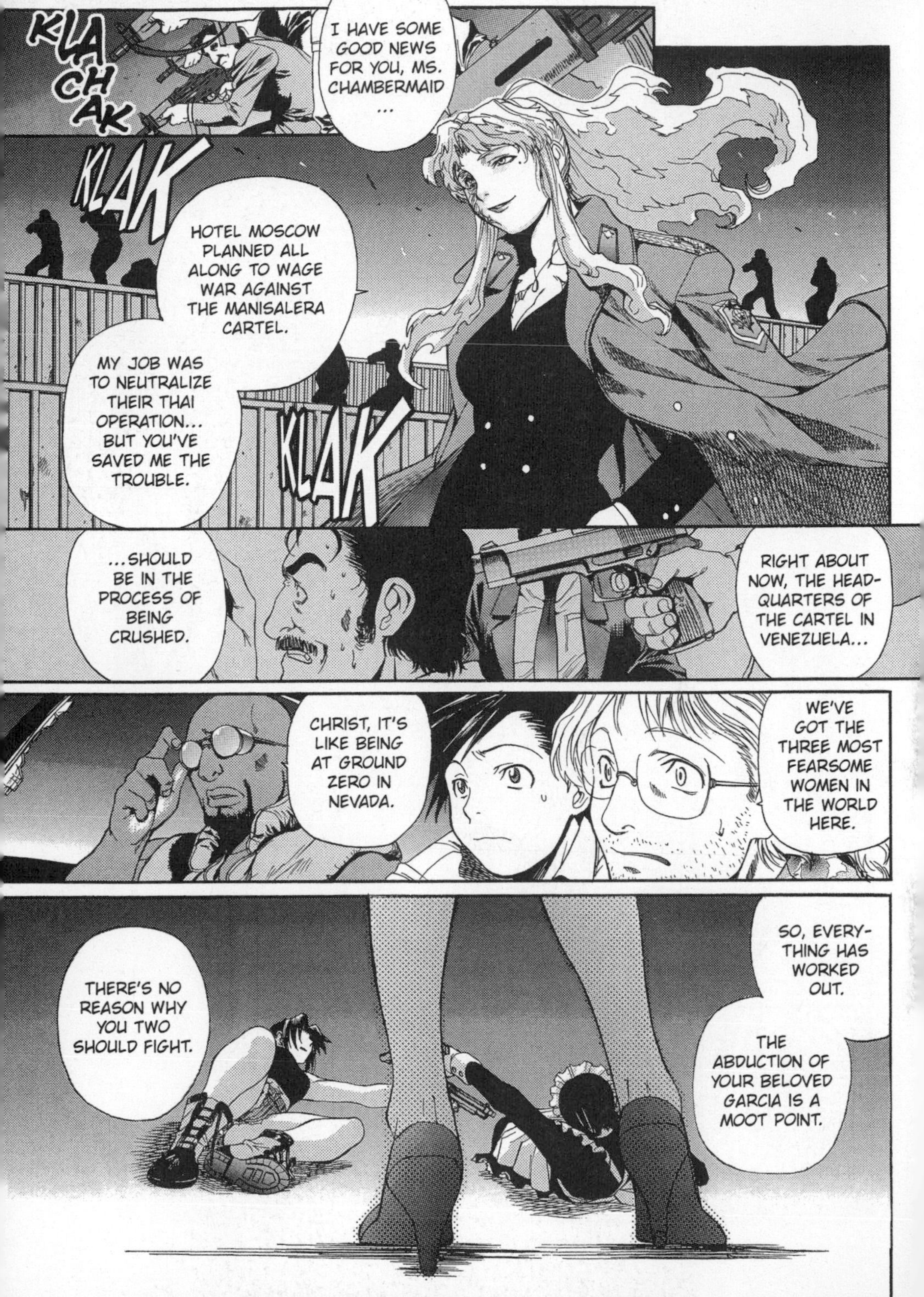
I HAVE SOME GOOD NEWS FOR YOU, MS. CHAMBERMAID ...
KLACHAK
KLAK
HOTEL MOSCOW PLANNED ALL ALONG TO WAGE WAR AGAINST THE MANISALERA CARTEL.
MY JOB WAS TO NEUTRALIZE THEIR THAI OPERATION... BUT YOU'VE SAVED ME THE TROUBLE.
KLAK
RIGHT ABOUT NOW, THE HEAD-QUARTERS OF THE CARTEL IN VENEZUELA...
...SHOULD BE IN THE PROCESS OF BEING CRUSHED.
WE'VE GOT THE THREE MOST FEARSOME WOMEN IN THE WORLD HERE.
CHRIST, IT'S LIKE BEING AT GROUND ZERO IN NEVADA.
SO, EVERY-THING HAS WORKED OUT.
THE ABDUCTION OF YOUR BELOVED GARCIA IS A MOOT POINT.
THERE'S NO REASON WHY YOU TWO SHOULD FIGHT.

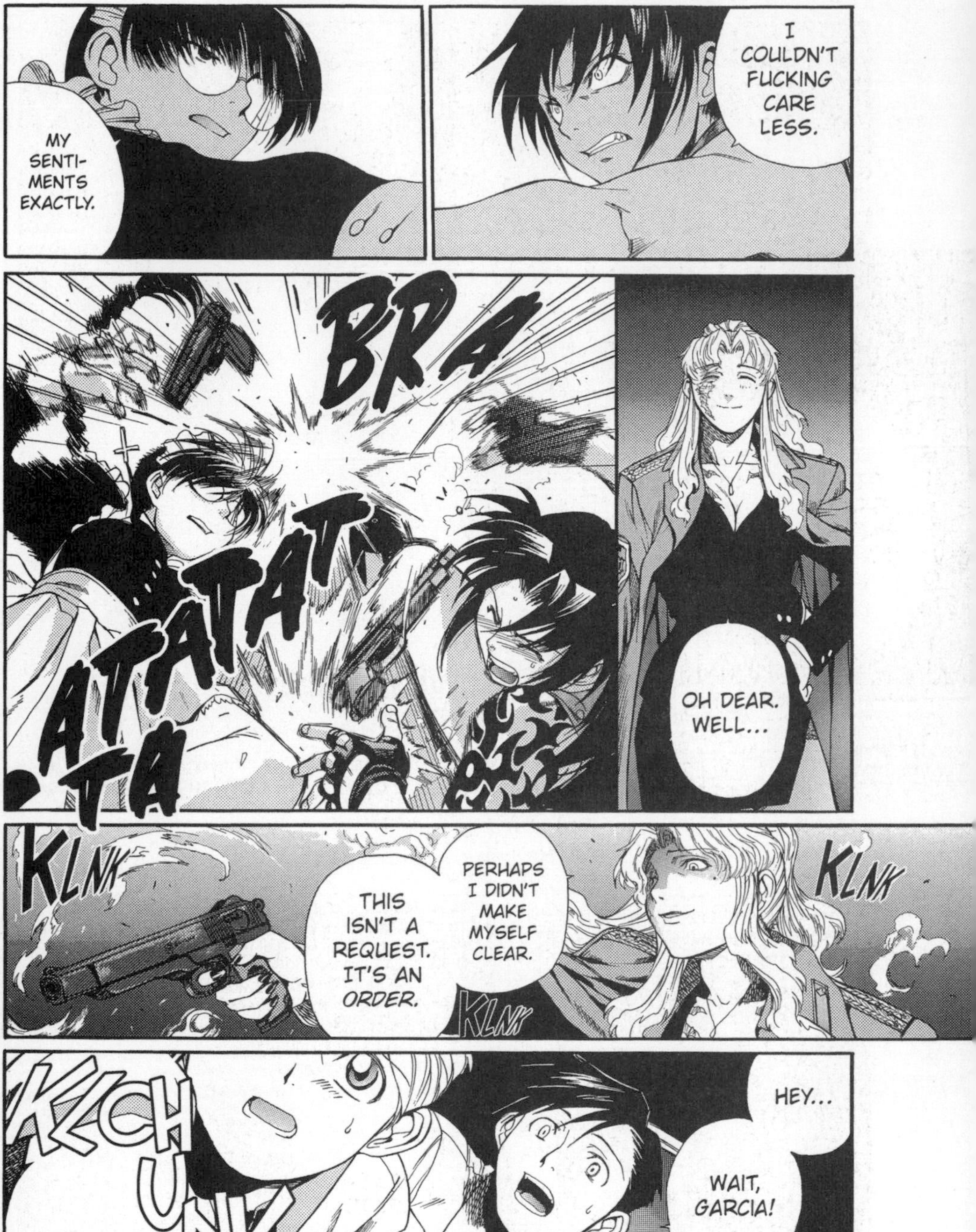
I COULDN'T FUCKING CARE LESS.
MY SENTI-MENTS EXACTLY.
OH DEAR. WELL...
BRA
TATATATATA
KLNK
PERHAPS I DIDN'T MAKE MYSELF CLEAR.
THIS ISN'T A REQUEST. IT'S AN ORDER.
KLNK
KLNK
HEY...
WAIT, GARCIA!
KLCHUNK

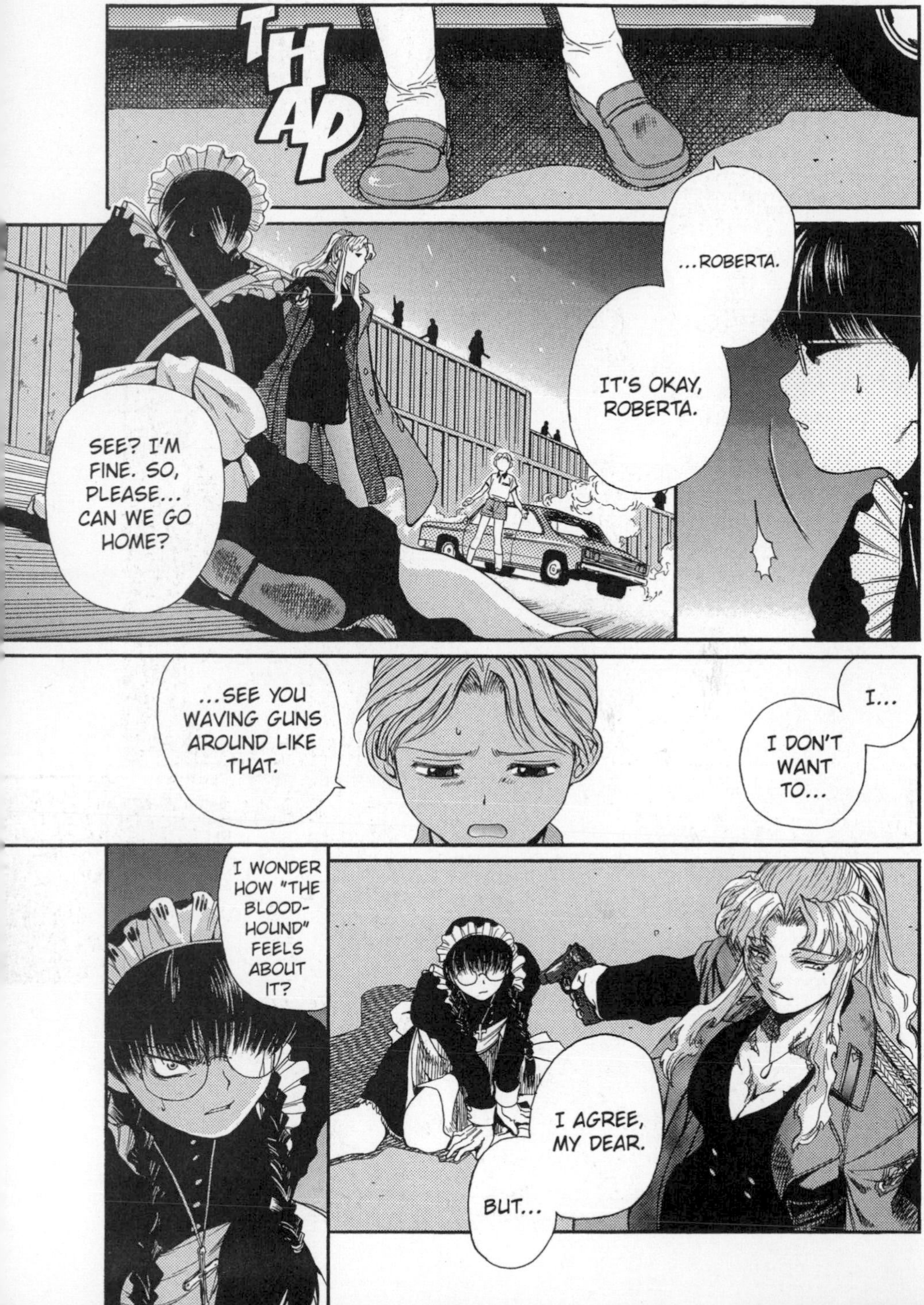
THAP
...ROBERTA.
IT'S OKAY, ROBERTA.
SEE? I'M FINE. SO, PLEASE... CAN WE GO HOME?
I...
I DON'T WANT TO...
...SEE YOU WAVING GUNS AROUND LIKE THAT.
I AGREE, MY DEAR.
BUT...
I WONDER HOW "THE BLOOD-HOUND" FEELS ABOUT IT?

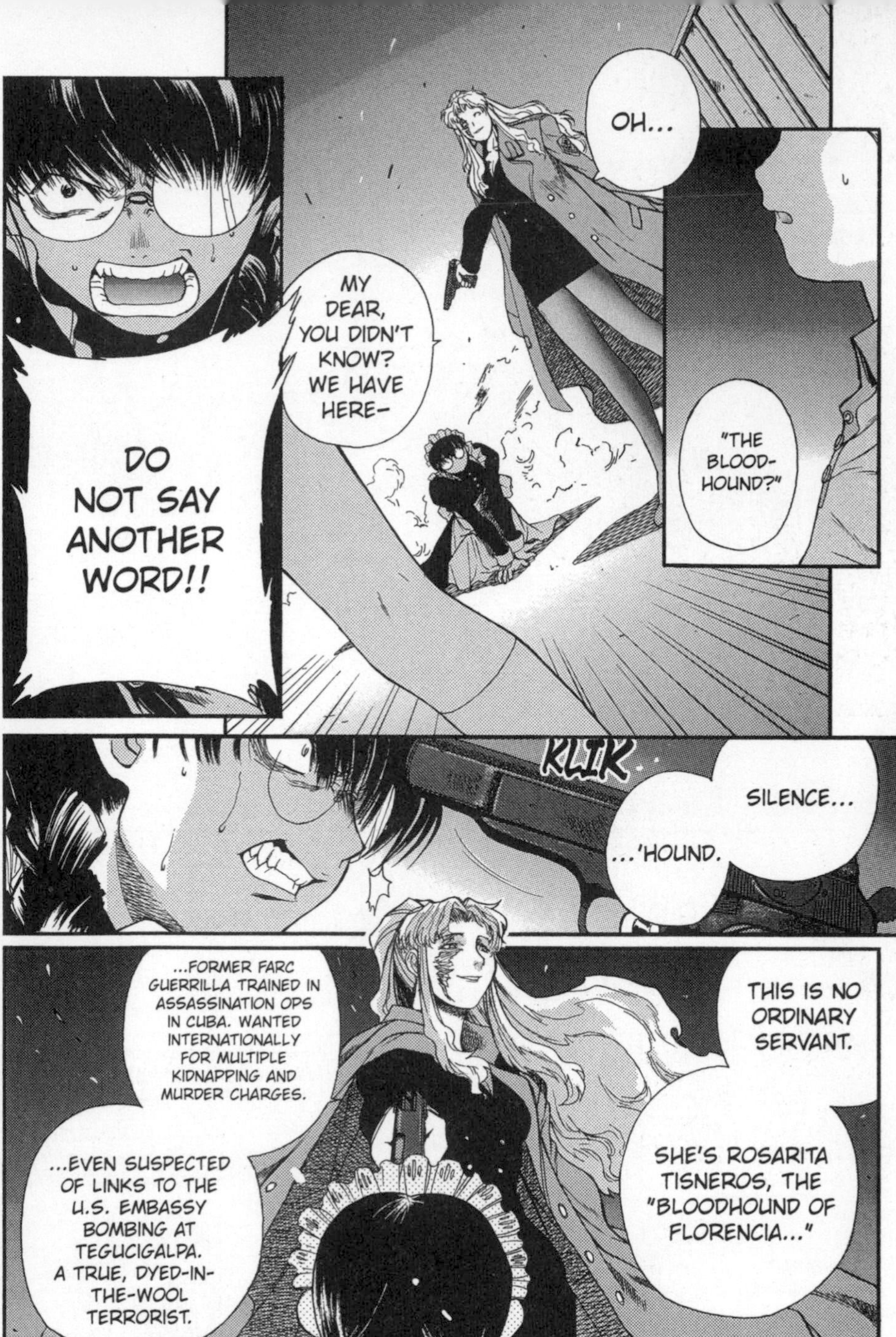
"THE BLOODHOUND?"
OH...
MY DEAR, YOU DIDN'T KNOW? WE HAVE HERE–
DO NOT SAY ANOTHER WORD!!
KLIK
SILENCE...
...'HOUND.
THIS IS NO ORDINARY SERVANT.
SHE'S ROSARITA TISNEROS, THE "BLOODHOUND OF FLORENCIA..."
...FORMER FARC GUERRILLA TRAINED IN ASSASSINATION OPS IN CUBA. WANTED INTERNATIONALLY FOR MULTIPLE KIDNAPPING AND MURDER CHARGES.
...EVEN SUSPECTED OF LINKS TO THE U.S. EMBASSY BOMBING AT TEGUCIGALPA. A TRUE, DYED-IN-THE-WOOL TERRORIST.

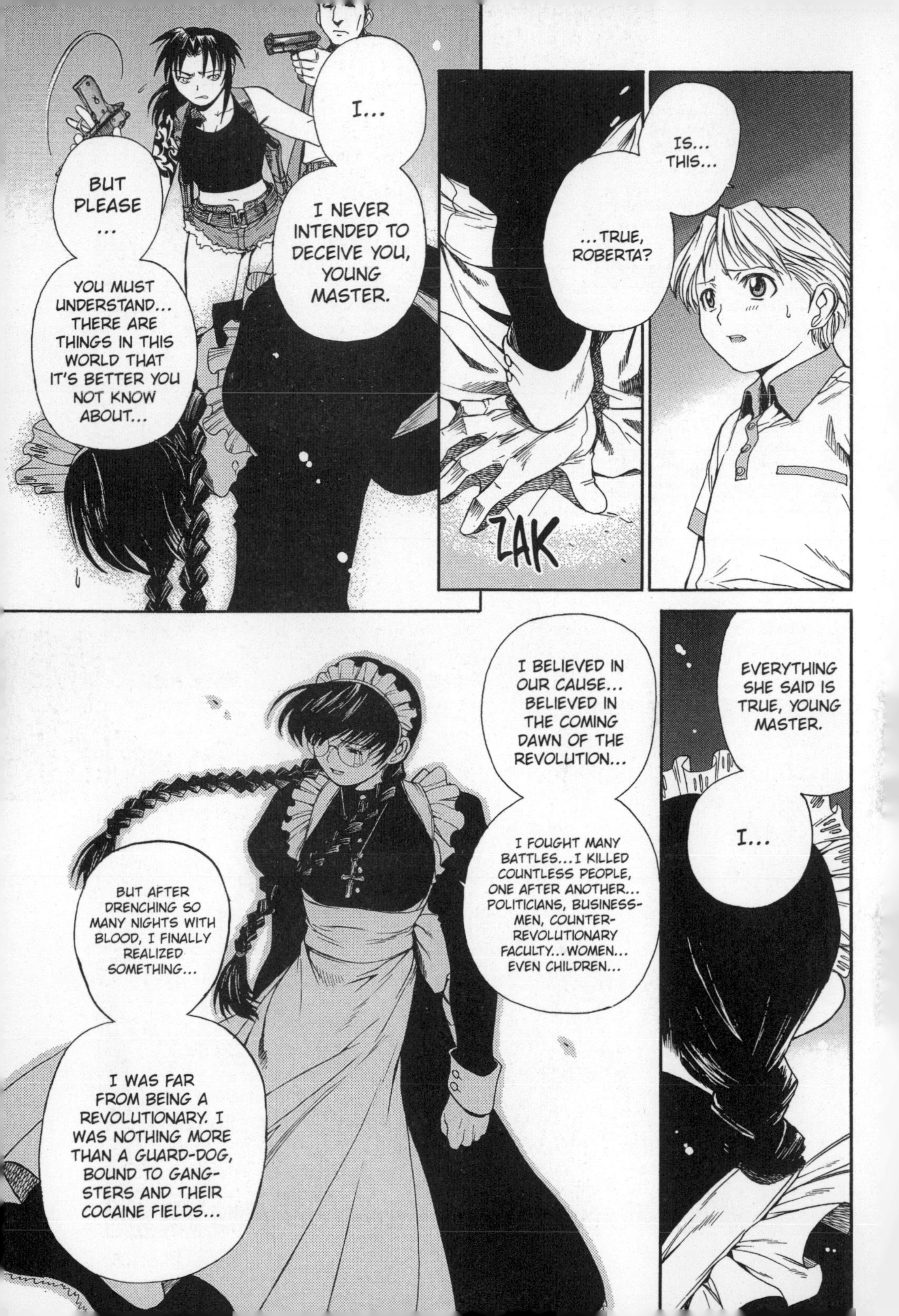
IS... THIS...
...TRUE, ROBERTA?
ZAK
I...
I NEVER INTENDED TO DECEIVE YOU, YOUNG MASTER.
BUT PLEASE...
YOU MUST UNDERSTAND... THERE ARE THINGS IN THIS WORLD THAT IT'S BETTER YOU NOT KNOW ABOUT...
EVERYTHING SHE SAID IS TRUE, YOUNG MASTER.
I...
I BELIEVED IN OUR CAUSE... BELIEVED IN THE COMING DAWN OF THE REVOLUTION...
I FOUGHT MANY BATTLES...I KILLED COUNTLESS PEOPLE, ONE AFTER ANOTHER... POLITICIANS, BUSINESS-MEN, COUNTER-REVOLUTIONARY FACULTY...WOMEN... EVEN CHILDREN...
BUT AFTER DRENCHING SO MANY NIGHTS WITH BLOOD, I FINALLY REALIZED SOMETHING...
I WAS FAR FROM BEING A REVOLUTIONARY. I WAS NOTHING MORE THAN A GUARD-DOG, BOUND TO GANG-STERS AND THEIR COCAINE FIELDS...

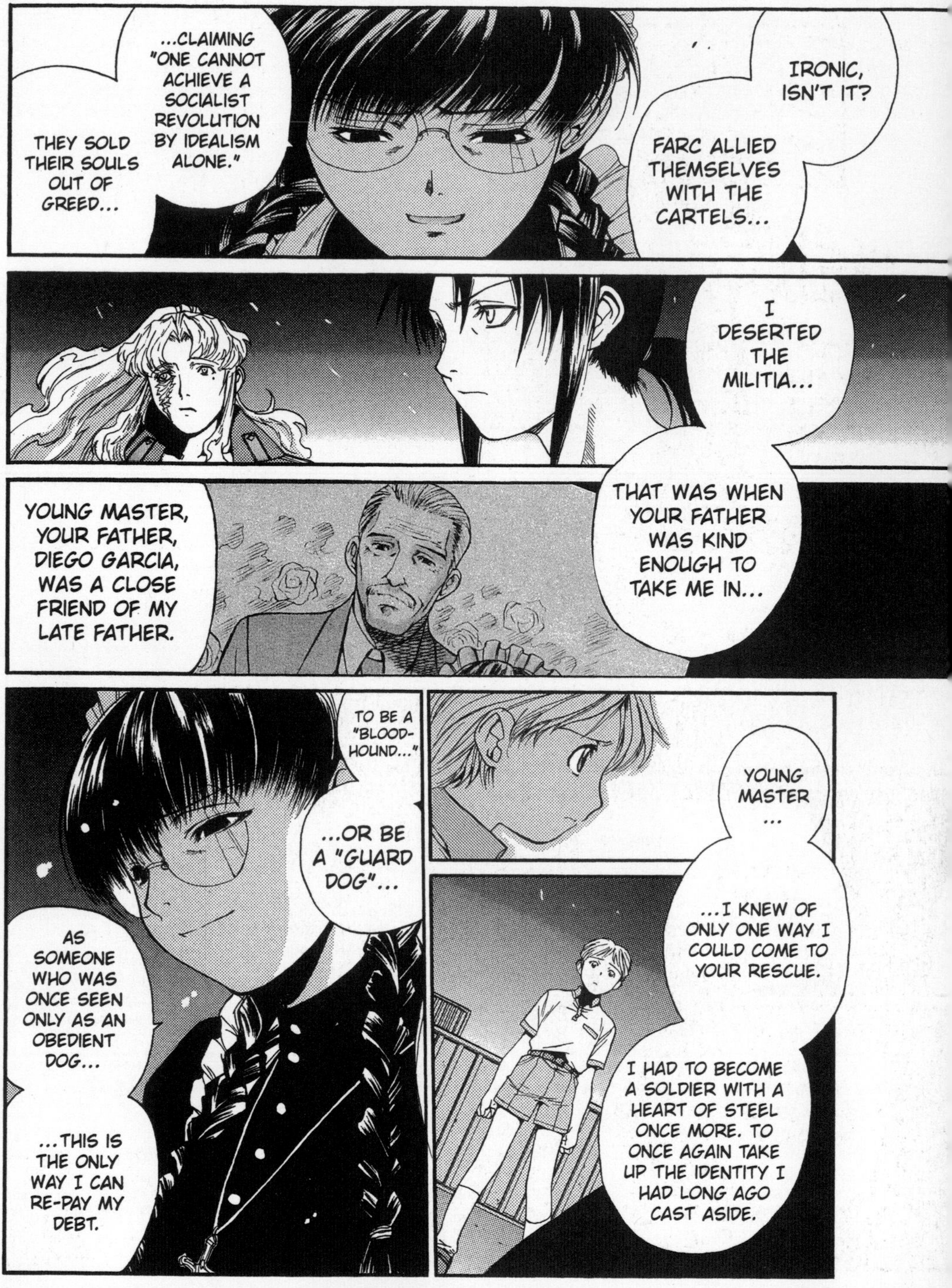
IRONIC, ISN'T IT?
FARC ALLIED THEMSELVES WITH THE CARTELS...
...CLAIMING "ONE CANNOT ACHIEVE A SOCIALIST REVOLUTION BY IDEALISM ALONE."
THEY SOLD THEIR SOULS OUT OF GREED...
I DESERTED THE MILITIA...
THAT WAS WHEN YOUR FATHER WAS KIND ENOUGH TO TAKE ME IN...
YOUNG MASTER, YOUR FATHER, DIEGO GARCIA, WAS A CLOSE FRIEND OF MY LATE FATHER.
YOUNG MASTER ...
...I KNEW OF ONLY ONE WAY I COULD COME TO YOUR RESCUE.
I HAD TO BECOME A SOLDIER WITH A HEART OF STEEL ONCE MORE. TO ONCE AGAIN TAKE UP THE IDENTITY I HAD LONG AGO CAST ASIDE.
TO BE A "BLOOD-HOUND..."
...OR BE A "GUARD DOG"...
AS SOMEONE WHO WAS ONCE SEEN ONLY AS AN OBEDIENT DOG...
...THIS IS THE ONLY WAY I CAN RE-PAY MY DEBT.

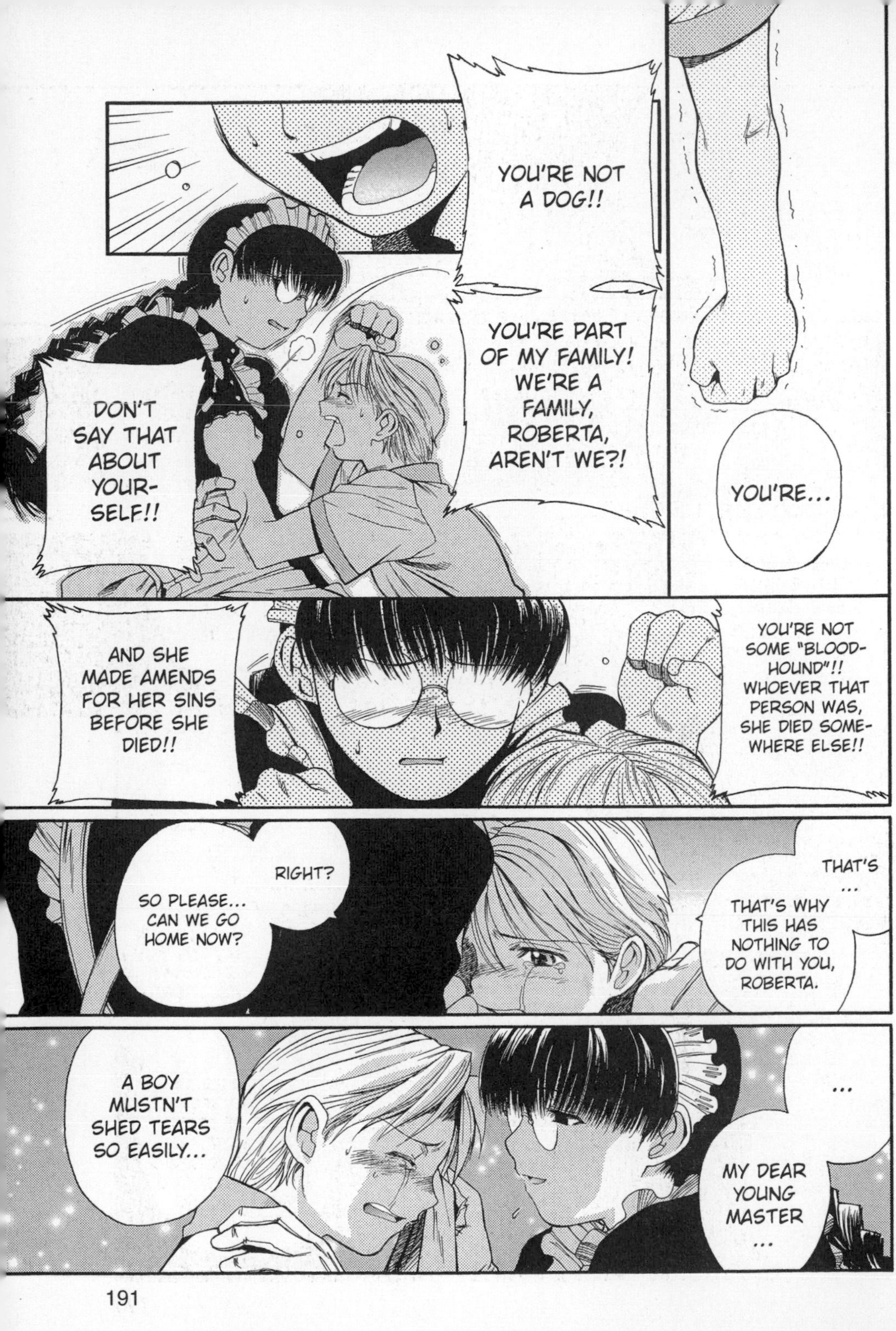
YOU'RE...
YOU'RE NOT A DOG!!
YOU'RE PART OF MY FAMILY! WE'RE A FAMILY, ROBERTA, AREN'T WE?!
DON'T SAY THAT ABOUT YOUR-SELF!!
YOU'RE NOT SOME "BLOOD-HOUND"!! WHOEVER THAT PERSON WAS, SHE DIED SOME-WHERE ELSE!!
AND SHE MADE AMENDS FOR HER SINS BEFORE SHE DIED!!
THAT'S ...
THAT'S WHY THIS HAS NOTHING TO DO WITH YOU, ROBERTA.
RIGHT?
SO PLEASE... CAN WE GO HOME NOW?
...
MY DEAR YOUNG MASTER ...
A BOY MUSTN'T SHED TEARS SO EASILY...

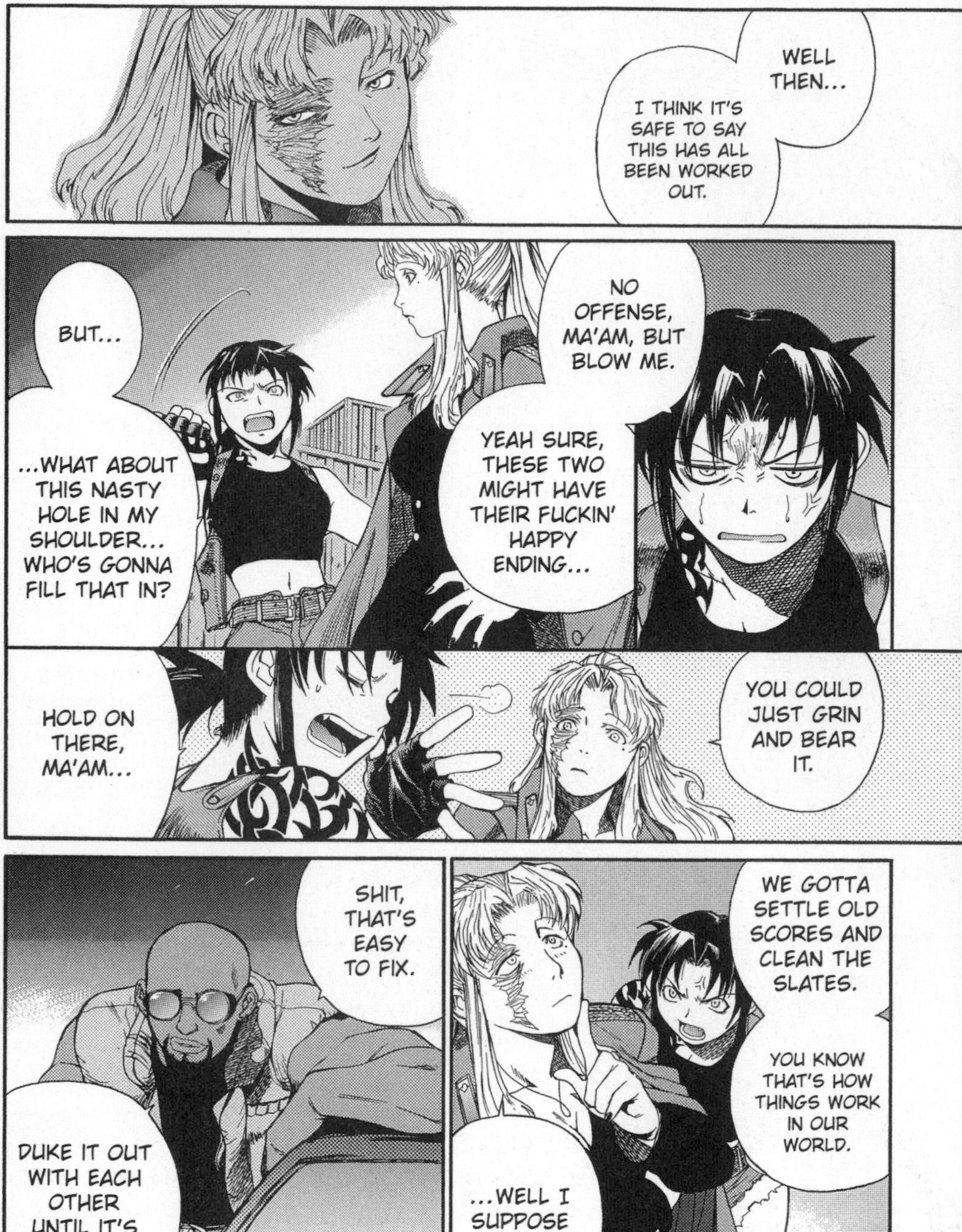
WELL THEN...
I THINK IT'S SAFE TO SAY THIS HAS ALL BEEN WORKED OUT.
NO OFFENSE, MA'AM, BUT BLOW ME.
YEAH SURE, THESE TWO MIGHT HAVE THEIR FUCKIN' HAPPY ENDING...
BUT...
...WHAT ABOUT THIS NASTY HOLE IN MY SHOULDER... WHO'S GONNA FILL THAT IN?
YOU COULD JUST GRIN AND BEAR IT.
HOLD ON THERE, MA'AM...
WE GOTTA SETTLE OLD SCORES AND CLEAN THE SLATES.
YOU KNOW THAT'S HOW THINGS WORK IN OUR WORLD.
...WELL I SUPPOSE SO...
SHIT, THAT'S EASY TO FIX.
DUKE IT OUT WITH EACH OTHER UNTIL IT'S SETTLED.

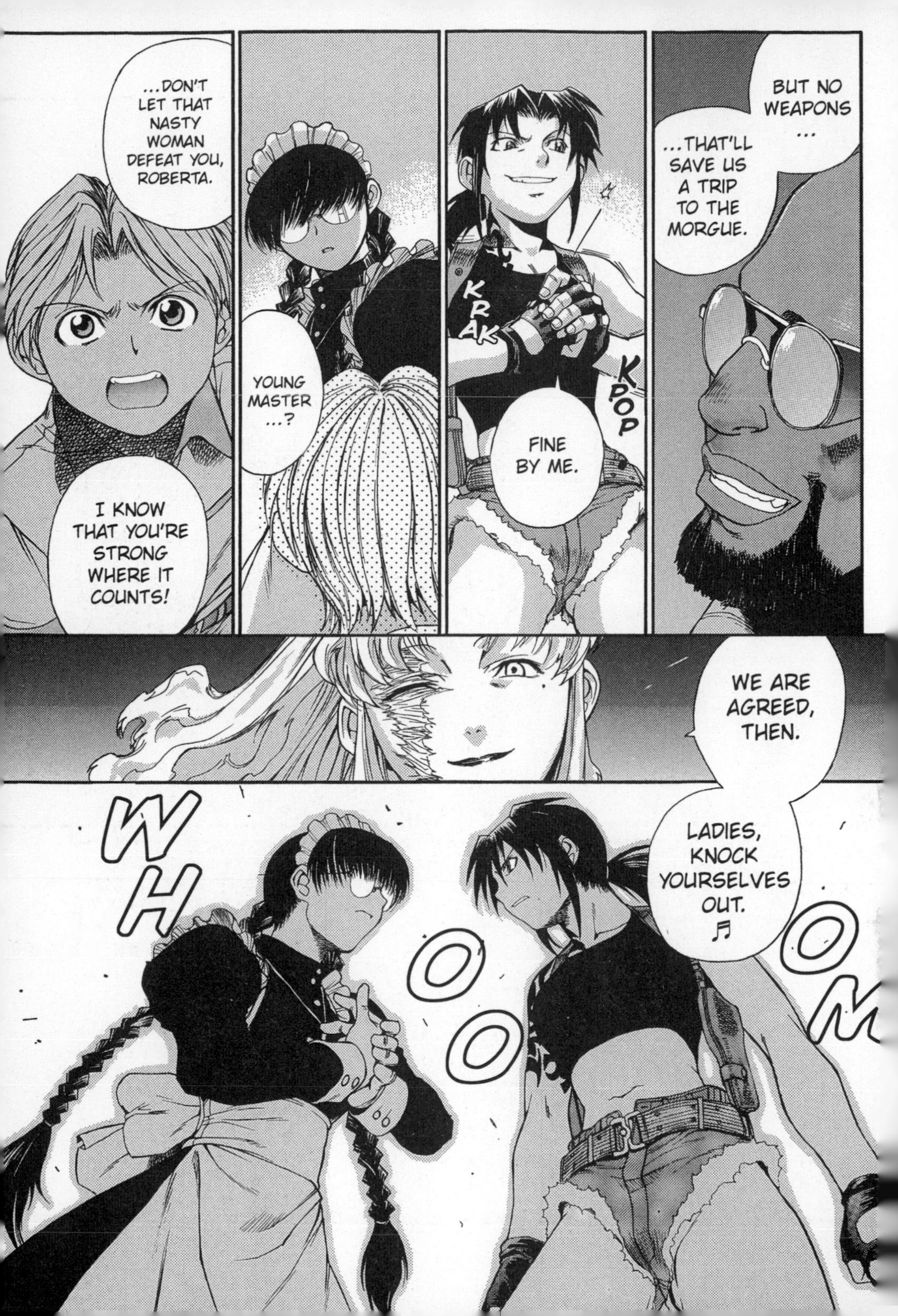
BUT NO WEAPONS ...
...THAT'LL SAVE US A TRIP TO THE MORGUE.
KRAK
KPOP
FINE BY ME.
YOUNG MASTER ...?
...DON'T LET THAT NASTY WOMAN DEFEAT YOU, ROBERTA.
I KNOW THAT YOU'RE STRONG WHERE IT COUNTS!
WE ARE AGREED, THEN.
LADIES, KNOCK YOURSELVES OUT. ♬
WHOOOOM

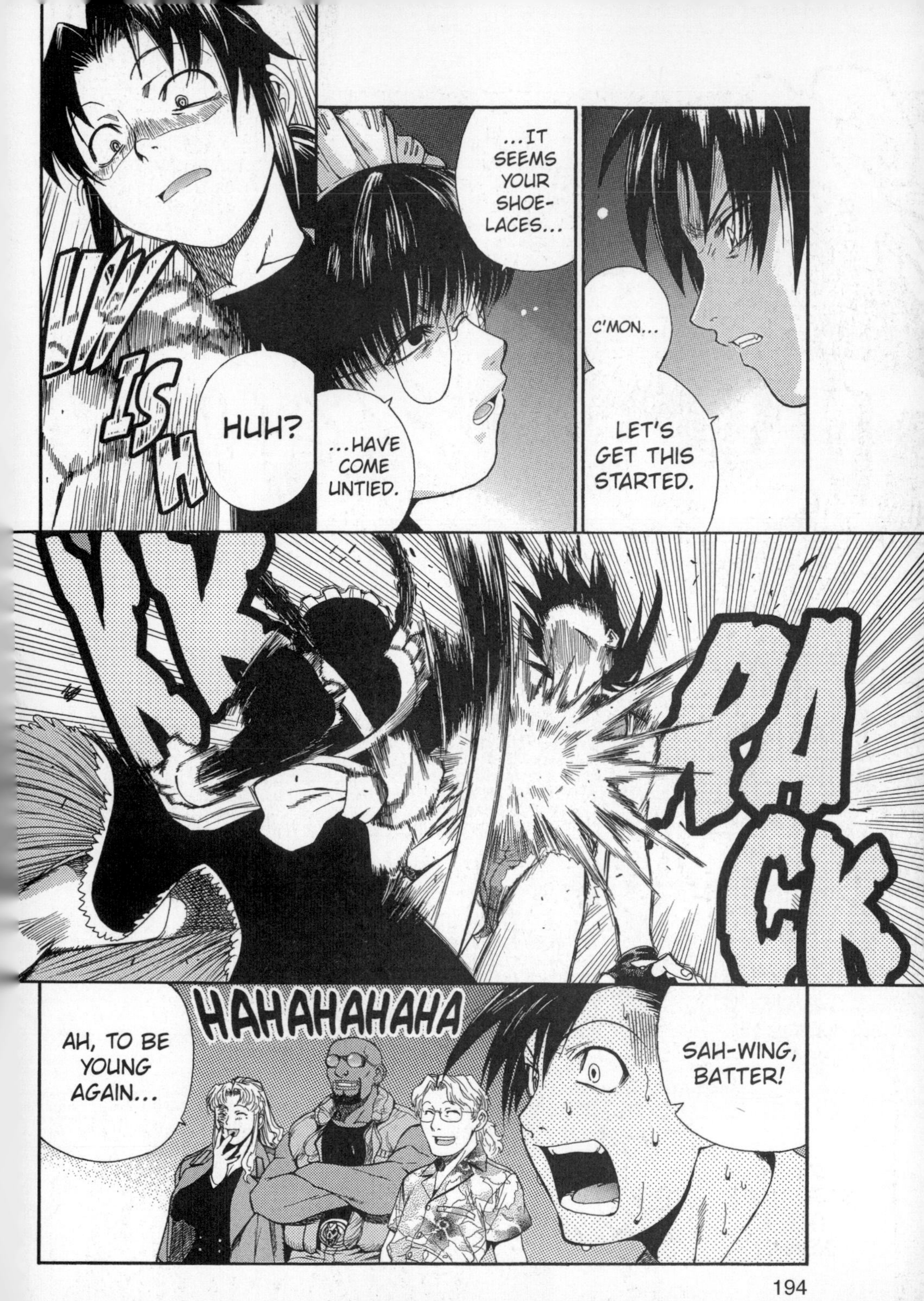
C'MON...
LET'S GET THIS STARTED.
...IT SEEMS YOUR SHOE-LACES...
...HAVE COME UNTIED.
HUH?
SAH-WING, BATTER!
HAHAHAHAHA
AH, TO BE YOUNG AGAIN...

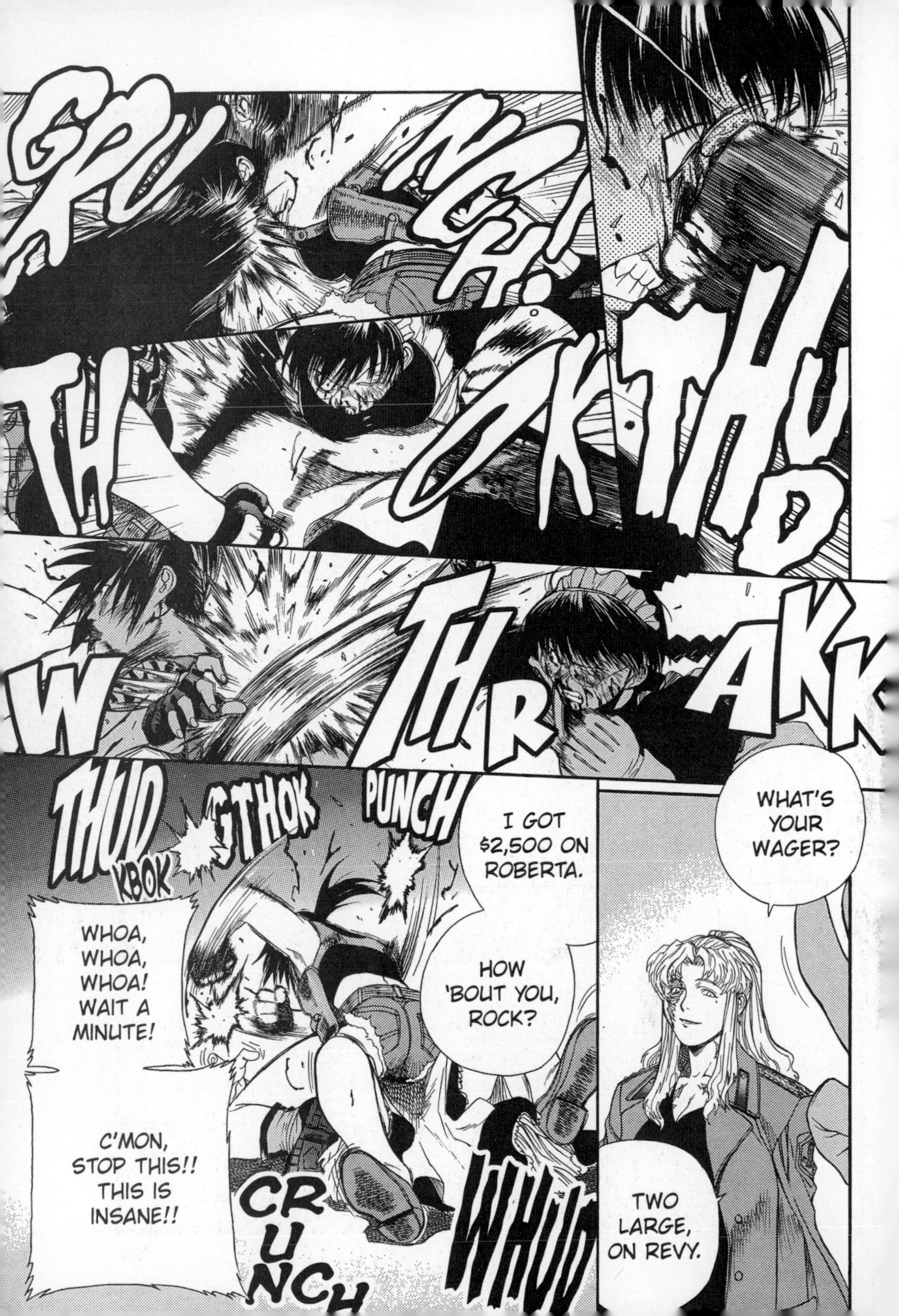
THUD
GRUNCH!
THAK
THRAKK
W
WHAT'S YOUR WAGER?
TWO LARGE, ON REVY.
I GOT $2,500 ON ROBERTA.
HOW 'BOUT YOU, ROCK?
PUNCH
GTHOK
THUD
KBOK
WHOA, WHOA, WHOA! WAIT A MINUTE!
C'MON, STOP THIS!! THIS IS INSANE!!
WHUD
CRUNCH

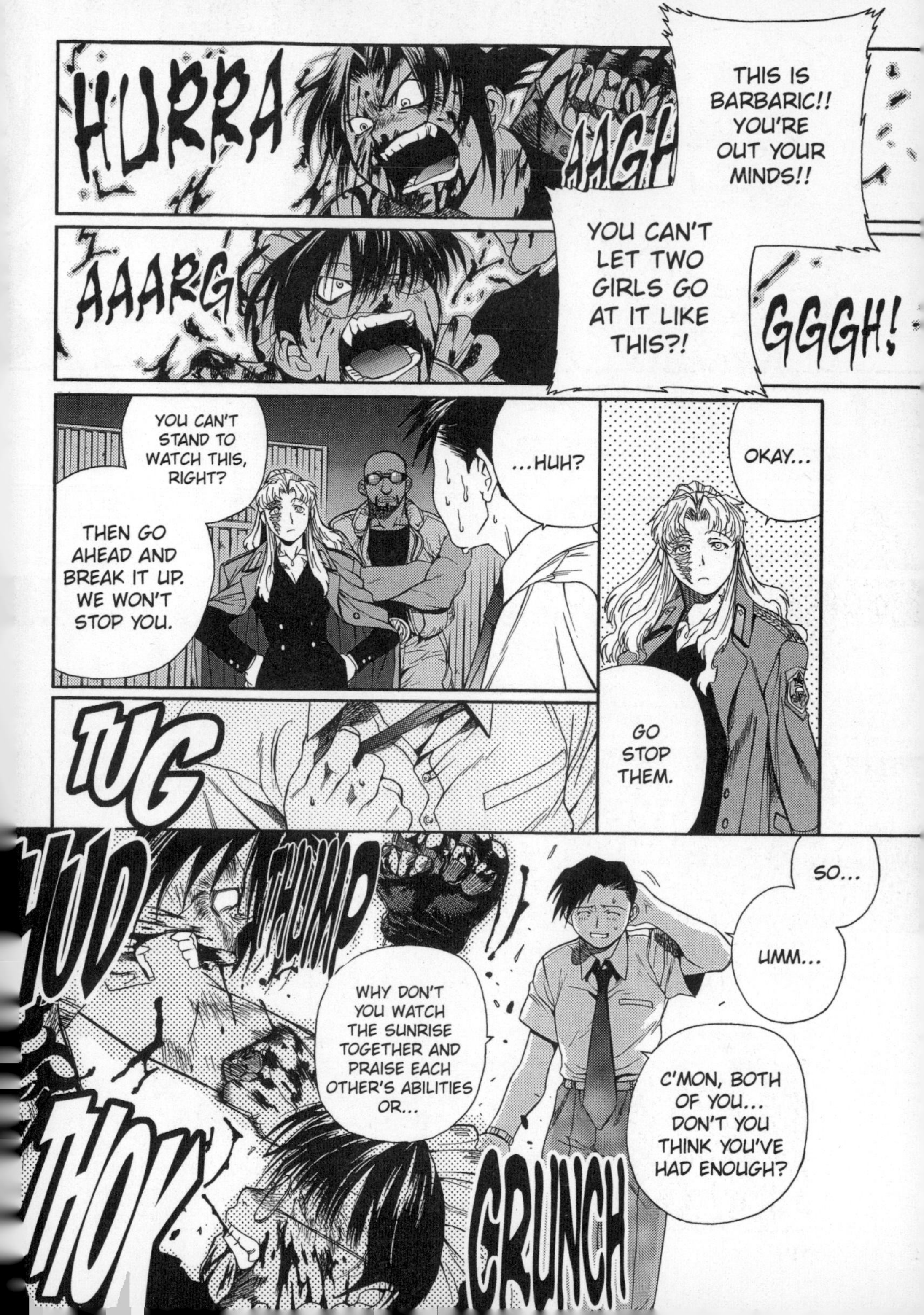
THIS IS BARBARIC!! YOU'RE OUT YOUR MINDS!!
YOU CAN'T LET TWO GIRLS GO AT IT LIKE THIS?!
GGGH!
HURRA
AAGH
AAARGH
OKAY...
GO STOP THEM.
YOU CAN'T STAND TO WATCH THIS, RIGHT?
...HUH?
THEN GO AHEAD AND BREAK IT UP. WE WON'T STOP YOU.
TUG
SO...
UMM...
C'MON, BOTH OF YOU... DON'T YOU THINK YOU'VE HAD ENOUGH?
WHY DON'T YOU WATCH THE SUNRISE TOGETHER AND PRAISE EACH OTHER'S ABILITIES OR...
CRUNCH
THUMP
HUD
THOK

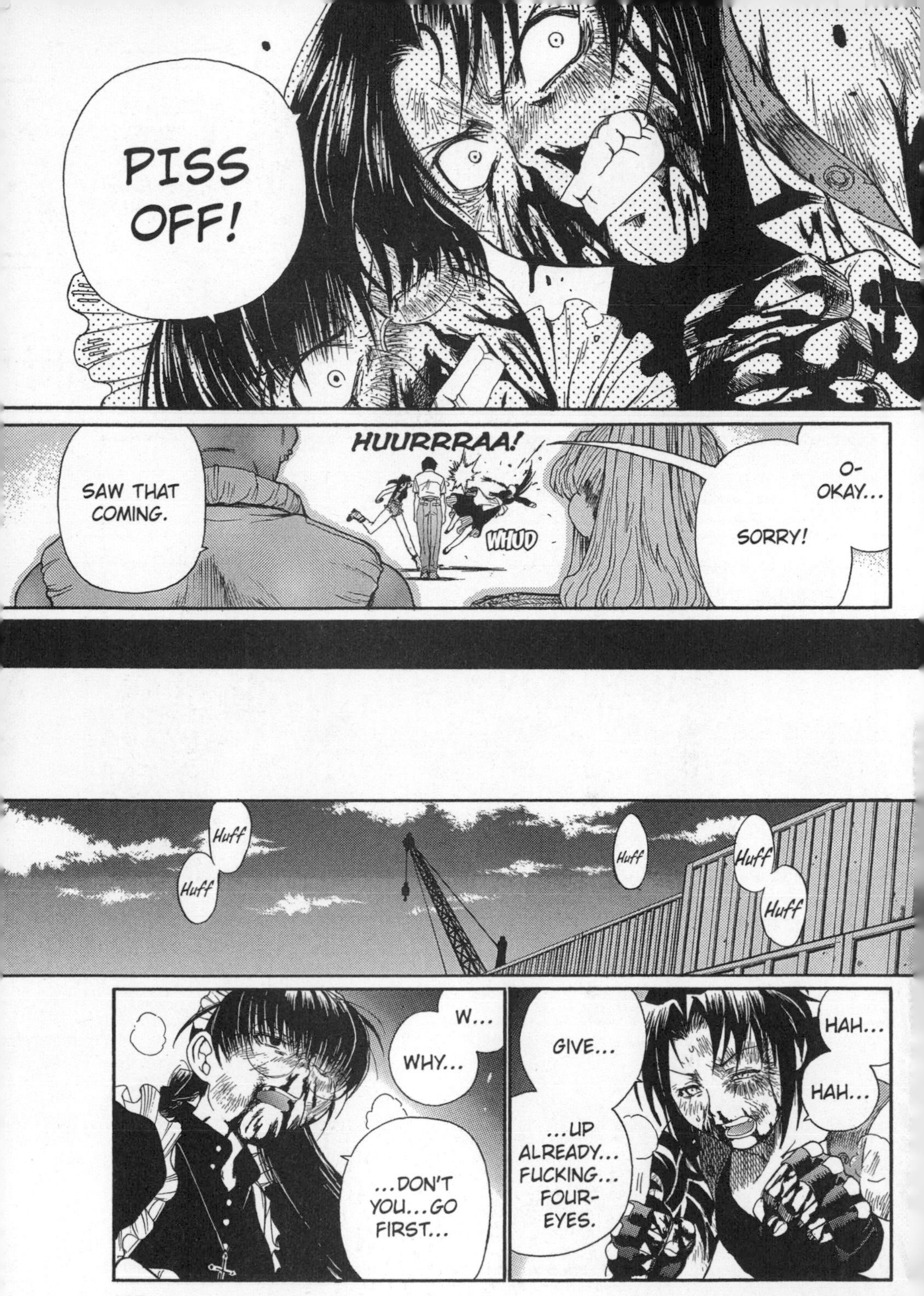
PISS OFF!
O- OKAY...
SORRY!
HUURRRAA!
WHUD
SAW THAT COMING.
Huff
Huff
Huff
Huff
Huff
HAH...
HAH...
GIVE...
...UP ALREADY... FUCKING... FOUR-EYES.
W...
WHY...
...DON'T YOU...GO FIRST...

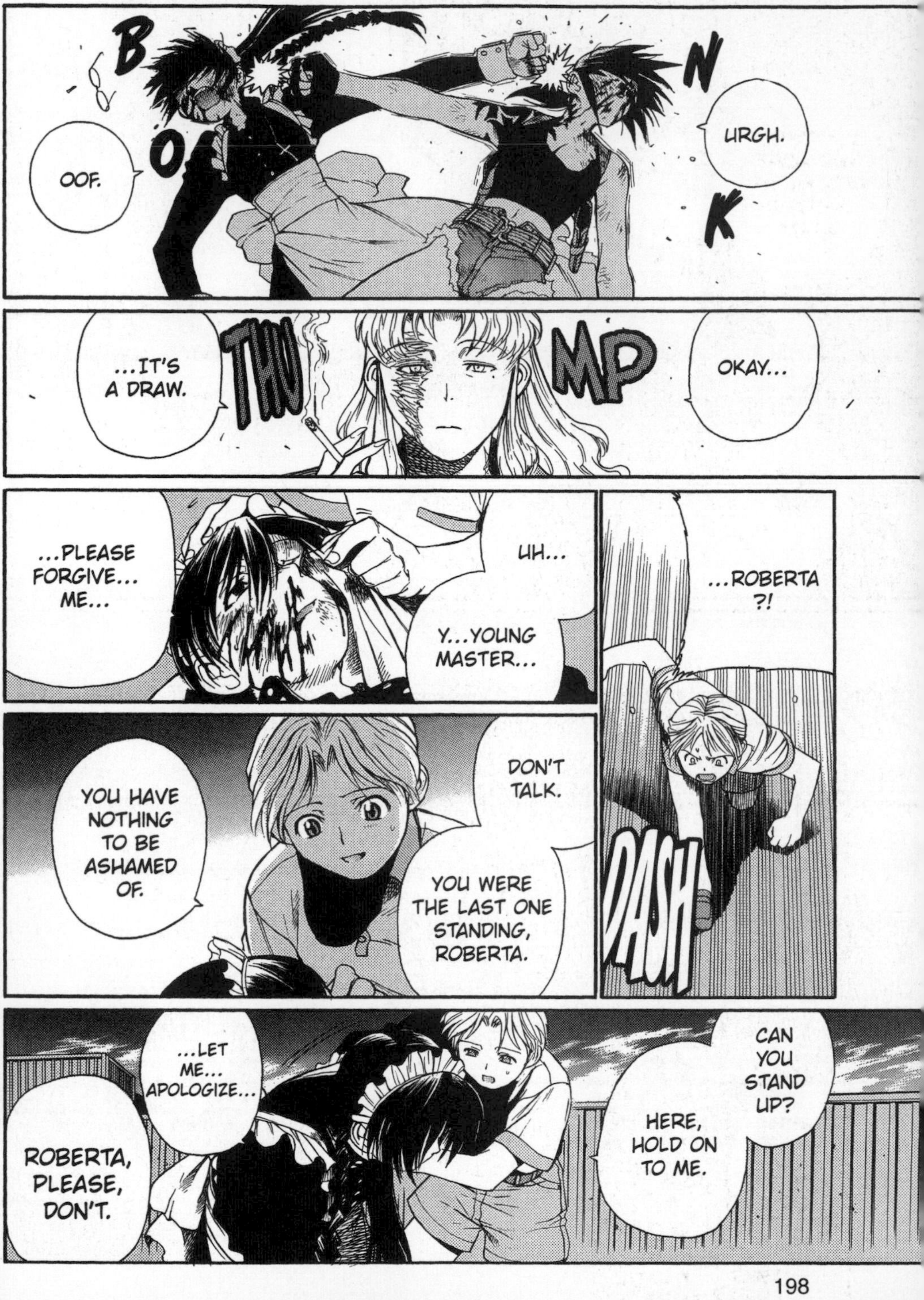
URGH.
BONK
OOF.
OKAY...
THUMP
...IT'S A DRAW.
...ROBERTA ?!
DASH
UH...
Y...YOUNG MASTER...
...PLEASE FORGIVE... ME...
DON'T TALK.
YOU WERE THE LAST ONE STANDING, ROBERTA.
YOU HAVE NOTHING TO BE ASHAMED OF.
CAN YOU STAND UP?
HERE, HOLD ON TO ME.
...LET ME... APOLOGIZE...
ROBERTA, PLEASE, DON'T.

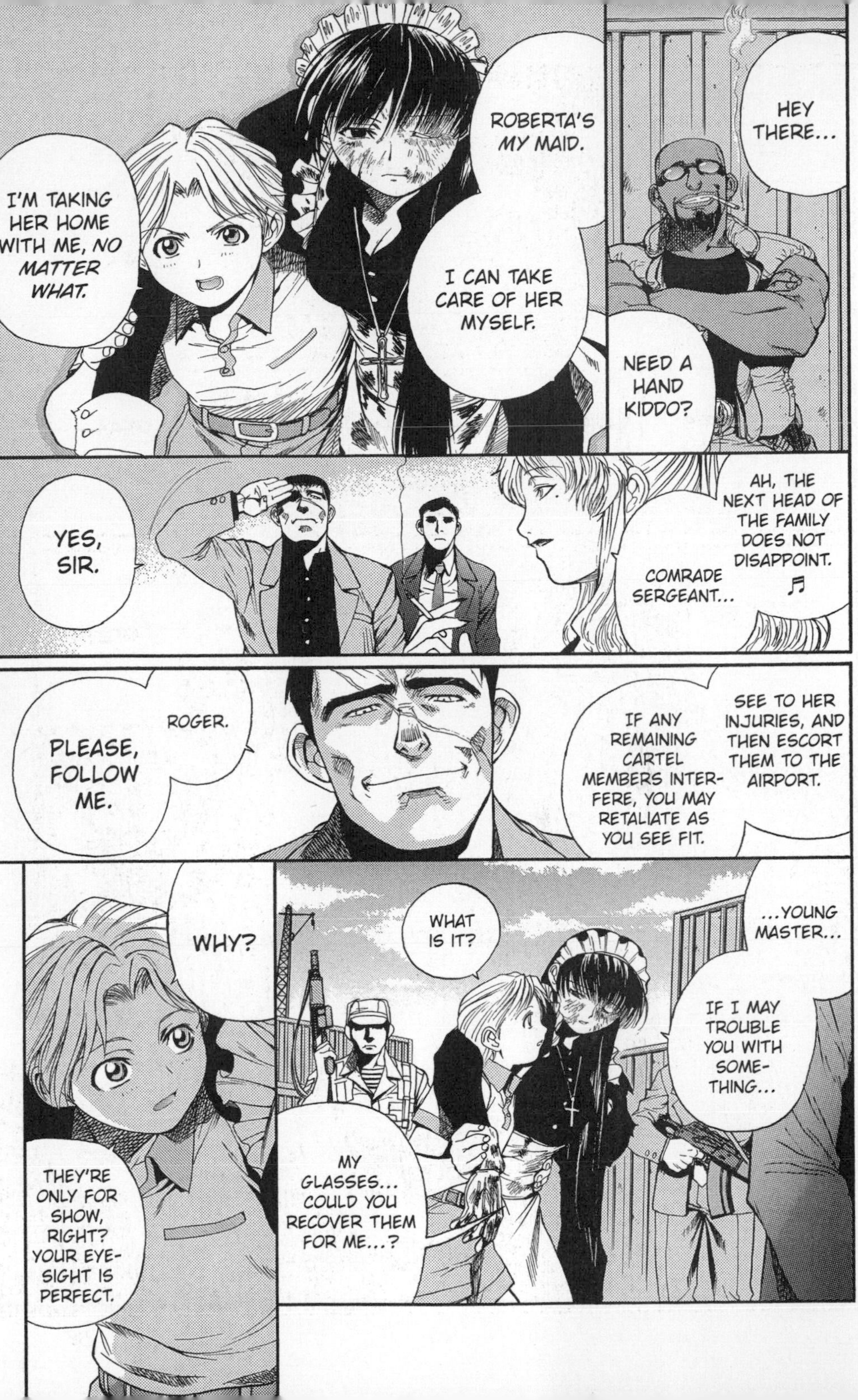
HEY THERE…
NEED A HAND KIDDO?
ROBERTA'S MY MAID.
I CAN TAKE CARE OF HER MYSELF.
I'M TAKING HER HOME WITH ME, NO MATTER WHAT.
AH, THE NEXT HEAD OF THE FAMILY DOES NOT DISAPPOINT. ♬
COMRADE SERGEANT…
YES, SIR.
SEE TO HER INJURIES, AND THEN ESCORT THEM TO THE AIRPORT.
IF ANY REMAINING CARTEL MEMBERS INTERFERE, YOU MAY RETALIATE AS YOU SEE FIT.
ROGER.
PLEASE, FOLLOW ME.
…YOUNG MASTER…
WHAT IS IT?
IF I MAY TROUBLE YOU WITH SOMETHING…
MY GLASSES… COULD YOU RECOVER THEM FOR ME…?
WHY?
THEY'RE ONLY FOR SHOW, RIGHT? YOUR EYESIGHT IS PERFECT.

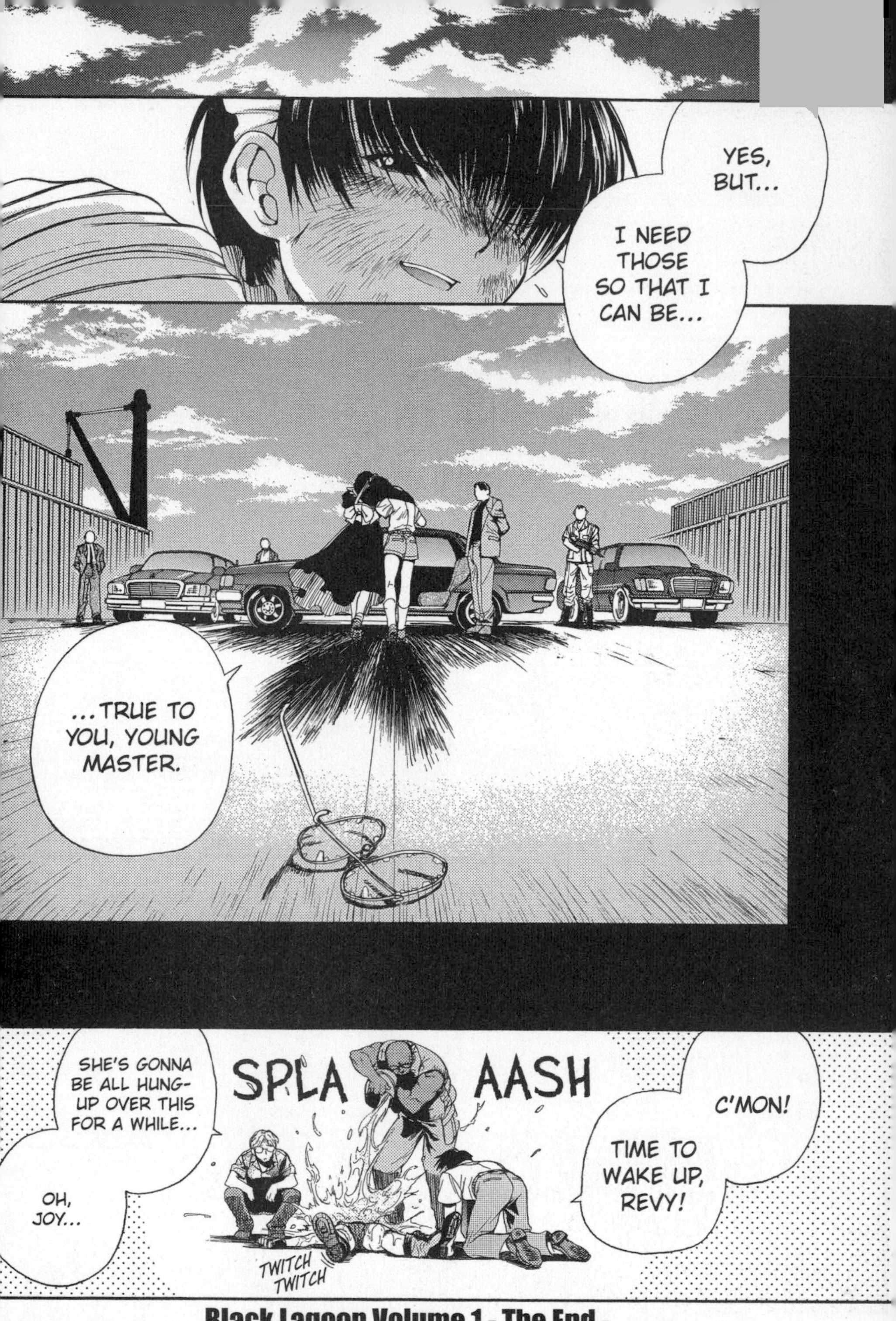
YES, BUT...
I NEED THOSE SO THAT I CAN BE...
...TRUE TO YOU, YOUNG MASTER.
C'MON!
TIME TO WAKE UP, REVY!
SPLA AASH
SHE'S GONNA BE ALL HUNG-UP OVER THIS FOR A WHILE...
OH, JOY...
TWITCH TWITCH

Black Lagoon Volume 1 - The End -

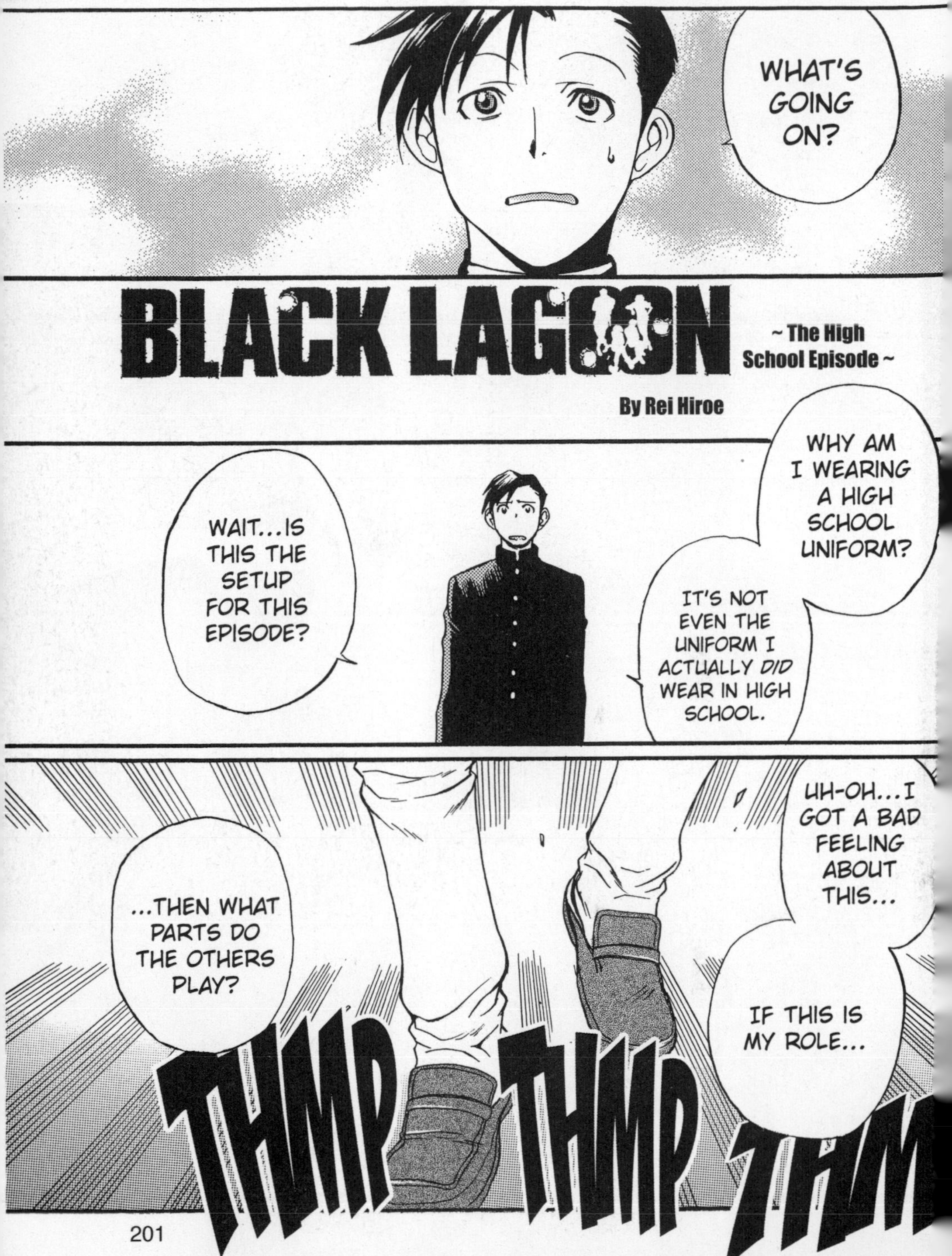
WHAT'S GOING ON?
BLACK LAGOON
~ The High School Episode ~
By Rei Hiroe
WHY AM I WEARING A HIGH SCHOOL UNIFORM?
IT'S NOT EVEN THE UNIFORM I ACTUALLY *DID* WEAR IN HIGH SCHOOL.
WAIT...IS THIS THE SETUP FOR THIS EPISODE?
UH-OH...I GOT A BAD FEELING ABOUT THIS...
IF THIS IS MY ROLE...
...THEN WHAT PARTS DO THE OTHERS PLAY?
THMP THMP THM

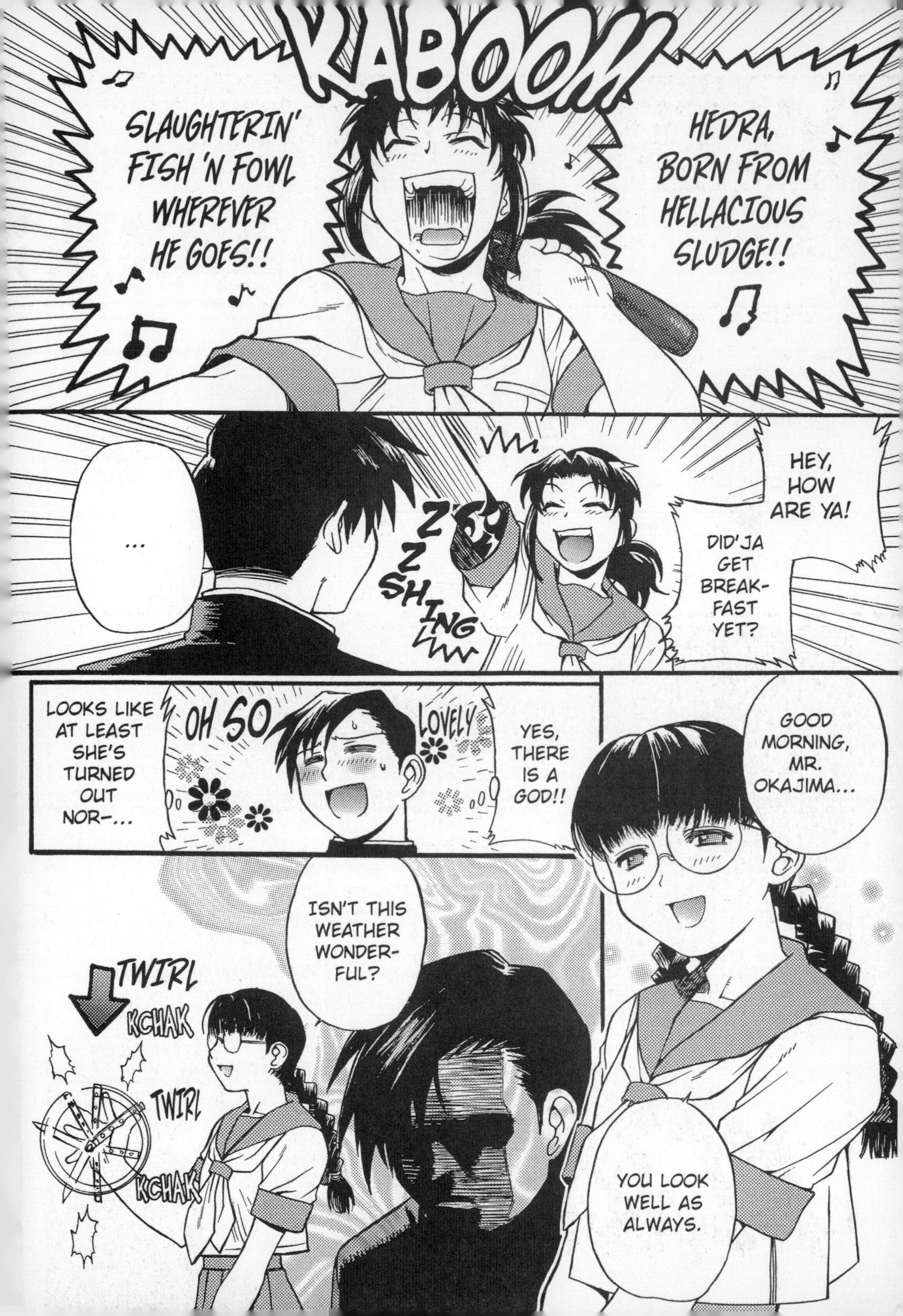
KABOOM!!
HEDRA, BORN FROM HELLACIOUS SLUDGE!!
SLAUGHTERIN' FISH 'N FOWL WHEREVER HE GOES!!
HEY, HOW ARE YA!
DID'JA GET BREAK-FAST YET?
ZZZSHING
...
GOOD MORNING, MR. OKAJIMA...
YOU LOOK WELL AS ALWAYS.
YES, THERE IS A GOD!!
OH SO LOVELY
LOOKS LIKE AT LEAST SHE'S TURNED OUT NOR-...
ISN'T THIS WEATHER WONDER-FUL?
TWIRL
KCHAK
TWIRL
KCHAK

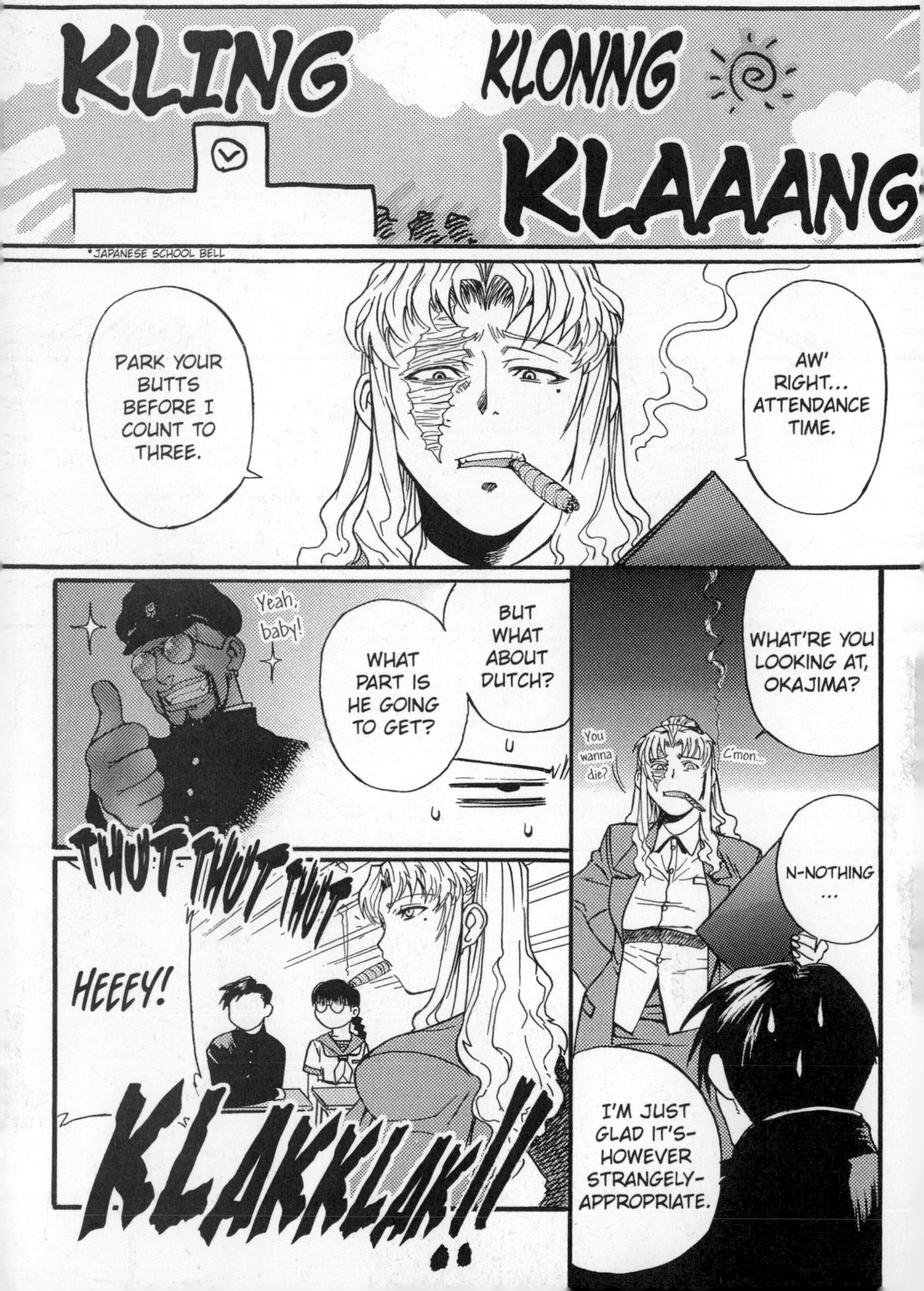
KLING
KLONNG
KLAAANG
*JAPANESE SCHOOL BELL
AW' RIGHT... ATTENDANCE TIME.
PARK YOUR BUTTS BEFORE I COUNT TO THREE.
WHAT'RE YOU LOOKING AT, OKAJIMA?
C'mon...
You wanna die?
N-NOTHING ...
I'M JUST GLAD IT'S- HOWEVER STRANGELY- APPROPRIATE.
BUT WHAT ABOUT DUTCH?
WHAT PART IS HE GOING TO GET?
Yeah, baby!
THUT THUT THUT
HEEEY!
KLAKKLAK!!

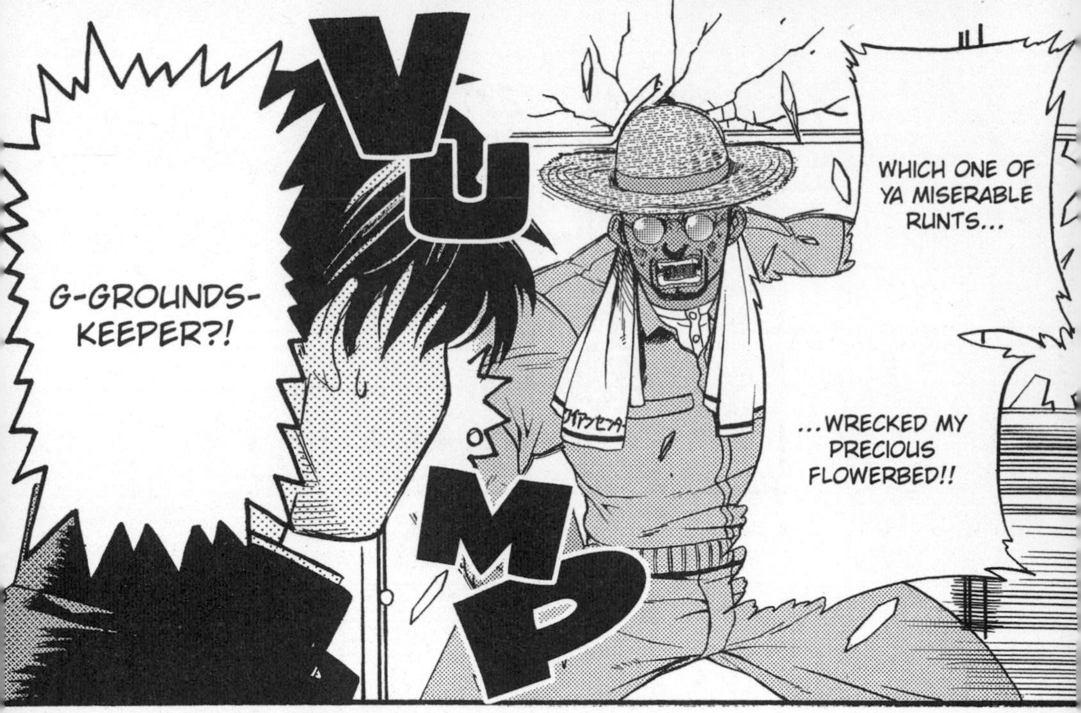
WHICH ONE OF YA MISERABLE RUNTS...
...WRECKED MY PRECIOUS FLOWERBED!!
G-GROUNDS-KEEPER?!
VUMP

MEANWHILE MR. BENNY...

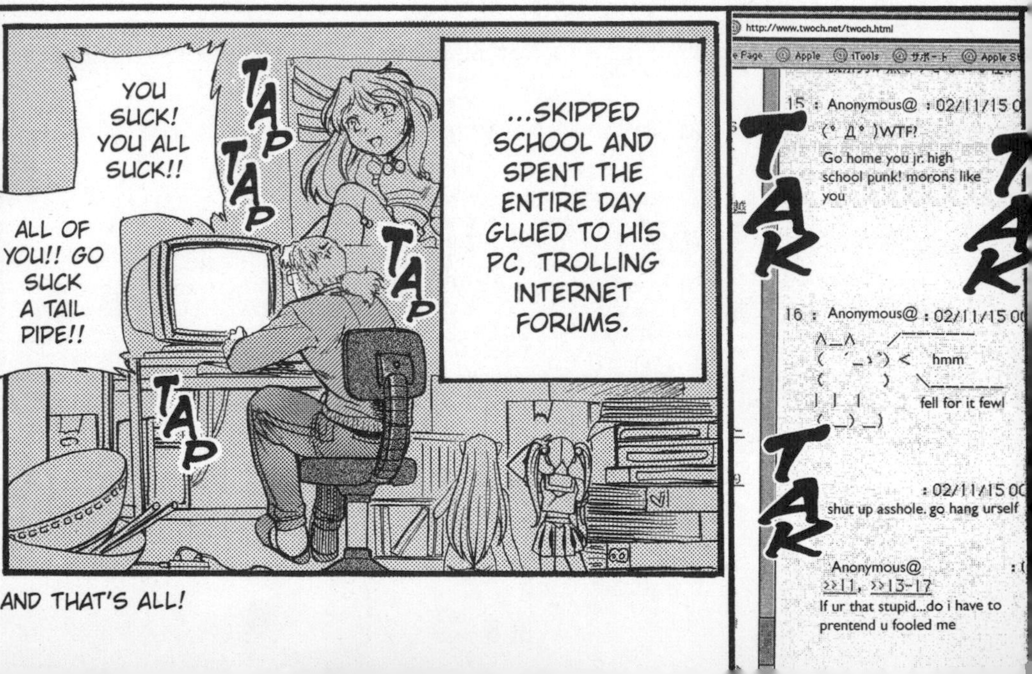
http://www.twoch.net/twoch.html
Apple iTools
15 : Anonymous@ : 02/11/15
(° Д°)WTF!
Go home you jr. high school punk! morons like you
TAK TAK
16 : Anonymous@ : 02/11/15
hmm
fell for it fewl
TAK TAK
: 02/11/15
shut up asshole. go hang urself
Anonymous@
>>11, >>13-17
If ur that stupid...do i have to prentend u fooled me
...SKIPPED SCHOOL AND SPENT THE ENTIRE DAY GLUED TO HIS PC, TROLLING INTERNET FORUMS.
YOU SUCK! YOU ALL SUCK!!
ALL OF YOU!! GO SUCK A TAIL PIPE!!
TAP TAP
TAP
TAP

AND THAT'S ALL!

THE WONDROUSLY CAPTIVATING ROBERTA
BY REI HIROE, 3RD GRADE, MS. BASINGER.

HEE-HEE!
FLIP
WHY, I NEVER ...!
YOU'VE BEEN A BAD BOY, YOUNG MASTER.
OWW.
PINCH
TWIST
DO I MAKE MYSELF CLEAR?
FLAP FLAP FLAP FLAP
I'M SORRY! I'M SORRY! I'M REALLY SORRY!
FLAP FLAP FLAP

CLOSING WORDS

BOY, IT'S BEEN A WHILE SINCE I LAST GOT A COMPILATION OUT. AND IT LOOKS LIKE I'LL BE ABLE TO HAVE ANOTHER ONE PUBLISHED TOO. I'M JUST GLAD IT SEEMS THINGS'LL WORK OUT FOR A WHILE. I HAVE TO ADMIT I'M RUNNING AROUND BLIND TO SOME DEGREE, BUT HOPEFULLY YOU'LL LIKE WHAT YOU SEE AND YOU'LL STICK WITH ME FOR A WHILE.

I'D LIKE TO EXPRESS MY APPRECIATION TO THE FOLLOWING PEOPLE:

I'D LIKE TO THANK MY MAIN ASSISTANCE STAFFERS: B-RIVER, MR. ITAKO, AND KAERU KOGANEI.

MY CREW AND BRAINSTORMING FRIENDS: GRAND MASTER MO'CHII, J-SAIRŌ, B1H, AND REIJI SAITŌ.

COOPERATION REGARDING FOREIGN LANGUAGE ISSUES BY: TOSHIRO ISHIYAMA, YŌSUKE FROM SPAIN, AND DAN KANEMITSU.

PLEASE STICK WITH ME IN THE FUTURE, OKAY? I'M BEGGING YOU. LET'S GO OUT AND DRINK AND STUFF.

I'D LIKE TO EXPRESS MY SPECIAL THANKS TO THE REGULARS THAT DROP BY THE BULLETIN BOARD ON MY WEB PAGE AND ALL THOSE KIND PEOPLE WHO SENT IN THE QUESTIONNAIRES INCLUDED IN THE MAGAZINE I WRITE FOR.

ALSO, TO MY COMRADE IN ARMS, WAR BUDDIES OF STEEL-THE SHINJUKU WAKŌ GANG, ESPECIALLY ENZU AND GASHIGE.

LOOKING FORWARD TO SEEING YOU ALL IN VOLUME 2.

--REI HIROE,
NOVEMBER 15TH, 2002.

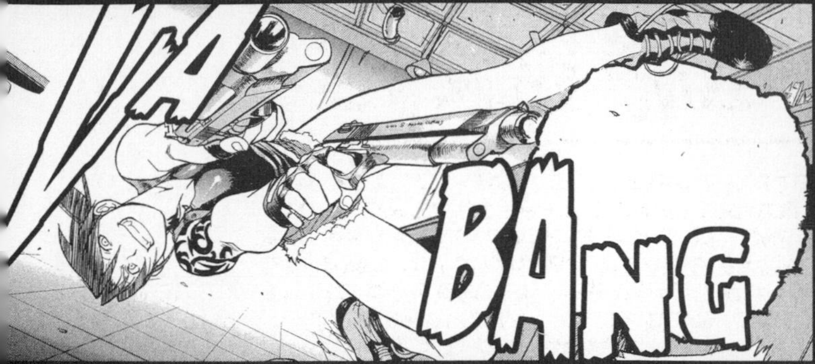
BANG

Revy "Two Hand"

Revy's two-gun style echoes the on-screen combat choreography (sometimes called the "bullet ballet") made famous in movies by John Woo. In real life, using two guns like this is highly impractical since it is virtually impossible to actually hit anything, especially if the target and the shooter are moving, and it's also difficult to reload. Of course, it looks totally *badass* on film, and in Rei Hiroe's stunning action-manga *Black Lagoon*!

Regarding the spelling of Revy's *nom de guerre*, it is indeed "Two Hand," not "Two Hands." This is a reference to a character from the hard-boiled crime novel *Run*, by Douglas E. Winter (which is a great read by the way).

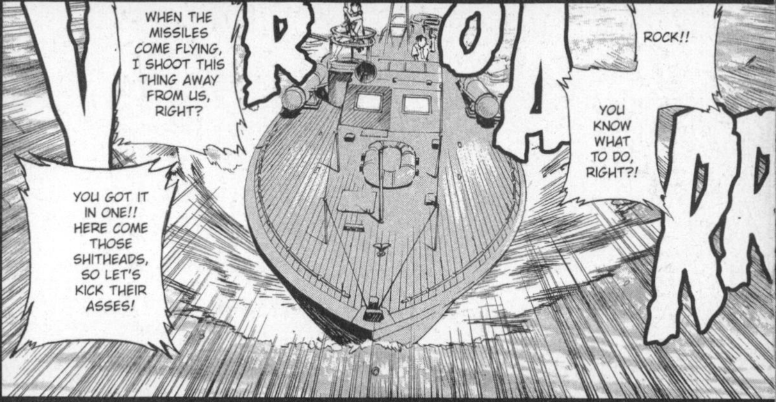
ROCK!!
YOU KNOW WHAT TO DO, RIGHT?!
WHEN THE MISSILES COME FLYING, I SHOOT THIS THING AWAY FROM US, RIGHT?
YOU GOT IT IN ONE!! HERE COME THOSE SHITHEADS, SO LET'S KICK THEIR ASSES!

The Black Lagoon

The *Black Lagoon* is a modified 80-foot Elco PT boat. First built for service in the U.S. Navy in World War II, the Elco PT boats were powered by three 1500 horsepower Packard Marine engines and could reach speeds of nearly 50 knots. PT boats were considered expendable (along with their crews) when used to attack more powerful warships. During WWII, they often served as couriers, scouts, and as transport for special reconnaissance teams inserted behind enemy lines. President John F. Kennedy was the skipper of one of these souped-up cabin cruisers, the famous PT-109.

In addition to the four torpedoes carried in tubes on deck, PT boats were armed with machine guns, anti-aircraft guns and depth charges—basically the crews bolted on whatever extra weaponry they could scrounge up! Dutch has removed all the original armament except the torpedoes (which get used very effectively and imaginatively in volume 1), but who needs all that when you've got Revy?!